P9-DIB-522

STAR WITNESS

BOOKS BY D. W. BUFFA

The Legacy

The Judgment

The Prosecution

The Defense

G. P. Putnam's Sons
New York

STAR WITNESS

D. W. BUFFA

This is a work of fiction. Names, characters, places, and incidents either are the product of the author's imagination or are used fictitiously, and any resemblance to actual persons, living or dead, business establishments, events, or locales is entirely coincidental.

G. P. Putnam's Sons
Publishers Since 1838
a member of
Penguin Putnam Inc.
375 Hudson Street
New York, NY 10014

Published simultaneously in Canada

Library of Congress Cataloging-in-Publication Data

Buffa, D. W., date.
Star witness / D. W. Buffa.
p. cm.
ISBN 0-399-15034-X
1. Antonelli, Joseph (Fictitious character)–Fiction.
2. San Francisco (Calif.)–Fiction. I. Title.
PS3552.U3739 S73 2003
813'.54–dc21 2002031801

Printed in the United States of America
10 9 8 7 6 5 4 3 2 1

This book is printed on acid-free paper. ♾

Book design by Victoria Kuskowski

FOR WENDY SHERMAN
AND DAVID HIGHFILL

"I invented a tragic story . . . because no one has written a tragedy about Hollywood . . . and doomed and heroic things do happen here."

—F. SCOTT FITZGERALD on *The Last Tycoon*

STAR WITNESS

1

EACH TIME I SAW HER she had the same strange haunting effect on me, arousing feelings of which I had scarcely been aware. From the very beginning I knew we would be perfect together; and sometimes, when she looked at me with those lovely, intelligent eyes, I thought she knew it too. Once, while she was dancing with someone whose name I might have known but have now forgotten, she looked over his shoulder and gazed right at me. In that moment she was not with him anymore, she was with me, clinging close, dancing to music that would never stop, through a night that would never end.

It seems odd now, but I never thought of her as having her own existence, separate and apart from my own, until I read in the newspapers the first reports of her death. She was thirty-two when she died. It surprised me that she was any age at all. She never changed, not in any way I could tell. It never occurred to me that she might not always be as beautiful, as utterly irresistible, as she had always been. Dreams may die, but they never grow old.

All over the country, thousands of people who had never met her, carefully, even tenderly, placed flowers at makeshift shrines as they mourned her passing. I did not do anything like that. To tell the truth, after I put down the paper, I did not think about her at all. Even had I lived in Los Angeles instead of San Francisco, I cannot imagine that I would have joined the huge crowd that began to form outside the gated entrance to the Beverly Hills mansion where early that morning her nude body had been found floating facedown in the pool. Drawn by curiosity, but also by the sense that they knew her in ways they did not know anyone else, they kept coming, more of them all the time, until it seemed that half of Los Angeles had joined in a long silent vigil for the woman known to the world as Mary Margaret Flanders.

She was born Marian Walsh, not the kind of name that would help make someone a movie star. The rumor, which in Los Angeles, where the truth of a thing is measured by how often it gets repeated, everyone claimed to believe, was that the name Mary Margaret Flanders had been chosen to appeal to both of the usually incompatible things men wanted most in a woman. Mary Margaret seemed a rather obvious allusion to the idea of the clean, fresh-scrubbed face of the proverbial girl next door, the girl you liked, the girl you thought you might one day want to marry. What was needed was a last name that would in combination conjure up the supposed dream of every American male that the angel on his arm would also be the whore in his bed. But not, if you will, a whore of ill repute. With an instinct for the popular mind, the anonymous publicist who supposedly first suggested it, understood that the name Moll Flanders had, as it were, entered the great collective subconscious of the American culture as a symbol of all the adventure and excitement of forgivable sin. And if that were a little too psychoanalytic, or if it suggested a level of literacy higher than could reasonably be expected, there was also the fact, the importance of which no one in Hollywood was likely to undervalue, that Daniel Defoe's famous novel had after all been made into a movie.

That was the rumor, but I doubt it's true; I doubt anyone gave any serious thought at all to what Marian Walsh's new name should be. She probably chose it herself, and probably for no other reason than that she liked the way it sounded, the whole three-word thing: Mary Margaret Flanders. From what I have come to know of her since her death, I doubt she would have tried to analyze it at all, much less to anticipate what an audience, or any part of an audience, might happen to like about it. Marian Walsh had always been what most men really wanted, and she had known it better than she had known anything else.

In her first few, otherwise forgettable films, Mary Margaret Flanders, eager and erotic, was in some of the most torrid scenes ever shown in a theater. They were low-budget, artistic disasters, shot in a few short days with a script made up of three- and four-word lines; but she somehow still managed a kind of vulnerability that conveyed more of the passion of love than the dull, straightforward mechanics of sex. There are some women men want to take to bed and never want to see again; after a night with Mary Margaret Flanders you would have married her in a minute and thought you were the luckiest man in the world.

She later claimed to regret them, but those early films made her someone people began to talk about. She was someone new, someone audiences wanted to see again. She did not play the lead in any of them; she was seldom even the principal supporting actress. She was the girl whose boyfriend leaves her, the girl who falls in love with the man she later finds out is married. She played a shopgirl, a clerk, a young woman who works in an office and struggles to get by; she never played anyone either well educated or rich.

It was the genius of Stanley Roth to recognize that women liked her because they thought she was just like them, and that men liked her because they knew she was not. Stanley Roth had often been right about such things. He had become one of most powerful men in the motion picture industry because he could always see just a little bit ahead of everyone else the kind of motion picture and the kind of star the public wanted next.

Stanley Roth was part of the myth of Hollywood, and not just of Hollywood: the myth that talent always leads to success. Before he was thirty he received his first Academy Award nomination for directing a picture about teenagers growing up in the hot Central Valley of California in the early 1960s. He won his first Oscar for a picture about a young boy who rescues a racehorse from the cruelty of its owner and, against impossible odds, rides it to victory. More than anyone else, Stanley Roth knew how to make the conventional something everyone thought they had to see.

The movies Roth made were all as successful as they were predictable. He gave the moviegoing public all the assurance they needed that good eventually triumphs over evil and that decent people inevitably overcome whatever adversity comes their way. There was no use pointing out that his films had nothing in common with reality; for millions of the people who paid money to see them, they were reality, or at least what reality was supposed to be. His movies made him a fortune, and when he had the money with which to do it, he walked away from the studio that had made it all possible and with two other rich and ambitious executives created one of his own. From the day Blue Zephyr Pictures opened for business it was, in the eyes of people who paid attention to the subtle shifts of power in the industry, the most important studio in town. Those who had experienced firsthand the absolute control he exercised over even the smallest details of production had to wonder, however, how long any partnership of which he was a member could possibly last.

There were those who had wondered the same thing about his marriage. Even before they were married, Stanley Roth and Mary Margaret Flanders were the leading couple in town. Whatever event they attended was by that fact alone a social success; when they hosted a gathering of their own it was, at least in Los Angeles, major news. They were among that relatively small number of celebrities mentioned rather frequently in the mainstream press, and they were often seen not only at major charitable events, but at those lavish political fundraisers in which Hollywood pretends it is made up of serious people and Washington pretends to believe it.

A photograph of the two of them at a black-tie event was a study in the subtleties of power and fame. Bright-eyed and effervescent, wearing something expensively simple, Mary Margaret Flanders would be talking to some well-known figure–a politician, an actor, a studio executive–while Stanley Roth stood a step behind or just off to the side, a look of cool detachment in his hooded half-shut eyes as if, a little bored with it all, he was appraising her performance. More interesting, and more instructive, were the faces of the people with whom she was talking. Their eyes were always on her, but you could tell they were already thinking about what they could say, what they could do, to make themselves noticed, not by Mary Margaret Flanders, but by the great Stanley Roth. Roth was the one who could decide whether to give them the chance to have everything they wanted–fame, money, power–or to make sure they would never have that chance at all.

They knew what Stanley Roth had decided about Mary Margaret Flanders, and they all knew what had happened to her. Roth had decided that she had that quality, that indefinable something that makes someone you might never notice on the street someone you can't take your eyes off on the screen. In the first picture she made for him, he gave her the starring role and spent millions promoting her as the next Hollywood sensation. The movie barely broke even, but from that point on, each of her movies made more than the one before; it was not long before the name Mary Margaret Flanders guaranteed the success of any movie she was in. She was making twenty million dollars a picture when they married, and there were those who thought that one reason he did it was to keep some of that money at home. Had Stanley Roth married entirely for love, that kind of calculation would still have crossed his mind.

I sometimes wondered what other thoughts must have crossed his ruthlessly analytical mind when he decided to marry a woman he had made famous by starring in movies in which half of America had seen her half naked. Stanley Roth could have had any woman in Hollywood he wanted. Would he have married her if he had not known that everyone who watched movies knew just how desirable she was? There was something strangely possessive in the idea of showing her that way to the public and then keeping her for your own; but then Stanley Roth was famous for taking what other people wanted, and sometimes what other people had. Whatever Stanley Roth may have thought when he married her, it was unlikely he ever imagined that it would end, just a few years later, not in divorce but in death, and that he would be the one standing at an open grave, wondering what had happened to make it all come to this.

The funeral was restricted to immediate family and close personal friends, but that apparently included every famous Hollywood star. Crowds stood respectfully outside the flagstone chapel during the service and then lined the black-paved streets as the body of Mary Margaret Flanders was taken to the cemetery. Like everything else known by the public about her, all of it was captured on film. I saw some of it that same night on the television news.

A small child, a girl of eight or nine, threw a last flower on the coffin as it was lowered slowly into the grave. A man in his mid- to late thirties with a straight, serious mouth and dark intense eyes stood next to the child, holding her hand. From the way he bent close and whispered to her just before she let go of the flower, I felt certain it must be her father, the first husband of the woman then called Marian Walsh. He was the only one with a face not famous.

Nearly twenty years older than his wife's first husband, wearing dark glasses and dressed in a dark suit, with deep furrows in his forehead and gray hair curling over the back of his shirt collar, Stanley Roth waited on the opposite side of the open grave for the flower to fall. Then, with a pensive expression, he tossed gently out in front of him a handful of dirt. It hit the lid of the casket, and a brief, barely perceptible shudder passed through him. Against his will, he took a sudden, half step back. When it was over, Roth acknowledged with a silent nod the condolences of the other mourners as one by one they slowly turned and walked away, until, finally, he was left alone at the graveside. I wondered what he called her, what name he used. I thought it must have been Mary Margaret. It was prettier than Marian, and I think for him it must have seemed more real.

I watched him, the husband of Mary Margaret Flanders, standing all alone at the side of her grave in the dying light of the late Los Angeles afternoon, watched as it dissolved into black. That was the last thing you saw, that long fading shot of the grief-stricken husband saying his final good-bye to the woman everyone loved. It was the kind of shot with which Stanley Roth had ended some of his best-known films.

Like most things that did not concern me directly, I forgot about Mary Margaret Flanders and Stanley Roth after I turned off the television set. I was just about to have dinner with Marissa Kane, the woman with whom I had been living for a little more than a year. That gives perhaps a false impression of what we were. If we had been much younger when we met–in our twenties or even our thirties–we might have become lovers and then, if we had been really quite fortunate, we might have become friends. We met instead when she was already a divorced woman with grown children and I had long since given up all thought of anything that could last.

We became friends, Marissa and I, when I came from Portland to try a case in San Francisco. Eventually we became more than friends, but just what name to put on what we had become was never easy to decide. I was not in love with her, not the way I remembered what that had been like; and I am almost certain she was not in love with me. Perhaps we had lost the capacity for the kind of passion that cannot see beyond itself; that believes it is the only thing that matters; that is convinced that it is the one thing that can never die. But we cared about each other, and as best we could we looked after each other. We even, to a point, understood each other. When the trial that had brought me to San Francisco was finally over, it did not take me long to decide that I did not want to leave, that I wanted to stay here, with her, for as long as it lasted. We lived in the house Marissa had owned for years: a chocolate-colored shingle-sided house on a steep hillside above the village of Sausalito with a view of the bay.

After I turned off the television, we had dinner, and after dinner, we went for a walk. A few restaurants were still open in the village, and from the doorway of a neighborhood bar the smoky sound of a jazz trumpet echoed out into the night. We kept walking, along the sidewalk and across the street, down by the shore where the water washed up against the rocks and the lights of San Francisco set fire to the bay.

We came here every night, an evening ritual, a last look across at the city, at San Francisco, the place where long before anyone had heard of Los Angeles, all the adventurers in the world, blown by the winds of heaven, had come, drawn by the chance to make their fortunes, and by making their fortune become someone else. That was why I had come, or why I had stayed; not to make my fortune, but to become someone else, someone I did not so much mind being. That was Marissa's gift: the way she made me feel about who I was.

"I don't like Los Angeles very much," said Marissa after I made some vague remark about the funeral of Mary Margaret Flanders. She slipped her hand inside mine. "It isn't really a place–not like this," she explained, raising her almond shaped eyes toward the city. "People come here–at least they used to come here–because they dreamed about San Francisco; people go to L.A. because they dream about themselves."

Under a sky filled with every star ever seen, the white lights of the city, like the souls of sinners released from perdition, burned bright in the darkness, lighting up the black invisible waters of the bay with an image of itself, an illusion that seemed as real as the city itself. It held you there, that late-night view of the city, and the more you looked at it, the more certain you were that it belonged to you in ways that it could never belong to anyone else.

We turned and started the slow walk home. Somewhere in the distance a woman's laughter broke the nighttime silence, and then, a little farther on, the sound of that same jazz trumpet prowled through the dark, nearly deserted street.

"Do you like it there–L.A.? You probably do, don't you?" asked Marissa as we walked along, holding hands, climbing the street to the house.

I laughed. "Why? Because I dream about myself?"

With her other hand she took hold of my sleeve and gave it a playful tug. "No," she said seriously. "Because you're always thinking about the next place you want to be, the place you haven't been."

"I like it here," I protested mildly.

"That isn't what I mean," she said with a cryptic smile.

When we reached the house we tumbled inside and went right to bed. Just before I fell asleep I thought again about Stanley Roth, bathed in the golden haze of the afternoon sun as he stood watching, while the child across from him threw a flower into his dead wife's grave. It was a fragmentary glimpse of something barely remembered, a quick glance backward at something I had seen early that evening. I did not know anything about Stanley Roth. He was someone vaguely famous married to a woman I never knew, both of them part of a world I knew only from a distance and only from the outside. When he woke me up in the middle of the night, I had at first no idea who he was or what he might want.

The voice, a voice I had never heard before, might just as well have said the name John Smith for all it meant to me.

"This is Stanley Roth," he said again.

I did not remember anyone named Stanley Roth; I certainly had not given anyone of that name my home telephone number.

"This number is unlisted," I said rather irritably. "How did you get it?"

"This is Stanley Roth. Do you know who I am?"

The voice was brusque and impatient. He had called me in the middle of the night and seemed to think I was somehow wasting his time.

"No," I replied. "Don't you?"

There was a dead silence at the other end. At any moment I expected to hear him hang up. It was the only reason I did not do it first.

"My apologies, Mr. Antonelli," he said presently in a clear, firm voice that was all business. "My name is Stanley Roth. My wife–perhaps you've heard of her–was Mary Margaret Flanders, the actress."

Turning on the lamp, I swung my legs around and sat on the edge of the bed.

"I'm terribly sorry, Mr. Roth. It's late, and I didn't realize . . ."

"Mr. Antonelli, I wonder if you might come to Los Angeles tomorrow. There's a matter I'd like to discuss with you. I know it's rather short notice, but it's really quite important. I'll send my plane up. My office will make all the arrangements."

He was used to having his way, and I think it never occurred to him that I might say no.

"What is it you want to see me about, Mr. Roth?"

"I'd really rather discuss it in person," he replied as if that should be the end of it.

And it almost was. I discovered that I was not as immune to the attraction of celebrity as I had thought. With a conscious effort I resisted the temptation to agree immediately to what he asked.

"I'd be very glad to see you, Mr. Roth," I said, taking refuge in formality, "but I can't possibly come there tomorrow."

Again he fell silent, but this time I did not expect him to hang up. He was thinking about what he was going to do next. When he finally spoke, there was a sense, not of panic exactly, but of concern, in his voice.

"What if I come there? Is there someplace we could meet privately? If I come to your office, someone is going to find out, and right now, I can't afford . . ."

He was talking faster, beginning to ramble, and, I thought, about to lose control.

"Are you in some kind of trouble, Mr. Roth?" I interjected, trying to sound as calm as I could.

The only response was a long, brooding silence. He had to be in trouble, serious trouble. Why else would he have called? No one, not even the supposedly enigmatic Stanley Roth, called a criminal defense attorney at midnight unless they were. How many times before had I been called in the middle of the night by people I did not know, people who could not wait until morning because they were afraid they might go crazy if they did not do something right away. I was still in my twenties, just out of law school, taking any case I could get, hoping I could make enough to cover the rent in the dreary two-room office in a nearly vacant Portland building, when those late-night calls started to come. Sometimes it was a drunk slurring his words from a pay phone in the jail; sometimes, as I began to acquire a reputation as a lawyer who almost never lost, the calls came from people accused of far more serious crimes. It was not long before I was the nighttime confidant of murderers, rapists, and thieves. Even after I could afford to take only the cases I wanted and had a number only a few people were supposed to know they still managed to call, desperate to talk, afraid to be alone with what they had done or what everyone was about to think they had done.

Rich or poor, famous or completely unknown, it did not matter: There was one thing they all had to say. Perhaps it was simply hearing themselves say it out loud that made them feel better. In that respect, at least, Stanley Roth was just like everyone else.

"I didn't do it, Mr. Antonelli; I swear I didn't."

They all said it, that simple, straightforward declaration of their innocence, but there was something about the way Stanley Roth said it that made me wonder whether the words had come to him unprompted, or whether he had recalled them from the memory of things he had seen, things he had heard, and perhaps even things he had written, in the movies he had made. I saw him again, standing at her grave, the last mourner left, husband and wife, director and star. And now I wondered, not what name he had called her, but whether in that last silent good-bye he had spoken any words about the way she had died or the reason she had been killed. All I knew was what everyone knew: The nude body of Mary Margaret Flanders had been found floating facedown in the outdoor swimming pool, a single silk stocking stretched around her neck, apparently used to hold her fast while a knife blade slashed deep across her throat.

"Have the police talked to you?" I asked, twisting the telephone cord between my fingers. "Or, rather, have you talked to the police?"

"Yes."

"When?"

"Yesterday, the day before the funeral," said Roth in a voice that now seemed tired. "They want to see me again. I think they're going to arrest me. They think I murdered my wife. I need your help, Mr. Antonelli. I'll pay you anything you ask."

I did not go to Los Angeles the next day. Stanley Roth was used to having people drop everything to do what he wanted. If I was going to represent him, I wanted him to know from the beginning that I would not take orders from him or anyone else. I wanted to establish a certain distance, an independence. I was the lawyer; he was the client: I decided what I was going to do and when I was going to do it.

What a fool I was. I should have known that it would be impossible to treat Stanley Roth the same way I treated anyone else. I should have known that this was going to be a murder case unlike anything I had ever seen before or would ever see again. I should have known from the moment I got involved that it was going to change things, including things about myself, in ways I could not then have imagined. Because of Stanley Roth I was about to become not only the best-known lawyer but perhaps the least understood man in America. But then, how could I have known–how could anyone have known–when I boarded the private plane that would take me to Hollywood that before it was all over one of the most talked-about movies of all time would be a movie about me.

2

FLASHING THROUGH THE BRIGHT MORNING SKY, the plane sent by Stanley Roth passed along the California coast and then, above Los Angeles, began its descent. We landed at the Burbank airport and taxied past the blue-and-white stucco art-deco terminal. For a moment it made me feel that I was back in the 1930s: I half expected to see Howard Hughes with his pencil-thin mustache, wearing goggles and a leather jacket, boosting himself out of the open cockpit of a two-seater biplane, back from a looping flight over the orange groves that once covered most of everything between here and the sand-covered Pacific beach. A few yards from where the plane came to a stop, a limousine was waiting. Holding his gray cap in his hand, the driver struck a languid pose next to the rear door. He looked like Howard Hughes, at least the mustache and the slick shiny black hair parted neatly high up on his scalp.

While the driver took my bag, I stood on the tarmac, glancing at the pale empty sky. The air was still and it was already getting warm. The heat was different here, the sun glistening hot and dry on the skin with none of the steaming humid sweating that makes other, eastern places miserable in the summer. It lasted all year long, the cloudless skies and the endless sun, as if nature and its harsh necessities had been banished by an act of imagination. Even the haze that hung across the horizon, a gritty gray during the day turned reddish orange at night, seemed less a reminder of the snarled long-distance traffic than of the way everything was always becoming something else, taking off one identity and putting on another.

At Blue Zephyr Pictures the guard waved the limousine through and the dark blue, gold-tipped front gate rolled shut behind us. The studio had the appearance of one of those military installations put up almost overnight during the Second World War and then never torn down because it was cheaper to maintain it than to build something more permanent in its place. Everywhere you looked there were odd-shaped hangarlike structures with round roofs and wire screen windows, flat-topped two-story barracks-style buildings, and enormous square-door garages, the kind that had once housed motor vehicles and munitions. We wound our way through a maze of almost uniform sameness, along a narrow two-lane road lined on both sides by palm trees taller than any of the buildings we passed. At the end of the street we came out onto a circle. Stopping in front of a small, unpretentious bungalow, the driver told me this was where Stanley Roth had his office.

We had passed the company headquarters, housed in one of the nondescript buildings on the way. Stanley Roth had most of his meetings there. It was where he did what he liked to call the company business. The bungalow was where he did what he called his real work, the work on the movies he still produced and directed. It had been built just for him, a perfect replica of the place he worked when he achieved his first success as a young director for the studio he later abandoned. It was the habit of superstition, the belief that you should never change anything once you had reached the point where each thing you did was as great, as successful, as what you had done before. Stanley Roth never let go of anything that had once brought him luck.

The five-room bungalow was not just where Stanley Roth did his work; it was a museum of what he had already done. As soon as you stepped inside the door you knew this place was all about the movies and all about Stanley Roth. The walls were covered with posters, the kind that when he was a kid growing up in the Central Valley he used to make a few dollars putting up on telephone poles advertising the movies then playing at the only theater in town. I did not know if they still did that, and when I saw them, one for each movie he had made, framed in identical silver frames, I wondered if he had had them made specially so he could have something to remind him of how far he had come.

The posters were only the beginning. The contract he had been given for his first job in the movies, assistant director on a picture I had never heard of and probably not more than a few people had ever seen, sat in a frame, one of a hundred different documents that chronicled with retrospective inevitability the steadily advancing career of Stanley Roth. There were letters written by famous people, including at least two Presidents, one of whom I had liked, acknowledging his importance; and photographs, hundreds of them, and all of them, as far as I could tell, related one way or the other to the movies he had made. In the room he used for his office, with a double set of French doors opening onto a private patio and a small pool, there were two photographs on the small bookshelf behind his desk. In the first, Mary Margaret Flanders stood next to him, beaming up at her husband, while he held aloft the Oscar he won that night for directing. In the second, with that same unforgettable smile, she stood by herself at the lectern, clutching to her bosom the Oscar for best actress she won two years later.

Roth followed my eye.

"I directed her in that picture." He assumed the expression of someone who always thought about what he said. "I directed her in all her pictures, all the ones that were any good."

The room was dark and cool. Roth sat in the shadows behind his desk, his ankle crossed over his knee, his arms folded loosely across his chest. He seemed almost too tired, or too preoccupied, to lift his head. When he spoke, he managed to raise his eyes, but then, when he finished, his gaze would drift away. He was not inattentive; he listened quite carefully to everything I said. His eyes would narrow and he would bite down on the edge of his lower lip, the attitude of someone concentrating on what he thinks may be important.

"I followed your advice, Mr. Antonelli. I told the police that I had already told them everything I knew, and that there was no point my telling them again."

He kept his eyes on me just long enough to measure my reaction, to see what effect this expression of confidence in my judgment had produced.

"Do you still think they're going to arrest you?" I asked.

His eyes came back to me. He nodded his head.

"Yeah. I'm almost sure of it."

"You told them everything you knew?" Before he could answer, I asked: "What exactly did you tell them?"

We stared at each other, searching each other's eyes, wondering how far we could trust one another, or whether we could trust each other at all.

"There's something I've been thinking about since the other night when we talked. You're one of the most famous criminal lawyers in the country. You never lose, and . . ."

"That's not true," I interjected with a quick shake of my head. "I've lost."

Roth had no patience for what he thought false modesty. He cocked his head and gave me an incredulous look.

"The murder of Jeremy Fullerton? The U.S. senator who wants to be President? The accused is a black kid no one in San Francisco wants to defend? The jury finds him guilty, and then you discover who the real killer is and you save an innocent man. You call that a loss? I call that a great movie."

A great movie? It seemed a strange way to characterize what had very nearly cost someone his life.

"I've lost other cases, Mr. Roth; but that case was the first time a jury brought back a guilty verdict against a defendant I knew had not done a thing. You may not think that was a loss–maybe it would make a great movie–but if you knew how I really found out who killed Jeremy Fullerton you might not be quite so certain that things always work out the way they should."

A knowing smile darted across his mouth. He seemed to think I had proved his point.

"Yes, exactly. Even when you lose, you somehow manage to win. That's what I've been thinking about. If you're my lawyer, won't people start to believe I must be guilty because why otherwise would I need Joseph Antonelli?"

Stanley Roth had spent his life convincing audiences that the way things looked was the way things were.

"The only thing that counts, Mr. Roth, is what the prosecution can prove. It doesn't matter what anyone believes."

"I meant before there is a trial, before I'm even charged." A trace of impatience began to creep into his voice. "If I already have you, won't people think I must have known I was in trouble, that I have something to hide?"

He was still clinging to the hope that he might not be arrested after all; that the police might change their mind and look elsewhere for the killer. If he hired a criminal defense lawyer, would he not in effect be telling them that they were right in suspecting that he had something to hide?

"Suppose we set aside for the moment the question about when–or even whether–I represent you. Let's talk instead about what happened, that night, the night your wife was killed."

Roth put both feet on the floor and planted his elbows on the desk. A plaintive expression fell across his face.

"I don't know what happened that night."

"You were in the house . . . when your wife was killed?" I asked tentatively.

Roth had a sense for the subtle changes in the meaning of words. He also knew that the silence between them sometimes said more than the words themselves.

"I was in the house; I don't know that she was."

"She?"

"My wife."

"Your wife?"

"Yes, Mary Margaret," he explained, wondering why he needed to.

"You didn't call her Marian?"

"No, of course not."

He said it as if he had never known her by any other name than the one by which the world had known her. He must have known that her name was Marian, but from the slightly incredulous look he gave me I began to think that after years of calling her Mary Margaret he might have forgotten that it was not real.

"What do you mean, you don't know that she was? Why would you not know whether your wife was home?"

"Mary Margaret had gone to a party. I'm in the middle of a picture–late nights, early mornings, very early mornings. I got in about eleven and went straight to bed. We were starting again at five and I had to be up at four. I was exhausted. If she came in, I didn't hear her. When I got up, I got dressed and left."

He paused, moved back from the desk, and turned a little to the side.

He was dressed in a light-colored pair of slacks and a faded tan sports jacket. The gray dress shirt he wore open at the collar revealed a few gray hairs curling from his chest. He had a deep tan, the kind that in Southern California seems never to fade away. His eyes, bluish gray and not very large, moved slowly from one thing to the next, taking their time.

"I was on the set when I first learned she was dead," added Roth as he lowered his eyes. In a gesture that seemed oddly out of place, he spread his fingers and appeared to inspect his clean, close-cut nails. He had spoken of his wife's death without emotion. I had assumed it was because of a decent impulse not to inflict upon someone still a stranger any of his own despair; now I was not sure what he felt, or if he felt anything at all.

"Your wife was out. You went to bed. Early in the morning you got up, got dressed and left. Is that right?" I asked, raising an eyebrow.

He searched my eyes to find out what he had not made clear enough for me to understand.

"You didn't notice that your wife was not there when you got up, when you dressed, when you left?"

He seemed almost relieved that it was so easy to explain.

"When I was working, when I had to get up that early, I slept in a different room."

He read something else in my eyes, something I did not know was there.

"I didn't say we didn't normally go to bed together. But I would sleep in the other room."

A slight smile hovered at the edge of his mouth, a brief advertisement of his own superiority, an admission that he knew everyone had wanted what he had. I started to ask another question, but he held up his hand and abruptly shook his head. He wanted to correct something he had just said.

"We didn't go to bed together very often." A wry expression took hold of his mouth. He looked at me with sudden interest. "Do you know why? Because she was not all that attractive, and because she wasn't all that sexy." He paused, smiling to himself. "You have a hard time believing that, don't you? You thought you knew her, Mary Margaret Flanders; you thought she was everything you'd ever want, didn't you?"

I started to protest, but he again cut me off.

"A lot of people who come to see me pretend they're not affected by what they see on the screen; that they're too smart, too sophisticated to fantasize about someone they saw in a movie. But you did, didn't you? I saw it in your eyes. That's when I decided you might be someone I could trust."

Roth glanced slowly around the room until his eyes came to rest on the Oscar that sat in the middle of an otherwise vacant bookshelf.

"You don't have to be very smart to do well in this business. I'm not saying you can be completely stupid, but it doesn't take what I would call serious talent. But one thing you have to have is an eye, the ability to see how someone will look on the screen. Or the way they can be made to look on the screen. I invented Mary Margaret Flanders. She was my best work. She was . . ."

He stopped, as if he had realized that he might be going too far.

"All I'm trying to say is that in person, without all the makeup, without all the clothes, without all the lighting, without the camera . . . That was it, the camera. I don't mean how she looked on camera, I mean the camera."

He hesitated, trying to think of exactly the right words to explain it.

"It's the way someone reacts to a camera. Most people–most actors–become self-conscious. I don't mean they shy away from it. It's the other way around: They become too aware of themselves. They think about the way they're going to look, and then they try to look a certain way. With her it was different. That's what I could tell about her, the first time I saw her. When she was on camera, everything came alive–and it was all instinct. . . . It was like watching a woman who has just fallen in love: the glow, the uncanny sense of precisely the right way to move, the perfect intuitive grasp of what the man she's in love with wants to see next–before he knows it himself. That's what she was: a young woman in love, but not with a man–with a camera: any camera, not just a motion picture camera. You've seen photographs of her. You couldn't take your eyes off her, could you? That's what she lived for: to be on camera, to be on film, to have other people watch her. You should have seen her, watching one of her own movies. She couldn't take her eyes off herself. She would sit there, in the dark, delighted, her mouth forming each of the words she was saying on screen, as if she was hearing them for the very first time."

Roth rolled his head from one side to the other and stared into space. A laugh, bitter and self-deprecating, escaped his lips.

"Sometimes I thought the reason she had so little interest in making love was because there wasn't a camera in the room. You know the story of Narcissus: He saw his own reflection in the pool and died because he could not stop looking at himself. Mary Margaret could have passed a mirror a thousand times and never given it more than a passing glance. She did not want to look at herself alone, she wanted everyone else to be looking at her. That's when she felt really alive, when she was up there on that screen, with all those other people huddled together in the dark, watching her."

Roth had become his own audience, listening to what he said like someone hearing for the first time things he had thought about but never put into words. In the silence that followed, he seemed to be thinking about what he had just heard, trying to decide how close it really came to what he knew about the woman who had, in his own mind at least, been the creature of his own invention.

"The marriage was . . . convenient," he said, looking up at me. It seemed deliberately ambiguous. Then he added, rather too quickly, I thought: "Don't misunderstand. I loved her, I really did; but it wasn't always easy."

I had the feeling he wanted to tell me more, but there would be plenty of time later to talk about his relationship with his wife; right now I needed to know more about what happened the night she died, and why he seemed so certain the police thought he had killed her.

"Who found the body? Who was at the house?"

"The maid. She found her–in the swimming pool."

"And the maid was there that night?"

"Yes."

"And she didn't hear anything, see anything?"

"No. Her room is just behind the kitchen, at the opposite end of the house. She goes to bed early. She doesn't speak that much English. I talk to her in Spanish. I asked her if she had heard Mary Margaret come in. She said she had not. I assume she told the police the same thing."

Though it would have been hard to imagine them living in anything else, I knew from the television coverage of her death that their house was one of those Beverly Hills mansions, hidden behind iron gates and tropical foliage, the only approach a long driveway curving up through a lawn tended with the same meticulous care lavished on the greens of country clubs that cater to the very rich. The house even had a name of its own, The Palms, given to it by its first owner, a star of the silent screen. For all those who believed in that shadowy, legendary epoch known as the Golden Age of Hollywood, it sounded much more romantic to hear that Stanley Roth had purchased The Palms as a wedding present for his wife, than that he had simply bought her a house.

"I assume you had a fairly elaborate security system?" I wanted to learn everything I could about how an outsider might have gotten in.

"No one broke in," said Roth, watching me closely, measuring my reaction. "There are sensors all around the perimeter. If anyone comes across the wall, if anyone climbs over the gate, a silent alarm is set off at the security office and someone is there within two minutes. Surveillance cameras are activated and everything is captured on film. Nothing happened that night. There was no alarm; the cameras never went on."

I looked at him sitting behind his desk in the cool darkness of the room where he did the work that had made him famous and where he decided who the moviegoing public would fall in love with next, and wondered if he had thought about his own situation with the same kind of detachment with which he must have gone through every script change in every film he had ever made. There were only two possibilities left and he must have known what they were.

"Everyone at the party said Mary Margaret left alone," remarked Roth. He held his hand in front of his mouth and with the tip of his little finger scratched his chin. A world-weary smile, the kind a gambler gets when he knows he has just lost everything, passed over his mouth. "The police seem convinced there were only three people in the house when she was killed: Mary Margaret, the maid, and me. I can tell you something else," he added, leaning forward, the smile a little larger. "No one thinks the maid did it."

It was not quite airtight; there was still a way a fourth person could have been there.

"Do the cameras operate whenever someone drives through the gate?"

The smile on Roth's face became intense.

"No, and that's how it happened; that's how it had to have happened. She may have left the party alone, but she brought someone here. The gate works on a combination. You enter the code, the system is deactivated, and the gate opens. The system is activated again when the garage door is closed. She brought someone home and whoever she brought home killed her."

"Did she . . . ?" I began tentatively.

"Did she often bring people home, late at night? I don't know the answer to that. Did she sleep with other men? I'm sure she did; but I couldn't say with any certainty who they were or when it happened. I imagine it happened every time she was away on location. It excited her to know that people wanted her."

The soft morning breeze rustled through the palm trees stretching high above the street outside. The light softened to a pale yellow as the shadows began to draw back across the thick green lawn. The scent of orange blossoms drifted through the room.

"No one broke in. There were no signs of a struggle. I'm the only suspect, because I'm the only one they know was there." He hesitated, as if he was struggling with himself, before he added: "I suppose there is something else you should know. I got into an argument with her–a bad argument–once. I lost my temper. I did more than that," said Roth, looking at me from under his lowered brow. "I hit her, I hit her hard. The truth of it is, I damn near killed her."

He raised his head and looked straight at me, as if he wanted to show me he would not back down from what he was about to say.

"I should have killed her for what she did. There were times after that I wished I had. But I didn't. I swear I didn't."

3

STANLEY ROTH SHOVED HIMSELF back from the desk and got to his feet. There was a trace of belligerence in his eyes, as if he expected me to say that there could not be a reason ever to strike a woman. He looked down at the floor, shook his head, and then moved to the open sliding glass door. Leaning his shoulder against the wall, he stared through the screen door which, like the frames on a roll of film, divided the visible world into a series of small, discrete images, each almost identical with the next. Somewhere not far away a lawn mower started up; and then, from a different direction, the fizzing, pulsating sound of a sprinkler shooting water, one burst after another, as it moved back and forth through a half-circle arc.

"I'm fifty-three years old. I've been married twice. The first time was a long time ago. I was just a kid. I'm fifty-three years old," he repeated as if, more than a measure of his own mortality, it was the mark of Cain. "Fifty-three years old, and I never had a child. I wanted one. We talked about it. We talked about it before we got married. That's the reason–one of the reasons–I did it: I wanted a child, and I thought she wanted one, too."

He fell into a thoughtful silence. The room was filled with the rapid, clicking sound of the sprinklers and the whirring noise of the lawn mower.

"The first I know she's pregnant," he said presently, "is when I find out she's had an abortion. She did not tell me; we never discussed it. I saw the bill from the hospital. That's how I knew: a bill from the hospital!"

His arms were folded over his chest; his mouth was a portrait in cynicism.

"You know what she said? That we could adopt. Adopt! A child to her was nothing more than a stage prop. It didn't matter to her where it came from, who it belonged to. It didn't matter to her who made it. It mattered to me, damn it! She had an abortion, and she's telling me we can adopt! She didn't want to be pregnant. That's what it came down to. She didn't want to be pregnant because she thought it would hurt her career. Her career!" he muttered with unconcealed contempt. "She should have been worried about her career."

Roth looked at me sharply, making certain, so I thought, that I was paying close attention to what he was about to say next.

"It was not even what she had done, or even what she said; it was the attitude, the 'Screw you, I'll do whatever the hell I feel like' attitude that did it. I don't know what happened. I know people say that, but it's true. I didn't think about it; it just happened. I hit her, I hit her hard. It surprised me how hard I hit her. I caught her on the side of the face. I think she must have seen it coming. She must have been moving backward; otherwise I think I would have really hurt her, maybe broken something. She ended up with a black eye, but nothing worse. I didn't mean to do it, but after I had done it, I didn't care. No, that's not true: I was glad I had done it. It was something real, something honest."

The telephone rang and with two quick steps Roth was at his desk to get it. Roth held the receiver to his ear and did not speak a word, not even hello.

While Roth listened intently, I thought about what he had just told me. He did not have to tell me that he had hit his wife or the reason why he had done it, and he certainly did not have to tell me that he had not had any regrets about doing it. Did he want me to know that if I became his lawyer he would not hold anything back? Or did he just want me to believe that he would tell me the truth? The distinction made all the difference in the world.

Roth's expression began to change. He started to tense. He glanced at me for an instant, then looked away.

"All right," said Roth finally, "let them through. But send them to the main building," he added, "not here. When they get there tell them I'm on the set and that you've already called. I'll be over in ten minutes."

His hand still on the telephone, he stared down at the desk, collecting himself. When he looked up there was a question in his eyes.

"The police are here. They have a warrant for my arrest. We have a few minutes. I need to know if you'll take my case."

I wonder if I would have made a different decision if I had known then what I know now. Another lawyer would have defended Stanley Roth, and the things that happened to me might have happened to him. And what happened to Stanley Roth . . . Well, I'm not sure anything could have changed that.

It is shameful to admit it, but the decision to represent Stanley Roth had already been made. It had been made the night he called. Perhaps in some strange sense it had been made a long time even before that, when I first saw Mary Margaret Flanders on the screen and when I first began to recognize Stanley Roth's name. Stanley Roth was a celebrity, and celebrity had become the most important thing in America, more important than wealth, more important than politics, sometimes more important than life itself. I wanted to know what it was like to be someone like Stanley Roth, and I wanted to know how Marian Walsh had become what she was, or, rather, how she had become what she seemed, and how, because of that, she had in a strange way even managed to avoid her own death. Marian Walsh might lay buried at Forest Lawn, but Mary Margaret Flanders was still moving, dancing, speaking, laughing, crying, making love, over and over again, from now until eternity, as long as anyone still cared to watch her films and there was still film to watch.

I knew what my answer was going to be, what it had to be, but I was not quite ready to tell Stanley Roth.

"When you do a picture, you insist on complete control. When I defend someone, I decide what we're going to do and when we're going to do it."

"Do whatever you have to do. That's all right. So long as you understand: If they want to accuse me of murdering my wife, they're damn well going to have to prove it," he said, thrusting his head forward to emphasize his point. "I'm not pleading to anything; I'm not going to take some deal because it'll be better for me than if I'm convicted."

I nodded my agreement and Roth picked up the phone. He spoke in a quiet, unhurried voice, a voice that, at least on this line with whomever was on the other end, was used to communicating in fragmentary phrases and half-finished sentences.

"Antonelli is in. Whatever he wants, anything he asks. Files, records." He paused, his face twisted up tight as he tried to think. "Make a list: Mary Margaret, friends, others. Anyone he should know something about." He paused again, but could think of nothing he wanted to add. "We're leaving now."

Despite his agreement that I was in charge, as soon as we left the bungalow and started walking toward the main building, he began to issue orders. They were couched in the form of suggestions, but made in the tone of someone used to having the final word.

"There are some people you might want to talk to. Start with Louis Griffin," said Roth, referring to one of his two partners in Blue Zephyr. "Next to me he knows more about this business than anyone; and he knows everything about this town. Anything you need to know about Mary Margaret, Louis can find out."

"There is a third partner, isn't there?" I asked as we walked at a brisk pace down the sidewalk.

Roth stopped and took hold of my arm. "Michael Wirthlin." Roth's eyes bored into mine. "Even if he could help, he wouldn't. He wants to run the whole thing himself."

He let go of my arm and I started to turn away, ready to resume the short walk to the main building. He caught hold of me before I could take the first step.

"He could not run this studio by himself for a week. He doesn't know anything more about this business than you do. And if you spent three weeks with me," he went on, nodding approval of his own conclusion, "I could teach you more about running a studio than he could learn in a lifetime."

Roth gazed beyond the row of palm trees lining the long, circling drive, to the large hangarlike buildings clustered close together below. The sound of the power mower came closer behind us and then, as it made its turn at the end of the lawn, gradually faded away. High above, a tiny silver speck slid across the sky, leaving behind a thin white trail dissolving into nothingness as the jet fell farther and farther away.

"Michael was brought in because he has a certain genius for money and how to raise it. But that's all he is–a money guy," said Roth as his eyes came slowly back to mine. He looked at me, making sure I understood; then he put his hand on my elbow and we again started to walk.

"All the money guys think they're really more than that," he explained with a caustic laugh. "There're two kinds of people with money in this town: people who made it because of something they did in the business, and people who either made it doing something else or had it to start with. The ones who made it in the business understand the difference between what they do and what they get paid for doing it; the others don't think there is a difference. Money is the only measure that counts. If you have more of it than someone else, that means you must be smarter. You have any idea how many people come out here–people with money–and try to buy their way in? They all want to be part of Hollywood. They like movies so they think they know how to make them. That's the strange part," said Roth, shaking his head. "How many people who like the symphony think they know how to conduct?"

We had reached the corner. On the other side of the street was a parking lot filled with automobiles, most of them Mercedeses or Jaguars, Bentleys or Rollses. Just beyond was the office building where the police were waiting to take Stanley Roth into custody.

"You didn't believe me back there, did you?" asked Roth. He stopped, his foot on the curb, peering at me, certain he was right. "You didn't believe me when I told you I didn't kill Mary Margaret."

It was an article of faith, an instinctive judgment made by nearly every defendant, the first thing–sometimes the only thing–they thought about: the demand that their lawyer believe them, believe it so intensely, so passionately that they would put everything else aside and fight for the acquittal of an obviously innocent man.

"That's good. Why should you believe anything I say just because I say it? We don't know each other. There's no reason for you to trust me–not yet, anyway."

He started to step off the curb, hesitated, and then looked at me again, this time with an expression, not of fear exactly, but of intense interest.

"What's going to happen to me–after they arrest me?"

"They'll take you downtown, to the jail. They'll take your fingerprints, your picture; then they'll put you in a cell. You'll have to stay in jail overnight. Tomorrow morning you'll be taken to court. That's when I'll try to get you out on bail."

Roth eyed me cautiously. "Try to?"

There was no point trying to hide the truth. "You might not get out at all," I told him. "It's murder; it's a capital case. They don't have to let you out on bail."

"I've been in jail before," said Roth, his eyes steady.

He saw my surprise, and it seemed to please him.

"Couple times. On location," he explained, the shadow of a smile flickering at the corners of his mouth. "A couple of weeks at Alcatraz in one picture; another time a month at the L.A. County Jail."

I felt like a fool saying it, but I said it anyway.

"The difference is you don't get to go home nights."

"You mean The Palms?" he remarked as we started toward the parking lot across the street. "I never much liked the place. Too much like a movie set," he added without apparent irony. "That's the reason Mary Margaret had to have it: The place was famous, part of 'old Hollywood.' It made her think that she had always been a part of it, that everything that had ever happened had happened because it was all leading up to her. She believed it, all of it, the whole Hollywood storybook dream."

We reached the main building, and a few minutes later, just outside his spacious studio office, we went through the ritual of surrendering to the police. I walked with him back outside the building to the police car and watched as they drove out the gate. I remembered seeing more than one movie that had ended with the suspect led away in handcuffs, driven off in a police car. Now that I thought about it, I thought about something else: My whole adult life I had been doing this kind of work and this was precisely where, instead of ending, the story always started.

"Mr. Antonelli?"

I turned around and found myself looking into the smart blue eyes of a young woman so striking that I immediately looked away, afraid that otherwise I would start to stare.

"I'm Julie Evans, Stanley's executive assistant. My car is just over here," she said as she began moving toward the parking lot.

She walked with her head held high, not a strand of the silky blonde hair that fell straight to her shoulders out of place. Dressed in a dark blue skirt and jacket and a soft white blouse, she moved with an easy assurance. She was used to being looked at, and she knew exactly what she was about.

"Stanley asked me to make sure you had everything you needed," said the confident Ms. Evans.

She was talking to me the way I imagined she would have talked to someone Roth–or Stanley, as she seemed to make a point of calling him–had asked her to show around the studio. If she was disturbed that Roth had just been arrested for murder and taken to jail she did not show it. We got to her car, a four-door white Mercedes with tan leather interior. As she backed out from the parking spot, she dialed a number on her cell phone.

"I'll be gone most of the afternoon," she said in a brisk voice, "but I'll be checking messages." She folded up the thin cell phone and put it back in her purse. "I thought we'd have lunch. Then I'll check you into the hotel."

"How long have you worked for Stanley Roth?" I asked as she drove out the front gate of the studio.

Whenever she spoke–even when, as now, she did not look at you–she raised her head and tilted it just slightly to the side.

"Almost four years. I started as a script reader at the other studio; I've been his executive assistant since he started Blue Zephyr. How long have you been a lawyer?" asked Julie without a pause.

In the presence of a beautiful woman vanity rushed forward like a coward running away. Instead of telling the truth, I exaggerated in the hope of making it seem a bigger lie than it really was.

"About a hundred years," I replied with a gruff laugh.

"You're in San Francisco now, but you used to be in Oregon–Portland–right?"

She knew the answer before she asked the question. It was her way of letting me know that she knew all about me, that she had probably been the one who had first suggested my name to Stanley Roth.

"Joseph Antonelli. Raised in Oregon, father a doctor. Undergraduate:

University of Michigan; law school: Harvard. Criminal defense attorney: Portland until a year or so ago, now in San Francisco. Never married."

Her eyes fixed on the road ahead. Both hands were on the wheel, but two fingers of her right hand tapped on it constantly, stopping only when she had something to say.

"Stanley says you're the best there is." For the first time, she glanced across at me. "What is that like–to be the best there is?"

This time it had nothing to do with vanity; this time I told her the truth, the real truth.

"After you've done something long enough, you acquire a certain reputation for it, and everyone thinks you're better than you really are. You win cases, and that's all anyone talks about–that you won; they don't know how many mistakes you made, how many times you did something, said something, and immediately wished you had not. They don't know how close you really came to losing. There's something else they don't know," I said as I looked out the window, watching all the cars jammed together on the freeway.

"What's that? What else is it they don't know?" I heard her ask.

I turned my head and looked at her, all shiny and new, too young to have won anything yet on her own, and still certain she would never have to deal with defeat.

"How often you win because the lawyer on the other side either isn't very good, or isn't willing to do what you have to do to win."

Her eyes brightened. A knowing smile flashed across her mouth.

"Be as ruthless as you are?" she asked, certain she was right.

It was not what I had meant at all.

We had lunch in a small French restaurant where everyone from the young man who parked her car to the middle-aged waiter who served us called her Miss Evans. As soon as we had been shown to our table, she whipped out her cell phone and in a voice filled with soft efficiency asked if anyone from Louis Griffin's office had called about this evening.

"Seven o'clock. His place on Mulholland. Good. Who else?"

She listened for a moment, leaning her shoulder against the sloping leather of the cylindrical booth, tapping her index finger on the white linen tablecloth, concentrating closely on what she was being told.

"No, don't send a driver. I'll bring him with me.

"You're invited to dinner. Louis Griffin. He's . . ."

"Yes, I know," I interjected. "Stanley Roth told me I should see him."

"Stanley asked me to set up a meeting." She lifted a glass of mineral water to her lips. "Louis is eager to talk to you," she went on after she finished drinking. "He's having a few people over tonight and was hoping you might come along."

"A few people?"

She proceeded to recite from memory the list of names she had just been given. The list began with Michael Wirthlin, the other partner in Blue Zephyr. The one Stanley Roth seemed to despise so much. It included an actor and an actress, both of them famous, it seemed, forever; each of them people about whom I had, like nearly everyone else, formed an opinion based on nothing but what I had seen on film and read in gossip columns. There were fourteen people, including the host and his wife. The dinner had been planned weeks before, and only because of the murder of Mary Margaret Flanders and the arrest of Stanley Roth had Julie Evans and I now been invited, in a manner of speaking, to take their places.

"What can you tell me about them–Griffin and Wirthlin?" I asked after we ordered.

"Stanley and Louis have known each other for years. Louis gave Stanley his first job as a director. They've both been in the business from the beginning. It's all they've ever wanted to do–make movies. Michael comes from a family that made billions in just about every kind of business you can imagine. When he was thirty, his father bought him a studio. A few years later, Michael sold it to the Japanese for a lot more than was paid for it and bought a company that owned cable television networks. He made another fortune on that. Then he came in with Stanley and Louis on Blue Zephyr. Michael is smart, very smart–but he doesn't know anything about making movies. Do you think he did it?" she asked, again without a pause. It was a technique which, whether or not she did it by design, managed each time to take me by surprise.

"Do I think who did what?" I asked cautiously.

The waiter brought the salad she had ordered and then began to serve me. She waited until he left before she explained.

"Do you think Stanley killed his wife?" she asked with astonishing nonchalance as she bent over the plate and lifted her fork to her mouth.

I watched her, wondering whether she had been asked by Stanley Roth to find out what I really thought about what he had told me, or whether she was asking on her own, hoping to become the one in whom I might confide things I would not tell even him.

"What do you think? You know him much better than I do. Do you think Stanley Roth murdered his wife?"

She put down her fork, lifted her head, tilted it slightly to the side and looked at me, a smile curling over her mouth.

"Yes, as a matter of fact, I do."

4

THERE HAD BEEN NOT the slightest hesitation, none of that deliberate troubled uncertainty by which people exhibit the reluctance they feel at saying what they have come to believe. Julie Evans had said she thought Stanley Roth had murdered his wife as if she had been asked a question about someone she had never met. I could not hide my surprise.

"I didn't say I thought he did it on purpose," said Julie as she took a small bite of her salad. "I wouldn't believe that at all. It wouldn't have been something he planned to do. But lose control–do it without thinking–do it because he got so angry he didn't know what he was doing until it was too late and she was already dead? Yes, I think that could have happened."

Laying down her fork, she placed both elbows on the table and laced her fingers together under her chin. Her blue eyes flared open; a rueful smile flashed across her mouth.

"They fought a lot–about money, about the movies she was in, about the movies she wanted to be in–about other men . . ." Her eyes moved past me, her smile becoming brittle, almost belligerent. Staring into the distance, she added, "About other women." The smile faded away, and when she turned to me there was a wistful look in her eyes. "They fought all the time."

"Other women?" I asked, searching her eyes, almost certain that she had been talking about herself.

"She thought so," answered Julie. "It's too bad she was wrong."

Why did I feel a slight twinge of disappointment? Was it was because the picture of Mary Margaret Flanders throwing an ashtray in a fit of jealous rage did not correspond to what I had thought she was like when

I watched her making love to other men, imagining she was making love with me? Was it because Julie Evans, tangible and real, and not some cinematic creation that flickered in the shared solitude of a movie theater, was as much in love with Stanley Roth, and as little attracted to me, as had been his movie-star wife? I did not know. All I knew for sure was that the three of them–the actress, the director, the director's assistant–lived separate and apart from people like me, people who could only watch and admire and even envy a little what they did.

After lunch, Julie drove me to the hotel where someone at Blue Zephyr had decided I should stay. I would wonder later if it had been deliberate, or like so many other things that happened in Hollywood, the kind of chance decision that eventually took on a meaning all its own. From the beginning, the Chateau Marmont had been a place where what people believed was the only reality that mattered. Out on a lonely stretch of Sunset Boulevard, where just a few small houses were scattered in the hills among the sagebrush and tumbleweed; out in the empty space between Los Angeles and Beverly Hills; out so far in the middle of nowhere that when it first opened the telephone operator told anyone who called that it was fifteen minutes from everywhere; a Los Angeles attorney who had fallen in love with a medieval castle on the banks of the Loire designed an apartment building meant to look like a French château. Seen from a distance it had looked a little like the false front of a movie set.

The apartments were too expensive and almost before it opened it became a hotel. The legends started at once. Everyone believed that Rudolph Valentino had been one of the very first guests, though when it opened in 1929 he had been dead for more than two years. Clark Gable supposedly proposed to Carole Lombard in the penthouse, though it turns out he never lived there. Lauren Bacall denied it, but before she married Humphrey Bogart they were said to have frequently stayed there together. Joanne Woodward claimed it was "pure Hollywood legend," but according to the legend, it was the place where Paul Newman asked her to marry him. Lucille Ball threw a valise filled with money at Desi Arnaz from the balcony of their suite at the Chateau Marmont as he walked away below. She missed him, the valise hit the pavement, and money flew all over the lawn. It was not the kind of thing anyone would ever likely forget, but no one was ever found who remembered seeing it. Bill Tilden was supposed to have been the tennis pro at the hotel, though the Marmont never had one. Proving the ultimate fiction of what everyone took for the truth, there was for a time a story that the Marmont was secretly owned by none other than Greta Garbo herself.

Julie glanced around the suite making certain everything was the way it was supposed to be. Then she pulled out a small leather-covered notebook and asked me what I needed.

I gestured toward one of the two silk damask sofas that faced each other in front of a marble fireplace. She sat at an angle on the edge of the sofa, her long sleek legs pressed together, her skirt just above her knees.

"It's been two hours since Roth was picked up. It won't be long before everyone knows he's been arrested. The calls are going to start coming in. Who is going to handle this at the studio?"

She had been looking at me with the efficient gaze of someone never caught short, someone always one step ahead, but she had not thought of this. Her lips parted and then closed, as she tried to come up with an answer.

"I want everything to go through you," I said as I got to my feet.

She started to object. "We have a whole publicity department." She thought of something else. "What about Louis Griffin? What about Michael Wirthlin? They'll insist any statement on behalf of Blue Zephyr is cleared by them first."

"Stanley Roth is head of Blue Zephyr, right?" I asked, looking down at her.

"Yes, but . . ."

"He speaks for Blue Zephyr, doesn't he?"

"Yes, but . . ."

"Well, I represent Stanley Roth, and I speak for him. So here is what we're going to do," I said as I walked toward the desk on the other side of the room. I opened my briefcase, took out a legal pad, and sat down. "We're going to draft a press release for Blue Zephyr Pictures and we–I mean you–are going to call a press conference at the studio for four o'clock this afternoon."

We wrote a simple, straightforward release in which the studio announced that Stanley Roth had voluntarily turned himself into the Los Angeles police department; that he was being charged with the murder of his wife, the actress Mary Margaret Flanders; that he declared categorically that he was innocent of those charges; and that he had no doubt whatsoever that after a trial by jury he would be exonerated completely. The last sentence read:

"Everyone at Blue Zephyr, everyone who knows Stanley Roth, knows he could not possibly have been responsible for the murder of Mary Margaret Flanders, the woman he loved, the woman whose death has left him devastated."

Julie cocked her head and raised an eyebrow.

"Everyone," I repeated.

We spent a few more minutes going over it, changing a word, adding a phrase, until we were both satisfied.

"Can you call it in, have someone at the studio put it out? Along with the announcement of the press conference?"

While she was on the phone, I went into the bathroom and put on a fresh shirt and a new tie. I threw some water on my face and tried to convince myself that I had agreed to defend Stanley Roth because I thought he might actually be innocent and not because, like some starstruck teenager, I wanted to be close to the famous people who made movies. The tie, a blue-and-gold regimental stripe, did not work: the line where the two colors met would look like a blur on television. I took it off and put on a solid, dark blue.

"I should have gotten a haircut," I remarked, irritated with myself, as we left the hotel.

I was still complaining about the way I looked when the car was brought round. Julie adjusted the rearview mirror. She ran her fingertip quickly over the lashes of her left eye, then briefly touched her chin. "Damn," she muttered softly. Reaching inside her purse, she found her lipstick. "There," she said, satisfied for the moment with the way she looked. She replaced the cap on the lipstick and put it away.

"You look fine," she added as she merged with the traffic on Sunset

Boulevard. A faint, teasing smile edged its way onto her mouth. "Would you like to have someone come over from makeup before the press conference?"

I felt a tinge of embarrassment, proof that I was as vain as she had suggested. Before I could think of some self-deprecating remark that might make her think that I did not take myself quite so seriously, she picked up her cell phone and called her office.

"You were right," she said as she hung up, her eyes fixed on the road as she maneuvered through traffic. "The story is all over the place. The phone has been ringing off the hook. The publicity people aren't sure what to do. They think the press release goes a little too far; they think . . ."

"I don't give a damn what they think," I said firmly. "That release goes the way it is. Call your office again," I insisted. "Tell them Stanley Roth said to do it. Have they announced the press conference?"

She was not sure they had. She called again, insisted the release go out at once and said that someone was going to have to answer for it if it did not. Whoever she was talking to then said something that for a moment seemed to take her breath away.

"Tell me that again," she said, her voice suddenly subdued. She turned off the phone, slipped it into her purse and stared ahead at the highway. Her hands gripped the wheel tightly and she fought back a tear. Slowly, bitterly, she began to shake her head.

"Those bastards," she muttered to herself.

"What happened?"

"They won't put out the release. They won't allow a press conference. They don't think the studio should be involved."

The traffic had come to a grinding halt. We were sitting in the middle of the freeway, going nowhere. Julie sat back against the leather seat and sighed.

"There's nothing I can do," she remarked, rolling her head a quarter turn until her eyes met mine. "The decision was made by both Lewis and Michael," she said, referring to Stanley Roth's two partners. "They'll do everything they can to help," she added, a cynical edge to her voice, "but the studio has to stay out of it. Whatever happens to Stanley, they're not going to allow it to jeopardize Blue Zephyr. There is too much at stake."

"What are they telling the reporters who call?" I asked as I thought about what to do next.

"Nothing, just the generic nonresponse: 'The studio has no statement to make at this time.'"

I started to smile. "Who do you work for: Stanley Roth or Blue Zephyr?"

Puzzled by my smile, she answered, "Stanley Roth is Blue Zephyr."

I picked up her cell phone and handed it to her. "Good. Now call the *L.A. Times*, call the television stations, call the networks, call everyone you can think of. The studio won't make a statement–we will."

"If I do that, it could cost me my job," said Julie.

"If you don't do it, it could cost Stanley Roth his life."

By four o'clock that afternoon the crowd of reporters and television crews at the main entrance to Blue Zephyr was so large no one could get in or out. The afternoon sun bathed the iron-gated front in a soft golden haze. Designed by Stanley Roth to look like what people remembered about the Hollywood of the 1940s, the studio was the perfect backdrop for the formal announcement that the director had been arrested for the murder of the star.

At my signal, Julie Evans stepped forward, and in front of a battery of microphones faced the cameras. She stood straight and tall, a single sheet of paper held in her left hand.

"I am Julie Evans," she announced in a low, quietly confident voice, "executive assistant to Stanley Roth, head of Blue Zephyr Pictures."

She held the sheet of paper in both hands and began to read, pausing after every few words to look into the cameras. A seasoned actor could not have done it to better effect.

"Earlier today, Stanley Roth voluntarily turned himself into the Los Angeles police department. Mr. Roth has been arrested in connection with the death of his wife, Mary Margaret Flanders. Mr. Roth has categorically denied any involvement in this awful crime. Mr. Roth has no doubt whatsoever that he will be fully exonerated."

Dropping her hand to the side, Julie lifted her chin and looked directly into the camera.

"I'm sure that I speak for everyone at Blue Zephyr, as well as everyone who knows him, when I say that Stanley Roth could not possibly have had anything to do with the tragic death of his wife. The police have made a mistake. We can only hope they do not compound it by failing to continue their investigation into who is really responsible for the death of our dear friend, Mary Margaret Flanders."

Julie looked down at the ground as if she needed to collect herself. "From this point forward," she said, lifting her eyes, "Joseph Antonelli will handle all inquires about the case."

I had a short statement of my own. I began with the one thing I wanted everyone who was going to see this on the news, including especially anyone who might be called as a juror, to hear and to remember.

"Stanley Roth swore to me that he did not murder his wife. He swore to me that he did not do it, and he swore to me that he does not know who did. He loved his wife and he was almost destroyed by her death; and now, as if he had not suffered enough, the police arrest him for a crime he did not commit because they can't find anyone else to blame and because they don't want to admit that they don't know what they're doing."

It was deliberately provocative, and, just as I hoped, it produced a response. From somewhere in the crowd a reporter shouted:

"Are you accusing the police of arresting someone they know to be innocent?"

I could feel on my face the glow of the hot dry sun. All around me, like a swarm of insects, I could hear the quick clicking noise as photographers snapped their cameras. At the far edge of the crowd one of the groundkeepers was holding his rake in front of him, watching with a look of disinterested detachment all the commotion. Things seemed more vivid, more real, everything more clearly distinguished, more sharply defined than I had seen them before. I was standing there, the center of attention, listening to the question, then listening to what I said in reply, an observer of my own performance, as detached, if not quite as disinterested, as that elderly stoop-shouldered Hispanic leaning on his rake.

I bent forward, staring straight into the television camera, and in a single sentence went as far as I could to put the police on trial instead of Stanley Roth.

"The police arrested the wrong man because they had no idea who the right man was and knew they never would."

"That's a fairly serious charge, isn't it?" demanded another reporter.

"Murder is a fairly serious charge," I countered. "One that shouldn't be made without an investigation that attempts to find the truth instead of one that starts out by deciding who you want to be guilty."

There was a stunned reaction, a brief pause while, like an audience that thinks with one mind, they grasped the full implications of what I had just said. Then they exploded into a raucous shouting match, each of them trying to be the first to ask the question that had simultaneously become obvious and imperative to them all.

"Are you saying the police framed Stanley Roth for the murder of his wife?"

I had not said that at all, but it did not bother me that they wanted me to say that I had. I waited for a second to reply, as if I were choosing my words with unusual care.

"I'm sure anyone who watches this trial will be able to answer that question for themselves," I said, adopting a slightly ominous tone.

The old man at the back pushed his straw hat farther down on his forehead and began slowly and methodically to rake the grass. None of the reporters jammed together in front of where he had been noticed he was gone.

"If Stanley Roth is innocent–if the police have really arrested the wrong man," asked a rumpled-looking middle-aged reporter in a transparently cynical voice, "then who murdered Mary Margaret Flanders?"

Without looking around, I could feel the eyes of Julie Evans, watching intently, waiting to hear what I was going to say. I turned until I was facing the reporter, singling him out.

"The killer of Mary Margaret Flanders was not her husband, but it was someone she knew," I said with perfect confidence. "It was someone she brought home that night." I paused just for an instant, and then, as if I knew a great deal more than I was going to say, added: "Someone she had known for a very long time."

It made them crazy. They were screaming, demanding to be heard.

Who had she brought home? Who had she known for a long time? Who was it? Who killed her? Who killed Mary Margaret Flanders?

I refused to say another word until they stopped; and when they did I still would not tell them what they wanted to know.

"The answer to that," I said with a grim smile, "will have to wait for the trial."

That was not good enough, not by half.

"Then you don't know who killed her, do you?" a voice yelled out.

"I've told you all I can," was my deliberately enigmatic reply.

Before anyone could ask another question, I made a second announcement.

"Stanley Roth has been arrested. Tomorrow morning, Mr. Roth will enter a plea of not guilty, and we will ask that a jury trial be scheduled for the earliest possible date. Stanley Roth wants to clear his name without delay, and he wants the police to begin a proper investigation into the murder of his wife."

I turned toward Julie Evans. She immediately stepped in front of me and announced that the press conference was over.

"For someone who just got here this morning, you certainly sound like you know everything there is to know about this case," whispered Julie as we slipped inside the gate and headed toward her studio office. "It sounds like you know who the murderer is."

The truth of course was that I did not know anything at all, except the importance of making it appear that I knew everything. That Stanley Roth had been arrested would be enough to make most people believe he was guilty. By insisting that the police were wrong, and perhaps even knew it; by claiming that the real killer was still out there, and suggesting that I had a pretty good idea who it might be, I had at least a chance to make a few of them think that Stanley Roth might not be guilty after all. First impressions are everything. When the television news first reported the arrest of Stanley Roth for the murder of his movie-star wife, the image I wanted them to see was not that of a killer finally caught, but of an innocent man falsely accused.

"At least they haven't changed the lock," remarked Julie as we entered her office.

There were three doors to Julie Evans's office on the second floor of the building that housed all of the studio's top executives. The one we had entered opened directly onto the hallway. The wooden door bore no markings of any kind, nothing to indicate who, or what, was behind it. Anyone with an appointment to see her went to the next door down the corridor, frosted glass with her name and title, executive assistant to Stanley Roth, lettered in gold. The third door connected her office to that of the great director and head of studio himself. It was closed and in the hushed atmosphere of her thick carpeted office I had the feeling that the only time it ever opened was when he came through it.

"We have an hour before we have to go," said Julie as she glanced at a cylindrical glass clock on the wall across from the rectangular glass table she used as a desk. It had no drawer, no place in which to file anything away. A telephone and a gold pen and pencil set were the only objects set on top. Behind her, a long credenza was stacked with what I assumed were movie scripts on which Stanley Roth was working and the countless memoranda of other things he wanted her to do.

Lifting the telephone, she whispered a word. A few moments later the door to the outer office opened and a well-dressed woman with silver-gray hair and thick glasses brought in an armload of shiny black plastic folders and set them on the desk.

"These are the studio files on Mary Margaret Flanders," Julie explained. After tapping them into a perfect rectangle, she rose from her chair and took them into her arms.

"Stanley said you should use his office," said Julie.

She waited for me to open the door and then led me inside. As she put the files down on Stanley Roth's desk, she stole a glance at me, eager to watch my reaction. I had never seen anything quite like it. Everything in the room, which must have been forty feet long and twenty or twenty-five feet wide, was white. Everything, not just the ceiling and the walls and a few pieces of furniture–everything: his desk and the chair that went with it; the plush, deep-pile wall-to-wall carpet; the fireplace, including the bricks inside; the two facing sofas; the lamps; the curtains; the blinds; even a white pen and pencil set prominently displayed in the middle of the front edge of the desk.

"Stanley is a traditionalist," explained Julie with a straight face. "Samuel Goldwyn's office was like this: everything white. It could be worse. David Selznick had everything green, and not a very nice green, either," she said as she moved toward the door to her office. "And not just his office: he had his car painted that color. Do you believe it?"

"And those were the people who made the movies I used to love," I said, shaking my head.

"Discouraging, isn't it?" she said with a conciliatory smile as she left.

There was not a great deal to be learned from the studio files on Mary Margaret Flanders, nothing that anyone who had seen her movies and read the gossip columns would not already have known. There were literally dozens of photographs, used over the years for publicity; endless press releases used to promote her pictures; and, of course, copies of all the contracts entered into between her and the studio for the films she had done for Blue Zephyr.

I had been there for perhaps half an hour when the door opened, not the one to Julie Evans's office, but another one, on the opposite side of the room. A man in a tan double-breasted suit with small dark eyes and a pinched mouth glared at me. He was short, five foot five if he was that. He kept staring at me, as if I had committed some unpardonable act.

"Mr. Roth isn't here," I said as I started to rise from the chair. "My name is Joseph Antonelli. Can I help you in some way?"

He glared at me with renewed intensity, as if what I had said had offended him even more. He turned on his heel and left, swinging the door shut behind him. I went back to what I was reading. Another thirty minutes went by, and I was nearly finished when Julie suddenly appeared.

"It's time we got started," she said, reminding me that in traffic it could take an hour to get to the dinner at the home of Louis Griffin.

I nodded and finished the last page.

"This is a contract for a picture that apparently hasn't been released," I said as I closed the file.

"Hasn't been finished. I'm not sure what's going to happen," she began as she gathered up the files to take them back to her office. "There were still a few scenes left to shoot with Mary Margaret. They either have to shoot around her or they have to junk the picture. That would be a disaster. It's already over budget, and the budget was a hundred million. Maybe we'll find out tonight," she said as we shut the door to Stanley Roth's office behind us. "If they don't shoot us first for what we did with the press."

5

THE HOUSE WHERE LOUIS GRIFFIN sometimes lived and frequently entertained was either the third or the fourth one built on what had originally been a chicken ranch on what eventually became Mulholland Drive. A silent film star bought the land a few years before the Depression and spent what was then considered a fortune on the construction of a Tudor mansion supposed to remind him of the England of his youth. That the actor in question had been born in Brooklyn with an unpronounceable Slovakian name had long since been forgotten, even, perhaps, by him. His career came to a gradual end and he lived a strange, embittered existence in which he scarcely ever left the house and was almost never sober. Sometime in the late 1930s–1938 or '39–by now a drunken wreck, he was running one of his favorite movies when the celluloid film caught fire, perhaps from a cigarette left unextinguished in an ashtray next to the projector. The house burned to the ground, and the charred remains of the actor, who had been too intoxicated to move, or too mesmerized by his own performance, was found in the chair in which he had been sitting, still facing what was left of the screen.

It sat there, during the long years of the war, three blackened, evil-looking chimneys towering high above a naked, twisted heap of jagged broken beams, coal gray bricks and melted leaded glass. In 1946, an industrialist who had been paid millions to develop faster fighter planes for the Navy, but had not produced even one of them before the war ended, bought the property and in place of the old Tudor mansion built a new Spanish villa. When he died forty years later, an old man who had outlived three wives and mistresses without number, the house had fallen into disrepair. Behind the bougainvillea, huge cracks spread over the walls. On the few days each year when the rains came, the broken tiles on the roof let the water drip through to the floor below. It had finally achieved the look that had appealed so much to the uninformed imagination of his middle age, a house that could be mistaken for one built under the Spanish land grants by which California had originally been divided.

Louis Griffin did not care how old it was, only that it was too small. Under the tutelage of his socially ambitious wife, he had become a collector of art, though neither he nor his wife knew all that much about it. By virtue of her husband's large contributions, she became a member of the board of The Museum of Modern Art; by virtue of his wife's insistent and very public enthusiasm, he became a major buyer of the works of almost anyone who had the wit to call what they did Postimpressionism. They tore down the forty-year-old Spanish villa and built in its place a glass and stucco contemporary with fifteen-foot ceilings and endless temperature-controlled corridors. Three months after it was finished, the house was shifted off its foundation and completely destroyed by an earthquake. Apart from a thin covering of dust, none of the pieces of their collection suffered any serious damage. Construction began again, this time with reinforced steel, and the house of Mr. and Mrs. Louis Griffin was given a second life.

We came around the bend and stopped at the gold-tipped black iron gate between two rows of boxed hedges that hid from view everything except the first few yards of the circular drive. Julie rolled down her window, and pushed the speaker button on a metal intercom. Harsh with static, a voice asked her to identify herself. Patiently, she gave both our names. A moment later, the gate parted in the middle, and each half slowly pulled back to the side.

It was seven o'clock precisely when we arrived in front of the house and turned the car over to the parking attendant. We were right on time, and we were the last to arrive. A Rolls-Royce, a Bentley, and three Mercedeses were lined up together in the area reserved for guests at the far edge of the drive. I exchanged a glance with Julie as we walked toward the large sculpted double doors at the entrance.

"It means everyone wanted to be here when you arrived." She pushed the doorbell, a wry, fugitive smile on her mouth. "As of about two hours ago, when that press conference was first carried on television, you became the newest famous person in town."

Like someone getting ready for a formal appearance, Julie straightened up, quickly running her hand over her forehead, sweeping out of the way a single strand of hair.

"Which means," she added, adjusting her smile for the enthusiastic greeting she was ready to exchange the moment the door swung open, "you're now the most famous person in town."

Without quite knowing why, I buttoned my jacket and slid my hand quickly across my shirt, making certain my tie was in place.

Though he had servants who could have done it, Louis Griffin usually answered the door himself.

"Hello, Louis," said Julie, beaming right on cue when the door opened. She kissed Louis Griffin on the side of his face and then, her hand on his arm, introduced him to me.

We shook hands; or, rather, I grasped his hand and he allowed me to do so, though only for an instant. Almost the moment I touched his soft, supple hand, he was letting go. Strangely enough, it did not convey unfriendliness, much less contempt; it seemed more an expression of discomfort, a kind of instinctive shy aversion to the kind of mauling, backslapping greeting often inflicted by people who want you to think you're friends.

Dressed in a tan jacket and a white dress shirt open at the collar, a pair of slacks slightly darker than the jacket, and a pair of brown woven loafers, Griffin was thin and angular. If you had seen him first in a photograph taken of him alone you would have thought him much taller than he actually was. In fact he was nearly as short as the man who had stared daggers when he found me sitting in Stanley Roth's office, five foot six at the outside. He had a high forehead and a rather querulous mouth, as if over the years he had come to expect unpleasantness. What caught your attention immediately, however, were his eyes, not the way they looked, but the way they worked. He would turn toward you and in a strange, rapid rhythm, quickly blink twice. Only then would he speak.

Griffin led us into the dining room where everyone had already been seated. As soon as we entered the room, they all circled around me, waiting to be introduced. Smiling to herself, Julie found her place at the table.

Three of the people I met were people I had seen before, in movies that as best I could remember went back at least twenty or thirty years, famous faces that were always there on the magazines at every airport and grocery store, faces I saw more often than all but a few of my friends. Two of them, Walker Bradley and the much younger Carole Conrad, were husband and wife. It was said that he married her because she was the last woman he had slept with when he was single and there were not any more left. Whether it was the result of his legendary amorous adventures, or the consequence of repeated cosmetic surgery, Bradley had the wide-eyed, tired look of someone who had just jumped out of the shower after not having gone to bed the night before. His wife, decades younger, grasped my hand with both of hers and looked at me with such gushing sincerity that her eyes, squinting tight, began to grow moist.

The other face I knew belonged to one of the loveliest women I had ever seen. If anything, Elizabeth Hawking was even more beautiful off the screen than she was on it. She had begun her career about the same time as Mary Margaret Flanders, but had not been quite so successful. She was considered too refined, too innocent, for the kind of explosive, sexually explicit parts that had made Mary Margaret Flanders such a box office draw. There was a sort of glittering eagerness about her that made you like her the moment you saw her. She was with a man I did not recognize. Melvin Shorenstein was the head of Universal Creative Management, UCM, the biggest agency in the business. Shorenstein represented Elizabeth Hawking. He had also represented, as he immediately mentioned, Mary Margaret Flanders. He shook my hand firmly.

"Stanley didn't do it," said Shorenstein with a quick glance at the other people gathered around. "You can believe me about that," he said earnestly, still gripping my hand. "Stanley didn't do it. Stanley was in love with her. You can believe me about that," he added as he finally let go.

Standing behind Shorenstein, waiting for him to finish, was an attractive couple in their early forties, William S. Pomeroy, the producer, and his wife, Estelle, a writer. He seemed vaguely familiar. Then I remembered that his father had been a prominent and widely respected senator from Michigan, married to the daughter of one of the early, legendary figures in the automobile industry. I remembered what Stanley Roth had said about the privileged sons of wealthy parents who tried to get into the movie business, but Pomeroy could have made it on his own.

Louis Griffin put his arm around my shoulder and turned me toward a tall, well-built man in his seventies with flowing snow-white hair and blue, curious eyes. An eager smile of baffled enthusiasm stretched across his strong mouth, lending him the look of someone determined to plunge ahead, confident in the belief that the good intentions of an honest heart will always triumph in the end.

"You're Robert Mansfield," I blurted out before I could recover from the surprise of finding myself suddenly face to face with the idol of my youth.

"Yes," he replied, pumping my hand like we were old friends meeting after a protracted absence. "Yes," he repeated, laughing heartily.

The laughter stopped. He looked at me intently.

"And you are?"

"Joseph Antonelli," I said quietly as if it was something that must just have slipped his mind.

Mansfield brightened immediately. "Oh, yes. Joseph Antonelli. Yes, yes; that's fine, just fine."

He pumped my hand twice more, then let go and turned to his wife, a handsome Latin woman of an age not much different than his own. She took her eyes off him only long enough to bestow upon me a gracious smile.

"And these two beautiful women," said Louis Griffin, putting his arm around both of them, "are my wife, Clarice, and Rebecca Wirthlin."

Michael Wirthlin was sitting at the table, talking to Julie. He was the only one who had not come to greet me. When I got a clear look at him, I was not surprised. He was the same man who had come into Stanley Roth's office and found me sitting at his partner's desk. When I sat down, we were introduced across the table. His only response was a single polite nod. Turning away, he resumed his conversation with Julie Evans, seated on his right.

The dining room faced out onto a courtyard and a long shallow rectangular pond filled with water lilies. A pair of white swans glided effortlessly from one end to the other. Three silent waiters served dinner, while a fourth appeared out of nowhere whenever a glass needed refilling.

"You've all had a chance to meet Joseph Antonelli," said Louis Griffin after everyone had started on their salad. He turned to me. "All of us are very interested in anything you can tell us about the case–what you expect to happen–whether Stanley will have to stay in jail until the trial."

Griffin hesitated. As an embarrassed smile flashed across his mouth, he thought about what he was going to say. He quickly blinked twice.

"This is a little awkward, of course; but I'm afraid that what has happened affects us all."

Griffin seemed to think that I knew what he meant. He waited for me to tell him, to tell them all, what I thought. Just as I opened my mouth to express my bewilderment, I heard the voice that years before had so often held my attention and captured my imagination.

"You know, Bogie was almost murdered," announced Robert Mansfield with that slightly astonished look he always had whenever he said something that had just occurred to him. "When he first started seeing Lauren," he explained. "It was his third wife–or was it his second?–Mayo, Mayo Methot. Yes, that was her name. By God, I never did know why he married her," he said, leaning forward, his arms stretched out on the table. He looked slowly from side to side. "She was not at all attractive. He came home one night after drying out at a place somewhere down on Sunset Boulevard–can't remember the name of it right now, but a lot of the fellows used to go there when they wanted to stop drinking for a while. Bogie comes home and Mayo is standing in the living room singing–singing, mind you!–'Embraceable You.' That was the song. Apparently, she sang it all the time, not because she liked it that much, but as a warning, a warning that she was going to do something. Well, she did something all right. She was holding a kitchen knife behind her back, singing 'Embraceable You,' and she lunged at him. She did not get him, though–not at first. Bogie ducked out of the way and tried to run. But she caught him, stabbed him in the back. He woke up on the floor, heard the doctor say it wasn't that bad, that he was lucky, only the tip of the knife had gone in. Then he passed out again. Wasn't like in the movies."

He was looking at me, that great baffled smile on his face, just the way I had always seen it.

"Do you like the movies?" he asked. The smile did not change, it did not move; but something behind it seemed to go away, and what was left was something lonely, something a little lost.

"Yes, I like the movies; although I have to admit I liked them a lot more when you were still making them. Those were my favorites. I haven't seen anything as good since."

Part of him came back. There was a glimmer, not of gratitude exactly; more like recognition of something we both understood, a fact on which we could both agree.

After the main course was served, Michael Wirthlin, who had not spoken a word to me, broke off a brief conversation he had been having with the actress Elizabeth Hawking.

"Mr. Antonelli," he said in a surprisingly rich, cultured voice, "Louis was asking your reaction about this terrible situation in which we now find ourselves."

He held his hands in front of him, dangling over the table, the tips of his fingers pressed together. A smile of purely artificial politeness covered his small closed mouth. Like a bookkeeper in the back room, his eyes began to take my measure.

"Let me explain," he went on, darting a brief glance to the end of the table, as if to signal Griffin that what he was about to say concerned him as well. "When Mary Margaret . . . died," said Wirthlin, consciously diplomatic, "we were just days away from finishing her last picture. The studio has over a hundred million invested in this project."

I kept looking at Wirthlin, but out of the corner of my eye I watched Julie's reaction. She had told me this was the thing with which the studio would be most concerned. Her face was a mask of indifference, as if she found nothing unsavory or even unusual in calculating the economic consequences of someone's death.

"I'm sure you understand. We could not just walk away from it; we have to finish. It's difficult, but Bill has pulled everything together," said Wirthlin, nodding toward William Pomeroy. "The writers have come up with a new ending, one that works without Mary Margaret. It shouldn't take more than a few weeks to finish."

Wirthlin permitted himself another brief, pointless smile.

"We had planned to release the movie as soon as possible."

I was beginning to understand. I crossed my arms over my chest and smiled back.

"While everyone still has her fresh in their minds," I ventured to say.

"Yes, of course," he said, glad that I was not wholly ignorant of the way things in his world worked. "When something like this happens," he added, just to be sure, "when someone famous dies, there is a period of time–a fairly short period of time–when that is all anyone wants to talk about. When Princess Diana died, for example. But wait a year, or even sometimes just a few months, and no one cares anymore. They have other things on their minds. It's almost as if that person who was so well known, so well loved, had never really existed at all."

Wirthlin paused, waiting for some kind of response. I made no reply, and then, as if to impress upon me that there was some as yet undefined sense in which I was involved in this as well, he added:

"It was Stanley's idea. He insisted upon it. No, he demanded that we finish the picture and get it out."

"As a tribute to Mary Margaret," said Pomeroy's wife, apparently without thinking.

Wirthlin shot a disapproving glance in her direction, like someone correcting a child.

"That's right," said Wirthlin, as if she had only been echoing what he felt. "We all want this, her last movie–which, by the way, we all think is her best–to be a tribute to her memory. But, now, with that unfortunate business today, there may be a problem."

"A problem?" I asked.

"Yes. It's what you said today, in that press conference, the one you held outside the studio. You said that whoever killed Mary Margaret was someone she brought home with her."

I wanted him to say exactly what he had on his mind. I stretched out my legs under the table, crossing one ankle over the other, and then lowered my head.

"How is that a problem?" I asked, narrowing my eyes as I looked at him from under my brow.

He pulled his head a little way back and for a moment searched my eyes.

"Because it suggests that there was something illicit going on."

"Christ, Michael, she was murdered! And you're worried about 'illicit'?" exclaimed Elizabeth Hawking in a sarcastic, high-pitched voice that was nothing like the smooth gentility of the one she used in her movies.

Wirthlin winced, but did not waste time on a look.

"Mary Margaret Flanders had a certain image," he went on, concentrating his attention on me; "an image carefully cultivated, and at considerable expense, over a long period of time. No one is minimizing the tragedy of her death, but–and I think Stanley would agree with this–the one thing that could make what's happened even worse is if her public were to turn on her because of some vague suspicions surrounding her death. I'm sure you can find a way to defend Stanley without subjecting his wife to innuendo and without damaging the substantial interests of the studio he helped to create and she did so much to make successful."

I took my eyes off Wirthlin long enough to glance at Julie Evans. Avoiding my gaze, she began to pick at her food.

My first impulse was to tell Wirthlin that it was none of his business what I did; my second was to let him know what I thought by ignoring what he had said. I turned away from Wirthlin and caught the eye of Walker Bradley.

"You knew Mary Margaret Flanders. Who do you think she might have brought home with her late at night, when her husband was already asleep and she knew she would not be disturbed?"

Even when he was not in a movie, Bradley always played himself. In the same way I had seen him do it dozens of times before, he moved his head a little to the side and, with his mouth partly open, ready to reply, waited while I finished the question.

"No," he insisted, "I don't know anyone she would have done that with." Holding his wife's hand, he drew himself up and with all the sincerity he could muster insisted again, "I can't believe it could have been someone she knew. Everybody loved her."

"Did Stanley love her?" asked Elizabeth Hawking out loud. "I wonder if he really did?"

"What do you mean by that?" asked Clarice Griffin, not so much offended, as interested, in the suggestion implicit in the question. Everyone around the table turned to see what Elizabeth Hawking was going to say next.

At first she did not say anything at all. A wistful smile floated across her mouth, the brief reflection of something remembered, some sorrow left in her own heart, made perhaps inevitable by who and what she had become.

"Rita Hayworth played the lead in a movie called *Gilda*, the movie that made her a star. . . ."

"Gilda!" cried Robert Mansfield with a sudden burst of energy. "Oh, yes, I knew Gilda!"

The spark was back in his wintry eyes. He was ready to regale us with another dimly remembered episode from his embellished past. His wife placed a cautionary hand on his sleeve. Suddenly subdued, he bent his forehead and instead of speaking, cleared his throat.

"Rita Hayworth supposedly said," continued Hawking, "that her problem with men was that they went to bed with Gilda and woke up with her. That's what I meant, about whether Stanley Roth loved–really loved–Mary Margaret. That's all."

I stole a glimpse at the aging Robert Mansfield. He was staring down at the table, a curious smile crossing his still remarkably handsome face, listening, I imagined, to all the things about Gilda he had now to keep to himself.

Michael Wirthlin's small mouth hardened into an expression of irritation. He put his hands once again in front of him, only now, instead of pressing his fingers together, he began to tap them against each other. His eyes were focused on them, or rather on something just the other side of them.

"So what you're saying," he said, his stare becoming more intense, "is that, contrary to what Antonelli here was telling us–what he was telling the world just a few hours ago–that she brought someone back to the house with her who killed her, Stanley Roth, the head of the studio, did it after all?"

Elizabeth had begun to laugh before he had finished; and when he had, she threw down her napkin and laughed some more.

"Christ, Michael," she said with a derisive grin, "that isn't what I said and you know it. Why don't you try listening to someone once in a while?"

There was a slight flash of embarrassment, not on the face of Michael Wirthlin, but on that of his wife. That was when I knew what everyone else in that room must already have known: Michael Wirthlin and Elizabeth Hawking had once been lovers. It explained why they now hated each other so much.

Louis Griffin tried to smooth things over.

"I'm sure no one thinks that Stanley had anything to do with Mary Margaret's death," he said in a solemn, ingratiating tone. "It's all a terrible tragedy, a tragedy twice compounded, really. First, the death of Mary Margaret, and now this."

He shook his head sadly, and then, as if to signal that there were other things, also serious, that had to be considered, he slowly lifted his eyebrows.

"But Michael is right. We have to concern ourselves with our own responsibilities and with those things over which we have some measure of control. I don't see that we have any choice but to release Mary Margaret's last film as soon as possible. With a hundred million into it, we can't really afford to wait to see how things come out at the trial."

He paused, a pensive expression on his face, and looked at me.

"This is such an awkward situation to be in. Michael and I–everyone at the studio–have just been beside ourselves. It's hard to know what to do, and we obviously haven't done very well so far. We don't mean for a minute that we don't want you to do everything you can to defend Stanley. Good God, Stanley is the best friend I have, and if it weren't for him, Blue Zephyr would not exist. And that is just the point, you see. Stanley Roth and Blue Zephyr are one and the same. We want to do everything possible to protect them both, Stanley and the studio."

Griffin's mouth closed tight and his eyes half shut into narrow slits.

Wirthlin nodded his agreement, though I had the impression his mind was on other things.

"The studio will do everything possible to help," continued Griffin, "anything at all. In exchange, I wonder if we might ask only that if there is anything damaging that might come out–about Mary Margaret, I mean–that you might let us know first? It could make a difference in what we do."

Leaning forward, I traced a circle with a fork in the tablecloth.

"Tomorrow morning, Mr. Roth is going to be brought in front of a magistrate and after we enter a plea of not guilty I'm going to ask for bail," I said, watching a moment longer the scratching movement of the shiny silver fork. I put it down and glanced around the table before my eyes came to rest on Louis Griffin. "But this is a capital case, and I'm not at all sure I'm going to be successful. If I'm not, then Stanley Roth is going to stay in jail, locked away, until the end of the trial. If that happens," I asked, "who is going to run Blue Zephyr?"

"Louis and I will run it together," replied Wirthlin immediately.

I thought for a moment Griffin was going to disagree, or perhaps at least distinguish the functions they would have in a way that, without injuring the other man's sensibilities, would make it clear that his would be the ultimate authority. If he had intended to say something like this, he changed his mind.

"Stanley is the head of the studio, but we've always agreed on everything," said Griffin diplomatically. "But I think you're wrong–I certainly hope you're wrong–about what's going to happen tomorrow. I can't imagine a judge doing that: keeping him in jail. Can you, Michael?"

Wirthlin's head snapped up. "Do you know which judge it's going to be?" he asked alertly.

"That won't make any difference," I replied.

Wirthlin gave me a strange look, as if there were things I did not know and he was not about to explain.

"It might," he said.

6

THERE WAS SOMETHING STRANGE about Judge Rudolph Honigman. It was not so much the way he looked, though his looks were a bit unusual. His eyes, for one thing, were different colors, one gray, the other blue. His nose was rather too prominent in profile, and, seen from the front, pushed too far off-center to the right. But though some of his features were a little irregular, the overall impression was still that of a distinguished man in his sixties with dark gray hair and a fine high forehead, a scholarly man who took himself seriously. No, it was not the way he looked that seemed strange: it was the way he moved, walking briskly, his eyes on the floor just ahead of his feet, as if he had to force himself to enter his own courtroom. This was Stanley Roth's first appearance. He was famous, his face as well known as any Hollywood actor. The courthouse was virtually under siege, surrounded by television trucks and satellite dishes, invaded by reporters not just from all over the country, but all over the globe, fighting among themselves for a place from which to watch the formal arraignment of Stanley Roth for murder. Struggling right along with them, some of the best known names in the motion picture industry squeezed their way onto the cramped wooden benches. It was the kind of scene seldom seen in a courtroom; and yet Rudolph Honigman never looked up, never once stole a glance at anyone there, as he hurried toward the bench.

He settled into the black leather chair as if he finally felt safe, and then carefully arranged the files and papers he had carried with him under his arm. When he finished, he paused, hesitating, as if he were uncertain what to do next. Finally, he looked up, but only to concentrate all his attention on the deputy district attorney who was at the counsel table to my right. He tried to smile but it dissolved into an ugly, awkward twitch. Instead of a seasoned trial court judge who had been on the bench for the better part of twenty years, the Honorable Rudolph G. Honigman seemed to be suffering from a potentially disabling case of judicial stage fright. He started to tell her to call the case, but before the first two words were out of his mouth, his voice broke and he had to try again. Dropping his eyes, he cleared his throat.

"Would you please call the case," instructed the judge in a voice that sounded hollow and lost.

Caught off guard by Honigman's peculiar behavior, the deputy district attorney stared at him, subjecting him to a scrutiny that he appeared not to appreciate at all.

"Call the case, please," he insisted in a harsh, irritated tone that left no doubt there would be serious consequences if she hesitated even a moment longer.

"The People of the State of California v. Stanley Roth," announced Annabelle Van Roten. She opened the file folder that lay on the table in front of her. "The charge is murder in the first degree."

She was tall, thin, with wide shoulders she made a conscious effort to hold straight; when she forgot, or when she relaxed, they sloped forward in a way that made her appear to slouch. She was one of those people who, because much of their appeal is in the energy they have and how animated they can become, are more attractive in person than when seen in a still photograph. She had large, dark eyes that flashed for emphasis when she spoke, and a wide, rather sad mouth that could break into a warm, ingratiating smile or a cold hard scowl of withering contempt. With a kind of elegant precision, her hands were in constant motion, gesturing even when she had nothing left to say. A beauty mark at the side of her chin added a touch of sensuality to the anger that entered her eyes as she began to argue that Stanley Roth should not be released from custody. She seemed to thrive on the presence of the crowd.

"This was a terrible crime, Your Honor," she said as she turned away from the bench and gazed slowly around the courtroom. "A young woman, a woman known all around the world, a woman who made a serious contribution not only to the motion picture industry, but to the community in which she lived, was brutally murdered in her own home."

A smile of weary resignation on her lips, Annabelle Van Roten looked back to the bench where Rudolph Honigman waited without expression.

"Murdered in her home, Your Honor; murdered in the one place where she should have felt safe; murdered, Your Honor, as the evidence will show, by the person whom more than anyone else she should have been able to trust with her life. Stanley Roth was her husband, but instead of protecting her, Your Honor, he murdered her. Instead of protecting her, he . . ."

"Your Honor!" I objected, springing to my feet. "The deputy district attorney seems to think she's in the middle of a trial, arguing her case to the jury. Perhaps she's confused because of the size of the crowd. Nothing she's said has anything to do with the question of bail, which is the only issue we are here to decide."

Honigman did not look at me; he did not so much as pretend to pay attention to what I said. Impatiently, he waved his hand in the air, motioning for me to stop, while at the same time he nodded at Van Roten, telling her to continue. I sat down, mortified and astounded.

Nearly as astonished as I, Van Roten forgot what she had been about to say.

"Your Honor," she began again, collecting herself, "the defendant in this case is, as we all know, one of the most famous and powerful men in Los Angeles. He is also one of the wealthiest. No amount of bail could stop him if he decided to avoid prosecution by fleeing the country."

Now, finally, Rudolph Honigman turned to me; but only long enough to let me know with a half-glance that I could, if I wanted, try to make a case for my client's release. I was standing at my place at the counsel table, still irritated at the way he had dismissed out of hand my attempt to object a moment earlier, waiting for a look, a civil smile, a few formal words of invitation to begin my argument: something to acknowledge the fact that I was there as an attorney entitled to at least the same attention he had given the other side, and all I got was this quick turn of his head, this blind glance of contempt.

It got worse. Honigman lowered his eyes, and kept them lowered, while I did what I could to make the case for releasing the defendant from jail. Not once did he look up; not once did he glance at Stanley Roth or anyone else in that hot, crowded courtroom. He kept his eyes, one gray, one blue, on the hard wooden surface of the bench below him, his lips pressed tight together, a strange twitch working silently at the corner of his mouth.

I was beside myself, angry at being treated this way, enraged by this blatant display of judicial bias. Placing both hands on the table, I bent forward, glaring at him, hoping by the sheer intensity of my stare to make him raise his head and look me straight in the eye. Not because I thought it would make any difference. No matter how many times you repeated it, the assertion that no one should be kept incarcerated for a crime for which he had not been tried, much less convicted, seldom carried great weight when balanced against the nightmare every judge feared: that someone who might already have killed once would, out on bail, kill again. The knowledge that all I could do was go through the motions made me angrier still. I fairly shouted the first few words.

"Stanley Roth is an innocent man falsely accused! He has never been convicted of a crime, charged with a crime, or even had it suggested that he might ever have committed a crime–any crime–not so much as a minor traffic infraction!" I exclaimed, as much indignant at the brazen disinterest of the judge as at the charge brought against my client.

It was maddening, the way he sat there, impervious to what I said, his eyes still lowered, his mouth still occupied by that strange, insidious twitch. I pulled my hands up from the table and in frustration threw them up in the air. I was angrier than ever and I did not think twice about the next thing I said.

"It obviously doesn't matter to the prosecution–and it apparently doesn't matter to this court–but Stanley Roth, one of the most respected citizens in this community, ought to be as much entitled to the presumption of innocence as some felon convicted of more crimes than anyone can count!"

In any other courtroom I would have been stopped by the gavel, lectured on my deficiencies as a lawyer and perhaps cited for contempt; but not here, not in the courtroom of the stoic Judge Rudolph Honigman who still refused to lift an eye. Nothing I could say was worth his time; no insult was worth the favor of a reply.

"Ms. Van Roten," I continued unabashed, "took it upon herself to describe Stanley Roth as famous, as powerful, as rich. She somehow failed to remember–or if she remembered, failed to report–that Mr. Roth is a member of virtually every major charitable organization in Los Angeles. She failed to remember–or she failed to report–that Stanley Roth has been a major source of financial support for the cultural and artistic life of Los Angeles for the past twenty years. Nor did Ms. Van Roten mention that Stanley Roth won't be the only one hurt if he is forced to languish in the county jail waiting his chance to prove his innocence at trial. Thousands of people depend for their livelihood on the work he does as head of Blue Zephyr Pictures. No one can step in and take his place without enormous disruption and delay of a sort that might ultimately threaten the ability of the studio to function at all."

I glanced over my shoulder. Louis Griffin was sitting in the first row, staring down at his hands.

"Louis Griffin, the second in command at Blue Zephyr, is here today, Your Honor, and I know he would agree with what I've just said."

I paused, took a deep breath and slowly let it out. There was nothing more I could say, except to make a promise on the defendant's behalf.

"Finally, Your Honor, I want to advise the court that Mr. Roth will agree to abide by any conditions the court might see fit to impose on his release."

There was not even the pretense of deliberation. The Honorable Rudolph G. Honigman did not glance from lawyer to lawyer as if he had found the arguments made by counsel interesting and persuasive and therefore difficult to decide between. He did not look at Annabelle Van Roten, and he certainly did not look at me. He did not look at anyone. His eyes stayed focused on the bench below him as he began to gather up the files and papers he had brought with him.

"Bail will be set in the amount of two million dollars," announced Rudolph Honigman as he rose from his chair. Pausing just long enough to announce the trial date, he rushed away from the bench as if he could not wait to get out of his own courtroom.

I don't know that I have ever been so astonished, so lost for words. Annabelle Van Roten stared in disbelief. Her mouth hung open as if, just about to protest, she had been struck dumb. When her voice came back, it did so with redoubled force.

"I object, Your Honor!" she shouted in a voice that ricocheted off the walls.

It was too late. The door to Judge Honigman's chambers had closed behind him. There was nothing she could do.

Whether it was an instinct, some sense of a thing dimly foretold, I suddenly turned round and in the crowded courtroom behind me saw Louis Griffin smiling to himself. He caught my look and tried to change his expression, to make it seem as if he had intended to smile at me all along. There was nothing I could put my finger on, nothing specific I could point to; just a feeling, a vague sense that something was going on, a kind of subtle intrigue about which I knew nothing.

I left the courthouse, ignoring the shouted demands of a swarm of reporters for answers to questions to which only a fool would have tried to respond and for which, in any event, I had no answers. What would all these intense reporters with their desperate eyes and frantic voices have thought–what would they have said?–if I had announced on the courthouse steps that I did not know a thing about the case, and that I was not sure what I thought about my client, Stanley Roth, whom I had with such postured indignation insisted was an innocent man falsely accused, the man charged with murder who had just been released from jail?

WE HAD AGREED to meet at his office around six. He had been arrested, kept overnight in jail, charged in open court. While that was still fresh in his memory, we were going to have the same conversation we had had before. This time, knowing what he faced, perhaps he would not try to hold anything back. At five o'clock I showered, changed, and rode the elevator down to the lobby of the hotel. As I stepped out, Julie Evans walked in the front door.

"I thought you might like to have dinner," she said as she came up to me, put her hand on my shoulder and kissed me gently on the side of my face.

The kiss took me a little by surprise. I did not know–I could not tell from her expression–whether it was simply the greeting she gave friends, or something more intimate.

"I'd love to," I replied, doing my best to ignore the self-conscious glow I still felt on my face, "but I'm on my way to the studio. I have a meeting with Roth."

She tilted her head and looked straight at me. "Stanley is tied up tonight."

Before I could say anything, Julie took me by the arm. "Take me into the bar and buy me a drink."

The hotel lounge was empty except for a small table in the corner where a young couple was engaged in a slow whispered conversation. Quiet laughter echoed soft and clear in the darkened stillness of the room. Julie sat at the bar and I stood next to her. The bartender took our order.

"Roth sent you here to tell me that he was too busy to see me? The day I get him out of jail?"

Her eyes flashed, and I wondered if she was mocking me as she barely suppressed a smile.

"Are you sure that's what happened?"

Before I could ask what she meant, her expression changed. "No, Stanley didn't send me. He told me to let you know he couldn't make it tonight, but I decided to tell you in person instead of on the phone. I didn't even tell him I was coming."

She glanced up at the bartender while he set our drinks down in front of us.

"I hope you don't mind," added Julie as she lifted the glass to her lips.

"Mind that you're here? Of course not. Mind that the great Stanley Roth is suddenly too busy to help with own defense? You bet."

The scotch felt good as it burned at the back of my throat. I took another drink.

"Maybe your friend Stanley better find himself another lawyer."

She was used to soothing the injured feelings of people Stanley Roth had offended.

"He didn't have any choice," she insisted.

Her shiny silk hair settled gently on her shoulder as she moved her head to the side. She peered at me through blue eyes that looked softer now than the day before when we had first met.

"He really didn't," she repeated. "They're all meeting tonight: Stanley–some of the people you met last night: Wirthlin, Griffin, Walker Bradley, Pomeroy–to decide what to do."

I still had no idea what she was talking about.

"What to do about Mary Margaret's last movie," explained Julie. "What to keep, what to cut; exactly how it should end. There are a thousand things they have to decide."

"I thought–someone said last night–that the writers had already written a new ending, that it would all be done in a few weeks?"

"You really don't know anything about this business, do you? The writers may have written a new ending, but Stanley watches the rushes every night while they're shooting, and more often than not decides to rewrite every scene. It may be done in a few weeks, or it may be done months from now. The point is, it isn't done until Stanley says it's done. You have to understand: He works all the time. If he hadn't gotten out of jail, I don't think he could have survived it, not being able to work, not being able to do what he does. It's what he lives for."

"All the more reason he better start taking this a little more seriously," I retorted. "I can't help him if he isn't willing to help himself."

"Oh, he's willing. He'll do anything you want," she said with confidence. "He said to tell you he could either meet you later tonight, midnight or a little later, after he's finished, or sometime tomorrow morning. Whenever you want."

"Midnight or a little later, whenever I want," I muttered to myself, half amused, as I tossed down more of the scotch and soda.

"Yes," she said, as if I had repeated it to make sure I had it right. "He said he would come here, to the Chateau Marmont, if you like. He doesn't know if he can get away from the reporters and the television people, however. They've staked out his home."

"The Palms?"

"Yes, and the studio."

She was about to tell me something more about the difficulties with which Stanley Roth had to deal when I stopped her.

"What did you mean when you made that remark–when you asked was I sure that's what happened when I said I had gotten him out of jail?"

There was a look in her eyes that told me she knew something I did not.

"Did someone do something? Did someone–Louis Griffin–get to the judge?"

"You mean–bribe?"

"You know damn well that's what I mean."

"No, of course not."

I bent closer, so close I could feel her breath, searching her eyes. "Then what . . . ?"

"I don't know. That's the truth."

"But you think something happened, don't you? What?"

"Louis contributes to a lot of things, and not just civic or charitable causes. He makes a lot of political contributions; and when Louis backs someone, a lot of other people do the same thing. Honigman wants to run for attorney general."

"You think he promised to help? That's still bribery."

"No," she replied, shaking her head in protest. "That's not how it works. Louis wouldn't have said anything. Louis is too honest for anything that crude. He didn't have to say anything. I was in court, standing at the back. I saw what happened. Why do you think Louis was there, sitting in the front row like that? To show moral support for Stanley? Yes, of course; but not to show Stanley–to show Honigman, to show him that this was something that meant a lot, not just to Blue Zephyr, but to Louis personally. God, do you think Louis Griffin makes it a point to wander around the county courthouse just to see what's going on?

"There's something else," said Julie rather tentatively. "Honigman has a daughter, an actress."

"And?"

"Do you think he wanted to jeopardize her career by keeping Stanley Roth in jail? Especially when, as you argued so passionately, he might be an innocent man?"

There was something insidious about it, something worse than bribery. It was the kind of influence that could never be traced; the kind that the people on whom it worked most effectively, the people it corrupted, were not always consciously aware it had worked at all. Rudolph Honigman would insist that his decision to release Stanley Roth had been based purely and entirely on the facts of the case, on the defendant's close ties to the community, on the absence of any criminal record, on the willingness of so many prominent people, including perhaps especially Louis Griffin, to vouch for Roth's promise to show up for trial. More than that, Honigman would believe that the lie he told himself was, underneath all the calculations of his own advantage, the truth; because he would believe–he had to believe–that he would have done the same thing for a man he had never heard of who could not possibly do anything of benefit for him.

We finished our drink and Julie began to make suggestions about dinner.

"Tell me something," I said as she began to run down a list of restaurants nearby where we might get in without too much of a wait. "What was she really like–Mary Margaret Flanders? There had to have been more to her than a woman who cared only about herself and fought all the time with her husband. I need to know everything I can about her. Why did she marry Stanley Roth if all she cared about was herself? And if the marriage wasn't any good, whom would she have brought home with her that night? Who would have wanted to kill her?"

Julie tossed her head and smiled.

"What was Mary Margaret Flanders really like? I suppose you'd have to find someone who knew her before she was a movie star. Because after that, after someone becomes a movie star . . . everything is different then. Everyone sees you in a different way, because however else they know you, they know you on the screen, and they keep trying to put the two things together–this idea they have from what they've watched you do in a movie and what you seem like in person. The thing is, almost everyone thinks the one they see on the screen is the real one, and that, off the screen, you're really pretending to be like everyone else. What was Mary Margaret Flanders really like? I'll be surprised if you find two people in this town who give you the same answer. She was like most movie stars: She was whatever she wanted someone to think she was. Now, come on," she said as she slid off the barstool and took my arm, "let's have dinner, and after dinner we can come back to the hotel and talk some more."

Then she put her other hand on my arm as well. "Or we can just come back to the hotel."

7

I HAD WRITTEN HIM THREE LETTERS and placed at least half a dozen telephone calls; the letters had all gone unanswered, and none of the calls had been returned. When I had first seen him, standing opposite Stanley Roth at the grave of Mary Margaret Flanders, holding the hand of that little girl as she listened to what he whispered in her ear and then let fall that single flower onto the casket that contained the last mortal remains of her mother, I thought him more interesting than any of the more recognizable people there. His was the only face not famous and the only one you found yourself coming back to again and again. Part of it was precisely because you did not know who he was, and part of it was because of the child; but mainly it was because of how different he was from the others in the way he looked, and in the way he stood at the edge of that grave as if he were there all alone, as if none of the others had for him any more tangible existence than the unremarkable faces of an anonymous crowd. Instinctively, the mourners closest to him edged away, creating what space they could, afraid that because he had no celebrity to share he might diminish their own. They treated him like the stranger he was; all, that is, except Stanley Roth, who after the others had finally taken their leave shook his hand and patted the little girl on her head.

For weeks I had tried to learn everything I could about Mary Margaret Flanders and the people around her who had known her best. The more I learned, the more intrigued I became with the man she had married first. If they said it in different ways, and in different tones, everyone I talked to who had known Mary Margaret Flanders when she was still called Marian Walsh all said the same thing: Paul Erlich had fallen in love with her the way you only fall in love once, if you ever really fall in love that way at all. It was curious the way they described it, sometimes almost with a touch of envy, and sometimes, for some of them, a touch of nostalgia. There was a sense that what Paul Erlich had felt was something more intense, more passionate, than what they themselves had ever experienced.

Everyone knew, or thought they knew, what happened to Marian Walsh after she became Mary Margaret Flanders; hardly anyone knew what happened to Paul Erlich after he was divorced from his wife. There was no reason to know. Erlich had the curious fate of belonging to what was tantamount to the prehistory of a famous woman; one of those names mentioned in passing in the early chapters of a thick film-star biography; relegated to the status of an early mistake in someone else's life, the kind of misjudgment that only in retrospect made possible her later triumphant success.

It is doubtful that Paul Erlich had read any of the biographies or any of the other things written about Hollywood life. He had left Los Angeles for Europe when his daughter was still an infant and did not come back until she was old enough to start school. He had been a graduate student at UCLA when he met and married Marian Walsh. After their divorce, after he left America, he studied first at Oxford and then at Rome. Though he could have taught anywhere he wanted, he came back to UCLA. I found him on the first day of fall term, in a lecture hall so crowded with students they were standing, packed together, in both the doorways that led inside. I pushed my way forward just in time to see him walk toward the lectern on the stage below.

Though it had passed out of fashion in most college classrooms, Paul Erlich dressed with a certain formality: a dark blue suit and a dark maroon tie. There must have been close to two hundred students crowded into a room built for perhaps a hundred and a half, all of them talking at once, laughing as they jostled against each other, settling into whatever place they could find. For a moment, Erlich stood still, slowly surveying his young audience. The noise dwindled down, began to subside; and then, when he opened his mouth to speak, stopped completely.

Soft as silk, his voice floated through the air and then, somehow, held you fast. You could barely hear him at first, his voice was that quiet; but the longer you listened, the more it seemed like a voice that was coming from somewhere inside your own mind, an echo of something that though you had not realized it, you must have thought before. What he said, at least at the beginning, seemed simple enough. Perhaps too simple.

"Let us begin at the beginning," said the young professor with gleaming eyes. "This is a course on twentieth-century European intellectual history. That means it is a course on nineteenth-century European intellectual history. More specifically," he continued with a quick decisive nod, followed by a quick emphatic smile, "all twentieth-century intellectual history–that is, all of it worth talking about–is dependent on Friedrich Nietzsche, who died, conveniently enough, in 1900; a date so perfect for the purpose of connecting the intellectual history–and perhaps more than just the intellectual history–of the two centuries together that it might make some among us wonder whether, despite what Nietzsche insisted, God is dead after all."

Erlich never waved his arms, never paced back and forth; there were none of those abrupt movements meant to show an audience how profoundly felt were the thoughts the speaker labored with such effort to put into words. When the words left his mouth they took on an independence, a life of their own.

"But if all of the most serious intellectual thought–including the most serious twentieth-century literature–is in one way or the other dependent on Nietzsche; all of the nineteenth century, including Nietzsche at the end of it and Hegel at the beginning, is in some sense a reaction to the eighteenth century, in part to Kant, but especially to Rousseau."

Pausing to flash a gentle smile, as if he shared the confusion they must have felt, he glanced from one side of the crowded hall to the other.

"We are beginning to see the problem. The twentieth century is dependent on the nineteenth; the nineteenth on the eighteenth; and, as I know you've guessed, it does not stop there. If we were really going to begin at the beginning, we would have to begin the study of twentieth-century intellectual history by taking up the study first of Plato, then of Aristotle. This would of course take us years, so we will simply skip over the beginning, which, I ask you to remember, Aristotle always insisted was 'more than half,' and do what we can. However," added Erlich, his eyes shining with mischief, "because he did not die until the year 1900, we are permitted, I think, to say just a word or two about the influence of Nietzsche on the rest. It is important, after all, to remember, especially as we read some of the things written in the twentieth century, that it is helpful to know not just what those authors wrote, but what they read themselves. For at least the first third of the twentieth century, anyone who wanted to think seriously, anyone who wanted to write something other people would take seriously, read Nietzsche.

"Let me give you three examples of his influence, three examples of the way the twentieth century was shaped by what he wrote. The most profound thinker of the twentieth century was Martin Heidegger. The best book he wrote is not the famous and unfinished *Being and Time*; it is rather the lectures that form his commentary on Nietzsche himself. The most profound novel of the twentieth century, *Dr. Faustus*–a novel its author, Thomas Mann, considered *the* novel of the twentieth century–a novel about genius and madness, takes as its central character a man who is unmistakably based on Nietzsche. It is perhaps one of the strange ironies of history that this novel, this great German novel, written by this great German author, was written not in Germany, but right here, in Los Angeles, after Thomas Mann was driven out of Germany by the Nazis.

"The third, and of course best-known, if perhaps least-understood, influence exerted by Nietzsche on the twentieth century is the way in which Hitler found in him a justification for what he wanted to do. Nietzsche was himself quite aware that nearly everyone who read him would fail to understand him, and that some who read him–or read what others wrote about him–would distort out of all recognition what he meant. But it is doubtful that even that astonishing intelligence could have anticipated that the will to power, by which he sought to understand the driving force in every form of animate and inanimate existence alike, would become the rationale for the mindless slaughter of tens of millions of human beings.

"It may be worth mentioning, that if there is a certain irony in the fact that the great German novel of the twentieth century was written in Los Angeles, it is hard to know quite what to think of the fact that perhaps the single most powerful and influential motion picture ever made was made in Germany, by a German, Leni Riefenstahl, with a title meant most emphatically to connect Hitler, whose coming to power was being celebrated in the film, to Nietzsche: *Triumph of the Will*."

Erlich stopped, glanced around the silent hall, then raised his chin and flashed a self-deprecating smile.

"I know this is UCLA, and I know this will disappoint many of you; but I'm afraid that was the last time we will mention film in any form for the rest of the term. Are there any questions?"

Before the end of the hour, I slipped out of the lecture hall to wait for Paul Erlich at his office. On both sides of a long corridor with painted white cinder-block walls and a gray linoleum floor, at regular intervals that could not have been more than ten feet and were probably closer to eight, dozens of yellow oak doors were closed shut. A clear plastic frame, open at the top so a three-by-five card could be inserted, was fastened to each of them, just below a narrow vertical window not more than three or four inches wide. On each of the cards was typed, sometimes without great care, the name of the professor whose office it was and the hours set aside for students who wished for some reason to see them. The corridor was deserted, the only sound a muffled conversation that drifted through a half-open door at the far end, next to the fire escape.

The elevator jolted open and the voices of two faculty members echoed ahead, exchanging a few casual remarks as they walked together to their offices. Just beyond the elevator there were footsteps on the stairs. With a slow, shuffling gait, Paul Erlich was coming toward me, one hand shoved in his pants pocket, while he held in the other a slim tan briefcase. His head was bent, his eyes on a point just in front of his feet; but if he had been looking right at me I do not think he would have noticed me. He was concentrating on something, concentrating so hard that, as he came closer, I could see that his lips were moving, silently, methodically, like someone repeating to himself a thought he did not want to forget. When he got to the door, he pulled out his key chain, and started looking for the one he needed to get in. He greeted me with his eyes as if he had been expecting to find me in that very spot.

"I noticed you in my class," he remarked affably as he first unlocked the door and then held out his hand. "You must be Joseph Antonelli. You aren't anything like what I imagined you'd be."

"How did you know . . . ?"

"Who you were?"

He held open the door, waiting until I passed in front of him. The office was more like a cell, barely large enough for the metal desk shoved against the wall and the bookcase on the far side of it. There was a swivel chair at the desk and a straight back metal chair on the side of it closest to the door. There were only two exceptions to the Spartan simplicity of the furnishings: a threadbare hand-knotted Oriental rug on the floor and a gilt-edged picture frame containing a black-and-white photograph of the child that was certainly his daughter.

Waving his hand toward the visitor's chair, he sank into his own.

"I don't see many students in my classroom wearing suits and ties; none, to be precise; and, if you'll forgive me, you're rather older than most of the students I get. If someone in administration had wandered in–lost–they might have on a suit, but never one as expensive as that," he explained with an appraising glance. "That's part of what I meant when I said you weren't what I expected. I'm afraid I tend to think of criminal defense lawyers as loud and flamboyant, not people who dress in well-tailored, understated clothes."

His face, especially his eyes, became more animated as he spoke, caught up in what for him was the obvious pleasure of explaining the peculiar way in which the mind–his mind–sometimes worked. From the way he held himself to the way each word came fully formed off his tongue there was about him a certain elegance. He was really quite extraordinary, every bit as impressive in the close confines of his office as he had been in front of two hundred utterly fascinated undergraduates. There was nothing the least pretentious about him; there was certainly nothing of the insufferable arrogance of intellectuals caught up in their own imagined importance. There was a kind of modesty about him, the kind found in someone not content with measuring himself against the shortcomings of others.

Erlich lifted his finely drawn chin and peered at me through steady, sensitive eyes, eyes that looked as if they could see right into the heart of things and not blink at the sight of what they found.

"I knew eventually you would come to find me," said Erlich in a gentle voice.

"Then why didn't you simply return a call, or answer a letter?" I was compelled to ask.

"Because I hoped you wouldn't," he admitted. "Come to find me, I mean. I understand why you had to; or why you might think you had to."

I almost felt an obligation to apologize, as if I had without reason trespassed upon his privacy.

"I'm just trying to find out what I can about . . ."

I hesitated, not quite sure how to put it; whether to call her by the name by which the world knew her, or the name by which he must have known her; whether to say something in sympathy for what after all the years they had been divorced was not the loss felt by a husband, and, for all I knew, might not even have been that felt by a friend. She was of course the mother of his child.

"Marian," said Erlich, sensing my discomfort. "I always called her that. Marian Erlich is the name she used on my daughter's birth certificate. Marian Walsh before I married her. But I imagine you know that, don't you?"

Reaching inside the desk drawer, Erlich pulled out a pack of cigarettes.

"Old habits die hard," he said as if it was some private joke he had with himself. "You don't mind, do you?"

He lit the cigarette, took a deep drag and then, closing his eyes, slowly let it out through his nostrils.

"It's against the rules," he explained. "I do it every day after class. Only one. It's my only criminal act, but you'll notice I do it over and over again. I'm what you call a repeat offender."

He took another drag, and looked at me through the column of smoke that was beginning its lazy, spiraling ascent.

"Do you think that's the reason some people become criminals, Mr. Antonelli? Because only by breaking the rules do they get any sense of being, any sense that they have an identity of their own? It was one of the strange phenomena of the twentieth century, the fascination with crime and criminals. Not this kind, of course," he added, nodding with an embarrassed grin toward the burning cigarette. "Serious crime, violent crime . . . murder."

From the look in his eyes I could tell that he knew as soon as I heard that last word I would think of the murder of his former wife. While he meant that, too, there was a broader point he wished to make.

"The twentieth century continued and intensified the movement away from the world as it presents itself and reveals itself to us as human beings. Everything has been covered over, buried under layer after layer of thought and language. I mean, just as an example, you can scarcely find anyone even willing to try to understand Plato or Aristotle as they understood themselves, as they understood the world as it revealed itself to them. But never mind that: think how seldom we see anything with our own eyes. We see everything through the eyes of someone else. The new technology–the technology that is supposedly the great contribution of the twentieth century–surrounds us with images, bombards us with them: radio, and the phonograph; then television; and yes, of course, the movies. Everything is artificial, done for effect. An act of violence, on the other hand, is real; it isn't done for an audience; it isn't done because of what others will think. People are fascinated with crime because the act itself, the violent assault on this artificial order of things, seems so spontaneous, so authentic, compared with the way the rest of us have to lead our lives."

A look of disdain creased his forehead. With narrowed eyes, he took a last drag on the cigarette and then snuffed it out on a small rose-colored ceramic glass he used as a makeshift ashtray.

"It was for a while the fashion among European intellectuals to extol the virtues of violence as the expression of individual refusal to become a useful, exploitable part of the social machinery."

Erlich closed his eyes, raised his eyebrows and sadly shook his head.

"Typical," he said, a world-weary look now in his eyes. "Bloodless voluptuaries, sitting in their offices, living out their tepid, tenured existences, thrilled at the thought that someone out there is equally contemptuous of the lives they take and of the consequences to themselves if they are caught."

He stared at me for a moment, then drew his head back slowly to the side as a secretive smile spread across his lips.

"None of us will admit it, but in a way we all admire the murderer, don't we, Mr. Antonelli? He's done something we don't think we would have the courage to do; not just the act of killing, but the courage to face what will happen to our standing in the world. Because of course, that thought, that eminently private thought, that the ability, the willingness to commit violence is a strength we don't have, is immediately suppressed, brought to bay by the moral certainty that murder is wrong and that anyone who does it is a coward."

He had followed his own thought, hunted it with a kind of single-minded fervor until he had taken the chase as far as he wanted to go.

"I'm sorry," said Erlich with a start, as if he had just realized what he had done. "I'm afraid I sometimes forget I'm not in class."

But then he thought of something else, something he had to explain.

"I said part of the fascination with crime was because it isn't done for an audience, isn't done because of what others will think. That's not entirely true, though, is it? There are cases–aren't there?–in which someone commits a crime precisely because they want it to be known, because they want to become known themselves. The ones who kill someone famous because they want to be famous, too; and they won't be if they kill someone no one knows. Wouldn't it be more interesting, though, if someone committed a crime–killed someone–because of what they hoped it would make others think of the victim?"

Abruptly, he shook his head, scolding himself for engaging in the same kind of digression for which he had a moment earlier apologized.

He had raised a possibility, however, that I had not thought of; one I was not sure I fully understood. I knew of course about situations in which someone famous had been murdered because the killer hoped in that demented way to share in the victim's celebrity; but what did it mean to kill someone to change the way other people thought of the man, or the woman, you killed? Erlich read the question in my eyes.

"The way Marian was killed, for example. Or perhaps I should say the way she was left after she was killed: her naked body floating in the swimming pool. Don't you think that creates a certain kind of impression? Don't you think that left a certain image in the minds of people who read about it, heard about it? And, my God, who didn't hear about it?"

Erlich winced at the memory of it. He looked at me sharply.

"It was all over the place. The first thing I did when I heard it was to get my daughter out of school. I didn't want her to hear about it the way everyone else was hearing about it. I took her for a long drive, out to the beach; and I told her there that her mother had died, that she had been killed. You see, I didn't want her to think what everyone else must have thought: that her mother was doing something she shouldn't have been doing and was murdered while she was doing it. That's what I meant, Mr. Antonelli; that's what I meant when I said that someone might kill someone to change the way people thought about her. If she had been killed in broad daylight, walking down the street, shot by some deranged fool, no one would think of her as anything but a beautiful woman, an accomplished actress; but slashed to death, late at night, naked; found in the morning floating facedown in the pool, her stocking still wrapped around her neck–it isn't the kind of death, even if a violent death, anyone is likely to associate with a respectable woman, is it? You've seen the tabloids. I try to keep my daughter out of grocery stores. It's everything imaginable: sex and murder–sex, drugs and murder. Whoever did it, Mr. Antonelli, destroyed what there was of her reputation. Whether that was done deliberately or not, I wouldn't know; but someone could have done it on purpose, couldn't they? Killed her in a way that made it look almost as if she deserved it."

It was an instinct bred from a thousand cross-examinations. I heard myself ask:

"Do you think she deserved it?"

Most people would have reacted with anger, even outrage; they would have shown some emotion, some sign of resentment at the implication that they could think anyone deserved to die. Erlich did not flinch. With his elbows on the arms of the chair, he folded his hands together.

"There were times when I thought so, Mr. Antonelli; there were times when I wished she were dead; not because of what had happened between us, but because of the way she treated our daughter. What do you really know about her, Mr. Antonelli? What do you know about Mary Margaret Flanders? She was not what you saw on the screen.

"We were young," said Erlich with a pensive sigh. "In some ways, though I was four years older, I was younger than she. I saw things in her," continued Erlich with a smile that was both rueful and nostalgic, "things that may not have been there; things I may have put there."

The smile softened, lost its regret, became more forgiving of youthful failure.

"We do that, don't we? See in others what we expect–or what we hope; invent someone, then fall in love with what we make. I did that with Marian, I'm afraid. She was intelligent–oh, she wasn't brilliant, or anything like that–but she had a clear mind, and she was interested in things, things she did not know anything about. That was it, you see: this gorgeous creature, eager to learn about everything. She made me feel like I was the most important person in the world."

A troubled look in his eyes, he struggled to find the exact words with which to clothe his thought.

"That was her real gift, her real form of intelligence: that ability to make other people feel something in her presence, something that made them feel important."

He was bending forward, his head cocked, looking at me with a kind of curiosity, as if there were things about her, and about the way he had felt about her, he still did not quite understand.

"I've never seen any of her movies except for the first one she made, and I left that one before it was over. It wasn't her, it wasn't her at all; but at the same time, it was close enough that . . . It was a little unnerving because, you see, I saw she could do it there, too: have that same effect she had on me; the effect she had on other people who came in contact with her; have it on the screen when there was, so to speak, no one there at all. It bothered me–no, it depressed me–more than I can tell you. A picture, a moving picture–she wasn't there, she wasn't real–and yet, as I looked around that theater, all those faces turned upward, watching her face on film, you could see it, the way they were drawn to her, the way she made them feel."

Erlich suddenly stopped talking. He picked up the photograph of his daughter and showed it to me.

"She has her mother's looks, doesn't she?"

She did look like her mother. She had the same high cheekbones and the same perfectly balanced bone structure; she had the same nose and the same mouth; but she had her father's eyes. Not the shape of them–that was like her mother's, too–but the depth, and though it may sound strange to say it of someone still so young, the intelligence.

"Marian did not have time for her; she did not have time for either one of us. Marian did not have time for anyone who was not part of what was now the only reality she cared about. The time she spent with us was time wasted, time she was not able to spend on her new career."

Carefully, Erlich put the picture of his daughter back in place.

"Marian had always wanted to be an actress, and she had taken that first, significant step, but until she got that part I thought she was giving up on it. She had a year left to go in school. We had a daughter. She talked about going to graduate school. She thought she'd like to become a teacher.

"Even after she got the part, I still thought that was what she was going to do. Then, when the movie was finished, when she saw herself in it, that is when it happened. She became addicted–and I mean that literally–addicted to what other people said, to what other people thought, to the way she was seen by other people. She could not pass a mirror without stopping–not to look at herself, not to see herself–to study her reflection, to see it from every possible angle, to see the way other people would see her in every conceivable situation.

"Shortly after the movie came out, we went to a party at the home of some producer. In that crowd of people, some of them quite well known, it was as if she was the only one there. She had that talent, that way about her that made everyone want to look at her. She would be talking to someone, and it was as if a camera was on her, filming a scene in which they were the only two people in the room."

With a pronounced air of discovery, Erlich's eyes blazed and he threw out his hands.

"Not as if they were really alone, you understand. No, it was as if they were the center of attention for the audience made up of everyone else.

It's the way someone holds herself, the way she moves, when she knows everyone is watching; the way someone walks down the aisle at the Academy Awards, their eyes straight ahead, completely composed, knowing all the time that every eye is on them; that thousands of people are watching; that hundreds of millions are watching on television. I had never seen her so beautiful, and I knew better than I had ever known before, knew with all the reluctant certainty of a broken heart, that the intimate affection of a husband–and perhaps even the innocent love of a child–could never compete with the thrill she got from the adulation of strangers."

Staring bleakly at the wall in front of him, Erlich for a moment reflected in silence on what had happened. I had the feeling that he did not blame her at all; that if he blamed anyone, he blamed himself for not grasping sooner how different were the things he thought important from what other people, no matter how intelligent, wanted for themselves. It was a kind of blindness on his part; born, I imagine, out of an unwillingness to accept how different he really was; a reluctance to face how lonely he was destined to be. That perhaps explained why he clung so tenaciously to the idea that he had somehow to protect his daughter from anything like what had happened to her mother. He must have been the only one alive who thought there was something to regret in the life Mary Margaret Flanders had been privileged to live.

Slowly pressing together the tips of his smooth, tapered fingers, Erlich turned to me, nodded twice and then let slip across his mouth a self-conscious smile.

"You have an interesting face, Mr. Antonelli. There's something about you that makes people want to tell you things about themselves. But you know that, don't you? It's part of the reason you're as good as you are at what you do."

The smile broadened and Erlich started to relax.

"You've scarcely asked me a question, and I've told you pretty much all I know; certainly more than I've ever told anyone else about what Marian was like then."

He had a slightly bemused expression on his face, as if he could not quite believe he had actually told me as much as he had. But he also seemed relieved that he had said it out loud; said it in a way that made sense out of it all. I do not believe that he thought it was the whole truth, but as much of it as any of us can hope to find about the things that happen to us that, for better or worse, change our lives forever.

"I wanted Chloe to have a chance at a normal life. I didn't want her growing up around Hollywood people. You see, Mr. Antonelli, I was the one who wanted the divorce. Don't misunderstand," he added quickly, "Marian would have–eventually. She was so wrapped up in what she was doing that she had not even begun to think that far ahead. When I told her it was not going to work out, that her career was already making too many demands on her, she did not disagree."

Erlich looked away, and then, biting his lip, shook his head.

"Marian seemed almost relieved when I told her I wanted custody of Chloe. She didn't object when I told her I was taking Chloe to live with me in Europe.

"On Chloe's birthday, and at Christmas, Marian sent her gifts, expensive gifts, gifts I suspect she had someone else pick out. She never came to see her. Once, when Chloe wrote to her–she was only five–she got back an autographed picture, the kind they send out as a response to fan mail. Marian did write once in a while, short little notes repeating over and over again how much 'Mommy loves her little girl.'

"It may have been a mistake taking Chloe away. I didn't want her to have any part of that kind of life; but in her mind, Chloe thought of her the way children think of a fairy godmother. She kept that autographed picture as if it were a promise of all the love in the world. She was certain nothing bad would ever happen to her because she knew her mother was always there with her, an unseen presence, more real than anyone, watching over her.

"We were gone nearly five years. We came back because it was time for Chloe to start school, and because without all the distractions of American life, her character had already taken form. She was six years old. She spoke English, French and Italian; she had been playing the violin since she was three. Two weeks after we got home I took her to see her mother.

"Marian–Mary Margaret Flanders–was at the studio, Blue Zephyr.

She was on a soundstage, shooting a movie; and we were taken to her dressing room to wait. Chloe was wearing her prettiest dress. I don't think I had ever seen her quite so excited. We waited half an hour and she was beaming the whole time, ecstatic that finally she was going to be reunited with her mother who, as she often told her friends, was the most famous, the most beautiful woman in the world.

"There was a commotion outside the door. Chloe's little eyes lit up. The door opened and Marian swept in, swearing a blue streak, while two assistants swirled around her, one of them working on her dress, the other trying without success to calm her down. She was beside herself about something that had just happened on the set. It was apparent from the look on the faces of the two assistants that they were used to these outbursts of ill temper.

"Chloe just stood there, her eyes wide open. She did not know what to do or what to think.

"'Hello, Marian,'" I said as calmly as I could.

"She wheeled around, angry that someone was there; angrier still that anyone would dare use that name. For an instant she stared at me, without any idea who I was. Then I saw in her eyes a flash of recognition; and I saw something else: that look you see when someone suddenly remembers they have an obligation to do something with you, something they would rather not do. As soon as she realized what it was, she did it the same way I imagine she had trained herself to do a scene: She looked down at Chloe, took her hands, and pretended she had a daughter.

"'Let me get a good look at you. You've become such a beautiful young lady. I'm so proud of you, Chloe," she said.

"She led her to a sofa and sat next to her, holding her hand.

"'You're going to have to tell me all about what you've been doing. But not right now. I have to get back to the set. We're making a movie. Isn't that wonderful!' Maybe she hoped Chloe would think so, too. 'But I made them all stop working just so I could come and see you,' she said. 'And I'm so glad I did.'

"Marian got to her feet, and with that smile with which, as they used to say so often in the publicity for her movies, she had captured the hearts of millions, broke the heart of a single little girl.

"'I have to get back now, but I'll see you again soon. We'll be able to spend a lot more time. I promise.'

"Then she was gone. Chloe did not say a word, not one thing, until we were outside the studio. She was quite calm; whatever disappointment she felt–and she must have felt more disappointment than anything I have ever known–had somehow been put away, hidden from the world; hidden, perhaps, even from herself. She was clutching my hand.

"'I don't think she likes me very much, does she, Daddy?'

"I could not look her in the eye; I had to look away. I mumbled something about of course she loved her, that we had just come at a bad time, that next time it would be a lot better. She gave my hand a squeeze, and I knew she did not believe me and that she wanted me to know it was enough that I had tried."

Resting the side of his head on the fingertips of his left hand, Paul Erlich narrowed his eyes into a desolate stare.

"Marian and I had a child together; but Marian did not exist anymore," said Erlich with the kind of conviction that has banished all doubt. "She was Mary Margaret Flanders and everything that had happened to her before had happened to someone else. They buried Mary Margaret Flanders the movie star last month; Marian Walsh, the girl I loved, the mother of my daughter, died ten years ago."

8

I AM NOT SURE when I first became aware of Jack Walsh; became aware of him, that is, as something more than the name of Marian Walsh's father. It was probably the same way I had first become aware of her, Mary Margaret Flanders. I must have noticed her right from the beginning–you could scarcely help noticing her; that was the gift she had: that talent for being noticed. I heard Jack Walsh's name a half dozen different times before I realized that he was suddenly everywhere, the grief-stricken father of the girl he claimed always to have loved, demanding that his daughter's killer get what he deserved.

He was at it again, explaining on yet another daytime television show how he had always known that his daughter, Mary Margaret, was going to grow up to be a star. That is what he called her: Mary Margaret. Maybe he had forgotten the one he had given her, become so blinded by her fame, seen her name so often and in so many different places, that he convinced himself it must have been the one he had chosen, the only one she had ever had.

I had just returned from Sausalito where I spent every weekend at home with Marissa, my only refuge from all the pressures of trying to prepare Stanley Roth's defense, and the only place where I could escape the prying eyes and the shouted insistent questions of reporters desperate to run down the latest rumor or start one of their own. Unpacking my suitcase in the suite at the Chateau Marmont, the suite that was paid for whether I stayed there or not, I was not really listening to Jack Walsh, but then he was asked why if he loved his daughter so much he abandoned her when she was still a child. Setting the armload of dress shirts down on the bed, I pulled a chair up in front of the television set.

"I did not abandon my daughter," insisted Walsh. "It broke my heart when her mother told me she didn't want to live with me anymore and asked me to leave. It didn't break my heart that she wanted a divorce. It wasn't a very good marriage, and I don't doubt that a lot of the blame for that is mine; but I never wanted a divorce. I was raised in a broken home and that was the last thing I ever wanted for Mary Margaret."

In his early fifties now, with gray hair streaked with brown, Jack Walsh had the kind of crude good looks that had taught him to believe that he could talk, perhaps not any woman, but any woman who was not quite as young, not quite as attractive, as she once had been, into almost anything he wanted her to think. What might have passed for sincerity and charm in the eyes of a lonely, middle-aged woman sitting in some suburban lounge out in the valley was lost completely on the smartly dressed talk show host who had both eyes focused firmly on the main chance. She pursued him with a relentless smile.

"Two years ago, I interviewed Mary Margaret Flanders myself. She told me then that her father had abandoned her and her mother when she was just a child."

She had called him a liar, but watching him you knew that of all the things she could have done, that was the one thing for which he was most prepared. There was nothing in his eyes, nothing in his expression, to signal any feeling of resentment; certainly none of that bristling indignation by which more prominent people react to anything that seems to question their integrity. Jack Walsh had never had the luxury of standing on his reputation or insisting on his due. A lifetime of small acts of duplicity had proven to him over and over again that instead of telling the truth it was always better to claim that he had through no fault of his own been grievously misunderstood. Benevolent and forgiving, he looked into her harsh stare.

"And if you had talked to her after that, you'd know that she now understood why I left. You'd know that the things she had been told by her mother . . . well, weren't all true."

Pausing, Walsh smiled sadly.

"I'm sure her mother meant well. She probably thought it was the easiest way to start the new life she wanted. She got married again, you know; about six months later, as a matter of fact. I think he was the kind of man she had always wanted: good job, steady, someone who could give her the things she wanted. I was always kind of a dreamer, I guess," said Walsh, shaking his head in a way that suggested that no matter how hard he tried, he was not the kind of man who could ever really settle down. "I just wanted something more out of life than a nine-to-five job somewhere. Mary Margaret was a lot like me that way, I think. As I say, I knew right away she was destined for bigger things."

He closed his mouth and clenched his teeth; his eyes became hard, unforgiving.

"And now he's ruined it; taken her away from me; taken her away from everybody. I'm not going to let him get away with it," said Walsh, glaring defiantly. "He may think he's going to get away with it; he may think he can bamboozle a jury with all his money and all his famous friends; but if Jack Walsh never does another thing in his life, I tell you he's going to make sure that the murder of his daughter does not go unpunished!"

In the daylight shadows of my hotel room, I crouched forward, my elbows resting on my knees, watching intently as Marian Walsh's delinquent father talked of outrage and revenge. It was astonishing how in such a short time Jack Walsh had learned to take any question and turn it to his own advantage. He had an instinct for publicity.

Stiff and alert, the host, someone who called herself Arlene Bascomb, made the obligatory gesture toward fair-minded impartiality:

"Mr. Roth has been accused of the murder of your daughter, but he insists he isn't guilty. He's entitled to the presumption of innocence, isn't he?"

"What 'presumption' did Mary Margaret get? What was she entitled to?" demanded Walsh angrily. "Oh, I know–I hear it every day–the 'rights of the accused.' What about the rights of the victim? What about the rights of my daughter? But of course it's too late for her, isn't it?" asked Walsh with withering sarcasm. "She's dead. Her killer is still alive, so everyone forgets about her and talks about him; about his right to a fair trial; about his right to be presumed innocent. Let them give him his fair trial," said Walsh scornfully. "I want him to have a fair trial; I want everyone to hear all the evidence: I want everyone to know what Stanley Roth is really like. I knew she should never have married him."

Ready with her next question, Bascomb had been waiting for him to finish, but this last remark took her by surprise.

"You didn't think she should marry Stanley Roth? Whatever you think of him now, you couldn't possibly have imagined that anything like this would happen."

He gave her a look that suggested she should not be so sure.

"You couldn't possibly have thought Stanley Roth was the kind of man who would murder his wife," she insisted.

"He did not love her," said Walsh emphatically, "he just wanted to own her. He wanted to control her. He wanted to control everything: what pictures she was in; what she did; who she saw; what she did with her money," he added with a contemptuous sneer. "That's why he killed her."

"That's why he killed her?" repeated Bascomb with a blank look. "Because he wanted to control her?"

"Because she wouldn't let him; because she was not going to put up with it anymore; because she was tired of it, tired of being beaten up."

I sprang to my feet, staring at the television set. Roth had told me about what he had done, how he had once hit his wife; but who had told Jack Walsh? Perhaps he was only guessing, jumping to the conclusion that if Roth had been willing to kill her, he might have committed some other act of violence against her before. It did not really matter. Jack Walsh had just told the world, and the world was not likely to insist on much in the way of proof before believing the worst about someone accused of murdering a woman as well known and as well loved as Mary Margaret Flanders.

"Mary Margaret was going to leave him. That's the reason he killed her. She was going to leave him and he couldn't stand that," claimed Jack Walsh. "No one leaves Stanley Roth."

Walsh had never said anything like this before. Bascomb's telephone was going to be ringing off the hook. Other reporters, other journalists, people from network news shows were going to be asking her what she thought about what Jack Walsh had said and whether she had known in advance that he was going to say it. She was going to be asked to appear on who knows how many shows herself. Careers had been made on less. She did what any investigative reporter would have done: She asked him how he knew.

"Because she told me," announced Walsh, raising his chin, a gesture of defiance to anyone who cared to challenge the veracity of what he said. "Just a week before he killed her."

Reaching for the small notebook I carried in the pocket of the jacket I had thrown over a chair, I started scribbling notes, trying to capture as close to verbatim as I could everything Jack Walsh had said.

Concealing behind the bland exterior of her professional personality the excitement she must have felt, Bascomb asked him why he had not said anything about this before.

"You've been interviewed quite a lot over the last several months, Mr. Walsh; why have you waited until your appearance here today to tell us that your daughter, Mary Margaret Flanders, was planning to divorce her husband, Stanley Roth?"

Walsh nodded as he listened, then stopped moving his head when she was through.

"I was not going to say anything until the trial, but when I read about what Stanley Roth was saying about how much they loved each other, I thought it was time to set the record straight."

Walsh bent closer, as if he were about to impart something equally devastating to the defense.

"If he was innocent, why would he have to get one of the most expensive lawyers in the country?" he asked with the smirking certainty of someone who knows already what the verdict should be. "You think the people Joseph Antonelli defends are innocent? You think all those people he keeps off death row are innocent victims arrested by mistake?"

The show went to commercial and I went into orbit. I picked up the telephone and called Stanley Roth at home. No one answered. I looked in my book for the other numbers I had for him when the phone started ringing for me. It was Julie Evans. She had been trying to reach me all day.

"I just got in," I explained. "Did Roth go on television this weekend while I was gone?"

She could tell I was angry, and I had the answer I needed by the hesitation I heard in her voice.

"Tell him to get another lawyer," I said abruptly. Without giving her a chance to reply, I hung up the phone.

Two minutes later, the phone rang again.

"I'm serious, Julie; tell him I'm through. I told him at the beginning that either he did what I told him or I would not take the case."

It was not Julie; it was Stanley Roth.

"Yes, you did; and you were right. I shouldn't have done what I did. If it makes any difference, I didn't do it on purpose. A reporter I know came to the house. I didn't invite her. She didn't have a camera. We just talked. Then she went on the air and told everyone what I said. I didn't say much; just that I loved Mary Margaret and she loved me."

I could hear in the background the muted voices of at least one woman and several men.

"Look, this isn't a good time to talk about this. Can you come over? That's why Julie was calling: We're at the studio. I've moved out of the house; I'm staying at the bungalow."

IN THE PALE YELLOW-GRAY LIGHT of a late Southern California afternoon, the heat rising from the sunbaked asphalt, I threaded my way across town. The traffic stopped and started, a great swirling mass that gave the illusion of everyone moving together in a single direction. Even when the jam had broken, and everyone was free to drive as fast as they wanted, there was not the same sense of frenetic urgency you felt when you were caught on a highway somewhere else. Maybe it was the weather; maybe it was the way everyone seemed to pay more attention to the conversations they had on their cell phones than to the traffic around them; or maybe it was just that here they spent so much time in their cars, moving from one unsettled place to another, that after a while they were more comfortable going somewhere than they were when they finally arrived.

Turning the corner from behind a block of modest white stucco apartment buildings lined sideways to the street, I came into view of the graceful high sloping palm trees in front of the studio. I had been here at least a dozen times, and, as I now realized, had never once wondered why it had been called Blue Zephyr or, for that matter, what it was supposed to mean. Perhaps it did not mean anything, perhaps it had been chosen because of the way it sounded, the way a baby, caught up in the first rhythms of spoken speech babbles nonsense with such great delight.

As I got closer I noticed the slender figure of Julie Evans waiting just inside the dark blue gold-tipped iron gate, next to the station where the security guard checked everyone who came in or out. Instead of flowing long and loose over her shoulder, her blonde hair was pulled tight along the sides of her head and tied at the back. Wearing dark glasses, she kept glancing up and down the street as if afraid someone might be watching.

The gate shut behind me, and Julie got into the car, a wry expression on her face. Reaching across, she patted me gently on the shoulder, her way of letting me know that she knew what I had said to Roth on the telephone.

"It wasn't Stanley's fault. I admit he probably shouldn't have talked to her at all, but Madeleine Madden is an old friend. She's an entertainment reporter, not a news reporter . . ."

Julie laughed at what she had just said, struck by how that distinction, in this town always incongruous, had with this case become nothing short of absurd.

"It was a mistake," conceded Julie with a gentle smile; "but I'm as guilty as anyone. I was there when she came to the house. I thought she was just there to give him moral support. Besides, it wouldn't have made any difference if he hadn't talked to her. Jack Walsh would have found another reason to go after Stanley."

She pointed up the narrow road toward the bungalow where Stanley Roth did his work.

"They're all there–screening the movie: Stanley, Wirthlin, Griffin, Bill Pomeroy."

I pulled up in front and turned off the ignition.

"That's the reason I was trying to reach you. Stanley wanted you here."

"To see her last movie?"

"He wants to know what you think–and he wants the others to hear it from you, too–about when it should be released."

"I thought they had already decided to release it right away, week after next."

Her response was to lift her eyebrows, flash a quick, doubtful smile and open the car door.

"Why does his father-in-law hate him so much?" I asked as we walked up the sidewalk toward the tile-roofed bungalow.

She turned to me, puzzled; then, when she understood, she laughed quietly.

"I don't think Stanley ever thought of Jack Walsh as his father-in-law. Why would he? Mary Margaret didn't think of him as her father. As far as I know," she added with a shrug, "she seldom thought of him at all."

She had not answered my question; or perhaps she had and I did not yet understand it. I asked again: "Why does Jack Walsh hate Stanley Roth?"

Julie gave me a strange, mischievous glance. "You mean other than the fact that he thinks Stanley murdered his daughter?"

The glance intensified. For a moment I had the feeling she was not going to say anything more.

"I don't know that Jack Walsh hates Stanley at all; I don't know that he isn't really a little grateful to him," she said finally. "Thanks to Stanley, he's becoming famous; and if you're famous, you must be important–isn't that right?"

In the bungalow, off the hallway that led to Stanley Roth's study, was a small projection room with eight thick padded theater chairs separated by a narrow aisleway into two rows of two seats on each side. The movie had just ended, the only thing on the blank white screen the shadow of cigar smoke curling through the air.

"It's her best movie," said Louis Griffin thoughtfully as the lights came on. He was sitting alone on the right side of the front row, a melancholy look in his eyes as he considered the talent that had been lost.

"It damn well better be," said a cold, caustic voice from somewhere in the back. It was Michael Wirthlin, hunched down in the seat, growling at the thought of how far over budget the picture had run. "We lost money on her last two pictures. We better make it up on this one."

Rising from his place on the aisle, Stanley Roth shook his head in disgust. He was about to reply to Wirthlin when he saw me standing in the doorway next to Julie.

"Come in," he said, approaching me with his hand extended. "You know everyone, don't you?"

Besides his two partners and William Pomeroy, Walker Bradley, whom I had met at Griffin's home, had come to watch the movie in which for the last time he co-starred with Mary Margaret Flanders.

"Sit down. You're just in time," said Roth as I took a chair across the aisle from where he had been sitting. His arms folded in front of him, Roth crossed one tassled loafer over the other and began to explain what they were trying to decide.

"Mary Margaret's last movie is ready to go," said Roth, glancing toward Wirthlin so he could confirm it. "We need to be candid about this," he added, looking at everyone in turn. "If we release it now, as scheduled, Mary Margaret is the story; if we wait until after the trial starts, then I'm the story and there might not be as much interest in the movie. From a strictly business point of view, there doesn't seem to me to be anything left to decide."

Louis Griffin, always attentive, always composed, sat forward.

"Yes, Stanley, we all agree on that: We all agree what should be done from a purely business point of view. But this can't be just another business decision. This is a good deal more than that. Which of course is the reason we wanted you to join us, Mr. Antonelli," said Griffin as he turned to me with a gracious smile.

"If we put this out now, what effect might it have on the trial? What does it do to Stanley's chances?"

I had often been asked how something might affect the outcome of a trial, but never anything quite like this. The honest answer was I did not have the slightest idea. Before I could confess my ignorance, Wirthlin did it for me.

"Nobody can answer that," he insisted with considerable irritation. "We shouldn't even try to answer that; we have to make the best business decision we can. We don't have any choice. We're the officers of the company–that's our obligation; not how it might or might not affect something else. Stanley agrees with that," added Wirthlin, directing his remarks to Griffin. "He said so at the beginning. We all agreed after Mary Margaret died that the quicker we got this into theaters, the better. And now, at the last minute, you want to talk about pulling it, waiting until the trial's over, whenever that might be?"

Visibly agitated, Griffin asked sharply: "What kind of business decision leaves out the long-term best interest of the studio? What do you think would happen to Blue Zephyr if–God forbid!–Stanley was to be convicted? And let's get something else straight. This was never just another business decision. We rushed everything through to a conclusion, we pulled people off of other projects, because we knew the public was going to be begging for a Mary Margaret Flanders movie after Mary Margaret had the great misfortune to get herself murdered. So don't tell me about our obligations as officers of this company! I've been doing this a lot longer than you, and Stanley has been doing it a lot better than either you or I ever could."

With a wrathful glance, Michael Wirthlin retreated into a sullen silence, waiting, as everyone turned to me, to see what I was going to say. When I admitted that I did not know, a brief, taunting look of triumph entered Wirthlin's small, calculating eyes.

"Then we go ahead, just the way we decided before," said Roth with an air of finality. He glanced across at a worried Louis Griffin. "It's all right, Louis. If Joseph thought it was any threat to my chances, he would have said so. Everything is going to be just fine. You'll see."

Nodding in agreement, Walker Bradley pulled himself out of his chair.

"It's a damn good picture," he said with a look of encouragement. He put his hand on Stanley Roth's shoulder and stared down at the floor. "Louis was right: It is the best thing she ever did."

"It may be the best thing you ever did, too, Walker," said Bill Pomeroy.

Rolling his head to the side until he caught his eye, Bradley gave the producer a searching look.

"It could have been better," said the actor in a way that suggested they both knew whose fault it was that it was not.

Pomeroy ignored it, or tried to. He looked past Bradley to Roth.

"It's the best movie I ever made, Stanley. I won't be surprised if both Mary Margaret and Walker are nominated."

"He says that about every picture he makes," whispered Bradley in a jaded tone as he passed in front of me on his way out. I had the feeling he would have said the same thing to the cleaning lady if he had happened to pass her instead.

Pomeroy, who seemed like a decent sort, began to talk to me about the movie, trying to assure me that releasing it before the trial could only help his good friend, Stanley Roth.

"The character she plays is so likeable, so extraordinary–Mary Margaret is madly in love, and he's madly in love with her; but she won't marry him. Then he finds out the reason is because she's dying and there is nothing anyone can do. She wants him to have a happy, normal life; she wants him to fall in love with someone else. He refuses. That's the character Walker plays. He tells her that it doesn't matter that one of them is dying; he wants them to be married forever. He doesn't actually come out and say he believes in heaven or the hereafter or eternal life–nothing that specifically religious–but it has that spiritual angle, you see. After people see it, they're going to think that the last person in the world who would ever hurt her, for God's sake, is the man who was lucky enough to marry her."

What would have been dismissed as the logic of a lunatic was in the mouth of a Hollywood producer almost persuasive.

While Pomeroy explained without self-conscious irony the way a fiction would provide the perspective from which we viewed the facts of someone's murder, Louis Griffin took Stanley Roth aside and spoke to him privately. Whatever they were talking about, Michael Wirthlin did not want to be left out. With barely controlled fury, he pushed his way between the two of them and began gesturing wildly as they all started to shout. Pomeroy stopped in midsentence and looked back over his shoulder. Julie Evans, who had sunk into a chair in the back, stood up, straining to hear.

"Not one damn dollar more!" yelled Wirthlin, red-faced and steaming, as he stalked out of the room. A moment later, the front door of the bungalow slammed shut behind him.

Griffin exchanged a worried look with Roth, and then, shaking his head, told Pomeroy they had better go.

"Michael isn't always a very pleasant man," said Griffin with an apologetic smile as he briefly shook my hand.

Roth walked them to the front door. Through the venetian blinds I could see them standing outside, talking quietly among themselves, as I followed Julie down the short hallway to the study.

"Want a drink?" asked Julie as she opened a cabinet on the other side of the room. She took a glass from a shelf and looked over her shoulder to see if I wanted to join her.

"Scotch and soda."

"That's what I'm having," she remarked just as Roth entered the room. She waited to see if he wanted something as well, but he hurried right past her, too preoccupied to notice.

Roth dropped into the wicker-backed chair at his desk. Immediately he started to tell me how he had been driven out of his house.

"I had to move out. Have you seen that street in front of my house? It's a campsite for tourists. Everybody in America wants to see where Mary Margaret Flanders was murdered," said Roth, his mouth curled back into a contemptuous sneer. He waved his hand in front of his face. "Tourists, reporters–they go around asking people why they're there. When I tried to get out, they surrounded the car, trying to get a better look. You should have seen those faces!" he exclaimed with a shudder. "They all think I did it. They looked at me like they wanted to kill me."

Julie brought me my drink and offered to Roth the one she had made for herself. He took it without a word and, as he continued his story, Julie went back to the small bar and made another one.

"I moved in here day before yesterday. I have everything I need," said Roth. "Julie brought me here. I had to hide in the trunk of the car."

Roth took a drink, and then, moving it around with his wrist, watched the ice rattle against the glass.

"As long as I'm inside the gates, they–the media, all those goddamn gawking tourists–can't get to me."

He raised his eyes and peered at me across the desk. With a pained expression he threw up his hands.

"I don't know if I'm going to live through all this. Mary Margaret–then they arrest me; and now I'm starting to feel the pressure here."

His eyes flashed with anger. He slammed his hand down on the desk. An ice cube flew out of the glass, slipped across the hard smooth surface and fell onto the floor.

"Do you know what that was all about? What Wirthlin is so upset about? What my good friend Louis Griffin is so worried about? Whether we can hang onto Blue Zephyr."

A look of alarm swept over Julie's face. "Stanley, I don't think . . ."

With a quick, irritated glance, Roth let her know he was not about to be told what to say. Chastened, Julie pulled back.

"We owe a lot of money, and a lot of what we owe is overdue. They won't come right out and say it–Wirthlin because he's a coward, and Louis because he's my friend–but they both think it's my fault, and maybe they're right. We lost a fortune on Mary Margaret's last two movies. The public doesn't know that; only a couple of people inside the studio know it. Hollywood accounting is an art form all by itself."

I did not quite understand why Roth's two partners would blame him for the financial failure of his wife's last two pictures. Roth was quick to read my reaction, but more than that, he assumed that I did not know anything about the way his business worked. It was an assumption I think he was used to making about nearly everyone, including people who had spent as many years in the business as he had. Like other enormously successful men, Stanley Roth, whatever he might say in public, did not, underneath it all, believe that his achievement owed anything important to chance.

"Mary Margaret got everything she asked for. If the picture had made money no one would have thought twice about it; but they lost money, and it doesn't look good. Mary Margaret made millions–my wife made millions–and the studio I run lost millions. I didn't negotiate those deals, by the way; Wirthlin did. It didn't work out and he resents it. Who else does he have to blame? They'll make it back with this picture," said Roth, staring past me, a bitter look in his eyes. "Everyone is going to want to see the last picture of the woman everyone was in love with. Don't you agree?" he asked, his eyes suddenly on me.

A mocking expression played on his mouth as if I had in that moment been selected to represent all the mindless sentimentality of that great amorphous mass of moviegoers on whose maudlin taste Roth had built much of his career.

"So long as they still think of her the way she was on the screen," I replied, staring hard at him, "and don't get too confused by reality."

The mocking expression faded from his lips. He looked at me a moment longer. For a second I thought there was something he wanted to say, something he wanted to ask; but then it was gone, replaced by the kind of cynicism that tries to pass itself off as irony.

"We release the picture, then we have the trial. Exactly right. That's what Wirthlin and Griffin both want; and I'm in no position to quarrel."

I took a drink of the scotch and soda, then put down the glass.

"What can you tell me about your wife's father, Jack Walsh? Why is he so damn certain you killed his daughter?"

Roth's head snapped back, as if he had just been hit with a jab. His eyes flashed with anger; his mouth pulled tight at the corners.

"You don't beat around the bush, do you? You know, I could get . . ."

"Another lawyer?" I asked, giving him back a little of what he had just given me. With both hands on the arms of the chair, I began to rise.

"No, no; you know I don't mean it. I'm a little on edge, that's all," said Roth, waving his hand for me to stay where I was. "You want to know about Jack Walsh? There have always been guys like Jack Walsh out here. There were guys like him in the gold rush, the ones who spent the rest of their lives talking about all the gold they almost found. They were here when I was a kid growing up in the valley: the quick-eyed speculators, the would-be investors in the latest sure thing. That's what Jack Walsh is–always just on the verge of the deal that is going to make him rich. That was the real reason he left his wife–he needed a little more money. He already owed everyone he knew, so he took the money she kept hidden in a shoebox on the shelf of her closet, got into the car she drove every day to work, and left her and his five-year-old daughter for good.

"That's what Jack Walsh is. He hadn't seen his daughter for years; he never tried to see her until she was famous. Then he shows up, after all that time, and gives her some phony excuse about how her mother wanted the divorce. What he really wanted was money. He told her about some deal of his that hadn't worked out and that he needed to pay off some of the people he owed. Her first mistake was to give him what he asked for, because of course he kept coming back for more. Finally, she had had enough. It wasn't the money–what was that to her? She just got sick of the sight of him, sick of remembering what he had done to her mother and what he had done to her. She cut him off, insisted she would never see him again. When I told him that he couldn't come back again, he refused to believe it was her idea. He blamed me instead. Now she's dead, and he goes around, the father of the victim, telling the world how wonderful she really was; how people would have loved her even more if they had known her the way he did. As if he knew her at all! You see what he's doing? If I'm the one who murdered his daughter, instead of a husband who lost his wife, then he can play the one who lost the only one he loved. It's one of the great hustles of all time."

Stanley Roth leaned back in his chair and gave me a strange look.

"Jack Walsh had nothing–no talent, no money, nothing. And now, because his daughter's dead, everyone is lining up to talk to him, ask him questions, hear what he has to say. The trial hasn't started yet and he's already got everyone convinced I murdered Mary Margaret. Who's Jack Walsh? Right now he's maybe the most powerful man in L.A."

9

STANLEY ROTH STOOD ON the front step of the bungalow as Julie Evans walked away down the narrow white sidewalk. High above, the palm trees whispered in the soft, insistent wind, blown from somewhere out on the Pacific, somewhere out beyond the far horizon, farther than the eye could see. Roth leaned his shoulder against the open doorway and followed her with his eyes, smiling to himself with the self-absorbed look of a man watching a woman who happened to catch his eye. It was Julie Evans, but it could have been anyone, anyone who was great-looking and knew it. That was essential–that she knew she was great-looking and that she knew everyone else knew it, too. It meant that she knew you were watching and that she wanted you to watch. It meant that for just that fleeting moment she had given you a kind of right in knowing who she was.

Julie turned the corner on her way to her car in the parking lot and disappeared from view. She was gone, but Roth was still staring at where he had seen her last, that same smile playing on his mouth like a song that after the music stops keeps echoing in your mind. I was caught up in the mood, standing next to him, watching a good-looking young woman the way I used to watch good-looking girls, girls I didn't know, girls I knew I'd never meet, wondering vaguely what might happen if I did. The summer scent of evening–the jasmine and the lush close-cut grass, the lemon trees and the orange trees, the bougainvillea and the daylong heat just slipping away–brought back memories of secret nighttime yearnings and shared and sometimes stolen frenzied intimacies.

Roth took a long look around, gazing up past the palms, out across the empty high-vaulted sky.

"That's what we did when I was kid growing up in the valley; that's what summer was: Go to a movie when you could afford it, then stand around and watch the girls you knew would never look at you because you didn't have a car and you weren't any good at football or basketball or anything else. The best-looking girls you ever see in your life are the girls in high school who wouldn't look at you twice."

Roth rubbed his nose with the back of his finger. He looked at me and smiled.

"Sonia Melinkoff–there's a name for you. I would have pumped gas in a service station for the rest of my life if she'd wanted to marry me. I don't think I ever would have regretted it, either."

He gazed again down the palm-lined street. The smile slowly vanished.

"Be careful what you say around Julie. She's completely loyal to me, but if the time comes when she decides that's not in her interest, she'll betray me, not only without a second thought, but without any thought at all. She's already told you she thinks I did it–killed Mary Margaret–hasn't she?"

"Is that what she told you?" I replied, not certain what he knew and what, for reasons of his own, he was trying to find out.

"She did, didn't she?" insisted Roth with a friendly grin, as if it were nothing very important; that it was, in fact, something he had always assumed–that everyone, at least everyone in that business, would always first look out for themselves.

"No, she did not."

It was not a lie, but it was not the truth, either; not the whole truth, anyway.

"She didn't say she thought you killed your wife. She did say," I went on, changing slightly the context of the conversation I had had with her that first day we met, "that the only way you could have done a thing like that is if your wife had driven you to it."

Before he could say anything in reply, I asked without any change of tone: "Is that what happened? Did she do something that drove you to it?"

I still was not sure. Sometime I did not think I knew anything about Stanley Roth beyond the bare surface–the opinions, the attitudes, the simple, straightforward facts of his life. Perhaps that is all we ever know about anyone, what we see–or what we think we see–on the surface. It had come, not exactly as a shock, but as a kind of surprise, when I first realized that instead of being wiser, more knowing, than the dream world he created, Stanley Roth might actually share with the audiences that came to his movies the same blind belief that things always worked out for the best and that evil never went entirely unpunished. That is what made it possible that Julie Evans had been right: that he could have killed his wife if she had done something terrible, something that provoked him into a rage and made him think that she deserved to die.

"You hit her–you told me you wished you had killed her–because she aborted your child," I reminded him when he began again to protest his innocence.

Roth stared hard at me; then, swearing into the night, marched inside the bungalow.

"Look," he said as he dropped into the chair at his desk; "if you want off the case, just get the hell off. But quit asking me if I did it. I've told you a thousand times: I didn't do it. Is saying it one more time going to make any difference?"

"You haven't said it a thousand times," I said sharply. "You've said it exactly three times: The first time was the first time we met, and the second time was two days ago–Friday–when I got the DNA results. The third time was just now."

Roth's arms dangled over the sides of the chair; his legs were sprawled out in front of him. With a look of exasperation, he emitted a low chugging sound, as if he was trying to extract something caught deep in his throat.

"I didn't do it," he said, in a voice suddenly lethargic. "I know it doesn't look good. I don't know how her blood got on that clothing, and I don't know how that shirt got into my closet. I didn't put it there."

It was difficult to believe, and if I had a hard time believing it, what was a jury going to think? The DNA results were beyond dispute, and as damning to the defense as anything the prosecution could have hoped for.

Roth claimed that because he had to be on the set early, he had been sleeping in another room the night his wife was murdered, but a bloodstained shirt had been found in a wicker laundry hamper inside Stanley

Roth's dressing room, just off the master bath. The blood belonged to Mary Margaret Flanders.

A sullen look in his eyes, Roth stuffed his hands inside his pants pockets and sank lower into the chair.

"I'd have to be pretty stupid, wouldn't I? First I murder Mary Margaret–slash her throat with a knife–and then, though I'm smart enough to get rid of the murder weapon, I leave a shirt with her blood all over it in the laundry hamper in my own bathroom!"

It made no sense, not to him anyway; and that was all the proof he needed, all the proof, he ventured to suggest, anyone would need.

"It's too obvious," he insisted.

Suddenly invigorated, he sprang to his feet.

"Want another?" he asked as he mixed himself a second scotch and soda. "Sure?" he asked when I declined.

He came back to his chair, but instead of sitting down placed his left hand on the back of it. While he took a drink he thought of how it worked to our advantage. In his director's mind, one scene always led to another.

"I wouldn't have done anything that stupid. Someone else had to have put it there. They wanted me to be blamed for Mary Margaret's murder. This wasn't some afterthought, some idea the killer got after the murder: This was something planned in advance. They came there that night, not just to murder Mary Margaret Flanders," he said, talking now in the third person, "but to have Stanley Roth accused of murder."

Roth looked at me, a somber expression on his face. He tapped his fingers together.

"Did you ever consider that possibility? That the real reason Mary Margaret was murdered was so that I could be blamed for it? That this whole thing was a plot to get me?"

"But who?" I asked. "Who would go to that kind of trouble–kill your wife–murder Mary Margaret Flanders–just so you could be blamed for it? Why would they murder her at all? If you were the one they wanted, why didn't they just murder you instead?"

Roth opened the middle drawer of the desk and removed a small, tarnished key which he then used to unlock a double drawer on the lower right side. Reaching down, he pulled out a manuscript, perhaps a hundred fifty or two hundred pages long. He put it under his arm and got to his feet. I caught a glimpse of a white label pasted to the dark blue cover. On it was typed a two-word title.

"*Blue Zephyr*? You're making a movie about the studio?"

Roth changed from his sports coat into a tan windbreaker. He put on a baseball cap and a pair of dark glasses.

"Come on," he said as he headed toward the door, the manuscript tucked under his arm. "Let's take a ride."

He was at the door before I could answer.

"We'll take your car," he said as I caught up with him. "Any reporter outside will think you're leaving and that I'm still here."

We drove out the gate, Roth crouching down in the front seat. He stayed there, the baseball cap shoved over his eyes until we were a few blocks away; then he pushed himself up, looked around to make sure no one was following and asked me to pull over. He hopped out and came round to my side.

"You mind if I drive?"

We changed places, but before Roth pulled away from the curb, he handed me the script for *Blue Zephyr*.

"There is one other copy. It's in a safe place. Take this one; read it. I've been working on it for three years, every chance I get. It's going to be the best thing I've ever done," he said with complete self-assurance. His eyes were fixed on the road in front of him. "It's going to be one of the best things anyone has ever done."

Roth drove to Santa Monica and parked on the street next to a public park. We sat on top of a picnic table, our feet on the bench below, looking out across a white sandy beach at the ocean. The sun had vanished below the wide, flat horizon. The first star was visible in the darkening sky. A breeze came cool and clean off the water. A few children were running half-naked in front of the waves, darting like shadows in the ankle-high surf. Holding her sandals over her shoulder by the strap, a pretty young girl of seventeen or eighteen kicked the sand with her feet, then scampered two or three steps ahead while an awkward young man struggled to keep up.

"When I first came here, just a kid who wanted to make movies, I lived here–just down the block. I grew up in the Central Valley, not far from Modesto. You ever been there? Hot, dry, flat, a hundred miles from the ocean. Might as well have been a million."

A look of nostalgia crept slowly into Roth's eyes. It was odd the way his eyes were the dominant feature in his face. He was not what anyone–man or woman–would call good-looking. Some men, when they reach their fifties, take on a certain air, have a way about them, something that, if it doesn't make them handsome, makes them look interesting, like men who know what they want and have become used to getting it. Stanley Roth had nothing of that. He had a thin, crooked mouth, and heavy-lidded eyes that drooped at the corners. His nose was too large, too broad; it gave him a ponderous, sluggish aspect. His chin was small, with a delicate, feminine shape suggesting indecisiveness and a natural timidity. His eyes changed everything, but even they did not produce an immediate effect. It was only after you had been with him a while that you began to notice how perfectly they matched the emotions of the moment. They moved scarcely at all, and never with the darting uncertainty of a nervous or excited reaction. It was more subtle than that, and more effective: a slight change in how open, or how closed, they were; a different shade of light, a muted change of color, as he lowered or raised his fine black lashes. He could look at you, his face otherwise immobile, and with his eyes alone tell you everything he felt, or perhaps more accurately, everything he wanted you to think he felt.

Roth stared out toward the edge of the sea that ran in a flat silver line between the night and what was left of the day.

"I used to come out here every night and sit here and watch the way the light changed; the way, when the sunset was over and the sky stopped burning red and orange, how the breeze would come up, quiet, cool; and then, for a little while, how everything–the sky, the ocean, the hills to the north–everything turned a kind of midnight blue."

He rested his chin on his hand, smiling at the memory of what it had been like, years ago, when all he had was the dream of what he wanted one day to do.

"That's why I named the studio Blue Zephyr. Strange, isn't it? It had so much significance for me, I thought it would have the same kind of meaning for other people too. It didn't. No one has ever even asked me what it meant, or why we called it that."

Clutching the edge of the table with his hands, Roth stared down at the bench on which he had planted his feet. He took a deep breath, let it out slowly, and raised his eyes again to the distant horizon.

"That's the color–not exactly midnight blue; more like the Duke Ellington song. You remember it–'Mood Indigo'? That's it–indigo blue. There's something melancholy, heartbreaking, about it, that mood, that color. And then, the way the breeze comes off the ocean this time of night. When I thought about what I liked most about being here, when I first came here, when everything about L.A. was brand new for me, this is what it was–here, at the ocean, at the end of the day, that hour between day and night, when you can hear the silence, when the wind brings back all the memories of all those other nights when you were young and the girls were all lovely and everything was always just the way it was supposed to be. That's why I called it Blue Zephyr: blue for the indigo night; Zephyr because it's the name for the west wind, the wind that carries the dream."

He stood up and took a few steps forward. It was as if he wanted to keep watching what was out there, at the far edge of the horizon, before it vanished finally forever into the night.

"I didn't want to be just another director; I didn't want Blue Zephyr to be just another studio," he said, turning back to me. "Thirty years ago, when I came here, I wanted to do something serious. I wanted to be the next Orson Welles; I wanted to make a picture as good as–no, better than–*Citizen Kane.* Thirty years later, what have I done?"

"You won an Academy Award."

"Can you tell me the name of the picture I won it for?"

I think he would only have been surprised if I had come right out with the name of it, instead of stumbling around for what I knew I would eventually remember if I had the chance to think about it for a while.

"But you remember *Citizen Kane*, don't you? It was a great picture–some say the best picture ever made. Whether it is or it isn't, it's a picture that's going to last forever; it's something people are always going to want to see. How long has Orson Welles been dead? You think when I'm dead that long anyone is going to remember any of the pictures I ever did? Yes, I know–I won the Academy Award. Take a look sometime at the list of each year's winners. How many of those pictures–how many of those names–do you really remember? And why should you? Most of them aren't worth remembering."

Night had fallen; there was no light left in the sky. The tall metal lamps near the sidewalk had come on. Roth was still wearing his dark glasses. Perhaps he was used to seeing things in the darkness. He turned up the collar on his windbreaker and shoved his hands into the coat pockets.

"Everybody thinks I'm lucky–or they did until Mary Margaret was killed. They all thought I had everything. Not just money, not just a movie-star wife, not just the Academy Award and the studio and everything that goes with it. No, more than all of that, more than all of it put together, I was lucky because I was me, Stanley Roth; because everyone knew who Stanley Roth was. I was famous. No," he said, shaking his head emphatically, "I was a celebrity, someone everyone thinks they know, someone everyone wants to be around. It's the damndest thing. I've never been on screen, never did what Hitchcock did and played a bit part in my own movie; but I'm on more magazine covers than any movie star. I can't go anywhere without someone asking for an autograph."

Roth rose up on the balls of his feet, tossed back his head, opened his mouth wide and gulped the air. With his hands still plunged in his pockets, he hopped stiff-legged twice, then stopped still. He batted his eyes as if he was trying to clear his mind of all the unimportant, inconsequential things that had made him lose sight of what he had once wanted to become.

"It wasn't my fault I became famous; it wasn't anything I set out to be. That first picture, the first one they let me direct–it was just a job, something I did to learn how to do it better. I didn't think it was going to do anything–break even, I hoped; but nothing like what it did. There wasn't anything interesting about it: just a simple story without any subtle characterizations, and everybody loved it. They loved it, and I was finished as a serious director before I began. No one wanted me to make movies that made anyone think, that made anyone uncomfortable. I had the gift of making the kind of movies everyone wanted to see, the kind that . . . Well, you know the kind," said Roth with a shrug that seemed to signal contempt for what he had done and what he had become because of it.

Roth paced slowly back and forth on the grass in front of the table where I sat, leaning forward, waiting for him to go on. He stopped and kicked half-heartedly at the ground.

"That was the whole reason for Blue Zephyr, the whole reason I wanted a studio of my own: to make the pictures I wanted. I wanted at least to try to do something important, something serious, something that people would remember the way they remember *Citizen Kane*."

"There have been other great pictures," I observed, struck by his apparent obsession with what Welles had done. "You never mention them."

"I studied *Citizen Kane*, studied it every way I knew," said Roth, a shrewd glint in his eye. "I watched it, over and over again; I read the script dozens of times. I wanted to know the reason it was such a great picture. I don't mean the technical reasons–the way Welles shot all those different black and white angles, the visual artistry of it. That was genius. No, I mean besides that. You can watch that movie now, fifty years later, and you're still drawn into it. Why? Because of who the story is about–William Randolph Hearst–and because of what Hearst was all about," said Roth, eager to explain it to me.

"Hearst was the first media celebrity, a man who did not just influence what people thought through the newspapers he owned, but a man who became famous because he didn't hide the influence he had. Think about that. It took me a while to figure it out, to understand what you would have to do to make a picture like that today. Who is there today like Hearst–a media celebrity–not a performer, not someone who plays a part–but the one who controls it all, all the parts of the story that gets told, the way Hearst used to control all the news that got published?"

I understood now whom he meant, and he knew it, too.

"Yes, exactly. Me, Stanley Roth. I'm Charles Foster Kane; and *Blue Zephyr*, the movie I'm going to make, is the next *Citizen Kane*. Read it," he urged. "See if I'm wrong. It's the story of how somebody who wanted to make great motion pictures got caught up in all the glamour, all the corruption, all the phony celebrity of Hollywood, and gave up everything he believed in because he got addicted to his own success. You want to know who would kill Mary Margaret to have me accused of murder? You want to know why they just didn't kill me if they wanted me out of the way? Because they can't kill me, they have to discredit me. They have to discredit me because it's the only way they can discredit the movie that will get made whether I'm dead or alive. The only way they can stop *Blue Zephyr* from destroying the careers of some of the most powerful people in this town is to destroy the reputation of the man who wrote it. And what better way to do that, than to have him convicted of the murder of his own wife?"

10

I READ *BLUE ZEPHYR*, and then I read it again. I read it the first time because Stanley Roth had written it, and said there were people who would do anything to stop it being made into a motion picture; I read it the second time because it was so much better than what I had thought it would be. *Blue Zephyr* was good; it might even be great; and the comparison Stanley Roth had drawn with *Citizen Kane* no longer seemed all that far from the truth.

Stanley Roth wanted to be what Orson Welles had been, what Orson Welles would be, not fifty years ago, but today; he wanted to make *Citizen Kane* all over again–now, today–not based on William Randolph Hearst, but on himself, Stanley Roth. The central character, the Charles Foster Kane of *Blue Zephyr*, is named William Welles.

In *Citizen Kane*, Kane is incredibly rich, just as William Randolph Hearst was incredibly rich. In *Blue Zephyr*, William Welles, like Stanley Roth, does not have much of anything. Hearst and Kane can have anything money can buy; Stanley Roth and William Welles have only their talent and ambition to sell. The first half of *Blue Zephyr* describes what Welles had to do; the people with whom he had to deal; the deals he had to make to get to the top, to have a studio of his own, a studio that would become the dominant force in the industry, and make William Welles the most powerful man in town.

Stanley Roth was right. *Blue Zephyr* was an indictment of Hollywood: the greed, the corruption, the indecent haste with which one person betrayed another, the ease with which disloyalty was disguised as an opportunity that might never come again. Roth spared no one, least of all himself, or, rather, his alter ego. William Welles just wants the chance to make pictures, the kind that were not being made anymore. He is not interested in money or power; and he is not thinking about one day having a studio of his own. Because he believes so fervently in his dream, he knows that others will believe in it as well. The young William Welles sets out to show Hollywood the kind of movies he can make.

He fails miserably. No one is interested in hearing what he thinks; no one wants to do anything except make pictures that make money. Disillusioned, he thinks about giving up, but he gets an offer to work as an assistant director to someone whose work he respects. The director is a much older man who has spent most of his life making pictures and remembers more than just one of the supposed golden ages of Hollywood. He tells him that the only way to survive is to make the movies the people with money, the people who own the studios, think are the movies people will pay to see. Welles learns a lesson, but not the one the director was trying to teach.

Stanley Roth thought he was writing a second *Citizen Kane*, but he was not writing about someone who had money and learned the limitations and the disappointments of power: he was writing about someone who had neither money nor power and knew he was better than those who did. Stanley Roth was William Welles, but William Welles was not Charles Foster Kane; William Welles was Julian Sorel. Without knowing it, Roth had written a second *The Red and the Black*. Like Julian Sorel, the young William Welles learns to keep his own counsel and make everyone believe he thinks the same way they do. He makes pictures that make money, and he does them so well that he becomes famous for it.

It was at this point in the script that I was first struck by how seriously I had underestimated Stanley Roth. He understood the way success makes prisoners of those who achieve it. William Welles had a name of his own, a famous name, a name respected in the industry; but instead of making the kind of picture he had dreamed of making, he keeps going on, doing the same thing over and over again, more obsessed than ever with making money. He tells himself that he needs it, that it is the only way he can have a studio of his own. He needs the money for the studio, and he needs the studio to make the kind of pictures he wants. He has to become rich because he wants to do good; and because he only wants to do good, it does not matter if he has to lie or cheat to get the money he needs.

Unscrupulous, remorseless, without a care for what happens to the people he uses, without a trace of conscience for what he does to the people he abandons once they have served their purpose, Welles gets the money he needs and then some. He becomes one of the wealthiest men in Hollywood, and then, finally, he gets a studio of his own. He calls it Blue Zephyr.

I do not know why Stanley Roth did this, called it *Blue Zephyr.* I suppose he had to if he wanted to make a movie about himself. Blue Zephyr was his signature, his stamp, his way of telling everyone that it was all about him. It added an authenticity to what he had done, gave it just a little more credibility; though, if anything, it was almost too believable as it was, too uncomfortably close to what must have happened at the other Blue Zephyr, the one I visited, the one where Stanley Roth now lived. Some of the most famous people in Hollywood were in that script. Their names were changed, though sometimes not by very much, and their characters were altered a little, but all of them were recognizable, even by an outsider like me.

William Welles has his studio, but he still does not make the kind of pictures he always thought he wanted to make. He has Blue Zephyr, but Blue Zephyr has to survive. The expenses are enormous, and he has a partner. Stanley Roth had two partners, Louis Griffin, whom he considered a friend; and Michael Wirthlin, whom he did not. In the script, Roth combines them into one character, a man who, like Wirthlin, brought money and the ability to raise more, and, like Griffin, was a friend of long standing, someone who could be trusted. He had to be someone Welles could trust: without trust there can be no betrayal, and the script of *Blue Zephyr* had no meaning if not the willing treachery of those you think you know the best.

The studio requires money, and Welles has to keep making the same kind of mindless movies he had been making before to get it. Then he meets her, Margaret Meyers–Mary Margaret Flanders–a young actress in whom he sees something no one else has seen, a quality that can be seen only through the lens of a camera. He does something utterly unexpected, but which, after he does it, makes perfect sense: he marries her.

It is an act of perfect cynicism, a way for Welles to take his revenge on the world of which he has become such a prominent part. He cannot make the movies he wants; he cannot be the kind of creative genius he thinks he could have been. He decides to show everyone how breathtakingly easy it is to succeed on the only terms Hollywood, and perhaps not just Hollywood, understands. He marries Margaret Meyers, this unknown actress of questionable talent, and by that single act makes her what everyone in Hollywood–and nearly everyone in America–wants so desperately to be: a celebrity, someone whose face is on the cover of glossy, colorful magazines; someone suddenly endowed with every virtue a publicity department could want or even God could invent. Welles does more than marry her. Ignoring all the conventional wisdom, to say nothing of the vehement objections of his partner, he casts his young wife, instead of an established box office draw, as the female lead in the most expensive movie Blue Zephyr has ever made.

Had Welles known that she would turn out to be as good as she was? Had he put her in that role to let everyone know that anyone could become a star if they were given the chance: that it was all an artifice, a parlor trick with lights and cameras; that the great American dream was nothing more than a kind of credible fraud, dependent on a willingness to believe what you knew was untrue? Whatever Welles thought he was doing–whatever strange, twisted thoughts of revenge he might have had–the woman he had first made a celebrity became with that single motion picture what the world thought of as a legitimate star. William Welles was now married to a woman suddenly more famous, more in demand, than himself.

This changed everything. Margaret Meyers was no longer dependent for her celebrity on being Mrs. William Welles. She was, however, still dependent on Blue Zephyr for her career. This is when we begin to find out what Margaret Meyers–and perhaps Mary Margaret Flanders–is all about. She begins an affair with her husband's friend, the partner in Blue Zephyr, and talks him–or rather seduces him–into starting a studio of his own, one where she can make the kind of pictures she wants. She leaves her husband, and she leaves Blue Zephyr. The studio Welles built is on the verge of bankruptcy. He stakes everything on one last picture, the one he has always wanted to make. He calls it *Blue Zephyr.*

Yes, *Blue Zephyr.* The whole thing is an imitation of an imitation, of art imitating–art. Stanley Roth wanted to make a second *Citizen Kane,* a movie about himself, in which he is the second Charles Foster Kane, William Welles, the most powerful man in Hollywood. Roth wanted to make a movie about himself, and that meant he had to make a movie about someone who ends up making a movie about . . . himself. The movie Welles makes in *Blue Zephyr* is the same movie Roth is making.

Or so it seemed until I turned to the last page of the script and discovered that Stanley Roth had written two alternative endings. Welles makes *Blue Zephyr,* the picture that is going to give the world an unvarnished look at the way Hollywood really works, but no one ever sees it. The night it is finished, Welles sits alone, watching it for the first time, the movie he always wanted to make, the one with which he hoped to save the studio he was otherwise going to lose. It is better than he had ever dared dream. He watches it by himself in his private theater at home; and then, at the very end, he slumps forward in his chair, the rhythmic clicking of the projector the last sound William Welles will ever hear. That is the way the movie ends, with William Welles dead. The two different endings deal with the way in which he dies. In one, Welles slumps forward, clutching his chest, dying of a heart attack, his eyes still focused on the screen. In the other, the camera draws away until all you see is the darkened silhouette of the back of his head, watching as the movie comes to an end. Then you hear it, a single gunshot, and the screen goes black.

IS THIS WHAT STANLEY ROTH had thought might happen to him–that someone might be willing to kill him to stop the movie from being made? Had he now changed his mind and decided that someone else had written a better ending? The death of William Welles might stop anyone from seeing the movie he had made; the death of Stanley Roth, like the murder of Mary Margaret Flanders, would almost guarantee that *Blue*

Zephyr would be shown in movie theaters all over the world. Stanley Roth did not have to be killed; he had to be destroyed, and what better way to do that than to have everyone believe he murdered the woman America had learned to love.

There was another difference between the script and the situation in which Stanley Roth now found himself. In the movie, it was not a secret that William Welles was making *Blue Zephyr*; but there were only two copies of the script Roth had written, one of which he kept locked in a desk drawer, the other of which he kept hidden in a place he thought secure. If Roth was the only one who knew it existed, it could not have been the motive for the murder of Mary Margaret Flanders as part of a plan to discredit him. Someone must have known, if not exactly what was in the script, then at least the broad outline of what Stanley Roth intended to do. He must have mentioned it to Julie Evans. He trusted her judgment, if he did not completely trust her. He had probably had her read it, wanting her reaction, and she, in turn, might easily have mentioned it to someone else. It was almost a week after he gave it to me that I had finally picked up the script and read *Blue Zephyr*; it was more than a week after that before I had a chance to ask Julie Evans what she knew about it.

STANLEY ROTH HAD INSISTED that I join his party at the premiere of Mary Margaret Flanders's last picture. Dressed in black tie, I stood in front of the Chateau Marmont under the sun-drenched Southern California sky, tapping my feet on the curb, getting more irritated with each passing minute. Half an hour late, Julie blamed it in her casual way on traffic. Wrapped in a long blue dress, her blonde hair pulled up and a diamond necklace fastened around her neck, she was so gorgeous I forgot how angry I had been about being made to wait.

"What can you tell me about anything that may have happened between Mary Margaret Flanders and either one of Roth's partners?" I asked as we pulled out into the street.

Her eyes glittered. A shrewd smile cut across her mouth.

"You mean, was she sleeping with one of them? The answer is, I don't know, but I wouldn't be surprised." She glanced across at me. "Why? That sounds more like a motive for a husband to kill his wife. You're supposed to be helping Stanley, aren't you?"

I ignored it, the only sign of my displeasure a brief, icy stare. For a few minutes neither of us said a word. Aware that she had overstepped herself, but unwilling to acknowledge a mistake, she added a slight qualification to what she had said before.

"She might have with Wirthlin. He would have jumped at the chance; not because she was Mary Margaret Flanders, but because she was Stanley Roth's wife. That would have appealed to him: the feeling that he could take her away from Stanley."

"But not with Louis Griffin?"

"Louis wouldn't have done it. In part because he's Stanley's friend, but mainly because he's something of a throwback, a man who thinks it's dishonorable to sleep with a woman married to another man."

A faint smile curled around the corners of her mouth, a reflection of a melancholy thought.

"It's nice to know there is still someone left like that," she added in a soft, rather husky voice. "Especially in this town."

I felt like a tourist, straining for a clearer view of a famous place. The premiere was being held at Mann's Chinese Theater. Not that long ago, Mary Margaret Flanders had knelt down on her knees and placed both hands on the wet cement that when it dried would make them, along with a plaque that bore her name, a permanent part of the movie-star procession in the sidewalk outside.

"Louis may have been the only man in Hollywood she didn't sleep with," said Julie with ill-concealed contempt. "She was fairly notorious that way, you know."

"That's interesting," I remarked in an offhand way. "In *Blue Zephyr*, the only affair mentioned is with William Welles's partner."

She seemed surprised.

"*Blue Zephyr*. The movie. The script Stanley Roth has been working on."

Julie glanced at me, her eyes full of caution. "Is that what Stanley told you?" She tried to sound nonchalant. "That there was one affair–the one with the partner?"

"No," I replied, curious about her reaction. "Stanley did not tell me; I read it."

A look, at first of astonishment, then of what seemed like anger, shone for a single, uncontrolled moment in her eyes.

"How much of it did he give you to read?"

There was an undercurrent of resentment, directed, not at me, but at Stanley Roth; as if by letting me see even a part of the script of *Blue Zephyr* he had somehow violated a trust or betrayed a secret.

I tried to make it sound as if I had not noticed.

"All of it," I replied, looking out the window on my side. "I read it straight through, then I read it again. I thought it was extraordinary. What do you think about it?" I asked, turning toward her.

Her polished lips were pressed tight together, her chin raised in an attitude of defiance.

"Am I in it?"

Her voice was quiet, ominously so.

"You haven't read it?" I asked, just to be sure.

Rather impatiently, she shook her head. "No one has read it. You're the first. I've read parts of it," she went on after she caught her breath, "a few pages at a time; a scene here, a scene there; none of it in sequence, never two scenes in a row."

The tension began to ebb. She looked at me, seeking confirmation.

"You're sure I'm not in it?"

"You didn't want to be in it?"

She looked like she wanted to laugh.

"Everybody knows about *Blue Zephyr*," she explained. "Everybody knows Stanley has been working on it for a couple of years now. No one has ever seen it–except you–seen all of it, I mean."

We were in front of the theater, waiting in line for the parking attendant to take the car. The handprints of once-famous people paraded silently down the street.

"Stanley has shown parts of it to people, people inside the studio; and he talks about it, what he wants it to be."

"The second *Citizen Kane*," I offered, in part to see her reaction, but also to see what it felt like, now that I had read it, to say it out loud.

"Is that what Stanley told you?" she asked shrewdly. "Is that what he thinks?"

Avoiding a direct reply, I told her only that reading the script it was impossible not to notice the similarities.

"Except that *Blue Zephyr* tells the story about the motion picture industry," she immediately remarked. "It's Stanley's dream–to tell that story better than it's ever been told before. That's the reason that it makes everyone who knows about it so nervous–the fear that he might tell the truth about the things he knows. But you're sure I'm not in it?" she asked with a visible sense of relief as we got out of the car.

Looking every inch the movie star herself, Julie took my arm as we entered the gauntlet of photographers and television cameras. Waving and smiling to the crowd surging behind the velvet ropes that cordoned off the red-carpeted walkway, she had them all thinking she must be famous as we made our way toward the entrance to the theater.

We went into the theater in broad daylight and when, two hours later, we came out, it was already dark. I do not know if William Pomeroy, the producer, had been right–I do not know if it was the best picture Mary Margaret Flanders had ever made–but knowing from the opening scene that this was the last time you would see her, the last time you would see her in something new, certainly made it the most memorable. Even when she was standing there, doing nothing, while Walker Bradley or one of the other actors held center stage, you kept watching her, waiting for what she was going to do next. When she dies at the end of the movie, in a scene shot at a distance using a stand-in after Mary Margaret Flanders had been murdered, the effect on the audience was something fiction alone would not have achieved. Though there were only a handful of people in the audience who had actually known her, the grief was real. People were still talking about it as we left the theater.

Outside, I stood off a ways, waiting while Julie ran up to tell Stanley Roth and the other studio executives gathered round him how much she liked the movie and how well she thought it would do. Just as she reached out to touch his arm, I heard it, that strident, unmistakable voice echoing above the noise of the swirling crowd.

"You're a murderer, Stanley Roth. You murdered Mary Margaret and you're going to pay."

I looked around until I found him, shaking his fist in the night, and then doing it all over again when the cameras turned toward him and the reporters came running fast. Tanned and meticulously groomed, dressed in a black tuxedo, Jack Walsh looked like someone who owned a studio of his own.

11

WE LOST A LONG TIME AGO the capacity to look at the world directly, seeing things as they are, rather than how they appear to be, refracted through the lens of the categories and conventions invented to explain experience. Still, for most of us, there are moments when, jarred by some accident, some unforeseen misfortune, we start to glimpse something we had not quite seen before and to look at everything else in a different light. Most people put on trial for their life rather quickly acquire a new perspective, one in which the only important question is their own survival. Dr. Johnson's famous dictum, "Tell a man he's to be executed in the morning, it concentrates his mind wonderfully," sums it up perfectly. But, then, Dr. Johnson had never met Stanley Roth.

After long, tedious weeks selecting a jury, the trial had finally begun. The prosecution had given its opening statement and I had given mine. Of all the other people I had ever defended for murder, I could not think of one who would not have asked what I thought about the way the jury had listened to the prosecution, the way the jury had listened to me. They always asked, they had to ask; they had to know how things stood, what I thought their chances were. Stanley Roth had a question, but it was not that; it was something else, a question no one but Stanley Roth would have thought to ask.

"Have you ever thought about becoming an actor?" asked Stanley Roth as I settled into what had become my accustomed place in the chair directly in front of his desk.

It was exactly eight o'clock, the time we started nearly every evening now. We might talk for a few hours or only a few minutes; once or twice we talked halfway through the night; but we always started at eight and we always did it here, in the bungalow where he lived and worked and tried not to think too much about what might happen when the trial was finally over. We met here every evening because the courthouse was a madhouse, full of cameras and reporters, all of them screaming about the public's right to know and each of them desperate to be the first one to tell. There was no place to go, no place to hide; the only time I could say something to Stanley Roth was in full view of the judge, the jury, and everyone who had fought their way into the courtroom, when I could lean close, my hand over my mouth, and whisper something in his ear.

Roth bent forward, holding his hands together in front of him. He had a look in his eyes, the narrow shrewdness of the streetwise charlatan who thinks he knows what you want before you do.

"It wouldn't be that much of a change," he went on, amused by the idea. "You're an actor already. You knew that, though, didn't you?"

"I'm not an actor, Stanley," I protested. "What I do is real."

Roth flashed a quick, dismissive smile. "Everyone is an actor, Antonelli. Everyone."

The pressure he was under had begun to take its toll. The circles under his eyes, barely noticeable when I first met him, had become dark, permanent shadows. His hands had begun to shake at odd times and for no apparent reason. His voice would now sometimes break in the middle of a sentence, and his speech would all of a sudden speed up like someone with a lot to say who is afraid of running out of time.

"You say you're not an actor; that what you do is real. But that opening statement I saw you make this afternoon went on for more than two hours and you never once referred to a note. Did all those smooth flowing sentences, all those well-organized paragraphs just come off the top of your head? You had to have spent . . . what? Days, weeks, working on that speech–drafting it, revising it, reworking it, memorizing it–learning it by heart until you could give it backward in your sleep. You're not an actor? You're one of the best I've ever seen!"

Roth paused and stroked his chin. He studied me through half-closed eyes as if he had been called upon to render a professional opinion about something on which he had unquestioned authority.

"I think you have a tendency to be a bit too formal at times. And that thing you do with your left hand . . . You know, when you have your right hand shoved into your pants pocket. You wave it around a little too much. Like this," he said as he flapped his hand in a loose, exaggerated manner. "Tighten it up a bit; make it more emphatic. Use it to underscore the words. Anyway, that's my take on it," he said, looking vaguely around the room, "for whatever it might be worth."

Slouching back against the chair, Roth put the palms of his hands on the seams of his pants, lifted his head to one side and looked at me with curious eyes.

"Really. How long did it take you to put that together–that opening statement you made?"

With a careless shrug and a halfhearted shake of my head, I dismissed the importance of what I had done in order to avoid discussing it. He had come close enough as it was.

"I didn't mean you were like an actor in the movies," he remarked; "more like an actor on the stage."

He folded his arms across his chest and moved his head farther to the side, an amused look on his face.

"Anyone can be a movie actor; not everyone can work on stage. . . . Mary Margaret had a hard time remembering two lines at a time; she could never have learned a whole script. But it didn't matter–it doesn't matter when you're making a movie . . . most of it is visual, anyway. All she had to do was memorize a few words. . . . We could keep shooting the scene until we got it right. But on stage! No, it would have been impossible."

He got to his feet, hesitated, and then slapped his hand hard on the corner of the desk. The sound of it was like the beat of a drum. He seemed to feed off it. His voice became more urgent, more insistent.

"Actors who do both always tell you they prefer the stage. They like working in front of a live audience. There is an energy about it, a passion they can't get when it is just them and the camera."

He stared through the window into the blue ambiguous night. I thought he had forgotten what he was trying to say; but then, suddenly, he wheeled around. He chopped the air with his left hand, doing it the way he had said I should.

"It's immediate. They live in the moment. They speak the words, play their part; they know while they're saying it they're the center of attention. They feel the response. It isn't their imagination, it's physical–you can feel it."

He looked at me sharply. "You felt it today, didn't you? When you were telling them what happened that night–how Mary Margaret was murdered while I was sleeping in the other room. I could tell you felt it. The look you had on your face–the scorn, the amused disdain–and your voice dripping contempt–when you said that the prosecution's case made sense only if I had set out to frame myself; when you insisted nobody could be so stupid. . . ."

Roth paused as if he had just remembered something. He lifted an eyebrow and looked at me.

"When you insisted nobody would ever have produced a picture in which the killer was so stupid as to murder his wife, go to all the trouble of getting rid of the weapon and then just casually drop his bloodstained clothes in the laundry hamper and go back to bed. That was an interesting touch. Something spur of the moment?"

"I wouldn't say spur of the moment, exactly," I mumbled.

"That's when you started to feel it, though, wasn't it? That's when you knew you had them, wasn't it?" he asked, keeping after me, certain he was right. "And not just the jury–everyone in the courtroom."

With a flash of intuition, Stanley Roth saw things in a new perspective.

"An actor–an actor on the stage–learns his lines, lines written by someone else, and speaks them over and over again, in every performance. Sometimes it goes on for years, the same play, the same part, the same lines, night after night. You write your own lines–or make them up on the spot," he added with a taunting glance as he began to walk back and forth. "You wrote the ones you gave today, though, didn't you?" he asked, peering at me from under his brow as he continued to pace nervously.

"I sketched out some of what I was going to say."

His smile told me he did not believe me. He was certain I had written it all out and then memorized every word of it. In the literal sense, he was wrong; but I did nothing to correct him. There were things he did not need to know.

"You perform it only once; and each time you do it–make an opening statement–you do it with a different audience, a different jury."

With a few quick steps he came back to the desk and dropped into the chair. One hand thrown lazily over the side, he sank into the opposite corner and, with his elbow on the arm, rested his chin on the heel of his hand. His eyes, moving languidly from a point somewhere above my shoulder, came to rest on mine; then, stirred by some other thought, moved back again. He removed his hand from under his chin. Unfolding his fingers, he gestured in a vague, desultory fashion into the distance.

"You're an actor who writes his own lines for a play that never has more than one performance. But you always play the same part, don't you?" asked Roth, his eyes, moving slower than his words, coming back to mine at the very end of the question. "Always the trial lawyer–or, rather, the defense attorney–pleading with your audience . . . that jury–each time twelve different people; but always twelve people you don't know, an audience of strangers–to do what you tell them is the right thing to do, though you know–don't you?–that sometimes it isn't the right thing at all. How do you do that? An actor has his lines–the lines of the play, the fiction being performed. But you–you have the lines you've written about something real, something that happened; and you're trying to convince the audience not just to enjoy the performance; not just to applaud how well you acted, how entertaining it has all been. . . . No, you want them to do something, to act, to decide whether one man, the defendant, your client, the man you represent, did or did not commit murder. The actor goes home after the play, satisfied with how well he has performed. How do you go home? Satisfied with your performance? Pleased with yourself if you've gotten your audience to do the right thing–or the wrong thing?"

He saw the look of anger in my eyes, the look I could not quite conceal, and it drove him on. He jumped forward, both arms on the desk and stared hard at me.

"Doesn't it bother you that you've learned how to act so well that you can persuade your audience to let a killer go free?"

"You mean, will it bother me if I convince this jury to let you go free?" I shot back.

"I knew you didn't believe me," he replied with an irritating sense of vindication; "that deep down you still thought I was guilty. I'm not, but it doesn't matter. It doesn't matter to you. That is what I did not understand before: that you don't care one way or the other. It doesn't change what you do, does it? It doesn't change how you feel about it. Because," he went on, that same shrewd look in his eye he had before, the look that told you he thought he knew your weakness and how to use it, "the only thing that matters to you–the whole reason you do this–the reason you love this–is the performance after all, isn't it? Isn't that the truth of it? You're an actor after all–a great actor–and like every great actor you become intoxicated with your own performance."

"You think everything is a performance; you think everyone is an actor. You don't understand the first thing about what I do," I protested as I got out of the chair.

I was tired of looking at him; I was tired of the way he thought he could put everything in categories of his own choosing, as if nothing existed unless he could first see it the way it would look on a screen. I stood at the open French doors, listening to the sound of a car pulling away from the studio lot below; the muffled voices of two women walking toward the gate, maybe two actresses–bit players–on their way home after a long day of shooting somewhere on the back lot; the low murmur of traffic from a highway a mile or so away. Everywhere the sound of normal life, or what we thought of as normal life, lived out beyond the edges of Blue Zephyr and its manufactured dreams.

"I'm not an actor," I said, turning around. "And I'm not–at least I hope I'm not–intoxicated with my own performance. But neither am I some cardboard character going through the motions, reciting the shopworn phrases about reasonable doubt and the questionable credibility of witnesses. I believe–really believe–in what I'm saying. That's the difference. I'm not reading lines; I'm not playing a part. I'm arguing a case. That's what I like about what I do: the argument."

"The argument?" asked Roth, confused.

Holding his hands together in his lap, he began to rub his fingers together as he waited with some impatience for me to explain. He had already decided what he thought; he was not really interested in hearing more about it from me.

"The argument," I repeated, jabbing the air with my left hand. "That is what a case is–civil, criminal, it doesn't matter–an argument about what the law is and what the facts are. You think I care about the defendant? You think I care what happens to him? You're right–most of them are guilty, most of them did what they're accused of doing."

I moved a step closer and fixed him with a stare.

"What do you think I have in common with most of the people I defend? Do you think I became a defense lawyer out of some public-minded democratic belief in the essential equality of everyone, whether the wisest, most honorable man I ever met, or some depraved bloodthirsty lunatic who would rape your mother and kill your father and not think twice about making you watch?"

Roth moved his head to one side, then the other, looking at me first from one angle, one perspective, then another.

"It isn't very often I lose sleep over what is going to happen to the defendant if I lose; I'm not losing any sleep over what might happen to you. I only worry that I might miss something, leave something out, forget something that could make the difference between winning the argument and losing the argument. That's what I worry about; not whether you're going to prison for the rest of your life, or whether you're going to wind up face to face with the executioner. . . ."

Roth had moved his chair a few inches to the right, toward the side of my face hit by the lamp light.

"What are you doing?" I asked, annoyed.

He shook his head, signaling that he did not want to be interrupted as he considered something.

"That's good," he said finally; "that anger. Not many people can do that–create the impression of genuine anger, real indignation. I saw a little of that this afternoon–in your opening; but this . . . this was good. You're a natural. Tell me this, though," he continued, sitting upright, stroking his small chin. "That business when we were picking a jury . . ."

"Voir dire," I said automatically, bewildered at the effect, or rather, the lack of effect my outburst had had on him.

He was impossible. Everything was a movie; everything some kind of act. I could have pointed a gun at him, and he would have thought only about how I should be holding it to make it look really authentic.

"Forget voir dire. I'm not an actor. This is not a picture show. There has never been a movie that comes close to what at the heart of it a trial–a murder trial–is all about. Orson Welles might have been able to do it," I added, willing to wound his vanity if that was the only way to get his attention. "He might have understood it: the way the argument works. He might have understood the way you have to take each fact and connect it with all the others; the way you have to make each point follow effortlessly, inexorably, from the one before it. Welles might have understood the way you try to take apart the argument on the other side, the argument by which the prosecution tries to convince that same jury–that same audience–that the facts, the evidence, proves conclusively–beyond that reasonable doubt–that the defendant is guilty. Yes," I said as if I was now convinced of it, "Orson Welles might have understood it: the way you take their argument and show how it doesn't prove guilt at all; that it proves instead–those same facts, that same evidence–that there is a reason to doubt, a reason serious people, people who take the law seriously, have to find the defendant not guilty; and do it, no matter how certain they are themselves that though they could not prove it the way they were supposed to prove it, the prosecution was right: the defendant was guilty, guilty as hell; guilty, guilty any way you can think, except by that one unimpeachable standard. That, Mr. Roth, is the argument. That's what I do. I make the argument. And if that argument helps you or anyone else–fine; and if it doesn't . . . Well, as I said before, I'm not going to lose any sleep over it."

Slowly tapping his fingers, Roth waited until I was finished. He bent his head to one side and looked at me with genuine interest.

"You said there hadn't been a movie made that really got to the heart of what a murder trial is all about."

It was astonishing. I should have realized when I said it that it would be all he could think about.

"What would it take?–I mean if someone wanted to make, not just a good movie, but a great movie . . . The kind Orson Welles might have made–about a murder trial?"

I suddenly remembered.

"He made one–*Compulsion*–about the Leopold and Loeb case. The murder of the boy in Chicago in the 1920s. Two older boys, college students, did it. They wanted to see if they could do it–kill someone; do it for no reason at all–to prove they were superior to the dictates of morality. They thought that's what you did if you were one of Nietzsche's supermen."

Roth was disappointed. He had worked for years on the script for *Blue Zephyr*, trying to outdo Orson Welles. For a brief moment, he must have thought there was something else he could do, something that Welles had not already done. His mood brightened when I suggested that *Compulsion* was not what I had had in mind.

"Welles played Clarence Darrow. There was no trial. Darrow pled them both guilty. The great scene is the speech Darrow gives in open court persuading the judge to sentence them to life in prison instead of death. It isn't what I was talking about: a picture that captures what it is like to be the defense attorney in a murder case; that sees things through his eyes; that shows what he does and how he does it. All the ones that have been made, including *Compulsion*, including *Witness for the Prosecution*–they're all concerned with the crime, or with the accused. You want to know how to make a great movie? Write a script in which the defendant may or may not be innocent, but everyone thinks he's guilty and all the evidence says he's guilty. Make it a case no one thinks the defense attorney can win. Make it a case where the defense attorney takes the facts proven by the prosecution and shows in his argument that they don't prove what the prosecution said they would. Do that, do it better than it's been done before–then you'll have a great movie."

A knowing smile edged across Stanley Roth's mouth as he sat back in his chair.

"The defendant may or may not be innocent; everyone thinks he's guilty; all the evidence is against him. You're talking about my trial. What a great idea! A movie about my case."

From behind my shoulder I felt the first cool stirring of the evening breeze, the wind, the western wind, the zephyr that Stanley Roth used to feel on his face when he stared out at the Pacific every night, dreaming about the movies he wanted one day to make. He still had not made them, and perhaps he never would; but it was still the thing he kept dreaming about, the thing that made him go on: the idea that he could do one thing well, as well as anyone ever had, and do it in a way no one would ever forget. Mary Margaret Flanders used to sit, mesmerized, watching herself on the screen; but Stanley Roth had watched right with her, watching not just her, but everything else he had created.

Roth's head was bent over the desk, his hand moving below him across a white sheet of paper, writing a note to himself. He wrote with a fountain pen, a gaudy gold and silver production, too large to be used with any facility for anything more than an elaborate signature or an occasional four-word flourish. With a slow, awkward stroke, wielding the pen more like a sculptor handling a chisel, Roth pushed on, determined to memorialize everything he wanted to remember. At the end, he paused, the pen suspended just above the paper, while he read over what he had written. He screwed the cap back over the nib and, holding it in both hands, appeared to study the barrel.

"That thing you did when we were picking the jury," he said very deliberately. He placed the pen on top of the sheet of paper and looked up. "Voir dire. Besides all that business about reasonable doubt, you always asked them–all of them–things about where they lived, where they went to school, how many kids they had. You were trying to make a connection with them, weren't you? Trying to make them comfortable with you. That way, they're more likely to think they can trust you. That's why you do that, isn't it? So they'll like you more than the D.A. She didn't do any of that. She didn't ask any of those kinds of personal questions. And you're still going to sit there and tell me you're not an actor, that it's all about the argument?"

He could not help himself. There was one thing more he had to say, one thing more he had to ask.

"Then, in the opening, after she goes through what the prosecution is going to prove–how I murdered Mary Margaret Flanders–you made it sound as if that was the single most outrageous suggestion you had ever heard in your life. If you're not an actor, then you must have believed it."

He sat there, looking at me, a mocking smile on his lips.

"But you don't believe it, do you? You don't believe I'm innocent. You don't believe I didn't kill her, do you?"

His eyes stayed on me. He tapped with his finger the page on which he had just a moment earlier finished writing a note to himself.

"How would you like to play the defense attorney in the movie I'm going to do when this is all over? You'd be terrific."

12

IT WAS HARD NOT to stare. Short and overweight, with a small mouth pinched into meanness and tiny, thick-lidded truculent eyes, the court clerk was as full of resentment as anyone I had ever seen. There were numerous specific functions she was required to perform, but she greeted each request with immediate suspicion, never quite certain she was not being asked to do something beyond the responsibilities, and beneath the dignity, of her position.

"Would you please bring in the jury?" Judge Honigman asked her with a tolerant smile.

Her pudgy hand on her hip, the clerk seemed to deliberate with herself about whether she would or would not. Then, muttering under her breath, she crossed in front of the counsel table on her way to the jury room. She stood in front of the door, drawing herself up to something close to an erect posture. With a harsh rap of her knuckles, she knocked once and then put her head inside and announced that it was time to start.

On the way back to the small desk she occupied below the bench on the side farthest from the jury box, she rapped her knuckles once more, this time on the edge of the table where I sat with Stanley Roth. In a voice freighted with all the burdens of martyrdom, she reported succinctly: "The jury, Your Honor."

Twelve jurors and two alternates, chosen in case a regular member of the jury had for some reason to be replaced, filed slowly into the courtroom. No matter how hard they tried, no matter how patiently each one waited for the juror in front, they could not help bump into each other as they crowded into the jury box. A single row of seven chairs would have been a tight enough fit; but fourteen people trying to squeeze themselves into the two rows into which that jury box had been divided was almost too painful to watch. There was no room to relax, no room to move around. One of the jurors in the back row, a tall, heavyset, middle-aged man with the thick arms and neck of someone who worked with his hands, had to sit straight up each time he crossed his legs. Each time he did it, a shudder passed through the elderly stiff-necked woman in front of him as his knee pushed hard against the back of her chair, forcing it forward.

The jury box was a crime, but so was everything else about this courtroom. There was nothing grand, nothing inspiring about this place with its acoustical tile ceiling and gray linoleum floor. The cheap wooden tables and the cheap wooden chairs; the army-green-colored metal wastebasket next to the armless chair where the sad-eyed court reporter worked; the sullen clerk with her permanent resentments; the broad-nosed female deputy sheriff standing off to the side, her stomach oozing over her holster belt, her dull eyes moving slowly from side to side on a blank patrol: all of it spoke of budgets and accountants, narrow-minded politicians who promised lowered taxes, and a public interested only in their own, private affairs.

When the jury finally squeezed themselves into their seats, Judge Honigman felt compelled to remark on their close quarters and offer what solace he could.

"I'm sorry there isn't more room. We'll try to take a short break from time to time so you can at least stretch your legs."

Honigman pressed his hands together and rested his cheek against them. He peered at the members of the jury, cramped together in the jury box less than three steps away.

"Yesterday, the two attorneys–Ms. Van Roten for the prosecution, and Mr. Antonelli for the defense–made their opening statements. I advised you then that those were statements made by the prosecution and the defense of what they expect the evidence to show, or not to show; I advised you then that those statements are not themselves evidence of anything. Evidence–admissible evidence–is that which tends to establish the existence, or the nonexistence, of a fact."

Honigman waited while the members of the jury thought about what that might mean. Without that pause they might not have thought anything about it at all. Honigman was better than I had originally thought; he was certainly better than most of the judges in whose courtrooms I had tried cases, judges who had said the same thing so many times before they did not ask themselves whether the words had any meaning to blank-eyed jurors who knew nothing about the technical terms of the law. Honigman seemed actually to want the jury to understand what they were doing.

"Opening statements themselves," Honigman repeated one last time, "are not evidence."

With that, he turned to Annabelle Van Roten and invited her to call the first witness for the prosecution.

Richard Crenshaw was in his late thirties, with evenly set brown eyes, and a firm, straight jaw. His nose looked a little too straight, as if it had been surgically altered; his teeth seemed almost too white, as if they, too, had been the subject of cosmetic work. There was nothing exceptional, or even out of the ordinary, about the color of his hair, but it had been cut with the kind of meticulous care I would not normally have associated with someone who lived on a police detective's salary. His nails were clean and cut short, all the edges polished smooth. His clothes–slacks, a sports jacket, shirt and tie–seemed at first what any detective might wear; then I realized that they were of a finer fabric, and fit him far better, than what could be found on a department store rack.

With the self-assurance of someone who had been there many times before, Detective Crenshaw settled into the witness chair. Under the helpful questioning of Annabelle Van Roten, he explained that he was a homicide detective and that he had been one for the better part of ten years. Two uniformed officers had arrived at the home of the victim, summoned by the frantic call of the housekeeper; but he was the first detective on the scene and had immediately taken charge of the investigation.

"And what exactly did you find when you arrived?" asked Van Roten, standing at the end of the counsel table, her right hand resting lightly on her hip, one foot crossed in front of the other.

"The victim–Mary Margaret Flanders–was floating facedown in the swimming pool," replied Crenshaw. "The water around her was full of blood. It was like a red cloud around her head. When we turned her over, you could barely see her face."

His answer seemed spontaneous and unrehearsed, a straightforward description of what he had seen; but there was something odd about his voice, as if he had practiced for a long time to make it sound always the same way: calm, controlled, a voice that carried with it a sense of unflappable confidence; a voice that would give whomever was listening confidence in him.

Van Roten knew what the jury must be thinking.

"Why didn't the two officers–the ones first on the scene–remove the body from the pool?"

Bent forward at a slight angle, both feet planted squarely on the floor, one a little in front of the other, both elbows on the arms of the chair, Crenshaw appeared to listen intently until the question had been asked. Then, turning only his head, a sober expression on his face, he looked at the jury.

"To prevent any contamination of the crime scene. We did not remove the body from the pool until the forensic people had done everything they needed to do."

He turned his head back to Van Roten and waited.

"Would you identify these photographs, please?" she asked as she stepped forward and handed him a large packet.

Without expression, he thumbed through the photographs.

"These are photographs taken of the body at the crime scene."

"This was the way she looked when you first saw her–floating facedown in the pool?"

"Yes," he answered in that calm, measured voice.

"Your Honor, I would ask that these photographs be entered into evidence."

Honigman waited while I glanced through them. It was strictly for show. I had filed a motion to keep them out of evidence and he had ruled against it.

"I would renew my objection, Your Honor," I said as I gave them back to the clerk. "The defense is willing to stipulate as to the manner of the victim's death and to the location of the body when it was found. These pictures," I added, shaking my head in disgust, "are an obscenity. They serve no purpose other than to inflame the emotions of the jury. They certainly do nothing to help prove any fact in dispute."

"Your objection has been noted, Mr. Antonelli," said Honigman as he gestured for Van Roten to continue.

"May the jury be shown these photographs, Your Honor?"

I had just sat down, and now I sprang up from my chair, barely able to contain myself.

"I should be glad to know precisely how these photographs–photographs of a naked woman with her throat slashed–a very famous naked woman, I might add–are supposed to assist the jury as it attempts to weigh the evidence in a purely rational manner?"

Honigman's eyes turned cold.

"Your objection was noted," he sought to remind me.

"My objection was to allowing them to be entered into evidence; the question of having them passed round the jury box at the beginning of the prosecution's case has never been discussed!"

His face reddened, and with the knowledge that he had not been able completely to hide his discomfort, it grew redder still.

"I'm asking that the jury see them now," interjected Van Roten, "so they can follow more closely the testimony of the witness, Your Honor."

I was trying to take as much of the shock out of seeing those photographs for the first time as I could; I had to make them sound even worse than they were. There was another reason as well, but I was not ready to reveal that either to Van Roten or the court: not yet, not until they had both come out in favor of letting the jury see things for themselves.

"Perhaps instead of these pornographic pictures of death, Ms. Van Roten would prefer to have Mary Margaret Flanders dug out of her grave so she can have the body passed round the jury box!"

"Your Honor!" shouted Annabelle Van Roten as she flew out of her chair, more stunned, I think, than enraged.

She need not have bothered. Honigman had already bolted forward, fixing me with a murderous stare.

"That is an outrageous thing to say."

I cocked my head and raised an eyebrow. "Passing those photographs around the jury box is an outrageous thing to do," I retorted with an insolence that made Honigman's face turn an even deeper shade of red.

"Mr. Antonelli," he warned, "I don't want to find you in contempt."

I threw out my arms and turned up my palms. I looked at him with a puzzled expression, as if the last thing I had intended was any disrespect.

"Forgive me, Your Honor. They're just words, words to express my frustration at my own inability to find other words, words with which to convey more clearly and more persuasively the concern I have that, as you were just a few minutes ago explaining to the jury, evidence, and only evidence, be the basis for their decision. I went too far, and I apologize for that."

His authority intact, Honigman could afford to show magnanimity. The tension that had held him rigid began to dissipate. The color in his face returned to normal. He had, or at least he thought he had, put me in my place. He became almost friendly.

"It's easy to become a little too intense," he said, assuming a diplomatic attitude. "Your objections have been noted. The photographs have been entered into evidence. Will the clerk please hand them to the jury."

Grumbling silently to herself, the clerk took the few short steps to the jury box. She flopped the short stack of black-and-white photographs in front of the first juror.

I watched as each juror leafed through them. What was going on inside their minds–what were they thinking–as they examined the pictures of a naked woman taken hours after her death? And not just a naked woman, but a woman all of them knew. Was it what I had felt when I first saw them? The strange sensation that someone had made a mistake; that this utterly ordinary-looking woman caught in the unfortunate exposure of violent death could not possibly be the same woman who had seemed so breathtakingly beautiful on the motion picture screen and so exciting and glamorous in the photographed pages of the movie magazines? It was in a way depressing to realize that she had really been no different than anyone else. If you had not known who she was, you would not have given her any more thought, nor been any more affected by her death, than anyone else you had never met.

Van Roten nodded perfunctorily toward the photographs being circulated in the jury box.

"Detective Crenshaw, these pictures were taken both before and immediately after the body of Mary Margaret Flanders was removed from the swimming pool at her home?"

Crenshaw waited until the juror holding the photographs glanced up.

"Yes."

"And these photographs accurately reflect the condition of the body as you saw it?"

"Yes."

"In . . . I believe it's the fifth photograph–the one taken of the victim lying on her back next to the pool–would you describe the mark that is clearly visible across her throat?"

With his left arm trailing across the arm of the witness chair, Crenshaw leaned toward the juror holding the photographs.

"The mark you refer to is a gash that runs from just below her left ear all the way across her throat to just below her right ear."

"In other words, Detective Crenshaw, her throat was slashed?"

"Yes, that's correct," he replied, turning his attention to her.

"With a knife?"

"With a sharp instrument of some sort; but, yes, probably a knife."

"We'll hear from the coroner a little later about the exact cause of death," said Van Roten, with a brief glance toward the jury. "But so far as you could tell, is that how she died?"

It was almost choreographed, the way his eyes followed hers to the jury.

"Yes; no question about it. Her throat was slashed, her larynx severed. It was a deep wound, as deep as any I've ever seen. It took some strength to do that, and some leverage as well."

"Leverage?" she asked, wheeling around as if this last remark was something of a surprise instead of something they had doubtless gone over again and again until they had it just right.

Crenshaw pointed toward the juror in the back row of the jury box who now had possession of the photographs.

"You'll notice that a silk stocking was wrapped around her neck, just above where her throat was cut. You'll also notice in one of the other photographs a bruise in the spinal area of her lower back. It appears that her killer held her from behind, holding onto the stocking with one hand, his knee against the small of her back, while he used his other hand–his right hand–to cut her throat."

"His right hand? How can you be sure of that?" asked Van Roten, turning until she was standing square in front of the jury box, her dark eyes blazing.

"Because of the angle of the wound, and because of the direction in which the larynx collapsed."

"You've testified that there was blood in the swimming pool. Was there blood anywhere else?"

"Yes, on the cement deck next to the pool."

"Did that blood also belong to the victim?"

"Yes."

"And was that the only other place in which you found traces of blood?"

"No. We found blood on some clothing as well."

"On clothing belonging to the victim, Mary Margaret Flanders?"

"No," replied Crenshaw, turning to the jury. "We found blood on clothing belonging to the defendant, Stanley Roth."

"One last question, Detective Crenshaw. You knew the victim, Mary Margaret Flanders, didn't you?"

"I was a consultant on a movie she made a couple years ago. I did not know her well; but, yes, I knew her."

Van Roten glanced at Stanley Roth and then looked back at the witness.

"And did you know the defendant, Stanley Roth, as well?"

"Yes. It was his picture."

I was on my feet the moment Annabelle Van Roten finished her examination of the witness, asking my first question before Judge Honigman could inquire whether I had anything I wanted to ask.

"That was it?" I asked with an incredulous grin. "A few bloodstains on the cement decking of the pool and blood on the clothing you claim belonged to the defendant?"

Richard Crenshaw rested his elbows on the arms of the witness chair and turned up his palms.

"As I testified," he said in that well-modulated voice, "we found blood belonging to the victim on the cement next to the pool, and we found blood belonging to the victim on clothing belonging to the defendant."

I tapped the corner of the table with the fingers of my left hand, and then, as if I had just become aware of a bad habit I was determined to break, shoved the offending hand into my coat pocket and stepped away from the table.

"You're sure? Blood next to the pool, and blood on the clothing you describe as belonging to the defendant? That is your testimony?"

Crenshaw crossed his ankle over his knee and clasped it with his hand.

"Yes," he replied warily, wondering if he might have missed something in the question or in the way I was asking it.

"Nowhere else?"

"No."

I lowered my eyes as I moved to the front of the counsel table. I was just a step from the jury box.

"You testified that when you first arrived, the body of the victim–Mary Margaret Flanders–was floating facedown in the swimming pool." I glanced up. "You testified–I think I remember the words exactly–that the water was like a 'red cloud.' That was the phrase you used, wasn't it–a 'red cloud'?"

"Yes, I believe that is what I said."

"And I take it you meant that there was a great deal of blood–the victim's blood–in the water, correct?"

He nodded grimly and waited for the next question.

"You also testified that the victim's throat had been slashed, slashed with such force that her larynx had been cut. You testified, I believe–and I think I remember your words exactly–that this had taken not only considerable strength but leverage as well. Is that what you said?"

Crenshaw let go of his ankle, planted both feet on the floor and bent forward.

"Yes, that's what I said," he agreed.

"From the pictures you identified–the ones passed around the jury box," I added with a brief grimace, "it's a fair observation, is it not, that the victim had lost a great deal of blood?"

"I wouldn't quarrel with that observation at all."

"Yet the only blood you found–other of course than the blood in the pool itself–was on the deck next to the pool and on some clothing you found. . . . Where exactly did you find that clothing?" I asked, staring hard at him.

"In the laundry hamper in the bathroom off the master bedroom."

I looked down at the floor, rubbing the back of my neck.

"Yes . . . in the laundry hamper . . . in the bathroom . . . off the master bedroom."

My hand on the railing of the jury box, I looked again at the witness.

"Well, I suppose that is in keeping with the defendant's extraordinary attention to good housekeeping." Lifting an eyebrow, I turned slightly to the side. "He murders his wife–slashes her throat–there's blood everywhere, all over his clothes, and yet, somehow, he manages to get all the way from the side of the pool where he killed her, across the deck, through the house, up the stairs, down the hall, into the bedroom and then into the bathroom. And he does it all so carefully that doesn't allow so much as a single miniscule drop to fall from his blood-soaked clothes onto the floor, onto the carpet; not even, please notice, onto any part of the exterior of the laundry hamper in which you claim to have found them!"

"Claimed to have found them!" exclaimed Annabelle Van Roten as she jumped out of her chair. Her dark eyes flashed anger and incredulity. Shaking her head, she turned from me toward the bench. "Counsel has not established any kind of foundation to make that kind of insinuation!"

Honigman's eyes came round to me. Before he could say anything, I asked: "Detective Crenshaw, did anyone see you find the clothing where you said you found it?"

"No. I searched the bedroom area alone. When I found the clothing with the blood on it I put it in an evidence bag myself."

"And the reason you made this search is because, as you testified earlier, you were the first detective on the scene?"

"Yes. I did not want to wait. I didn't know what–or who–might still be in the house; and I wanted to make sure that if there was any evidence in the house it would not be interfered with."

"And you went to the bedroom because the victim was found naked in the pool, and you assumed for that reason that she must have undressed somewhere and the bedroom would be the most logical place?"

"Yes, basically that's right."

"Would it be fair to say that you were very much on the alert as you moved through the house, checking for anything that might have some value–some evidentiary value–in helping solve the crime you were there to investigate?"

Crenshaw followed me with his eyes. "Yes, it would be fair to say so," he replied cautiously.

"Then when you found that clothing covered with the victim's blood you must have been completely mystified, weren't you?"

"Mystified?"

"Yes, mystified. It is what I said before, Detective Crenshaw: all that blood, the victim's blood, all over the clothing, and despite looking everywhere you did not find a single drop anywhere between the place where the body was found and the laundry hamper. Didn't that mystify you, Detective Crenshaw? Didn't you wonder how someone could get blood all over his clothing from slashing a woman's throat and not leave a trace of it anywhere while he raced through the house, ran upstairs, took off what he was wearing and tossed it into the laundry hamper where, according to your testimony, you claim you found it?"

He was shaking his head, ready to dismiss out of hand the suggestion that there was anything unusual in the absence of blood between where the murder had occurred and where the clothing had been found. I did not give him the chance. I asked a question that stopped him cold.

"At exactly what time was the clothing put in that laundry hamper?"

His face went blank. He shifted uneasily in the chair. Biting on the inside of his lip, he made a brief, failed attempt at calculation.

"She had been dead for a few hours when we got there, so . . ."

"No, Detective Crenshaw," I interjected, "not what time was the victim killed: what time was the clothing put in the place you say you found it?"

Convinced I must be confused, he tried to clarify things for me.

"The clothing was put there right after the murder," explained Crenshaw in a patronizing voice. "The defendant killed her, ran upstairs to the bedroom, got out of his clothing and tried to clean up. That's why there wasn't any blood anywhere else: He went directly to the bathroom and took off his clothes."

"You're here to offer evidence, Detective Crenshaw, not to give us your opinion about what you think the jury's verdict ought to be. Now, once more: What evidence–what facts–can you give us concerning the exact time the clothing you found was put in the laundry hamper? It must have been sometime after the murder, correct? They might have been put there hours after the murder, isn't that true?"

Angry and frustrated that I was twisting things out of context, he vigorously shook his head.

"No, you're wrong. It's a reasonable inference from all the facts and circumstances of the case. She was murdered. He was the only one–other than the maid–in the house. Her blood was found on his clothing, and his clothing was found in the laundry hamper where I said I found it!"

"Move to strike, Your Honor!" I demanded, wheeling around until I was face to face with the judge. "The witness is here to testify about what he has observed, not the inferences he claims to have drawn from those observations."

Honigman's eyes darted toward Annabelle Van Roten. She rose slowly from her chair, a measured smile pasted on her mouth.

"I'm sure the witness would answer directly any question Mr. Antonelli cares to ask, if he would ever ask one." She arched her slender neck. Her fingers grazed the edge of the table below her. "I must say, Mr. Antonelli seems at times more interested in asking rhetorical questions than in hearing what the witness might have to say." The smile, faint and obscure, became thoughtful and almost seductive. "He has, it is true, quite the most wonderful voice I've ever heard; which I suppose is the reason he seems never to tire of listening to himself speak."

In the unspoken competition for the sympathy and respect of the jury, Annabelle Van Roten had just struck a blow. I had to do something.

"Do you really like my voice?" I asked hopefully.

Her face reddened, though just slightly, and her dark eyes smoldered. She looked away, trying to ignore me; but I kept staring at her, waiting with a kind of boyish eagerness, as if I had to know whether she had really meant it. She threw me a contemptuous glance, and turned to the judge.

"One last time, Detective Crenshaw. You did not yourself observe the defendant place the clothing into the laundry hamper, did you?"

Her fists clenched petulantly at her sides, Annabelle Van Roten stamped her foot.

"Your Honor!"

Honigman had turned to watch the witness.

"Yes?" he asked, looking over his shoulder.

"You haven't ruled on my objection," explained Van Roten.

"You didn't make one," said the judge as he swung round to face her. "Mr. Antonelli moved to strike. You made a response." A formal smile, the kind a physician might use to tell a patient that there is nothing wrong, crept over his mouth. "Your response must have been persuasive: By asking the next question Mr. Antonelli has, sub silentio, withdrawn the motion."

Honigman's face fairly glowed. In the heat of the moment, Annabelle Van Roten had forgotten that she had not made an objection and I had forgotten that I had ever made a motion. But we were in a manner saved from our mutual mistakes by the vanity of a judge who could not wait to invoke one of those phrases the law employs because it sounds so much more impressive in Latin than it does in English.

"Sub silentio," I repeated gravely, like someone grateful to have been understood exactly the way he meant to be understood. "Yes, precisely. Now, Detective Crenshaw," I said, shifting my attention back to the witness, "if you would be so kind. Did you observe the defendant place the clothing in question into the laundry hamper?"

Crenshaw's eyes were sullen, observant, engaged in a game of watchful waiting. He listened carefully, weighing each word in the hope of finding something he could use as a weapon.

"I observed the clothing; I observed the blood on the clothing."

I stood squarely in front of the jury box, gazing down the two rows of faces flattened in my vision into a single, crowded tier. I smiled to myself.

"You didn't observe the defendant put them there, though, did you?" I asked softly.

"No," I heard him answer.

"You found the bloody clothing belonging to the defendant in the laundry hamper in the bathroom of the bedroom," I said, gazing at the faces in front of me. "Where did you find the knife, the weapon which the killer used to slash the throat of Mary Margaret Flanders? Was that also in the laundry hamper?"

"No, it was not in the laundry hamper."

Slowly, deliberately, I peered into the eyes of first one juror, then the next.

"Then where did you find it?"

Crenshaw cleared his throat, the only sound in the silence a creaking echo as he changed position in the leather witness chair.

"The murder weapon was never found," admitted Crenshaw, doing his best to dismiss it as a matter of little importance.

I kept looking at the jury, staring into their eyes, telling them by the way I looked at them that Crenshaw was wrong and that he knew it; that the failure to find the murder weapon was a matter of the greatest importance and that they should not forget it. I put my hand on the jury box railing and lowered my gaze, smiling again to myself like someone enjoying a private joke of his own.

"So you didn't find the knife? You didn't find it in the laundry hamper? You didn't find it anywhere in the house?"

"As I said," replied Crenshaw with an air of undisturbed confidence, "the murder weapon has not been located."

Furrowing my brow, I shook my head like someone who has suddenly realized that what had seemed so simple and straightforward is actually complicated and even confusing. My hand still on the railing, I stood straight up and looked right at him.

"But you are convinced–as you were so eager to testify just a few minutes ago–that the defendant is the one who put the bloody clothing in the laundry hamper, where even the most cursory search of the premises would find them?"

"Yes, I am," replied Crenshaw without hesitation, seizing on the opportunity to repeat his opinion that Stanley Roth had murdered his wife.

"It's puzzling, isn't it, Detective Crenshaw? If you're right, Stanley Roth murdered his wife, tossed his bloodstained clothing just about the first place anyone would look, but then took such great care, went to such great lengths, to dispose of the murder weapon that despite all their efforts the police still haven't found it. Don't you find that just a little strange, Detective Crenshaw? That a man would go to such trouble to hide some of the evidence of his crime and at the same time almost go out of his way to make certain that other evidence of his crime would be found?" I asked in rapid-fire succession. "Isn't that just about the strangest, most inexplicable conduct you've ever seen in all your years as a homicide detective?"

"Your Honor!" shouted Annabelle Van Roten from her chair. "How many questions does he get to ask before the witness is given a chance to answer?"

"I apologize, Your Honor," I said before Honigman could answer. "I was going too fast." I turned back to the witness.

"Let me try again, Detective Crenshaw. How do you explain the inconsistency: that someone would carefully hide a murder weapon but leave bloodstained clothing the first place anyone would look for it?"

By now he had had enough time to think about it. He thought he had an answer. In a smooth, fluid motion he turned his shoulders until his gaze rested on the jury.

"This was not a murder planned very far in advance, if it was planned at all. Whatever reason Mary Margaret Flanders was killed, she was killed in a hurry, and . . ."

"And answer my question, Detective Crenshaw! I did not ask about your theory of the case."

His head swung around until his eyes met mine.

"You asked me to explain how he could hide the knife and not hide the clothing. It could have happened any number of ways. Think about all the things that go through the mind of a killer just after he's murdered someone–all the fear, all the emotion, the rush. . . . Yes, I know, it's not the kind of thing we like to talk about, but it's true. You've just killed someone; your heart is beating like a hammer; you can't hear anything; you can't see anything. The only thing you know is what you've done; the only thing you think about is what you have to do next."

Crenshaw's eyes were large and defiant, and perhaps, I thought, even excited. He held onto the arm of the chair, gripping it hard with his hand as he leaned as far forward as he could, straining to make his point.

"He has just killed her. He races inside the house, he gets upstairs and only then realizes he is still clutching in his hand the knife he used to kill her. He doesn't know what to do with it; it's all he can think about: how to get rid of it, where he can hide it, where he can throw it away where no one will ever find it. He doesn't even remember taking off his clothes, much less what he did with them: all he can think about is getting out of there, getting out of that house, and getting rid of the knife. He leaves his clothes in the laundry hamper because that's where he always puts them and then he showers and changes and leaves the house.

"That's how it could have happened, Mr. Antonelli. Or maybe he just thought no one would search his things; maybe he thought he would have plenty of time later on to get them washed. It could have happened any number of ways. I'm afraid I don't see anything inconsistent in it at all."

I stood there with my mouth half open, a stunned expression on my face, like someone left speechless by an argument with which they had never been confronted before and to which they could now offer no reply. Silently, I walked the few short steps to the counsel table and placed my hand on the shoulder of Stanley Roth.

"You're right," I admitted, nodding toward Crenshaw. "He could have done it, and done it just the way you described it. He could have killed her; he could have run back in the house; he could have thrown off his clothes; he could have been so concerned with what he had to do to get rid of the knife that he never noticed–or if he noticed, didn't worry about–his blood-covered clothes. You're right, Detective Crenshaw; you're absolutely right."

A look of self-satisfaction started in his eyes, then pulled at the corners of his mouth, twisting it back into a smug, caustic grin which, despite a conscious effort to do so, he could not entirely control. I let go of Stanley Roth's shoulder and stepped to the side of the counsel table. I was right next to the jury box, directly in front of the witness stand.

"It could have happened that way, or–what was it you said? Oh, yes. That way, or any number of ways. And one of those ways, one which is at least as consistent with the facts of this case–with the only facts that have been proven about this case–is that someone else, someone other than Stanley Roth, murdered Mary Margaret Flanders, and then, in order to make sure Stanley Roth was blamed for it, took some of his clothes, wiped them in the blood from her throat and then put them in the laundry hamper where the only person who wouldn't think to look for them would be Stanley Roth himself; because, after all, if he didn't kill her, he certainly wouldn't have any reason to imagine that any of his clothing would have any of her blood on them, would he, Detective Crenshaw?"

He did not answer and I did not care if he did.

"It's consistent with the evidence, and it's more consistent with itself, isn't it, Detective Crenshaw?" I demanded, taking a step forward. "Instead of a killer who conceals the murder weapon but doesn't notice he's covered in blood, we have a killer who covers his tracks so well that he manages to convince the police to arrest the wrong man for the crime!"

13

THERE WERE A FEW MORE questions I wanted to ask Detective Crenshaw but I was not allowed to ask them. At the beginning of the trial Judge Honigman had promised the jury that each day's proceedings would end promptly at five. When the clock struck that hour he interrupted me in midsentence to announce that court would stand adjourned until nine-thirty the next morning. With a menacing glance, the clerk warned me not to do or say anything that might keep court in session a single needless moment longer.

"That was very well done," said Louis Griffin as he put one hand on my shoulder and shook my hand with the other.

Griffin came every day to court. Somehow he had arranged to have a seat in the first row, directly behind the counsel table where Stanley Roth sat next to me. Usually, he stayed only a short time, sometimes just a few minutes; but he was always there, every day, at the beginning, lending moral support to his friend and partner.

"I should have been back at the studio hours ago," he explained; "but I wanted to watch your cross-examination, and, well, after you started I could not stop watching."

Griffin looked at me with his gentle, quiet eyes, eyes that made you feel comfortable and secure. His left hand was still on my shoulder; his right was still clasping mine, when Stanley Roth got to his feet and without so much as a glance at his partner said it was time to go.

We ran the gauntlet of cameras and reporters on the steps outside the courthouse the way we did every day now, Stanley Roth looking straight ahead while I tried to wave everyone off as we burrowed through the crowd to the waiting car and then sped off, the same meaningless questions about what had happened that day and what we expected to happen the next, hanging unanswered in the warm enveloping Southern California air.

As if he were trying to put off just a little longer the conversation he knew we had to have, Stanley Roth sat huddled in the corner of the back seat, his face turned toward the window.

"Why didn't you tell me you knew Crenshaw? Why didn't you tell me he knew your wife? The last thing the prosecution asks him, the last thing I hear before I have to start my cross-examination, is that he knew your wife and that he knew you. Every time I asked him a question I kept wondering what it meant; whether there was something about the fact that he knew both of you that might make a difference; whether there was anything I could use. But I couldn't ask–I couldn't take the chance–because I didn't know; and I didn't know because you never told me. Why would you hold that back from me? What reason could you possibly have had? You must have known the prosecution would know. It's the first thing he would have told Van Roten when she started to prepare him to testify."

Roth gave me a strange look. "I would have thought it would have been the last thing he would have told her."

"You thought he'd keep it a secret? He worked as a consultant on a movie you made. Your wife was the star. Even if he wanted to, how could he have kept that a secret? Other people would have known."

"No one knew. It never happened. He never worked as a consultant; he didn't have anything to do with that movie. He was never on the set."

"What are you saying? That he lied under oath–about that?" I asked, incredulous. "Why?"

Roth leaned back against the soft leather seat. Wearily, with his thumb and finger, he stroked his brow. He was in his early fifties, but he was starting to look older now. His gray hair was no longer the stylish curly cut of a famous and powerful man, but more like the disheveled appearance of someone past caring how he looks. His fingernails had been bitten down to a jagged edge; the skin on the back of his hands seemed to sag from the tendons and had a ghostly, transparent look. The side of his face, just below his ear, was stained with small dark red splotches. When he opened his mouth to speak, his teeth, instead of glittering white the way they had when we first met, were coated with a dull, yellowish haze. Stanley Roth did not just look older: he had the look of someone who had begun to lose his health, someone who had begun to doubt whether he had any reason left to live.

Roth bit his lip, scraping his teeth over the edge of it, again and again, while he peered intently into the distance. He stopped, took a deep breath to calm his nerves, and looked across at me.

"I suppose strictly speaking he didn't lie at all. He was a consultant; at least that's how it went on the books–but he never worked on that movie. Crenshaw came to my house that night–the night I hit Mary Margaret, the night I wanted to kill her."

"The night you found out she had aborted your child?"

"That's right," said Roth, nodding.

"She called the police and they sent a homicide detective?" I asked, trying to make sense out what he was saying.

"No. They sent two uniformed cops in a patrol car. I was furious. I wouldn't let them through the front gate. That's when Crenshaw came. I suppose they thought a detective would have more luck. He was smooth, very smooth. He told me on the phone they had to get in, that there had been a call to 911, that they had to follow up. He said he knew it couldn't have been anything serious, that a lot of people called 911 in the middle of an argument and said things–made accusations–they didn't mean. He was very persuasive. I let him in."

Roth tossed back his head, his mouth twisted into a look of disgust.

"I think he knew what he was going to do before he ever got there, before he was called. As soon as I answered the door, he turned to the uniformed cop who had come up the drive with him and told him he could go."

Roth brought his head back down. With a shrewd glance he let me know that it had not been difficult to figure out what Crenshaw really wanted.

"He wanted to be helpful," explained Roth with a low, rumbling laugh. "He had to see Mary Margaret, of course. She had called; she had asked for help. As I told you, I had hit her, all right; hit her hard. Her eye was all cut and bruised. Any normal cop would have arrested me on the spot; if I had been anybody else, Crenshaw would have arrested me on the spot. But I'm not anybody else, am I? I'm Stanley Roth, and everybody–at least everybody in this town–knows what I can do. People will do anything to get into this business–anything."

Roth's gaze drifted away. He seemed to remember something, something about himself, when he was one of those people on the outside, so eager to get in, so desperate to be a part of a world that helped form, and then haunted, the imaginations of all those other, less fortunate people, caught in the routine of everyday life.

"And Crenshaw really didn't have to do anything to get what he wanted. All he had to do was pretend that nothing had happened, that no one had been hurt; that it had been nothing more than a little domestic quarrel–a little too much to drink–nothing worth a formal report, much less a formal charge. He took one look at Mary Margaret–I remember how he almost stood at attention when she walked into the room holding an ice pack on her eye–and said to us both that she should have it looked at. That was all: looked at. He didn't ask how it happened; he didn't ask if I had hit her; just, 'Better have it looked at.' Then he started telling me about a screenplay he had written and how he had not had much luck getting anyone to look at it."

Roth did not need to tell me what happened next.

"And you said you'd be glad to take a look at it."

"What else was I going to tell him? He sent it over the next day. I never bothered to read it. I called him on the phone and told him the studio wanted to take an option on it. I asked him how much he wanted, and that's what I gave him."

"But you said you put it on the books as a consultant?"

"An option runs for a set term, usually a year. Then a decision has to be made whether to renew it. I didn't want anyone else in the studio to get involved. There was another reason. Normally there's a little publicity when we take an option on something. Crenshaw didn't object when I suggested it might be a little early for that and that because of the way we met it might be misinterpreted."

Roth looked out the window, smiling to himself.

"Misinterpreted! Not by him. He understood perfectly. Except for one thing," added Roth, cocking his head as he looked back at me. "I don't think he thought he was blackmailing me into anything. He thought that screenplay of his was worth every penny of the quarter million I gave him. He did! I know it. I could tell it from the way he talked about it, from the look in his eyes, from the tone of his voice. He has a kind of confidence, a self-assurance, an arrogance, I suppose, about himself. You saw how he was on the stand; how certain he was of everything. He knows I hit her–he doesn't know why I hit her: Mary Margaret was not about to breathe a word about that–and because I hit her, he thinks I killed her. But he can't tell anyone, because then everyone will know about him: how I hit her but he didn't do anything about it because he wanted something for himself. And I can't tell anyone about him, because then everyone will think the same thing he does. It's what we used to call a Mexican standoff."

It explained why Crenshaw had lied, or at least not told the whole truth, about how he happened to have known both the defendant and the victim. There was, however, one point on which I was not quite clear. Roth had made it seem that he had bought Crenshaw's silence, met blackmail with bribery, but even by his own account it had not been as simple as that. Crenshaw had given something beyond his silence in exchange for what Stanley Roth had given him. It seemed likely that he wanted more than just money in return.

"You never looked at what Crenshaw gave you? Didn't he want to know what you thought about it?"

The iron gates of Blue Zephyr were two blocks ahead. Roth sat up straight, ran his fingers through his hair, and then adjusted the lapels on his blue suit coat.

"He got his check," said Roth in the apparent belief that this answered the question.

"But he thought his screenplay was worth every penny of what you paid him."

He gave me a condescending glance. "And?"

"And which is it? Did he want the money or did he want his screenplay made into a movie? You said people would do anything to get into this business. Isn't that what Crenshaw wanted–to get into the business? You took an option on it. That's what you told him. I understand he got his check–but what about later, after he got the check? Didn't he ask you when you were going to decide whether you were going to exercise the option? Didn't he want to know if you were going to make it into a movie? Didn't he want to know if you thought he should make any changes in it?"

A crowd of photographers, along with a handful of screaming protesters waving handmade signs calling Stanley Roth a murderer and a woman hater, had gathered at the entrance. Roth made certain his tie was in place and then sat back and stared straight ahead while the gates swung open. Cameras were flashing all around us. Voices, muted by the thick glass windows, shouted their incomprehensible questions and their stupid, self-righteous accusations; and faces twisted into strange, inhuman contortions as they struggled with each other for the attentions of a man who resolutely refused to look their way. It was like a mob scene in a silent movie, the veins on the forehead of each actor bulging out as they did their best to impersonate ruthless, coldhearted rage.

The gates shut behind us, and the photographers, all their frenzy spent, shuffled around, waiting to be told what to wait for next. The protesters, their energy and their anger spent, drifted off, dragging their posters behind them. Stanley Roth lowered his window. Turning up his face, he took a breath of the still, late afternoon air, heavy with the lush scent of orange and lemon, and the tension finally began to let go. It happened like this every day when we passed through the gates of Blue Zephyr. It was like watching someone come home at the end of the day when, free of what other people thought he should be, he could be himself. He pulled his tie down far enough to get to the top button of his shirt. Drawing the tie from under his collar, he folded it over several times until it was small enough to put into the pocket of his coat.

"Charlie will take you to the hotel," said Roth as the car pulled up in front of the bungalow where he now not only lived and worked, but spent all the time he did not have to be in court.

"You didn't answer my question," I reminded him as he started to get out.

He stopped and looked back, waiting for me to remind him what that question had been.

"Didn't Crenshaw want to know if you were going to use his screenplay? Isn't that what he wanted? Wasn't that the real reason he did what he did, more than the money?"

"I don't know what he wanted. All I know is that he had gotten all he was going to get out of me," said Roth with a shrewd look in his eyes. "He took the money, and once he had done that, he had more to lose than I did if the story ever came out."

Roth still had not told me what I wanted to know.

"He never asked you if you were going to use it? He didn't call you up and want to know what was happening with his script?"

Roth shrugged. "Yeah, he called."

"You didn't take his calls?"

"What for?"

"Did it ever occur to you that he might have come to your house that night–the night you hit your wife, the night you wanted to kill her–and decided just to do the both of you a favor, because he might have understood how damaging that kind of publicity could be? Did it ever occur to you that when you said you would read his screenplay–the one on which he had worked so hard and so long–he thought you were doing him a favor, too? And then he finds out you weren't doing him a favor at all: You were insulting him, paying him off like a cop on the take."

"He took the money," insisted Roth, starting to get angry.

"Why wouldn't he think it was for what you said it was for–an option? Don't you think that is what he wanted it to be? You remember what it was like–how difficult it was to get a start? You remember what you wrote–what you gave me to read–*Blue Zephyr*? You wanted to do something better than *Citizen Kane*. Richard Crenshaw wanted to do something, too; and you did something worse than tell him no: you told him yes, and then you took it all away. He got the money, all right–and he kept it–but, my God, how he must have hated you for it. And then what do you do? You give him the best way in the world to get even. Crenshaw gets to help convict you for the murder of your wife! Don't you see the irony in it? He doesn't want to be a cop; he doesn't want to be a detective. He wants to be a writer, a screenwriter; but instead, thanks to you, he has to stay a cop, stay a detective, the detective who helped convict you, the great Stanley Roth, for the murder of the great film star, Mary Margaret Flanders."

I was taunting him with what he had done, perhaps because I was angry that he had not told me about all this before, and perhaps because I thought he deserved it for assuming he could buy his way out of trouble, that he was too important to be treated like anyone else. Whatever the reason, the more I said, the more I wanted to say. I leaned closer.

"And if he does help convict you of murder, guess what's going to happen then? While you sit in prison, waiting for the executioner, wondering what would have happened if you could have made *Blue Zephyr*, wondering whether you could have done something better than Orson Welles, maybe Richard Crenshaw will be writing another screenplay, this one about the detective who solved the murder of one of Hollywood's biggest stars."

Roth put his hand on my sleeve, a calm, remorseless look in his eyes, like some fastidious assassin impervious to either pity or fear, an assassin who knows exactly what he is going to do and precisely how he is going to do it.

"I'm not going to be convicted of anything. You never lose, Antonelli; and I didn't kill Mary Margaret. I don't give a damn what Crenshaw wanted; I don't give a damn how he feels. I offered him money and he took it. That's all there was to it."

Roth hopped out of the car and started to walk away. He thought of something that made him laugh. He turned around and opened the door.

"But if you're right–if he did hate me that much and for that reason–you'd be right again, wouldn't you? What you were suggesting in court today: that someone else put those blood-soaked clothes in the laundry hamper; that someone was trying to frame me for the murder."

A harsh, bitter smile cut across his mouth and then, quick as a glance, vanished from view. He looked at me now with the eyes of someone convinced that he had been right all along, that he had been cheated, and that he was the only one who understood that he had.

"Remember what I told you that night, the night I gave you *Blue Zephyr* to read: that they murdered Mary Margaret to destroy me? It isn't that much different than what you just told me, is it?"

Roth shut the door and signaled the driver it was time to go. The car turned around in the small cul-de-sac. Stanley Roth, his hands plunged despairingly into his pockets, walked toward his white stucco bungalow like a tired salesman home from a long day of failure, trying not to think too much about tomorrow. Just as he reached the steps to the porch, Julie Evans, who must have been waiting for him inside and seen him coming, burst out the front door. She stood directly in his path, gesticulating wildly, her face all twisted up. He listened for a moment, and then, as if that was the end of it, abruptly shook his head and pushed his way past her. She stared after him, her mouth open in amazement. Out of the corner of her eye, she became aware of the long limousine moving on the street behind her. She pulled herself together and in firm, decisive steps walked quickly up the steps and followed Stanley Roth inside.

Whether Julie Evans was angry or just upset, there was no trace of any emotion that might have disturbed her self-possession when, a little over an hour later, she picked me up at the Chateau Marmont. She asked about the trial; she wanted to know everything that had happened that day. She listened politely, but three sentences after I began to tell her about Detective Crenshaw and his testimony, she suddenly turned to me and asked if I would mind if we did not have dinner alone.

"There's trouble at the studio. Louis wants me to come to the house. He wants you to come, too."

"What about Stanley?"

She shook her head. "No. Michael is going to be there, and Louis didn't think it would be a good idea."

"And he wants me there?"

"Maybe he wants to make sure that whatever happens, there is somebody Stanley will trust to tell him the truth about it." She paused, looked back at the road, smiling a little to herself. "No, I think the real reason is that he's come to rely on you in certain ways."

"Rely on me?"

Her chin tilted up, the smile on her mouth a bit brighter, a bit more certain of itself.

"He feels more confident about things when you're around. You have that effect on people, you know." A kind of soft melancholy shadowed her eyes as she drove along in the failing light of evening. "You have that effect on me."

Cars swarmed all around us, darting in and out, like fireflies in the night, dashing off into the distance and then, somehow, out of nowhere, coming so close you think you can grab them with your hand.

Julie started to say something more, then changed her mind. She did not say anything for a while, and then, with a serious, businesslike expression, she explained:

"Michael Wirthlin is threatening to pull out of the studio. If he does that, Blue Zephyr is finished. Without his money, without his ability to raise money, it can't survive."

"Is that what you were telling Roth outside the bungalow?"

Perhaps she had not realized I had been in the car, or perhaps she did not want me to think she had known I had been watching her. She turned to me as if she were surprised.

"Yes."

"How did he take it?" I asked as she gazed back at the twisted lines of traffic ahead of us.

Julie tossed her head, a reluctant smile of grudging admiration on her mouth.

"He said he didn't give a damn what Michael Wirthlin did. He doesn't believe Wirthlin will really do it–pull out of the studio; not while he thinks there is a chance he might get it all for himself."

"You mean, if Stanley Roth is convicted. But if that were to happen, why would Wirthlin end up with it? What about Griffin?"

"Michael has always known that there was no point fighting Stanley on anything because Louis would always side with Stanley. Michael has always thought he was smarter than Louis; and with his control of the money–the sources of money–he doesn't think Louis would dare try to stand in his way."

"Then why is he threatening to pull out? Roth doesn't think he's serious. Is he just trying to make trouble?"

"Michael never does anything without a reason, and he isn't just trying to make trouble. Stanley is wrong about him; Stanley is wrong about a lot of things," said Julie with a distant look.

We were on Mulholland Drive, less than a quarter mile from Louis Griffin's sprawling glass-and-stucco contemporary house, where no one now remembered either the Spanish villa or the English Tudor mansion, both of them built to last forever, that had stood there before, and only the hawks that circled the daytime sky seemed not to have forgotten the chickens that had roosted there long before that. Julie pulled off the side of the road and switched off the ignition. All of Los Angeles was spread out below us, like a flat, empty desert running straight out to the edge of the sea, glistening under the shelter of the bronze-colored sun.

"Stanley is wrong," said Julie.

She lay her head back against the glass, a wistful expression on the smooth white contours of her face.

"He thinks when the trial is over everything will be back to normal. He doesn't understand that nothing is ever going to be normal again. Blue Zephyr is finished. Michael Wirthlin knows it. I think Louis knows it, too, though he doesn't want to admit it. The only one who doesn't know it is Stanley. He spends every night in that bungalow of his, cut off from everything, carrying on as if he was still in charge and that nothing was ever going to change. He doesn't understand that it doesn't matter if he's acquitted. What matters is that everyone thinks he's guilty. No one is going to risk their careers or their money on a man the world thinks murdered a woman everyone loved. Michael was not just making a threat to hear the way it sounded. He's going to do something; it's just a question of when. Blue Zephyr is dead. All that is left of it is the dream, the one Stanley still carries around in his head."

14

LOUIS GRIFFIN SEEMED DISTRACTED. He greeted us at the door with the same smooth polished smile and that soft touch of his hand as he gave it to you and then, just as you began to take hold of it, pulled it away; the by now unconscious reaction to the social necessity of allowing even perfect strangers to touch him. It was nothing like the way he had shaken my hand in the courtroom just a few hours earlier. Louis Griffin was worried, worried that something had happened and that, for all his experience at negotiating arrangements that left everyone reasonably content, this time he might not be able to put all the pieces back together again.

"I meant what I said to you today. I may not know much about the law, but I know something about performances, and what you did with that detective was one of the best I've ever seen."

"Stanley thinks he should become an actor," teased Julie.

It was an offhand, casual remark, made for no reason than to put us all at our ease; but it made me wonder how much she knew, how much Stanley Roth told her about the conversations we had had since I first became his lawyer. It bothered me, the idea that he did not view what was said between us as a confidence that had to be kept.

Griffin thought about what Julie had said. With a shrewd glance he suggested Stanley Roth was wrong.

"I don't think our friend here would be willing to follow anyone else's direction. I don't even think he'd be able to follow a script." He shifted his gaze from Julie to me. "You know where you want to go when you're examining a witness, don't you?" asked Griffin rhetorically. "But you don't always know in advance how you're going to get there. Isn't that right? You don't always know the next question until you have the last answer. True?"

"Not even always then," I laughed as Griffin led us into the dining room.

When I had come here that first time with Julie–when, as she had put it, after that press conference in front of the gates of Blue Zephyr, I had been the newest famous person in town–everyone had crowded around me, eager to meet me. Perhaps because we had already met, or perhaps because the murder of Mary Margaret Flanders now seemed less of a mystery and the innocence of her husband no longer quite so easy to insist upon, no one left the table to greet me. Instead, I stood next to Louis Griffin while, with one hand on my arm, he gestured in turn to each of his guests.

"Of course you know Walker and Carole," he went on, nodding across the table at Walker Bradley and Carole Conrad.

His mouth half open, Bradley had a slightly pained expression, like someone who had been struggling with a thought and getting nowhere with it. Squinting her eyes, Carole Conrad looked up from her nearly empty wineglass and pushed out her hand as if she was trying to reach across to mine and gushed a quiet hello. She pulled back her hand and stared again into her glass.

William Pomeroy stood up and shook my hand. His wife, Estelle, the writer, gave my sleeve a gentle tug when she said hello. They were friendly, and I liked them both; but there was something in the way they looked at me, not a warning exactly, more like a hint that there might be trouble and that I had better be careful.

I had just finished saying hello to Griffin's wife, Clarice, when he let go of my arm.

"Michael of course you know," he said in a voice suddenly hollow and cold. "And I'm sure you remember his wife."

Michael Wirthlin was hunched over the table, running his finger along the edge of the plate in front of him. He did not look up. A look of growing irritation on his mouth, he kept watching his finger as it moved slowly first one way, then the other, back and forth. I began to talk to his wife, a few stray remarks, a brief, inconsequential conversation that with each word made him more upset. He pulled his hand back from the plate and raised his eyes.

"We were just talking about you. Louis was telling how well you did today in court, cross-examining that detective, the one who found Stanley's blood-covered clothing."

Wirthlin swung around in his chair and put his elbow on the back corner of it. He fixed me with a grim, defiant stare.

"Do you think you'll do that well with me?"

I knew what he was talking about, but from the puzzled expressions on the faces of several of the other people there it appeared I was one of the few who did.

"Michael has been subpoenaed as a witness for the prosecution," explained Louis Griffin.

I went to my place on the other side of the table. While everyone else talked about this latest bit of news, I looked out through the glass wall into the courtyard where the pair of white swans were gliding silently across the smooth, unruffled surface of the pond.

"But why have you been subpoenaed as a witness, Michael?" asked William Pomeroy. "And why as a witness for the prosecution and not for the defense?" he asked, darting an inquiring glance at me.

I tried to dismiss it as a matter of at best only minor importance, something that was merely routine, the sort of thing the prosecution did in every case of this kind.

"I imagine they want to get into the financial situation at Blue Zephyr," I remarked with a show of indifference. "The obvious person with whom to do that is the chief financial officer of the company."

"You don't seem surprised," observed Pomeroy.

"No," I replied as I plunged my fork into the salad that had just been served. "The prosecution has to give me a list of the witnesses they intend to call. I've known for quite a while they were going to call Michael Wirthlin."

"Well, I haven't known it for 'quite a while,'" spat Wirthlin, glaring at me from his place two seats down on the other side of the table. "You might have mentioned it. I was subpoenaed yesterday."

I finished swallowing, and then replied:

"I'm not your lawyer, Mr. Wirthlin; and I don't go around advising witnesses for the prosecution that they're about to be subpoenaed."

"But I still don't understand," said William Pomeroy. He was sitting forward, trying to concentrate. "Why would the prosecution want to know about the financial situation of the studio? This is a murder case. What difference would it make?"

Wirthlin looked at him like he was a fool. He looked at a lot of people that way. It was one of the things I disliked about him most.

"They think he might have killed her for the money," said Wirthlin.

Resting his hands in his lap, he lifted his chin and gazed pensively into the distance as if he were considering the sufficiency of the motive and the circumstances in which it might apply. Dressed in a dark, double-breasted suit and a white, collarless shirt fastened at the top, he had the fashionable look that, as he must have known, marked him out as a major Hollywood player.

"They have a point," said Wirthlin, his eyes coming back into focus. "Mary Margaret's death did bring with it certain financial advantages."

"Michael, I think that's quite enough!" exclaimed Louis Griffin, tossing his napkin down on the table. "I understand you're upset about being subpoenaed to testify. I don't blame you. But, for God's sake, that's no reason to start talking as if you actually believe Stanley had anything to do with Mary Margaret's murder."

With an intense, malevolent stare, Wirthlin sneered: "I don't know if he did it or not; but if you think I don't think he could have done it; that he was perfectly capable of doing it . . ."

I was not sure which of them would break it off first, which of them would finally look away, they seemed so determined not to give pride of place to the other.

"That doesn't say anything at all," I said derisively; "that Stanley Roth, or anyone else, could have done something, or was capable of doing something."

Angrily, Wirthlin wheeled around.

"After all," I went on before he could speak, "you could have said the same thing about yourself, couldn't you?"

Whatever he was going to say, this stopped him. The anger seemed to dissipate. He became cautious.

"Exactly what do you mean by that?" he asked, carefully searching my eyes.

I smiled and waited while the salad plates were removed and the next course was served. The conversation moved back into more normal channels. There was talk about how well Mary Margaret Flanders's last movie had done, not only at the box office but with the critics. Pomeroy was more convinced than ever that there were going to be several Oscar nominations. He repeated what I had heard him say the night of the first private screening: that it was the best film Mary Margaret had ever made and the best work Walker Bradley had yet done. This time Bradley did not disagree.

There was an almost tangible sense of relief that nothing more was being said about either the trial or Stanley Roth; but there was also a sense of foreboding, a tension that underlay everything that was said. It was as if everyone was just waiting to see who would bring it up first. A strange kind of frenzy took hold. People laughed at the slightest hint of something funny and the laughter itself had a certain manic quality, as if they were all afraid that when it stopped the screaming would begin. Everyone was drinking, some more than others and no one more than Michael Wirthlin who never laughed at all. He sat there, barely talking, keeping to himself, all the time aware that the atmosphere around that table had been darkened by his mood. That was the fact of it: all the others–the actor and the actress, the director and the writer, certainly Julie Evans, but even the gracious Louis Griffin and his socially anxious wife–were one way or the other dependent on Michael Wirthlin, their lives in some measure affected by what he decided to do, and by nothing so much as what he decided to do about Blue Zephyr.

"Walker has been subpoenaed, too," announced Carole Conrad with an eager smile. As soon as she said it, her cheeks began to color, as if she realized too late that she should not have said anything.

"What do they want you to testify about, Walker?" asked Louis Griffin.

Before Bradley turned to Griffin, he patted his wife on the wrist, assuring her that there was nothing to worry about.

"I think they just want to know what she was like . . . what she talked about . . . that kind of thing–the few days before her death. At least that's what the investigator they sent to talk to me wanted to know."

"This is terrible," remarked William Pomeroy, visibly agitated. "This won't look good at all. You're going to testify against Stanley, after how close the two of you have always been? You must feel awful, having to do this."

Bradley waited, his mouth partway open, and then replied with a shrug. "Yeah, well, we've known each other a long time, that's true. But I wouldn't say we were ever all that close."

For the first time, Wirthlin laughed. He bent forward, both elbows on the table, twisting his head until he was looking straight down the table at Louis Griffin. With a smug, vindictive smile, he nodded toward Bradley.

"You see, Louis. You're the only one left; the only one who still believes Stanley didn't do it."

Wirthlin glanced around the table, an expression of amazement on his face, as if astonished that anyone, even Louis Griffin, could still believe in the innocence of Stanley Roth.

"I'll bet even his lawyer thinks Stanley did it, murdered Mary Margaret." Wirthlin's eyes met mine and immediately moved away. "But it doesn't matter. It doesn't matter what anyone thinks. The fact is, as I was trying to tell you earlier, three out of four people–and we have the surveys to prove it–now think Stanley murdered Mary Margaret."

It took a moment for me to be sure I had heard him right. They had done a survey–taken a poll–to see whether the public thought Stanley Roth was guilty of murder? What conceivable difference did it make what people who had not spent any time in the courtroom, had not heard any of the testimony and did not know anything about the witnesses yet to appear, thought about Stanley Roth? They were not going to decide what happened.

"It doesn't matter how many people out there think Stanley Roth is guilty," I reminded him forcefully. "It doesn't matter if everyone thinks he's guilty. The only opinion that counts is the opinion–the unanimous opinion–of the twelve members of that jury; who are, by the way–unlike the members of your supposedly scientific statistical sample–listening to all the evidence and not just to what they hear from some self-proclaimed expert's twenty-second sound bite!"

I might as well have suggested that he believe in miracles and the power of faith. Michael Wirthlin was far too sophisticated to believe there was anything more important or more powerful than public opinion. That the opinion of the public might be wrong was simply beside the point. He dismissed what I had said with a contemptuous glance.

"Even if Antonelli does what he's paid to do," said Wirthlin, taking in the table with his gaze, "and gets Stanley off, everyone is still going to think he did it. The public–the moviegoing public–has turned against him. And we all know what happens in this business when that happens. He'll be an outcast; no one will want to have anything to do with him; no one is going to be willing to invest any more money in Blue Zephyr–not while he's still running it."

Wirthlin paused, a glimmer of self-satisfaction in his eye. He had just thought of something that would prove his point.

"Tell me, Walker; are you interested in making another movie at Blue Zephyr?"

Bradley tried to put the best face on it he could, but for all his stammering good intentions, all his quietly self-righteous insistence that he was not going to prejudge anything, it was clear that he had already done precisely that.

Louis Griffin could not resist getting in a little of his own. "You needn't worry, Walker. Stanley has already decided that he needs someone else for the lead in the next movie he is going to make." He looked up from his coffee. "Someone younger."

Bradley raised his thick eyebrows, smiled knowingly to himself, and then, like a bored adolescent, slouched in his chair, both hands shoved down between his legs. He began to laugh, again, like the smile, more to himself than for the benefit of anyone else.

"Michael is right," he said finally. He raised his eyes just far enough to get a sideways glimpse of Louis Griffin sitting over his coffee at the far end of the table. "There isn't going to be another picture. Stanley won't be able to raise the money."

Griffin continued to sip his coffee, serene and quietly assured. He put down the cup, sniffed once and then looked at his guests, a thoughtful expression in his eyes.

"I'm afraid Michael isn't right at all, Walker. Oh, you may be right, Michael, that Stanley won't be able to hang on to Blue Zephyr; but what I think you've never quite understood is that for Stanley at least, Blue Zephyr isn't that collection of sound stages and equipment; it isn't the dressing rooms and the offices and the costumes and the special effects; it isn't all the buildings and all the land. No, for Stanley Roth, Blue Zephyr was never anything tangible: it was never something on which someone could set a value, a price. That's what you never understood, Michael; what you'll never understand. Stanley Roth is the closest thing to a genius I've ever known in this business. Stanley Roth is Blue Zephyr–the idea of it, Michael; the idea, the idea that becomes the movie–that's what Blue Zephyr stands for: the idea that you can invent a story, imagine what it will look like, feel how all the parts of it will work together, see it the way an audience will see it when it's finally finished and be able to do all that before the first foot of film has been shot. Money can buy you a studio, Michael; money can buy you almost anything if you have enough of it; but it can never buy you that, it can never buy you genius. You only get that the way Stanley Roth got it: you're born with it.

"You can leave, Michael; you can pull out your money and you can make sure no one else provides the kind of financing necessary to keep the studio running. You can do that, Michael: you can close the studio. But there is one thing you can't do: You can't stop Stanley Roth from making another picture. Stanley and I started out making movies when we didn't have any money at all, and now Stanley and I have all the money either one of us could ever want, and maybe more than anyone should ever have. No, Michael, we can make another movie. And, frankly, I wouldn't mind if we had to do it that way–with our own money and whatever we could borrow from a few friends. When you reach my age, Michael, the idea of starting all over again has more attraction than you might believe."

Every face was turned to Louis Griffin, listening in astonishment to this politely phrased act of defiance; all, that is, except Michael Wirthlin. He kept stirring his coffee, methodically, like someone sitting all alone in a crowded restaurant, barely aware of the noisy conversations going on all around him, lost in thoughts of his own. That at least is what he wanted everyone to think: that he was, if not entirely oblivious, then largely indifferent to what was being said to him. It was an impression that became more difficult to sustain with each word Louis Griffin spoke. Wirthlin's eyes grew hard, cold; his jaw clenched tighter and tighter until the color began to drain from his lips. When Griffin finally finished, Wirthlin let go of the spoon. With both hands he carefully pushed the cup and saucer a few inches forward on the white linen tablecloth. He straightened up, shook his head like an adult marveling at the willful stupidity of a child, and proceeded, one by one, to study the faces around him, as if he wanted to make sure they understood the true meaning of what they had all just witnessed.

"You don't know what you're talking about. You don't have any idea what you're talking about," said Wirthlin with a withering dismissive glance at Griffin. "This isn't the same business it was when you started; maybe it never was. You and Stanley–always talking about the way pictures used to be made! Pictures cost money–serious money–the kind you have to raise in the financial markets, not the kind you get by going around borrowing it from your friends. You think Stanley Roth is Blue Zephyr? There wouldn't have been a Blue Zephyr if I hadn't come in, and there won't be a Blue Zephyr after I'm gone."

Griffin had kept Wirthlin under his steady gaze. He never once looked away, never once tried to create an impression of anything except unwavering patience and the good manners of a well-bred man.

"I agree, Michael, that without you, Blue Zephyr could not have been started. I also agree that it is now time for you to go."

Wirthlin did not quite believe it; did not quite believe that Louis Griffin was willing to see him pull out of Blue Zephyr. A smile started, then died stillborn on his lips. His eyes seemed to turn inward, as he calculated what to do or say next. With his hands on the sides of the seat, he moved his chair back from the table, ready to get up. He was just about to say something when from down the hall came the sound of the front door being slammed shut and the hurried shouts of voices coming quickly closer.

"I can find my way without your help!" cried an angry, familiar voice.

With a helpless, embarrassed look, the Japanese butler held open the doors as a drunken Stanley Roth reeled into the dining room and immediately began searching for Michael Wirthlin.

"There you are you miserable son of a bitch!" he exclaimed, waving a sheet of paper he was clutching in his hand.

Roth started to say something more, something even more unpleasant, when it caught his eye, that paper he was waving in the air, as if he had just become aware he was doing it and was not sure what it was. Then he remembered, and a shrewd look of triumph entered his eyes. He started to laugh, stopped, staggered a step forward, and stopped again. A sheepish grin on his face, he stared down at the floor.

Louis Griffin began to rise from his chair. "Stanley, I . . ."

Roth's head snapped up. His mouth twisted back at the corners.

"How could you have done this?" he demanded of Griffin.

"Done what? I haven't done . . ."

Roth wheeled around until he was face to face with Wirthlin.

"You really thought I'd sign this?" he asked, shaking at him that sheet of paper he held in his fist.

"What is it, Stanley?" asked Louis Griffin, standing at the end of the table. His voice was calm, but firm. He knew Stanley Roth, knew him far better than I did, and from the way he was watching him I knew he was worried.

"What's in that paper you're holding? I swear I don't know."

Roth did not turn to look. He kept staring across the table at where Michael Wirthlin sat trying to look unconcerned.

"You know what's in it, though, don't you?" insisted Roth as he tossed it underhand, a crumpled ball of paper that bounced on the table and rolled into Wirthlin's waiting hands.

"What is it, Michael?" asked Griffin in a tone so commanding that Wirthlin did not even think to hesitate before he answered.

"My last attempt to save the studio." He took his eyes off Stanley Roth just long enough to explain: "It's a dissolution agreement. Stanley leaves, gives up all interest in Blue Zephyr. The partnership remains, but there will be only two partners, not three."

That look down the table was all Stanley Roth needed. Pushing Julie Evans aside, he picked up her chair with both hands and sent it sailing over the table. Wirthlin managed to duck out of the way. The chair grazed his back and flew against the window behind him, shattering the glass into a thousand pieces. Shrieks and shouts filled the room as everyone dove for cover. Instinctively, I pulled my arm in front of my face. When I looked up, Roth was already on the other side of the table, right next to where Wirthlin was crouching down, shielding his head with his arms. Roth reached for an open bottle of wine, grabbed it by the neck and raised it high in the air. In a way it was almost funny. He had turned the bottle and I could see the label. There was a color drawing, a Parisian dancer in the Moulin Rouge, a redheaded, high-stepping can-can dancer with her thick fluffy dress pulled up in front. Held in Stanley Roth's threatening hand, the bottle and the label were upside down and it struck me that her dress was going to fall right over her shoulder and off her head.

That is all I remember: that redheaded dancer with her flashing eyes and flying legs, upside down on a painted label. I do not remember diving across the table, trying to stop Stanley Roth, trying to keep him from smashing a bottle over the head of Michael Wirthlin. I do not remember hitting the floor when I tackled Stanley Roth, and I don't remember anything about the way it felt when the jagged edge of the broken bottle cut its way into my face. All I remember is lying flat on my back in a strange bedroom while a doctor dressed in a business suit wove a needle and thread in and out of my skin. He was humming to himself as he worked, a song I kept trying to remember, a song I thought I knew. Then, just as I thought I had it, everything went dark and I did not care anymore what it was. I did not care about anything at all. Nothing.

15

"THE DOCTOR SAID YOU WERE LUCKY."

Sunlight was streaming through the bedroom window. I shifted position until it was out of my eyes. Louis Griffin was sitting in a square, low-backed chair. I started to raise my head off the pillow, but it began to throb with a harsh, relentless pain.

"Lucky?" I mumbled, laying as still as I could, hoping that if I did not move the throbbing would stop.

"Let me close the blinds a little. Perhaps that will help," said Louis sympathetically.

As the light grew dimmer, I began to feel a little safer, a little more confident that I could look around without my senses being struck with the same violence as before. At first I did not do anything but move my eyes. I was in a large bed, and the bed was covered with a quilted pink satin comforter. The sheets were smooth and slick, gray satin sheets that seemed to slide underneath me each time I moved my legs.

I must have looked surprised. Louis laughed quietly and explained that it was not the room they normally used for guests.

"It was my daughter's room. We thought you would be more comfortable here."

He placed a second pillow behind me as I managed finally to sit up. The throbbing was still there, but it was nothing like as severe as before and it lasted only until the movement was complete and I was once again perfectly still.

"You took quite a fall. It would have been bad enough hitting the stone floor the way you did; but the bottle hit it first and broke and you landed on the glass. That's why the doctor said you were lucky. A fraction of an inch lower and instead of a gash along your eyebrow you could have lost your eye."

I ran my finger across the line of stitches furrowed into my head, wondering if anything that felt that grotesque could ever really heal and what I was going to say about it when I got to court. Then I remembered. I slid my legs across the smooth satin sheets and put my feet on the floor. I had moved too quickly and for a moment I was blinded with pain. My hands shot to my temples. Gritting my teeth, I stared at the floor. Louis was at my side, helping me back into bed.

"You need to rest."

"I have to get up," I protested. "I have to be in court this morning. What time is it, anyway?" I asked as the pain began to subside.

"Court has been cancelled today," said Louis in a soothing voice.

"Cancelled? Why?" I asked blankly.

Adjusting the blinds, Louis let in a little more light. On a bureau underneath a mirror, a simple framed color photograph sat at an angle, a picture of a teenage girl in riding gear holding the bridle of her horse.

"Cancelled because the defense attorney had an accident last night," explained Louis. "He tripped on the steps after dinner at a private home in Los Angeles and suffered a mild concussion."

"There were other people here last night," I said skeptically. "You don't think any of them are going to tell anyone they saw Stanley Roth try to kill Michael Wirthlin?"

Griffin glanced around the bedroom once occupied by his now grown-up daughter, but he was not thinking about her, and he was not really thinking about what had happened last night. He was thinking, if I'm any judge of that look of nostalgia in his eyes, about something that could not be defined by any one thing or any one person. He was thinking about his whole life, and what it had come to, and whether, really, it had any meaning at all.

"You did a very brave thing," he said as his eyes came back to mine. "You didn't hesitate, not for an instant. I admire you for that. You thought you were saving someone's life. But–and this doesn't change at all how much I admire what you did–Stanley was not going to hit Michael with that bottle. He was threatening him," he added before I could object;

"warning him. He might have thrown that bottle–the way he threw that chair–right past him, close enough to scare the hell out of Michael. He could have hit him with that chair, you know," insisted Griffin. "He could have come around the table and hit him with it, but he didn't do that. He threw it through the window instead, didn't he?"

He wanted me to agree; he wanted me to say that his partner, his friend, the great Stanley Roth, never intended to hurt anyone, after I had seen him with my own eyes hurl a chair straight at Michael Wirthlin's head and then pick up a wine bottle to finish the job.

"I saw him do it. I saw him throw that chair. He wasn't trying to miss. I saw him grab that bottle, saw him lift it up. He wasn't doing that to scare him–he was doing that to hit him."

Griffin sat down. He nodded his head, agreeing, not with what I had seen, but with my belief that that was what I thought I had seen.

"Yes, exactly; that's what you saw, because that is what you thought you saw."

Griffin placed both feet on the floor, put his hands on his knees and bent forward, an earnest, wise look on his face.

"You don't know Stanley Roth the way I do. He's temperamental, volatile; but he would never hurt anyone on purpose. He isn't that kind of man." A subtle, cunning smile traced its way across Griffin's mouth. "He's too intelligent, too selfish to do that." He paused. "He has too much ego for it. He can go into a rage, throw things around, break a few windows if he feels like it–but deliberately strike someone? No, that would suggest he didn't have any other way to deal with them; which in turn would suggest that they were more powerful, more important, than he was." Griffin raised his eyes and laughed softly. "A long time ago, when he was just starting out–long before he had Blue Zephyr, long before he had any reason to think he would ever have a studio of his own, he had an idea for a picture, something he really believed in. He must have been turned down by every major studio in town; not just turned down, but ridiculed, insulted, told to his face that what he wanted to do would never work, and that even if he did get it made, no one would ever pay money to see it. At the end, when there was no place left to go, no one else to ask, he went on a two-day drunk.

"He showed up at my house–the way he did last night–in a rage. He stalked all around the living room. I tried to calm him down, but I don't think he heard a word I said. He kept ranting about how he was going to get even, how he was going to make them all pay. And he meant it, too. You could see it in his eyes. He had the look on his face of someone who knows what is going to happen, knows that things are going to work just the way he imagines, knows it with such absolute certainty that he has already begun to enjoy the way it is going to make him feel. Stanley Roth had been told–told by everyone, everyone who counted–that he didn't have the talent to make a movie on his own, and yet there he was, convinced, and jubilant in the conviction, that he was not only going to make a movie on his own but that he was going to make that movie, the one they had all turned down. That was his idea of revenge: to make them feel what fools they had been, to make them sorry they had treated him the way they had. That's what I mean when I say he has too much ego, that he's too selfish."

Griffin's eyes roved around the room, like someone looking at things he had not seen in a very long time.

"Stanley Roth doesn't want to hurt anyone; he wants them to know they made a mistake, that they underestimated him, that he now has the power to ruin their lives, or at least destroy their careers. The last thing he would ever do is kill someone he really wanted to hurt."

The way he said it made me wonder whether Stanley Roth had ever done anything like that to him. If Roth was too selfish to commit an act of violence; if he had too much ego to give anyone the satisfaction, such as it was, of believing that it was the only way he could deal with them; then what about all those people, like Louis Griffin, who were required constantly to submit to whatever the great man decided he wanted to do? Was there a point at which any of them ever had enough; a point at which they were willing to risk his displeasure and tell him what they really thought about the way he treated them and the others around him? Or were they all, except for those like Michael Wirthlin who could always buy his way into another studio, another project, afraid to do anything that might jeopardize their chance to remain a part of that Hollywood life they thought everyone wanted to have?

I lay there, in that silk and satin bed, watching in the stillness how the light filtered through the shutters behind Louis Griffin and placed him in the shadows, softening his features, making him seem somehow near at hand and yet far away. It was that distance I had noticed about him from the very first, that sense that he was someone you could trust, someone who would help you any way he could, but someone who had too much pride ever to ask you to do anything for him.

"Did he make that movie?" I asked for no other reason than to break the silence.

Griffin smiled. "Yes, he made it. He won the Academy Award for it." He paused. "He gave quite an eloquent acceptance speech. 'Not everyone thought this could be done.'"

It amused him, the way those few quoted words sounded when he spoke them out loud in the quiet privacy of this room, years after he had heard them.

"'Not everyone thought this could be done.' That was the first line, the very first thing he said that night when he stood there on the stage, holding the Oscar for Best Picture. He must have felt this tremendous sense of satisfaction, had this incredible feeling of vindication, but the only people who felt the full sting of what he said were the ones who had turned him down, the ones who ridiculed him, told him he would never make it in their business–yes, 'their business.' No one else, only them, because he immediately added, 'Which makes my debt to those who did believe it could be done, who not only believed it but helped make it possible, all the greater.'"

Smiling to himself, Louis Griffin rubbed the back of his hand with his other thumb.

"That night Stanley Roth owned this town, and everyone knew it. They knew something else as well," said Griffin, looking up. "They knew he was going to own it for a long time to come."

I was feeling a little better and found that if I did it slowly I could raise my head without any appreciable discomfort. As carefully as I could, I sat up in bed.

"You better not try to get up just yet. The doctor said you should stay in bed all day. Why don't I leave? Perhaps you can get back to sleep. It would do you good."

"No," I said as he started to get up from the chair. "I'm sure the doctor is right, but stay a while longer if you can. I know you have other things to do, but I'm interested in what you have been telling me."

"A few more minutes; then you better rest," said Griffin as he let himself back down into the chair.

He began to glance around the room, a pensive expression in his eyes, until he got to the picture of his daughter. He seemed to stop still. Raising his hand to his mouth, he pressed his fingers together, his face a blank stare.

"I used to come in here sometimes late at night," said Griffin wistfully; "when my daughter was still a child. I'd sit here, in this chair, and watch her sleep. Not for very long, just a few minutes; but it was for me the best time of the day, those few minutes in the nighttime quiet, watching her sleep, knowing that there was nothing better in the world. I would have liked for it to last forever, having a child in her childhood, a young–well, perhaps not really a young–father. I was nearly forty when she was born."

He looked again at the photograph of his daughter. From what he had just said, it must have been taken some years before, yet it was the only photograph in the room. There was nothing to show what she looked like later, nothing to commemorate any of the events that mark the normal stages in a young girl's life. Perhaps they were in some other part of the house, her parent's bedroom for example; but then why was everything else–the pink satin comforter, the white lacquered dresser, the simple mirror–the way a girl of that age would have wanted it and not what she would have wanted when she was older, a young woman beginning to lead a life of her own?

"You've been wondering why–or perhaps even how–I've stayed on such apparently good terms with Stanley; why, given the way he behaves, we have managed to remain friends," said Griffin, his eyes coming slowly back to mine. "It's because of her, my daughter. Stanley saved her life. You won't find that in any of the biographies or any of the magazine articles about him. He never told anyone; he made me promise I'd never tell anyone. She was three years old. We weren't living here then. We lived in Pasadena on a residential street. She was playing in the front yard. It was fenced, but she went out on the sidewalk. A dog–just a puppy–had gotten loose and was running down the street. She went out in the street to touch it, to pet it. She ran right in front of a car. Stanley had just pulled into the driveway. He saw it all happen. He went after her, dove in front of the car, shoved her out of the way. The car hit him and broke his shoulder, but he saved her life. So, you see, Stanley Roth can come over here and throw a dining-room chair through my window; he can in one of his frequent fits of temper say things to me I wouldn't take from another human being on the face of the earth; he could even–though I don't for a moment think he did–murder his wife, and I would still do anything I could to help him; because, you see, Mr. Antonelli, there are some debts that can never be repaid. Ever.

"But I should also tell you, that even if that had never happened, even if he had never saved my daughter's life, I would probably still consider myself fortunate to be his friend. Talent doesn't excuse everything, but it excuses a lot. I mean real talent, the kind that Stanley Roth has. Yes, yes, I know: it's Hollywood we're talking about; it's not really art. The strange thing is, I tend to agree with that. Most of what's done here is a travesty: crude, moronic, the kind of thing no sensible person would waste his time watching; or, if he mistakenly began to watch, would immediately walk out of, embarrassed that anyone would stay."

Lifting his chin, Griffin studied me for a moment.

"Do you ever read the newspaper accounts of a trial you're in? Have you read, for example, what's been written in the L.A. papers during this trial? If you read that you conducted a 'brilliant' cross-examination of a witness, don't you find yourself, if only just for a moment, thinking perhaps just a little more highly of that particular cross-examination than you did before? We all do that, don't we?–think of ourselves the way others think of us; or, rather, think of ourselves in terms of what others say about us. It's a strange phenomenon when you think about it: we may think someone a fool, a liar, a person who wouldn't tell the truth even on the off-chance he figured out what it was–but let him tell you that he thought something you did was great and he becomes immediately the embodied voice of all the intelligence, all the wisdom in the world."

Folding his arms across his chest, Griffin leaned against the side of the chair, striking a languid pose.

"We all do it–believe the things we want to hear and invent a thousand reasons why the things we don't want to hear are wrong. But if it's always difficult not to be influenced by the opinions of others, it's almost impossible here, in this town, especially if you become successful. You don't make good movies, or pretty good movies: you make great movies, some of the greatest movies ever made. And you are not–if you're Stanley Roth–a perfectly capable, or quite a competent, director, someone who can bring out the talent of the actors with whom you work. No, you're a great director, and everything you do is something no one else could have done as well.

"There is no sense of proportion here, no sense of the small degrees of difference that make up the distinction between better and worse. Stanley Roth is one of the few men–maybe the only one when you really get down to it–who doesn't believe any of it. And do you know why? Because he knows he's better than the rest of them, and because he also knows that he isn't anything like as good as he should be."

Griffin drew a breath. His eyes moved slowly from side to side as he thought about the implications of what he had just said.

"Didn't something like that happen to you? When you realized you were better than other lawyers, but that you also made mistakes? When you knew the mistakes you had made, the things you could have done better, in that cross-examination the newspapers called brilliant?"

Griffin smiled as he remembered what he had said to me himself.

"The cross-examination of Detective Crenshaw, the one I thought was so great: You would have seen flaws in it, thought of things you should have done differently; perhaps even become angry with yourself for not having seen something you only thought about when it was too late. That's what I'm trying to tell you about Stanley: He doesn't depend on what other people think, because he knows more about it than they do. It doesn't make him very easy to be around sometimes, but then I don't imagine you're always very easy to be around all the time, either. I don't think it's very easy for Stanley to be around himself. It's the price he pays for being what he is; it's the price he pays for that astonishing talent he has. I admire that; I wish I had some of it myself. So I sometimes put up with things perhaps I shouldn't. So what?"

With a slight shift of his shoulder Griffin seemed to dismiss any suggestion that Stanley Roth could ever have done anything that would make him reconsider the loyalty he felt toward him.

"Was Wirthlin right?" I asked, touching the lump above my eye. There did not seem to be quite so many sutures as I had thought before, and the stitched path they formed not nearly so jagged. What I had feared might be disfigurement now felt no larger than a minor cut.

"Was he right that Stanley Roth is finished? No, I won't believe that until it happens. Is he right that Blue Zephyr is finished? Probably." He paused. "I suppose it was finished the day we started. Bringing Michael in. I was against it. I thought we should wait a while longer, until we could finance it on our own. I could tell Michael wouldn't be content with letting Stanley–or anyone else–run the show. He said all the right things; he insisted he understood that Blue Zephyr was Stanley's studio, that Stanley would decide what pictures to make and how to make them; but–well, you've seen Michael enough to know–he wasn't going to let anyone do anything if he disagreed with it, not if there was any way he could stop it. I think Michael really thought that once Stanley got to know him, he'd start to see that Michael knew what he was talking about. The problem was that the more Stanley got to know him, the more convinced he was that Michael didn't have any idea what he was talking about. And as you can imagine, Stanley wasn't shy about telling him so.

"Stanley knew that it was only a matter of time before Michael would decide to pull out; but he thought by then we wouldn't need him anymore: that the studio would be making enough money that we wouldn't need much in the way of outside financing."

"What do you know about Stanley's screenplay, *Blue Zephyr*?"

Griffin's eyes lit up.

"The next *Citizen Kane*? I know it's what Stanley has always wanted to do. I know the rough outline of the story, but if you're asking if I've ever read it–no, I haven't. Have you?"

He did not seem surprised when I told him that I had, and even less surprised when I told him how good I thought it was.

"Has he told you what he's working on now?" inquired Griffin, more than a little curious.

"No, I have no idea. To tell you the truth, I didn't know that he was working on anything in particular. I know he works, at night, after the trial, in that bungalow of his; but I just assumed it was on the routine business of the studio."

"Whatever it is," said Griffin with a sigh, "it isn't routine. He won't tell me what it is, except that he's thoroughly engrossed in it and he's determined it's going to be the next movie he makes. How did he put it? Yes, even if it's the last movie he makes. He's spending all his time on it, all the time he isn't in court or otherwise occupied with the trial. Every night, sometimes till three or four in the morning–and all weekend long. I don't know when he sleeps. I think the only rest he gets is when he's sitting next to you in court, when he can't do anything else. Whatever he's working on, he seems to think it can't wait."

I thought I understood the sense of urgency, the fear that he did not have much time. He was on trial for murder, and these might be the last days of freedom he had left. But when I suggested that to Griffin, he disagreed. He assured me that Stanley Roth could not possibly be convicted.

"That's what Stanley believes; that's what he hopes," I said, attempting a clarification.

"No, it's what he's convinced of. He knows he didn't do it," said Griffin before he added with a slight, deferential nod, "and he knows what you can do."

A glance passed between us and for a moment we were both reminded of what he had been telling me earlier about believing ourselves to be what others said about us.

"In *Blue Zephyr*," I said presently, "the head of the studio has a partner–just one partner–who has an affair with his wife, because his wife, a movie star he created out of a minor actress, wants the partner to have a studio of his own where she can do what she wants."

"And does he? The partner, I mean. Does he leave Blue Zephyr and set up a studio of his own?" asked Griffin pensively.

"Yes, and the actress goes with him, and Blue Zephyr is about to go under and William Welles–that is the name of the character, the name Stanley Roth gave himself–makes one last picture, the picture that will tell the truth about Hollywood and save the studio. He calls the picture . . ."

Griffin had been following intently.

"Blue Zephyr."

He said it in a way that startled me. He knew it, and not because he had known, as he put it, the rough outline of the story. He knew it with a kind of inevitability, as if he had known Stanley Roth so well, understood him so thoroughly, that he knew instinctively what he would have called–what he would have had to have called–the movie made inside the movie.

"Nobody but Stanley Roth could have done that," said Griffin, calmly shaking his head in admiration. "Even if they had thought of it, nobody else would have had the guts. *Blue Zephyr.* Astonishing, isn't it? How simple it seems, after it's been done."

Griffin sat straight up. His nostrils flared as he took a short, decisive breath.

"You want to know if I think Mary Margaret was having an affair with Michael Wirthlin. You want to know if she was going to leave Stanley and leave Blue Zephyr. She might have had an affair with Michael, but it wouldn't have meant much if she had, at least not to her. I'm sure you've been told lots of different things about Marian, but . . ."

"You called her Marian?" I asked, unable to hide my surprise.

There was a brief, awkward silence, and in the shadows of that dimly lit room I thought I saw a slight flush of embarrassment on Louis Griffin's finely sculpted cheek. He closed his eyes and began to run the fingers of his right hand over his forehead, slowly, back and forth, the weary gesture of someone remembering something he would have given anything to change, something he tried not to think about, because each time he did it broke his heart all over again. He stopped rubbing his forehead and opened his eyes, disappointed in himself for exposing, if only for the moment, what he had intended to keep private.

"There was a time when we were very close, closer perhaps than I've ever been with anyone," he remarked, holding his head high.

He saw the question in my eyes, the question I had to ask but did not want to put into words.

"No, nothing like that at all. I had just lost my daughter. She . . . died. I was inconsolable; my wife was . . . well, it was even harder for her. Everyone, of course, tried to be helpful, but it's difficult to know what to do. There isn't anything anyone can do. Except for Marian. She used to come every day. Sometimes she would just sit in a chair and not say anything–just be here, just in case I wanted someone to talk to. I called her Marian because, quite simply, that was her name, her real name, not the name of the movie star everyone went to see; the name of the young woman who had the decency to make me feel there was some reason to go on living. She became in a way a second daughter to me. She told me things about herself I don't think she had ever told anyone before."

His eyes were filled with anguish and his voice heavy with sorrow when he added: "You can have no idea how much it hurt when she died, too."

Rubbing his hands together, he stared down at the floor, collecting himself.

"She might have left Stanley one day, but it would not have been for Michael," he said, lifting his eyes. "If she had left, it wouldn't have been because she wanted out of the studio. She had everything she wanted, and she knew she always would–at least so long as I was there. The only way she would have left Blue Zephyr is if she had decided to get out of the business altogether."

He made it sound like something she had actually thought about doing. When I asked him, he gave me a strange look, as if the answer was more complicated than that.

"Stanley made her a star, and she was grateful to him for that. But she also resented him for that. She was famous, she was idolized, she was what every young woman wants to be–and she resented him for that, resented him because she did not really want any of it, not after she had it. She thought she did, when she was growing up, when she was going to school, when she was trying to become an actress. But even then it wasn't because she wanted it so much for herself. She told me about growing up, abandoned by her father, with that alcoholic mother of hers telling her all the time she had the looks to be a movie star. It was her mother's dream before it was hers. Then, when she went to college, she falls in love and gets married and that's what he wants, too."

"Paul Erlich? Her first husband? She thought that's what he wanted–for her to become a movie star?" Then it came to me, like an echo in my mind, something Erlich had said about the way he felt when Marian Walsh was still auditioning for small parts in stock productions.

"He didn't mind the idea, her trying to become an actress. It never occurred to him that she might succeed, that she might really become a movie star."

Louis Griffin sadly shook his head. "And she was doing it all because of him, because she thought that was what had attracted him to her, made him want to be with her–what she could become. And then she became what she thought everyone wanted her to be, and ended up with everything except the only man she ever really loved."

"And her daughter," I added.

Griffin glanced away, his gaze settling on the photograph on the dresser.

"Yes, and her daughter."

16

STANLEY ROTH ACTED AS IF nothing had happened, and perhaps, in his mind, nothing had. He inspected the discolored gash sewn shut along the line of my eyebrow as if he were only dimly aware of how it had gotten there.

"I'm sorry about the accident," he said in a whispered voice just as the bailiff announced the impending entrance of the judge.

I had barely time to give him a quick, incredulous glance before the door at the side opened and Judge Rudolph Honigman began the short three-step march to the bench. Was Stanley Roth trying to tell me he did not remember how I had been hurt; that he did not remember that he was about to hit Michael Wirthlin with a bottle or, if I was to believe Louis Griffin, merely threaten him with it; that he did not remember anything about the way I had tried to stop him, the way we had both been thrown to the floor by the force of our collision? Or was that just the way he chose to describe what he did? That he had not meant to hurt anyone; that it was an accident, one he regretted, one for which he felt responsible, but nothing for which he should be expected to feel guilty?

"Mr. Antonelli," said Honigman. He studied me with a benevolent, worried gaze. "The court was quite distressed to learn of your unfortunate accident. We're glad to see that you're apparently all right."

"I'm fine, Your Honor. Thank you. I'm sorry to have caused a delay."

Honigman nodded to his clerk. Grumbling beneath her breath, she shoved herself up from her chair and reluctantly made her way to the jury room.

After the jury squeezed themselves into their tight-fitting chairs,

Richard Crenshaw was brought into the courtroom and reminded that he was still under oath.

"Mr. Antonelli," announced Honigman as he turned his attention to a bulging file folder he had brought with him into court, "you may resume your cross-examination of the witness."

The first time Crenshaw had taken the stand he had worn slacks and a sports jacket. Today he was dressed in a dark blue suit. Even more forcibly than before, I was struck with how much time he appeared to spend thinking about how he looked.

"That's a very nice suit you're wearing, Detective Crenshaw," I remarked as I rose from my chair.

He flashed a consciously modest smile. "Thank you."

"A very expensive suit, I would think."

He shrugged as if to say that it was not anything worth talking about.

"No, I mean it, Detective Crenshaw: That is a very expensive suit." I hesitated, like someone not quite certain of something but willing to guess. "You must do fairly well consulting on movies. How many of these consulting jobs–besides the one you did on the movie with Mary Margaret Flanders–have you had?"

"Just the one," replied Crenshaw in that careful even-toned voice.

I pretended surprise. "You were a consultant on a movie produced by Stanley Roth–a movie starring Mary Margaret Flanders–and you've never been asked to do another one? Why is that, Detective Crenshaw? Wasn't your work very good?"

He dismissed the question, and the suggestion, with a condescending glance. I shifted ground and came at him from a different angle.

"Did you enjoy the work? I assume you were there to advise on–what? Police procedure . . . that sort of thing?"

He nodded, but without enthusiasm, as if it had been nothing more than a job which, like any job, was sometimes interesting and sometimes not.

"Yes–to both questions."

"I see. Well, tell us this, then, Detective Crenshaw: What was she like?"

His wrists rested on the arms of the witness chair, his hands dangled over the ends. He seemed at ease, confident, perhaps a little too confident. A smile played at the corners of his mouth as he called attention to the ambiguity in my question, not because he did not know what I meant, but to show the jury he could hold his own with a lawyer.

"What was who like?"

"Mary Margaret Flanders. You worked with her. You told Ms. Van Roten that you knew her. What was she like?"

He drew his eyebrows together, knitting his brow, and pursed his lips.

"She seemed like a very nice person," said Crenshaw after a short pause. "She was certainly very nice to me."

Lowering my head, I drifted toward the jury box.

"Did you talk to her very often?' I asked, my eyes still focused on the floor.

He tried to make it sound that the last thing he had meant to suggest was that they had become anything more than casual acquaintances: two people who just happened to be working at the same place.

"No, not very often. A couple of times, perhaps–not more than that."

"On the set?"

"Yes."

I leaned against the railing of the jury box and raised my head. I smiled to myself in a way to make him wonder what I knew, or what I thought I knew.

"You're sure you spoke to her on more than one occasion?"

"A couple of times," he replied with a look of indifference.

"Do you remember what you talked about?"

"Nothing in particular: just casual conversation."

"So she never said anything to you like: 'I think my husband wants to kill me'? Nothing like: 'I'm afraid of my husband: I think he wants to hurt me'? Nothing like: 'He's hurt me before and I'm afraid he'll hurt me again'?"

Crenshaw's expression did not change: it was that same impassive look, the look of someone always in control of himself and of any situation in which he found himself. But I thought I saw in his eyes a slight alteration, like the kind of correction someone makes when they decide they might have been just a little off in the way they measured a distance, and begin to recalculate because they want to get it exactly right.

"She never said anything like that to you, did she? She never said anything that made you think she might be in any danger, did she?"

"No," he had to admit, "she did not."

I started to walk back to the counsel table; then, as if I had just thought of it, I stopped and asked: "Who hired you to be a consultant on that picture?"

"Someone from the studio. I don't remember the name."

"I see. Then it wasn't Stanley Roth, because I assume you'd remember his name, wouldn't you?"

He let his silence speak his agreement.

"You had this one consulting job and no others. Have you done anything else in connection with the motion picture industry? Have you taken acting lessons, for example?"

"Some. A few years ago."

I do not know why it surprised me, but it did. Everything about him suggested a self-conscious effort to achieve a certain effect: the clothes he wore, the way his hair was cut, the way he carried himself. Each movement, each gesture practically screamed for approval, if not for how well it was done then for how often it had been practiced; and none of it more obvious than the way he had trained his voice. He used it to make himself sound like someone who knew what he was about, someone who, like the talking heads on the evening news, could give an air of authority to two or three short sentences of otherwise doubtful importance.

"You had acting lessons. Then you aren't particularly interested in remaining a police officer? Excuse me–a detective?"

He answered with an indulgent smile.

"I had some acting lessons a few years ago because one of the television networks wanted to do a pilot for one of those real-life police shows. They thought I might be the narrator. So I went to an acting class–the one they sent me to–for a few weeks. But nothing came of it. They didn't make the pilot, and I didn't become an actor."

"I don't know if I'd go that far, Detective Crenshaw. Given the way you handle yourself in court, I'd say that you learned those lessons fairly well."

Annabelle Van Roten rose straight up from her chair. She put her right hand on the corner of the table, and with her left made an expansive gesture meant to demonstrate that her dissatisfaction with what I had done was not confined to some narrow, arcane point of law.

"I realize, Your Honor, that Mr. Antonelli received a rather nasty knock on the head–and perhaps that explains why instead of asking questions he keeps making statements, but . . ."

"I thought you liked my voice," I interjected with a slightly bewildered look.

A couple of jurors laughed. Van Roten turned a little red. Honigman gave me a mildly disapproving look. Van Roten quickly got control of herself.

"The prosecution would have no objection to another day's delay if Mr. Antonelli needs more time for his recovery."

I stood there, staring at her, stammering silently like a long-lost lover, waiting until her eyes left the bench and came triumphantly back around to me.

"I don't suppose you'd believe me if I told you I slipped and fell because I was thinking about you?"

The dark eyes of Annabelle Van Roten flashed with anger, but also with a certain proud defiance. It suddenly struck me that she was–at least when she was not animated by a strong emotion–a remarkable-looking woman.

"Sorry," I mumbled, embarrassed by what I had done. "I shouldn't have done that."

Quick to see her advantage, she did not hesitate to make the most of it. The corners of her mouth turned down. Her eyes mocked me with the staged pretense of disappointment.

"You mean you weren't thinking of me?"

The same jurors who had laughed before laughed again. The court clerk frowned and checked the time.

"Perhaps the two of you could fall in love over dinner in a restaurant somewhere instead of in my courtroom," Honigman dryly remarked. "Now, did you have an objection you wanted to make, Ms. Van Roten?"

"Yes, Your Honor, I was . . ."

"Mr. Antonelli, perhaps you could try to limit yourself to asking questions of this witness," instructed the judge, stopping her before she could finish.

I bowed to his wishes and picked up where I had left off.

"You had acting lessons in preparation for a pilot that did not get made. Was there a script you read for the part of the narrator, the part they thought they wanted you to play?"

"Yes, there was a script."

"When you served as a consultant on that one movie, the one during which you first met Mary Margaret Flanders, did you review a script–to make sure what it said about police procedure was accurate, or at least not too far removed from the way things are actually done by police detectives?"

"Yes," he replied, a question in his voice, as if he wanted to know why I was asking.

"You have some familiarity, then, with the mode, the style, or perhaps I should say, the way in which a script is organized, the way each scene is described and the dialogue written within it. Is that correct?"

"Yes, I have some familiarity with that."

"Did you ever think that perhaps you could write one of your own, one that was at least as good as the ones you had seen?"

Crenshaw turned up the palms of his hands as if to show that this was far beyond any ambition of his own. "I wouldn't mind trying that someday. I think it might be interesting."

I stared at him, incredulous. "You wouldn't mind doing that someday," I repeated slowly. "You're trying to say you haven't . . ."

I caught myself. I had thrown up my left hand, that gesture Stanley Roth had told me I did all wrong. I started to laugh, and I looked across to the counsel table to see if Roth had noticed it as well. He was sitting with his arms folded, lost in thought. He had not seen anything. He had not once looked up, neither today, nor the day before yesterday, while Richard Crenshaw was on the witness stand. Quickly, I turned back to Crenshaw. He was waiting for me, waiting to see what I was going to do next. Then I realized that he had not looked at Stanley Roth either, not once, from the first moment he stepped up to the stand. Stanley Roth had been right about him.

"I have no further questions of this witness, Your Honor."

Richard Crenshaw was halfway to his feet when I added: "But I do intend to call him later as a witness for the defense."

His arms braced on the chair, Crenshaw cast an inquiring glance toward Annabelle Van Roten. She had no more idea than did he about why I might want him back. She looked down at the file folder open on the table in front of her, running her eye down the long list of names scheduled to be called as witnesses for the prosecution. Crenshaw stood up, threw back his shoulders, and remembered to smile one last time–a modest, friendly grin–at the jury. But when he turned away he became far more subdued. He was worried about something, and I thought I knew what it was.

When the door at the back of the small, crowded courtroom had closed behind Detective Crenshaw, Annabelle Van Roten stood up. "Your Honor," she announced, "the People call Jack Walsh."

I never knew whether Annabelle Van Roten really wanted to call Mary Margaret Flanders's father as a witness, but I suspect she did not. Walsh was too full of his own–how shall I put it?–posthumous importance; too convinced that he should be seen almost as much a victim as his daughter, to confine himself to the truth. He would embellish things to put himself in the best possible light. A defense attorney would not have much trouble turning what he said into a marked advantage for the other side. Van Roten was intelligent and cunning. She had to have seen the danger, but she may have thought she had no choice. Jack Walsh had spent months promoting himself as the spokesman for his dead daughter and as the only person to whom she had confided her secret but real fear that Stanley Roth was going to kill her. It did not take much imagination to figure out what Jack Walsh would do if he was not called to testify and if Annabelle Van Roten then failed to convict Stanley Roth of murder.

Walsh took the witness stand eager–too eager–to begin. Before Van Roten finished asking him to state his name and spell it for the record, he blurted it out. His voice was harsh, discordant, the harping echo of all the emotions swirling inside him.

"Jack Walsh," he repeated, forcing himself to say it again when Van Roten finished the question.

"Jack Walsh," he said a third time, the sound of it finally normal.

It was curious, the way he worked, feeling his way, becoming a little more confident with each question he was asked. His answers, at first hesitant, uncertain and brief, became forceful, self-assured and endless. He began to deliver monologues. He testified for hours and it seemed like days. He managed to bring in everything he had ever said in public and, as near as I could tell, everything he had ever thought in private, about his daughter and about Stanley Roth. He told the jury–told them the way he would have told his twelve closest friends–if he had ever had that many friends–that whole lamentable story about his marriage and his divorce and how he had thought, perhaps mistakenly, that his daughter would be better off if he disappeared from her life. He told them how she had always had that something, that he had always known she was going to be a star. He told them how after all those wasted years of being apart, he had finally found her again, found her in time to tell her what had really happened: that he wouldn't have left her for anything in the world if her mother had not been so insistent on a divorce. He told them how he had never liked Stanley Roth, and he told them how glad he was when his daughter told him, shortly before she died, that she was going to leave her husband.

"That's why he killed her."

Van Roten hesitated, certain I was going to object. She looked at me over her shoulder when I did not.

"Do you wish to object?" asked Judge Honigman.

I blinked. "I'm sorry," I said with a perplexed expression. "I must not have been listening. Object to what?"

Honigman's head snapped up. He searched my eyes, trying to discover what I thought I was doing.

"The witness just testified that the victim was going to leave the defendant and, quote, 'That's why he killed her,' unquote. Do you wish to object?"

I laughed. "Is that what he said?" I looked at Van Roten and smiled. "No, no objection, Your Honor." Then I sat down.

"And what was the reason your daughter gave you when she told you she was going to leave her husband, the defendant, Stanley Roth?" asked Van Roten, turning back to the witness.

Walsh did not answer immediately. He slowly turned his shoulders and glared at Stanley Roth.

"She said he had beaten her and she was afraid he was going to kill her."

I thought I heard a barely audible sigh of relief from Annabelle Van

Roten when she announced to the court that she was through with the witness. The direct testimony of Jack Walsh, which had begun in the morning, had lasted into the middle of the afternoon, broken only by lunch. The small, creaking noises from the jury box, as the jurors tried to shift position to give some relief to their stiffening limbs, had, despite their self-conscious attempts to do it quietly, become more frequent and more noticeable. Honigman, clearly embarrassed by the inadequacies of his courtroom, was merciful. As soon as Van Roten had finished, he declared a ten-minute recess.

I stood up to stretch. Van Roten, facing the opposite direction, was standing right next to me, so close that her arm bumped against mine.

"There's a rumor," she whispered under her breath while she smiled at someone in the courtroom crowd, "that what happened to you wasn't exactly an accident. Should I call you as a witness about your client's predisposition toward violence?"

She stepped away and began to confer with the assistant district attorney who was sitting second chair for the prosecution. Was there really a rumor, or had she guessed? Or had she just made it up, trying to cost me my concentration just before I began the cross-examination of the prosecution's witness? She was capable of it: of inventing a lie to make me wonder if it was the truth. She was smart, and she knew it; she was good looking, and she knew that, too. I doubt that she had ever in her life thought there was any reason not to exploit any advantage she had. She would toss her head, tease me with her eyes, the whole time measuring me, seeing what she could do to get me off my guard. She reminded me of women I had known in college, the ones who would get you to call them and ask them out so they could say no and then laugh about it with their friends.

Huffing and puffing with each slow step her stubby legs took, the clerk led the jury back into the courtroom. She cast a malevolent glance toward the bench and retreated to her desk. The jurors struggled into their accustomed places, smiling their apologies as they banged against each other.

"Do you wish to cross-examine the witness?" asked Honigman routinely.

Jack Walsh was waiting for me, sneering defiance. He was certain that after what he had already said, everyone was on his side.

"You testified that your daughter told you that her husband had beaten her," I reminded him in a quiet voice as I got to my feet.

"That's right," he replied. His eyes followed me as I moved to the end of the jury box farthest from the witness stand.

"She told you this?"

"Yes," insisted Walsh with a trace of annoyance. He did not want anyone to think that he would not be offended if someone questioned his word.

"That her husband, Stanley Roth, had beaten her?"

Walsh looked at Annabelle Van Roten, certain she should object. She was jotting a note to herself. She did not look up.

"Did she tell you why she didn't report this to the police?" I continued. "Or did she tell you why she didn't leave him right then, when he beat her, if, as you testified, she was afraid he was going to kill her?"

With a scowl, he crossed his arms, acting as if it was up to him whether he would answer or not.

"How long had your daughter been married to Stanley Roth when this happened?"

The question seemed to confuse him.

"Well, how long had they been married when she died?"

He could not help himself. "You mean, when she was murdered?"

"How long?"

He hesitated, trying to calculate the time.

"Does five years sound about right to you?" I asked.

"Five years," he said, making it sound that he had just come to that very same conclusion on his own.

"She had a child, didn't she?"

"Yes."

"A child from another marriage?"

"Yes."

"You're that child's grandfather, correct?"

"Yes."

"Tell us, then–tell the jury–when was the last time you saw your grandchild?"

He seemed almost to shrink back into himself. His chin sagged onto his chest. His hands fell limp into his lap. Biting his lip, he lowered his eyes.

"I was out of my daughter's life for a long time," he mumbled. He looked up. "I've already testified that after her mother divorced me I . . ."

"Have you ever seen your grandchild?"

"No," he admitted.

"Do you know how old she is? Never mind," I said, waving my hand in the air. "Tell us this, instead: Your daughter was married to Stanley Roth for five years, but they had no children. Did your daughter not like children?"

He said what he thought he was supposed to say; what any decent, caring father would say about his daughter.

"She loved children."

My hand on the jury box railing, I lifted an eyebrow. "Her only child, however, lived with her first husband. He had custody, correct?"

"Yes."

My hand still on the railing, I took a step forward, drawing just a little closer to him. "But she loved children. I take it, then, that she wanted more; wanted children with her second husband, Stanley Roth?"

"Yes, of course."

"But she didn't have any children with Stanley Roth. Do you know why? Was it perhaps because she was too preoccupied with her career?" I asked tentatively, like someone honestly searching for an answer.

Whatever Jack Walsh had talked about with Mary Margaret Flanders, I doubt the question of children had ever come up, not with the way he had treated her, his only child. But this was the kind of thing a daughter might be expected to talk to her father about; and Jack Walsh was never reluctant to pretend he was what he thought others thought he should be.

"She wanted children," he insisted. He bent forward, a look of anguish in his eyes. "She wouldn't tell me the reason they didn't have any." He darted an angry glance toward the counsel table behind me where Stanley Roth was sitting quietly. "I had the feeling he couldn't have any."

For a moment I did not say anything. Sliding my hand along the jury box railing, I moved another step closer.

"You had the feeling he couldn't have any," I repeated. "You just testified that your daughter never told you the reason they didn't have children, but you 'had the feeling'?" I stared hard at him. "You have no more idea than anyone else here why they didn't have children. Your daughter never talked to you about it: not just the reason she didn't have children with Stanley Roth–but any of it. She didn't talk to you about anything, did she? You showed up, asked her for money and she gave it to you. And then, when you kept asking, she finally got tired of it and said she didn't want to see you again–isn't that what happened?"

"That's not true!" exclaimed Walsh, bolting forward until he was on the very edge of the witness chair.

"Did she call the police?"

It came so quick–it was so unexpected–it took him completely unawares. He must have remembered what I had asked him before, about why she had not called the police, the question I had not given him time to answer.

"No," he said without hesitation. "She didn't want anyone to know."

"She told you that? She told you she didn't call the police because she didn't want anyone else to know?"

"Yes," insisted Walsh, bristling with hostility.

I looked down at the floor, smiling to myself as I stroked my chin.

"Are you sure?" I asked as I raised my eyes.

There was a glimmer of uncertainty, a moment of doubt. He tensed, like someone who suddenly suspects a trap. It was too late. The last thing Jack Walsh would ever do is admit a lie.

"Yes, I'm sure," he insisted angrily.

I nodded as if I had agreed with him all along.

"Well, that would explain it–wouldn't it? Why there is no police report about any such incident; why there is no one on the prosecution's witness list to testify that any such report was ever made."

I returned to the counsel table and stood with my hands on the back of my empty chair.

"But it wouldn't explain–would it, Mr. Walsh?–why the defense is going to call a witness who will testify that your daughter–the daughter you abandoned when she was only five years old–in fact did call the police."

"Then he did hit her!" Walsh cried, as if in comparison with that, any lies he may have told were simply unimportant.

"Yes, he did. Once. When he found out, Mr. Walsh, that behind his back your daughter had aborted his child, the child he was desperate to have.

"No more questions," I said, turning my eyes toward the bench, but no one heard me say it. The courtroom was bedlam. Honigman was pounding his gavel. Annabelle Van Roten had risen to her feet, but then something held her back. Her mouth still open, she wheeled around, peering at me from suspicious eyes, trying to figure out what I thought I was doing by telling the world that my client, Stanley Roth, accused of murder, was a violent man.

For Jack Walsh all it meant was vindication. Outside the courtroom, surrounded by cameras and reporters, he insisted over and over again that everything he had said was the truth, that his daughter had told him Stanley Roth was a dangerous man, and now Stanley Roth's own lawyer had admitted it.

17

WITH MY HANDS SPREAD APART, I leaned against the tile shower stall and let the hot, pulsating water beat against the back of my neck as I tried to forget everything that had happened. All day long in court I had concentrated on each word spoken, weighing it in my mind, measuring it against everything else the witness had said–everything everyone involved in the trial had said–afraid I might miss that one misstatement, that single, seemingly unimportant inconsistency, that minor inaccuracy, that could change the outcome of the trial. Then, when it was over, when the judge and the jury left for the day and there was nothing left to listen to, I started listening to the same thing all over as it played itself back in my mind, doing it again and again over my fierce objection until through sheer exhaustion the question, the answer, all the vivid memories of what happened that day gradually began to fade into the background and I could try to think about what was going to happen tomorrow when I had to do it again.

Every trial was different, every trial had something that set it apart from the others; but the trial of Stanley Roth was so far removed from anything in my experience that there was really nothing to which I could compare it. Stanley Roth was famous, powerful, and rich; but he was also intelligent, and so obsessed with what he thought was the importance of what he did that he viewed the trial–the trial in which he might be found guilty of murder–as a kind of minor annoyance that in some strange sense had very little to do with him. If there had been a way around it, I don't think he would have attended the trial at all. He would have left the whole thing to me, the way I imagine he left to other producers, other directors, movies made by Blue Zephyr in which he had no particular interest. Sometimes, during a lull in the trial, when a witness was being sworn or had just been excused, I would turn to see how he was. It would take a moment before he realized I was looking at him. It was like being back in college, sitting next to someone so bored with the lecture that while he pretended to be taking notes was actually reading something from another class.

I turned off the water and stepped out of the shower. With the heel of my hand I rubbed a clearing in the steam-covered bathroom mirror. The stitches above my eye looked stiff and crooked, woven in and out of the eyebrow matted wet to my skin. When I first started practicing law, defending the kind of people who settled everything with violence, I used to think that some day, because I had lost their case or made the mistake of telling them what I really thought about them, one of them might try to kill me, but none of them ever had. They let me alone and nearly always treated me with a certain respect. I had to wait for Stanley Roth before I finally got into a situation where I needed the help of a doctor. And then he sat there, pretending that he did not know anything about what had happened, pretending that I had had an accident, that I had slipped and fallen, the way it had been reported to the court and to the press.

With two fingers, I pushed tentatively against the cut to see if it was still tender. It did not hurt, and I pushed harder. There was still no pain; and I felt better because of it, indulging myself in the illusion that I was still young enough to heal quickly.

The telephone was ringing. I walked into the bedroom, a towel around my waist. It was Stanley Roth.

"You're mad at me, aren't you?"

He was like an eighteen-year-old who knew he could always talk his way out of trouble because he knew that everyone liked him and that they knew, or at least wanted to believe, that no matter what he might have done, it was never with the deliberate purpose of hurting them or anyone else. Age had changed nothing. Gray hair curled up over the back collar of his shirt and deep lines were embedded in his forehead and along the sides of his face, but beneath all the charm and all the ruthlessness, beneath all the polished civility and all the explosive, primitive rage, he was still the same eager adolescent he had been that first time he had stared out at the Pacific, dreaming about the movies he wanted to make.

"You're mad at me," he repeated when I did not answer.

"What do you want, Stanley?" I asked. I sat at the edge of the bed, watching the tendons stretch like bowstrings when I flexed my toes.

"Are you coming over tonight, so we can talk about the case?"

I crossed my ankle over my knee and began to massage the sole of my foot.

"No."

I was not going to give him a reason, but then, almost against my will, heard myself doing precisely that.

"I've got too much to do to get ready for tomorrow."

"You're mad at me, aren't you?"

I let go of my foot.

"You're damn right I'm mad," I said firmly as I stood up. "This case is difficult enough without having to defend you against yourself. You could have killed Wirthlin! And for what?–because you got upset?"

"I knew you were mad at me. Louis told me what you did–how you thought I was going to smash Michael's head with a wine bottle–how you jumped over the table to stop me–how you got hurt."

There was a silence and I knew he was listening in his mind to the way what he was about to say was going to sound, and wondering what I would think when I heard it.

"Louis bends over backward to make excuses for me," he said, speaking with deliberate care. "Someday I'll tell you why. But you were right: I was going to hit that son of a bitch with that bottle; hit him as hard as I could. Did I want to kill him? I don't know. I came over there because I wanted to tell him what I thought of him: to let him know there wasn't any way I was going to walk away from Blue Zephyr and let him have it all. But then, when I saw him sitting there–that smug, stupid face of his–I knew there wasn't any point to it, that nothing I could say would make any difference. That's why I did it; that's why I went after him. If you hadn't stopped me, maybe I would have killed him. I know damn well I would have hit him."

He paused, and when he spoke again, he sounded tired and discouraged.

"I know you're mad. You have every right to be. But for what it's worth I'm sorry about what I did."

He laughed quietly, a low, self-deprecating laugh, a detached commentary on his own mixed emotions.

"I'm not all that sorry I went after Michael; but I'm damn sorry you got hurt because of it. And you're right: you did defend me against myself, and it isn't your job, but I'm grateful, and I'll always be grateful, that you did. Nobody else there did. They were all too busy worrying about themselves. Except Louis," added Roth immediately. "That is one of his failings: He always thinks first about other people and only then about himself."

It seemed a strange thing to say under the circumstances. "You think that's a failing?" I asked, a little irritated. "After what he did for you?"

"It's a failing in this business. If you don't think about yourself first, no one else will."

I wondered if he meant it, or if it was something that his own sense of who he had become had taught him to say. Stanley Roth, the cynical manipulator, the one in charge, the one who could give everyone what they wanted or take it all away: the great Stanley Roth who did not give a second thought to what happened to anyone.

"Sometimes, Stanley, you talk like a character out of one of your own movies."

He did not disagree. To the contrary, he seemed to think it the most normal thing in the world.

"Doesn't everyone? I mean, talk like someone else? Act like someone else?"

I did not have a chance to respond; though if I had, I'm not sure what I would have said.

"I didn't call you to get into a long discussion about the 'effect of the media on modern American life,'" he said, invoking the phrase with the clear derision of someone who had been challenged on that particular point more often than he cared to remember. "I called to apologize, and to ask if you could come by sometime tonight. There are some things I want to talk to you about," said Roth with the kind of vague ambiguity he used when he wanted me to think that I was one of the few people he could trust and that it would be a kind of betrayal if I did not go at once to see what he had to say.

"I accept your apology; but I have a lot of work yet to do and I need a decent night's sleep."

"It's about Blue Zephyr." Roth's voice was quiet, ominous, as if those two words would by themselves impress upon me how important it was that we talk.

"The script–or the studio?"

"Both," replied Roth with the utmost seriousness.

Curious, I felt myself starting to yield. I threw up a half-hearted objection.

"I'm supposed to have dinner with . . ."

"With Julie. Yes, I know. Go ahead, have dinner. Come later on," he insisted, certain he had gotten his way. "Don't worry about the time. I'll be up."

He made it sound like he was doing me a favor, and for a moment I almost felt he had. Once again he had persuaded me to do something I had had no intention of doing. I laughed about it, or tried to; but there was nothing all that funny about the way I let myself become subject to the changing moods, the sudden whims, the capricious demands of Stanley Roth. I could not stay mad at him, even after what he had done two nights before when I could have lost an eye. He was irresponsible, a grown-up, self-indulgent child; but that was who he was. He scarcely made a secret of it: He did everything short of bragging about it. I knew what he was; I had known it–or at least I should have known it–from the first time we talked. Yet I still could not quite bring myself to say no–to say no and mean it–when there was something he really wanted, especially when what he wanted was to tell me something about himself he had not told anyone–or at least not very many others–before. I could scream at him, swear at him, tell him to his face that he was a liar and worse; but I was never able simply to walk away. He was too interesting for that.

No, it was something else. Actually, there was not much about Stanley Roth that was interesting at all. He could not carry on a conversation for five minutes, unless it was about the motion picture industry; and he could not carry that on for more than ten minutes unless it was about a movie he had produced or directed. He had no serious interest in literature; and yet, despite that, some of the dialogue in that screenplay of his had held me riveted to the page. He had no interest in the arts; he was not even one of those people who admit they do not know anything about it, but insist they know what they like. Roth was always too wrapped up in what he was doing, what he was working on, to notice. He could not describe something he had seen happen right in front of his eyes without, so to speak, rearranging it to fit on the screen. His work was his life; but his work was fantasy and his life a kind of fiction, a story he seemed to rewrite every day as if it could always be whatever he wanted it to be. That was what was so interesting: not what he was–I'm not sure he was anything–but the way everything around him always seemed to be changing, and the way he made you believe he was the only one who knew–really knew–what was going to change next, and who was, for that reason, the only one you could be certain would not be left behind.

It was false and it was empty and I knew it, and I still could not quite resist. I told myself I was his lawyer; that I had to put up with his unusual demands and erratic behavior; that it was the only way to keep his confidence, but I knew it was a lie. I had been drawn to Mary Margaret Flanders, a woman I had never met, in a way I had seldom been attracted to any of the women I had known, because, I suppose, she had come to represent in those dreams I had shared with everyone who bought a ticket to see her, what I thought I wanted a woman to be. I was drawn to Stanley Roth because he had helped create those dreams. Or, if he did not create them, then convey them, promote them, do more than anyone else to make them the common categories by which the vast majority of us had come to look at the world around us. Because there was, after all, nothing terribly original about Stanley Roth. Not once had I heard him express a thought or voice an opinion I had not heard, not just from someone else, but from nearly everyone else before. I had started out wondering if he really believed any of the sentimental nonsense that characterized so many of his films; it was not long before I had begun to wonder if he had ever believed anything else.

It only seems a contradiction to say that Louis Griffin was right: that Stanley Roth was a genius. He was a genius, but not because of any new insight he had into the nature of things. He was a genius because, in some way he could never explain, he understood what people wanted before they knew it themselves, and because he could tell on the screen a story everyone already knew in a way that made it seem they were seeing it for the very first time. *Blue Zephyr*, the film that was going to rival *Citizen Kane*, was far better than anything Stanley Roth had ever done–better than anything almost anyone had done–but it could not have been written if *Kane* had not been written first.

Among the other riddles of Stanley Roth's existence I could never quite solve was the precise nature of his relationship with Julie Evans. I had seen him look at her the way he had once looked at girls in high school, the good-looking girls he knew he could never have; look at her from a distance with a kind of dreamlike stare. But then, when they were in the same room, he seemed not to notice her at all; and when he did remember she was there, it was usually to tell her in that short, abbreviated fashion of his what she was supposed to do next, or with barely concealed contempt remind her what she should have done already. He must have known she was in love with him, and yet he was the one who warned me that there was a limit to her loyalty, and that, if she thought she had to, she would not hesitate to abandon and perhaps even betray him.

I had the feeling that Roth was right, that she might eventually leave him, but not because of some cold assessment of her own self-interest. It was not that she was incapable of looking to her own advantage. She had that gift, not dissimilar to Stanley Roth's gift, of knowing instinctively the next thing that was going to happen and which among the thousand different threads of power and influence would be the one that unraveled all the rest. If she had not been in love with Stanley Roth I think she might not have had any conscience at all. But she was in love with Stanley Roth, and she was not going to do anything that would jeopardize whatever chance she thought she had with him until she was either convinced he was never going to fall in love with her or something happened that simply gave her no choice.

Was that why she asked if we could have dinner tonight, I wondered as I watched her step out of her car and walk toward me in front of the Chateau Marmont? I was supposed to meet her in the lobby, but I liked watching her walk: I liked the way she looked, sleek and glistening in the golden light, moving toward me, one long leg in front of the other, blonde from head to toe. She saw me, and I knew what she was going to do next: She looked at me and kept looking at me, her mouth a half-mocking smile, the way a woman stares up at you while you help her out of the car so you won't look anywhere else, her eyes teasing you, laughing at you, with the knowledge of your temptation.

Julie took my arm and tugged thoughtfully on my sleeve. "You were great the other night."

I was still thinking about the way she had looked at me and what it had made me remember. And now this. I started to laugh.

"The way you reacted; the way you stopped Stanley before he could . . ." She shook her head, obviously still troubled by what had happened. "Stanley was crazy. I've never seen him like that before."

"Louis Griffin has," I said in a tone of voice that suggested I did not quite believe her. "Stanley has a temper. You know that as well as I do. You're the one who told me he might have killed his wife, remember? Might have done it in a rage–because of something she had done?"

Julie was looking down at the ground, holding my arm lightly with both her hands, idly swinging her foot.

"I know he has a temper," she replied, her eyes hidden beneath her lashes. "And I know what I said–about what he might have done. But the other night was the first time I've ever seen him actually try to hurt someone–physically. It surprised me."

Julie let go of my arm and raised her head. "I made a reservation."

The restaurant, small, but not too crowded, was tucked into a side street not far from Rodeo Drive. It was a few minutes past seven, and under the nighttime sky the stores, thronged with customers, were bursting with artificial, man-made light.

I ordered a scotch and soda. Julie thought for a moment, and then ordered one as well.

"I need this," she explained with a grim smile when the waiter returned with our drinks.

She took a fairly healthy dose of it, then put down the glass. Frowning, she searched my eyes.

"Can Stanley win?"

I tapped the edge of the table, wondering not so much about what might happen at the end of the trial as at the apparent urgency with which she wanted to know.

"It's important," insisted Julie, biting her lip.

I kept tapping the edge of the table, waiting for more.

"Blue Zephyr is finished." A look of confusion entered her eyes. "No, it isn't finished yet; but it may as well be. Stanley resigned. Apparently, he did it yesterday, late in the afternoon. He didn't tell me–he didn't tell anyone. Michael told me, this afternoon, before Stanley got back from court."

At first I could not believe it; not after what had happened the other night.

"He was ready to kill Michael Wirthlin for even suggesting it; now he's gone ahead and done it? What for?"

Even as I asked the question, I began to suspect the answer. It was precisely because of what had happened the other night. By attacking Wirthlin, Roth had put himself into Wirthlin's hands; and Wirthlin, it had become all too apparent, would not hesitate to exploit any weakness he found. It was not difficult to guess what Wirthlin had threatened to do.

Julie had not guessed; she had not thought about it. Her mind was on other things.

"I don't know why he did it," she replied absently.

She took another drink. A look of distaste spread over her rather wide mouth. Shoving aside the glass, she beckoned the waiter. She ordered a glass of wine to replace the scotch, then changed her mind and, with a glance at me to see if I would share it, told him we wanted a bottle.

"I have to make a decision," said Julie, laying her head back against the leather booth. "Michael plans to reorganize everything. He wants me to be in charge of day-to-day operations. He's offered to make me head of the studio."

The waiter arrived with a bottle of Artessa Pinot Noir. Julie tasted it, nodded her approval, and waited while he filled our glasses.

"Take it," I said with indifference.

She seemed surprised.

"You don't think Stanley can . . . ?"

"Win? What does that matter?" I was a little annoyed at being asked what I thought was going to happen to Stanley Roth by people who were interested only in how it would affect them. "All right, you asked. He's going to win. He's going to be acquitted," I announced with all the confidence I could muster. "He didn't murder Mary Margaret Flanders. I thought you knew that."

Julie's eyes flashed with anger, but only for an instant. She bent forward, glancing around the restaurant to make sure no one was close enough to overhear.

"I don't know that; I don't know anything, except that I'd rather take my chances with Stanley Roth–even if he doesn't have the studio–than with anyone else in this town. But if he isn't acquitted, then . . ."

I sat back, my hands at my sides, watching her struggle with the sudden realization that whatever she did might be a mistake. Without much sympathy, I summed up her dilemma:

"You can take your chances: leave with Roth, show everyone how loyal you are; or you can stay where you are and become head of the studio. It's a great-sounding title, and without Stanley Roth the only person you would have to deal with is Michael Wirthlin. He may be difficult, but probably nothing like as demanding as Stanley Roth. And besides, you probably know more about this business than anyone except, maybe, Stanley Roth himself. Has he asked you to stay with him, to leave the studio?" I asked abruptly.

"No," replied Julie; "but he'll expect it."

It was none of my business what she did, and that was the reason that I now told her the truth: that I could not even hazard a guess what the jury might ultimately decide, weeks from now, when the trial was finally over. She nodded as if she had known it all along, and I suspect she had. I think the only reason she had asked was to confirm that very point, to be sure about the precise extent of her uncertainty as she measured the risk Stanley Roth expected her to take.

Julie shut her eyes and pressed her lips together. Her body tensed and a shudder passed through her. She opened her eyes, and with an icy, malicious stare directed at some imaginary figure sitting next to me, remarked:

"I've done things for him I never thought I'd do for anyone."

She kept staring at that spot, but the malice in her eyes was replaced with the look of someone who has made a decision and, having made it, wonders why it had taken them so long to do it. When her eyes came back round to me, a smile had begun to form at the corners of her mouth, an easy, teasing smile, as if she did not have a care in the world. She sipped on the wine, and as she did, the glow came back on her cheeks.

"I'm not really hungry. Are you?" she asked. Her voice was soft, insistent, with none of the tortured self-doubt that had been there just a few minutes before. "Let's go somewhere else," said Julie with a rush of enthusiasm.

We left the restaurant and without a word about where we were going or what we were going to do, Julie began to drive. We drove for miles, part of an endless caravan of yellow-eyed machines sailing through the purple crystal night, making our anonymous way across what not that many years ago had been a vast forgotten desert on the western edge of the civilized world.

There had been something I had wanted to ask her, something I was certain she knew.

"What happened to Louis Griffin's daughter? He told me she died, but the way he said it . . ."

"Louis likes you," said Julie, her eyes, blue and shiny, fastened straight ahead. We had left the freeway and a few turns later had entered a narrow, winding road that led into the Hollywood hills. "He doesn't talk about that with anyone," continued Julie. "She was killed."

"Murdered?"

"Yes."

"When?"

"Six years ago next month."

Julie's eyes stayed fixed on the road. She did not glance across at me; she did not make any gesture by which to show how she felt. She spoke quietly, concisely; careful, as I thought, not to say anything more than she had to.

"She was murdered–six years ago? Why didn't I read anything about it?"

"I suppose because Louis Griffin isn't Stanley Roth. It was in the papers; it's just that it wasn't on the front page, and it never became a major story.

Not many people outside the industry know who Louis is. The police never found the killer, so there was nothing else to report, nothing else to cover. And besides," she added in a cryptic tone, "Louis didn't want any publicity. No one did."

Sensing my confusion, Julie explained:

"His daughter–Elizabeth–was kidnapped. She was a sophomore at USC. They think it must have been someone she knew, at least knew well enough to get into a car. One of her friends saw it happen, saw her get into the car late on a Friday night, a few blocks from campus. They asked for a million dollars; made the usual threats about not bringing in the police. Louis did what he was told–or, rather, Stanley did. Louis was going to call the police, but Stanley told him not to take the risk. Stanley got the money–it was his money–and he paid it. He took it to where it was supposed to go, left it where he was supposed to leave it. They killed her anyway. They left her body in a place where it wouldn't be found for a long time. Poor Louis, he had to identify her. He's never gotten over it, and I'm afraid he never will. He never talks about her–ever. And you have to know that he thinks about her all the time. She was his whole life."

"Does he blame Roth–for convincing him not to call in the police?"

"No, he doesn't blame Stanley at all. Stanley loved her almost as much as he did. He doesn't blame Stanley, but Stanley does. To this day he thinks it's his fault; that if he hadn't talked Louis out of calling the police, Elizabeth would still be alive."

Julie turned to me, and with her eyes asked for a promise.

"No one knows any of this. I only know it because one night, years ago, I found Stanley late at night in the bungalow, drunk and crying and he told me then. You can't ever . . ."

"No, of course not," I assured her. "But that wasn't the reason Griffin didn't want any publicity. He wasn't trying to conceal the fact that he had paid the ransom instead of calling in the police or the FBI?"

"He didn't want it to happen to anyone else. Look, everyone here is vulnerable. All these famous people, walking around, going places, out in the open; their children going to school; and all those lunatics out there who want to get famous or want to get rich–Louis didn't want someone like that to find out just how easy it was, how easy to take a girl off the street, make all that money and get away with it. Stanley thought they ought to do everything they could to let everyone know what happened. He thought it might help find whoever killed her. But by that time the last thing he was going to do was tell Louis he was wrong."

We kept driving along the narrow road, past clusters of small houses tucked away in the hills, until we came to a cottage set back in a tangle of manzanita trees.

"This is where I live," announced Julie as she pulled into the carport and turned off the engine.

When we got inside, Julie poured me a drink.

"Tomorrow's Friday," she said as she sat on the sofa beside me. "I thought I'd drive up to Santa Barbara for the weekend. There's a place I go up there when I have things I need to think about."

She pulled one knee onto the sofa and rested her arm against my shoulder.

"Why don't you come with me?" She smiled, and then added: "Or do you have to go back to San Francisco?"

At that moment I did not want to go anywhere. She took the glass out of my hand and put it down on the coffee table. She took my hand and got to her feet.

"In the meantime, why don't you stay here tonight? I promise to get you to court on time," she said in a low, husky voice as we began to walk toward the other room.

18

STANLEY ROTH WAS NOT ANGRY at all. If anything, he seemed a little amused.

"You didn't show up last night," he said as I settled into the chair next to his. I removed from my briefcase a black loose-leaf notebook and a yellow legal pad.

"It was late when I finished dinner," I explained, rapidly scribbling a note about something I wanted to ask the prosecution's next witness. "And I still had a lot of work to do."

I kept my eyes on the sheet of paper in front of me, watching my hand race across the page, leaving in its wake the scratch marks of my indecipherable scrawl. For a while Roth did not say anything; but I could feel him watching me. I knew he did not believe me.

"Just remember what I told you about her," he said presently.

I stopped writing. With the pen poised to resume its work, I turned my head. He was not giving me a warning to stay away from her; he certainly was not threatening to do something if I did not. He was telling me to be careful around a woman who could be trusted only within limits, if she could be trusted at all.

Stanley Roth expected loyalty and he expected sacrifice, and he was too convinced of his own importance and the importance of what he did to imagine anyone could think him a hypocrite, or learn that they had better look out for themselves, each time he discarded someone he decided was no longer necessary or useful. I knew I could not fully trust Julie Evans, but it was not because of anything Roth had ever told me. I had become more involved with her than, for a lot of reasons, I should have; so involved, I'm afraid, that whatever regrets I might have about it were not likely to stop me from seeing her again. I was the willing prisoner of my own lingering illusions about what I thought I could still be in the eyes of a beautiful young woman.

"I'll keep that in mind," I said rather brusquely to Roth.

I quickly finished the note I was writing to myself, and then put down the pen. Pushing my chair back at an angle, I bent toward him so none of the jurors who were twisting into their places in the jury box could hear.

"Why did you resign?" I asked, peering intently into his pale blue eyes. "Did Wirthlin threaten to tell the D.A. what happened the other night?"

There was no response. Roth started to look away.

"Wirthlin is the prosecution's next witness." With a slight backward movement of my forehead, I gestured toward Annabelle Van Roten at the counsel table behind me. "She told me yesterday there was a rumor that what happened to me was not an accident. Where do you think she heard that?"

The jury was finally seated. Roth turned away from me, facing them. In the first row, the third juror from the left, a woman in her early thirties who had once done a little acting and whose smooth, well-shaped hands had appeared in several soap commercials, smiled discreetly. She began to converse with the juror next to her, a heavyset, middle-aged woman. Roth placed his arms on the table and tapped his fingers together. On the bench, Judge Honigman arranged the case file, getting ready to start the day's proceedings. Below him, the clerk crossed her arms and retreated into a daydream of her own. I put my hand on Roth's shoulder and did not let go until he turned around.

"I need to know," I whispered insistently. "What is he going to say? Is he going to tell the jury that you tried to kill him?"

Reluctantly, Roth shook his head from side to side. "I don't know what he's going to say, but he won't say that."

He said it with a kind of paid-for certainty, and we both knew what the price had been. I started to say something, but Roth stopped me.

"He was not supposed to say anything. No one was supposed to know about the studio until the trial was over. But he couldn't wait to tell Julie, and then Julie told you."

The sound of shuffling papers came to a stop. Rudolph Honigman cleared his throat. While he invited Annabelle Van Roten to call the next witness for the prosecution, I tried to remember everything I could about Michael Wirthlin.

Perhaps it had been just a rumor, something Van Roten had heard, something she had used to see what reaction she could get from me; perhaps it had been a rumor started by Wirthlin himself, forwarded to the district attorney's office through some anonymous informant to gain what leverage he could with Stanley Roth. Van Roten did not use it. She asked Wirthlin a great many questions, but she never asked him if he had ever been assaulted by Stanley Roth. Wirthlin had extracted a high price for his silence; too high, I thought, not to see how far he would lie.

Wirthlin was on the stand most of the day, answering questions, some of them quite technical, about the financial condition of the studio and the arrangements that had been made to insure against the possibility of the death or incapacity of its leading star. Used to well-appointed, softly lit rooms, it had taken him a while to adjust to the glaring lights of the crowded and numbingly utilitarian courtroom. At first, he kept glancing nervously at the jury; astonished, I think, that this was what real people looked and dressed like. He seemed to be afraid that simply by being there he might be mistaken for one of them. When it was my turn to take the witness, I asked him if he wanted a glass of water; I think he would have preferred that I had asked him if he wanted to wash his hands.

"Mr. Wirthlin," I began, still sitting in my chair, "you've testified that the studio, Blue Zephyr, in which you're one of the partners, is in some financial difficulty; and that it has in fact lost a great deal of money over the last several years."

Through narrowed eyes, I peered at him as if I were trying to reconcile an apparent inconsistency in what he had said. Using my left hand for support, I rose slowly from the chair.

"You testified that most of this money was lost because of projects directly involving Stanley Roth."

I stepped carefully to the end of the counsel table closest to the jury box and directly to the right of where Roth had been sitting all day, watching his partner contribute without any obvious reluctance to the case against him.

"The last three or four pictures of Mary Margaret Flanders–the last three or four released while she was still alive–lost money. Isn't that what you testified?"

"Yes, that is what I testified," replied Wirthlin matter-of-factly. He lifted his head and sniffed the air. Then he lowered his eyes and began to study, one by one, his manicured nails.

"The studio was in danger of going bankrupt?"

Wirthlin glanced up. "It could have come to that."

In the small space in front of the witness stand I began to pace: three steps to the court clerk's desk, where I immediately encountered a sullen, possessive stare, and three steps back. Three steps in any direction and I was in danger of stumbling into something. I shook my head in embarrassment. A couple of the jurors smiled knowingly. I pulled myself straight up, turned sideways to the witness, and faced the prosecutor.

"Apparently, Ms. Van Roten is attempting to establish a motive; though, frankly, it is still a little unclear to me what it might be."

Annabelle Van Roten sat back in her chair, resting the side of her face on the tapered fingers of her left hand.

"The studio was losing money. Then Mary Margaret Flanders was killed and two things happened: the insurance policy the studio carried on her paid off; but far more important, the picture–what everyone now knew would be the last picture Mary Margaret Flanders would ever make–was a huge financial success."

Slowly, and as it were, reluctantly, I turned away from Annabelle Van Roten and again faced Michael Wirthlin.

"The suggestion, I guess, is that Stanley Roth murdered his wife to save his studio. Is that the way you see it, Mr. Wirthlin? Stanley Roth murdered his wife because it was the only way he could keep Blue Zephyr?"

Though my back was to her, I could hear the chair scrape along the hard linoleum floor as Annabelle Van Roten rose to object. Before the words were out of her mouth, I waved my hand in the air, signaling my contrition. Quickly, I retrieved a document from the file folder on the counsel table.

"Would you look at the last page and tell us if that is your signature?"

I handed him the document and waited while he glanced at the bottom of the page where he had signed his name.

"Yes, that's my signature," he said as he let the document hang limp in his hand.

"Not Stanley Roth?"

"No, I negotiated the contracts."

"In fact, you insisted on that, didn't you?"

"I was the chief financial officer. That was–is–part of my job."

"But you didn't decide that Mary Margaret Flanders–or anyone else–was going to be cast for a part in a Blue Zephyr film. Stanley Roth–or some other producer or director–made that decision. Then you worked out the details–the financial details–correct?"

"Yes, to a point." Wirthlin was anxious not to be thought as having had no role in the more creative side of the business. "In any major picture–with any major star, we–I mean, Stanley and I and a few other people as well–would usually talk about what kind of budget we had to work with, who among the people we wanted might fit within that budget. Sometimes, if the project was particularly interesting, we might be able to get someone for less money up front in exchange for a percentage of the gross. So it wasn't, you see, like a lot of other businesses where you need to hire someone and you call up personnel and tell them to find someone. We were all involved in deciding who it should be and how much we should spend."

I looked over at the jury and smiled; then I turned back to the witness.

"I see. And you were all involved–weren't you?–I mean, you and Stanley Roth and Louis Griffin–in the decision about what to do with Mary Margaret Flanders's last picture, the one she didn't finish, the one she was making when she was killed."

"Yes, we were." Wirthlin furrowed his brow. "It was a very difficult decision," he added in a voice designed to emphasize the solemn nature of the task.

I stared at him, incredulous. "Oh, but it wasn't difficult for you at all, Mr. Wirthlin!" I insisted forcefully. "You knew right from the beginning that you wanted the picture finished. You knew from the beginning that you wanted that picture–Mary Margaret Flanders's last picture–released as soon as possible. Difficult? It wasn't difficult, Mr. Wirthlin; not for you, anyway. You were the one–not Stanley Roth, not Louis Griffin–who insisted it had to be put out while the public was still mourning her death; had to be put out before she was forgotten; had to be put out, Mr. Wirthlin–and I believe these are almost the identical words with which Stanley Roth described to your face what you wanted–'before the public became more interested in his murder trial than in her last picture.' Isn't that true, Mr. Wirthlin? Aren't you the one who, more than anyone else–certainly more than Stanley Roth–was concerned about how to make money from her death?"

Van Roten was on her feet before I had finished, objecting as strenuously as she could.

"The witness isn't on trial, Your Honor! If Mr. Antonelli has a question, let him ask it–but this kind of personal attack has no place . . ."

Honigman raised his hand, letting her know she had said enough.

"Mr. Antonelli, perhaps . . ."

"I'll rephrase the question," I replied, my gaze still fixed on Michael Wirthlin.

"Would it be fair to say that you were in favor of finishing Mary Margaret Flanders's last picture as quickly as possible?"

The ferocity with which I had come after him had taken him somewhat by surprise. He planted both feet on the floor, hunched his shoulders and eyed me with suspicion. He listened to the question carefully.

"A great deal of money–nearly a hundred million dollars–had been invested in that picture. When Ms. Flanders died, there were still several scenes left to shoot, but it was almost finished. We had to finish it: Too much money had been spent to stop."

Growing more confident as he spoke, Wirthlin straightened his shoulders and raised his head. He turned to the jury.

"We also thought it was the best picture Mary Margaret had made. We thought we owed it to her public to make sure it was finished."

"You haven't answered my question, Mr. Wirthlin." I paused long enough to let him know I was going to insist that he did. "You wanted to finish it as quickly as possible, didn't you?"

"Yes."

"Because you wanted it released as soon as possible?"

"Yes; I thought it was important that her public not have to wait to see her last, best picture."

"Important for the public," I remarked, smiling in admiration at the way he made it all sound so utterly noble and disinterested. "And important for the studio as well, wasn't it? You had to know, didn't you, Mr. Wirthlin–a shrewd businessman like yourself–that with everyone still talking about her death her last picture had to be a huge box-office success? You knew that, didn't you?"

"I thought people would want to see it–yes."

"Not everyone agreed, though, did they?"

"That people would want to see it?" he asked with a superior smile.

"Not everyone agreed that it should be released as early as it was. Your other partner, Louis Griffin, didn't think it should be released until after this trial was over. Isn't that right, Mr. Wirthlin?"

"There were discussions, but in the end we all agreed on when it should be released."

"Louis Griffin objected, didn't he?"

"Louis had some reservations."

"Some reservations?" I repeated skeptically. "He thought the early release of that film might have an adverse effect on this trial, didn't he? He thought it might add to the already existing atmosphere of suspicion and doubt that always surrounds a defendant in a murder trial. He thought it would hurt Stanley Roth's chance for a fair trial. Isn't that right, Mr. Wirthlin?" I demanded energetically.

"We couldn't be concerned with that!" Wirthlin shot back. "It was a business decision. Stanley agreed. Stanley insisted on it."

Drawing back a step, I placed my hand on the jury box railing and cocked my head, as if he had said something that made it necessary to look at him from a new perspective. I narrowed my eyes and slowly stroked my chin.

"Stanley Roth insisted on it because he wanted to save the studio, even if it meant it would jeopardize his chance for a fair trial?"

It took him a second fully to grasp the implication of the question I had just asked.

"He said–and I believe you said the same thing–that it was impossible to tell what effect–or whether it would have any effect at all–on the outcome of the trial."

"In other words, he was willing to take that chance–a chance that could cost him his life–because his wife's last picture, if released early enough, would help save the studio?"

"Yes."

"And so were you–ready to take a chance on his life . . . to save the studio, weren't you?"

"Your Honor!" protested Annabelle Van Roten from the table behind me.

"Withdrawn," I shouted back. I folded my arms across my chest, crossed one foot over the other, and for a few moments gazed silently at the floor.

"You've known Stanley Roth for quite some time, haven't you?" I inquired, shoving my hands deep into my pants pockets. Without raising my eyes, I waited for his short, one word answer and then asked the same question about Mary Margaret Flanders.

"And did they love each other?" I asked, looking up at him.

He struggled to find an answer, and I asked him again.

"That's a little difficult for me to say. I imagine they must have, but I'm not sure I'm in a position to know what either one of them felt about the other."

I lowered my eyes and began to move the tip of my right toe from side to side, sliding it back and forth over the gray cracked linoleum floor. It was warped along the edge, pulling back from the bottom of the jury box railing, leaving behind a narrow gap filled, as I now noticed, with a greasy layer of dirt and dust. A tiny spider, reddish brown and not much bigger than the flat end of a pin, waited motionless just inside.

"You were with the two of them on occasion–had dinner with them; were at various social and charitable events with them?"

"Yes."

"You were a guest in their home?"

"Yes."

"They were guests in your home?"

"Yes."

"And you also knew them, of course, not just as a couple, but individually: Stanley Roth because he was your partner; Mary Margaret Flanders because she was a motion picture star with whom you worked professionally. And yet, you still can't tell us," I asked, moving my arm in an expansive gesture toward the jury on my right, "whether they loved each other?"

He started to answer with the same kind of evasive, indecisive testimony he had given when I had asked him before. Out of patience, I cut him off and changed the question.

"Did they in your presence ever engage in acts of affection? Did they ever, for example, hold hands?"

With an awkward smile, he said he was certain they had. He was also certain that he had seen them with their arms around each other. He admitted that on a number of occasions he had witnessed Mary Margaret Flanders kiss her husband.

"Usually on the side of the face," he added for no apparent reason. "Mary Margaret was a very affectionate person. She often kissed people on the side of the face."

"So they were–at least outwardly–affectionate?"

"Yes, they were."

"Let's come at this from another point of view," I said, my head down, scuffing the floor with the tip of my shoe. I looked up. "Did you ever see him hit her?"

"No," replied Wirthlin, somewhat startled by the question.

"Did you ever see him try to hit her?"

"No."

Pulling my hands out of my pockets, I moved close enough to put my right foot on the step below the witness stand. I put my left hand on my hip and peered directly into his eyes.

"Has Stanley Roth ever hit you?"

His eyes darted past me to Stanley Roth at the counsel table and then, quickly, came back to me.

"No, of course not."

"Has he ever tried to hit you?"

There was a slight twitch on his lower lip, an involuntary reaction to the lie he was about to tell; but I was the only one close enough to see it. His eyes seemed to grow smaller, as if trying to withdraw to a place of safety.

"No."

"Have you ever–even once–seen Stanley Roth engage in an act of violence?"

It was all he could do to stop himself from blurting out the truth. I could see it in his eyes, how much he wanted to strike back: to tell the world what Stanley Roth had tried to do to him just the other night; to tell the world how violent Stanley Roth could be.

"No, I have not."

Wirthlin had kept his end of the bargain he had made with Stanley Roth. It had not occurred to him–or to Stanley Roth, either, for that matter–that their agreement had nothing to do with me. I had not given a promise to anyone about anything, and I was far beyond the point where I had the least interest in helping either one of them keep theirs.

I walked the few short steps to the counsel table and poured myself a glass of water. Everyone was watching, waiting to see what I was going to do next, when I finished drinking and resumed the cross-examination of Michael Wirthlin. My eye wandered around the courtroom. There were none of the blank stares seen on the upturned faces of a crowded movie theater; none of the dull-eyed vacancy of someone gazing at a television screen. These people were alive: interested spectators fully engaged by the questions, the answers; following not only the words, but the looks, the gestures that accompanied them and sometimes changed their meaning. As I put down the glass my eye settled for a moment on Louis Griffin, sitting in the same first row seat that seemed always to be waiting for him. A brief smile crossed his lips. I smiled back, and then, without quite knowing why, tried to warn him with my eyes. I did not want him to be taken by surprise–or, rather, I did not want anyone to notice if he was–by the question I was now about to ask Michael Wirthlin.

"Tell me, Mr. Wirthlin," I said, slowly turning toward the witness stand, "are you familiar with *Blue Zephyr*?"

He spread open his palms and shrugged his shoulders. "Could you be a little more precise? It's a very large studio, and I'm not sure . . ."

"Not the studio, Mr. Wirthlin–the movie, or rather the screenplay for the movie. The movie Stanley Roth wants to make."

"Oh, that. Yes, I'm familiar with it."

"Have you read it?"

"No. Stanley–Mr. Roth–has been working on that off and on for some time now. I believe he has shown parts of it to a few people at the studio; but, no, I haven't read it."

"Do you know what the story is about?"

Wirthlin waved his hand, a gesture of uncertainty, and then shook his head. "Something to do with the business–the movie business, I mean."

"Yes, you could say that," I remarked as I stepped out from behind the counsel table and took a position at the end of the jury box farthest from the witness stand. "But he called it *Blue Zephyr*, didn't he? You just now said that you'd heard of it. That suggests–doesn't it?–that you must have known, or must have guessed, that it had something to do, not just with the movie business, but a very specific part of the movie business–a single studio, for example."

"I think it was just a working title. I doubt that is what he was going to call it if it ever actually got made," explained Wirthlin with a dismissive air.

"No, Mr. Wirthlin; it's more than a working title. I've read *Blue Zephyr*."

Out of the corner of my eye, I could see Stanley Roth shifting position, leaning forward, resting his right elbow on the table. With his thumb under his cheekbone and the other four fingers of his right hand spread across his forehead, he stared straight down, trying not to show the jury or anyone else what he felt.

"*Blue Zephyr*, Mr. Wirthlin, is the story of two men who are partners in a studio–a studio just like Blue Zephyr. It is the story of how one of them betrays the other: first by sleeping with the other's movie-star wife; and then by pulling out his own financial support from the studio to create one of his own, one in which the woman he wants–his partner's movie star wife–can do what she likes. I have read it, Mr. Wirthlin. It's an extraordinary story. It's certainly the best thing I've ever read about how Hollywood really works. How much of it do you imagine is based on fact, on things that actually happened to Stanley Roth?"

Wirthlin's mouth stretched into a taut, thin line, like a rubber band ready to snap back, stinging whatever it hits.

"I wouldn't know. I told you: I haven't read it."

Smiling and unperturbed, I wagged my finger.

"But the first part is true, though, isn't it? You did sleep with Stanley Roth's wife, didn't you?"

His eyes still fixed on the table below him, Stanley Roth began to rub his forehead with his fingers.

"Answer the question, Mr. Wirthlin! You're under oath. Did you or did you not sleep with Mary Margaret Flanders while she was married to the defendant, Stanley Roth?"

"Relevance, Your Honor!" demanded Annabelle Van Roten as she rather wearily got to her feet.

"Relevance?" I exclaimed, casting a mocking glance in her direction. "Let me count the ways. First, it goes to the bias of the witness; second, it goes to the issue of who besides the defendant might have had a motive; third . . . well, how many more reasons does the court require?"

Honigman folded his hands in front of him, nodding thoughtfully, as if he had been asked to make some Solomon-like decision instead of rule on a simple, straightforward question of evidence.

"I'll allow it," he said, nodding one last time to underscore the finality of it.

I looked at Wirthlin and waited.

"We were very good friends." His voice, when he said it, was richer, deeper, than it had been. I had heard him use that voice before, the cultured, definitive sound of his considered judgment, the final statement that brought all discussion to a close.

"Is that a yes or a no, Mr. Wirthlin?" I asked impatiently.

"I think that's all I care to say about it," replied Wirthlin, sitting back in the witness chair.

"Your Honor!"

Honigman leaned across the bench. "The witness will answer the question."

Wirthlin did not move.

"Or the witness will be held in contempt. That means, Mr. Wirthlin, that you will sit in jail until you decide to answer the question you have been asked."

"Yes," angrily snapped Wirthlin. "I slept with Mary Margaret. What of it?"

"You slept with your partner's wife. So that part of the screenplay is true, isn't it? Now, the second part, remember, is that this same partner–the one who slept with the other one's movie-star wife–wants a studio for his very own. He doesn't want a partner anymore, certainly not the one he has, the husband of the woman he wants. Tell us, Mr. Wirthlin, is this part true as well? You slept with Stanley Roth's wife. Did you also want Stanley Roth's studio?"

"Your Honor!" cried Annabelle Van Roten. "This is . . ."

Honigman did not take his eyes off the witness. "No, I'll allow it."

I bore in on Wirthlin, taunting him, daring him to deny it. "You did, didn't you? You wanted the studio; you wanted Blue Zephyr. You wanted it so bad you were willing to do anything to get it, weren't you?"

"No, that's not true," protested Wirthlin vigorously.

"That's not true? You didn't, just two days ago, demand that Stanley Roth resign? Didn't you insist that because he was on trial for murder no one would want to do business with the studio: no investors, no important performers? You didn't tell him that if he didn't resign there wouldn't be any more financing, that Blue Zephyr would go bankrupt?"

Wirthlin was livid. He sat at the edge of the chair, grabbing the ends of it with all his might as if it was the only way to keep himself from flying out of it.

"That isn't the way it happened; that isn't what happened at all," he sputtered incoherently.

"But it is a fact–isn't it, Mr. Wirthlin?–that Stanley Roth has now done exactly what you demanded he do. Isn't it true, Mr. Wirthlin, that just yesterday, your partner, Stanley Roth, the man whose wife you were sleeping with, resigned, and that you, Michael Wirthlin, are now, for all intents and purposes, in charge of Blue Zephyr?"

Clenching his lips together as hard as he could, Wirthlin sat rigid on the edge of the chair, refusing to say another word.

"In *Blue Zephyr*, the movie star wife leaves her husband; but Mary Margaret Flanders did not leave Stanley Roth for you, did she? But it still all worked out for you, didn't it? You didn't get her, but neither did anyone else. She's dead, and because she's dead–and because her husband, and not somebody else, is accused of killing her–you get the studio. You get everything–don't you?–the fame, the power, all of it. And Stanley Roth? He's lost his wife, he's lost his studio, and, if he's convicted, he'll never be able to make *Blue Zephyr*, the movie that tells everyone what you did to him. So it isn't really too difficult to see precisely who benefited from the death of Mary Margaret Flanders, is it, Mr. Wirthlin?"

19

I SAT ON THE EDGE of the bed, staring at the telephone on the nightstand next to me. It was quarter past six in the evening and I told myself I had time to get out of my clothes, time to take a shower, time to collect my thoughts, time to talk myself into believing that I really did have too much work to do and that this weekend at least I had to stay here. I was supposed to be on the seven o'clock shuttle for the one-hour flight to San Francisco. Marissa always met me at the plane. I should have called from the courthouse during the lunchtime break, but my mind had been too full of the trial to think about the weekend or the lies I was going to tell. It had given me the perfect excuse to delay even longer the point at which I had to decide. It allowed me to indulge in the vain pretense that I would not make the call at all; that I would do what I was supposed to do–what part of me wanted to do–that I would get on the plane at seven o'clock, fly home for the weekend, and go on as if what had happened with Julie Evans the night before had not happened at all.

I picked up the telephone, quickly dialed the number and while it rang took a deep breath. My dismal gaze wandered across the bedroom to the sitting room. Strewn over a table, the various notebooks and files I used each night preparing for the next day in trial had the aspect of something in progress, something only briefly interrupted. I tried to feel all the fatigue of my imaginary labors. By the time Marissa finally answered the only thought in my mind was the single juxtaposition of the arduous, lonely task that awaited me here and the relaxed comfort of the house in Sausalito overlooking the bay. I had to make an effort not to sound too sorry for myself.

"I'm glad I caught you," I said. "I was afraid you might already have left."

Marissa was understanding, sympathetic, and did not seem to mind too much that I had to spend the weekend away. In my pathetic self-absorption I discovered I would have liked her to mind just a little bit more.

I lay on the bed, staring at the ceiling, relieved it was over and that it had not been nearly so difficult as I had feared. It had gone so easily it made me wonder whether Marissa might have suspected the truth, that I was seeing someone else. The thought seemed somehow unfair, as if it would somehow be more wrong of her not to trust me, than for me to deceive and betray her. But then I was used to my own imperfections and the way in which I had learned to overlook them. I suppose that was the reason I had not much liked the way Julie had asked whether I had to be in San Francisco when she invited me to Santa Barbara: it almost seemed as if she took a kind of pleasure, reminding me of my infidelity.

Outside the Chateau Marmont, I put my overnight bag on the sidewalk and in the reddish warmth of the evening sun waited for the first sight of the shiny white Mercedes. Julie was going to pick me up at seven. We would be in Santa Barbara by nine. I ran my fingers across the thick, rough trunk of a palm tree, and then brushed away a few dull splinters from my hand. Lazily, I walked a few steps, stopped, looked down the street, and then walked back. With my foot, I nudged the overnight bag, pushing it just an inch or so across the smooth cement. I checked my watch. She was ten minutes late. In Los Angeles, she could still claim to be early. My mind a blank, I kept watching the curving shadows of the palm trees as they slowly lengthened under the lavender sky. After a while I went into the bar.

A different couple than the one I had seen the night I had a drink with Julie played the same soft, laughing scene of seduction, eager to capture in the night all the illusions of their own enchantment. Before I realized it, I had finished a scotch and soda and ordered a second. I left the glass on the bar and went to the front desk.

"A Ms. Evans called," said the clerk with a cursory glance at the message. "She asked if you could call her at this number."

He handed me the square piece of monogrammed paper and pointed toward a phone booth opposite the far corner of the desk. I took two steps toward it, crumpled the message in my fist, and returned to the bar. I could grab a cab and catch a plane. I drank a little more scotch. There was a flight every hour, and though it was Friday, it was late enough that I could be sure of getting a seat. And if I didn't get one on the first flight, I'd certainly get one on the next. Even if I didn't get back before midnight, I would still have the weekend, and after everything that had happened—the trial, the collision with Stanley Roth, the concussion—it would be nice to be home for a few days. All I had to do was call the airline. I took another drink and checked my watch. It was eight o'clock. I finished what was left in the glass and went out to the telephone booth in the lobby.

I dialed the number, hesitated, and then waited while it rang.

"I'm sorry about tonight," said Julie in a hurried voice. "Something came up. I couldn't get away as early as I had hoped."

She did not sound particularly apologetic, and I did not feel especially understanding.

"I'm still at the studio," she explained when I made no reply. "I've got about an hour more I've got to do. I can be there by nine-thirty."

She paused, waiting for me to tell her that it would be all right.

"We'll still be up there before midnight," she added rather tentatively, her voice growing indifferent as my silence continued. "Or we could wait and go in the morning . . . Or not go at all."

"I have a lot of work to do myself," I said finally. "Tomorrow might be better. Why don't I call you then?"

The silence now came from her end. I could hear the slow rhythm of a pencil, or a fingernail, tapping against something hard, something glass or metallic.

"I think I'm going to go up tonight," said Julie abruptly. "I need to get away, and I like driving at night."

We drifted through another speechless space, a silent test of will, measuring not so much what we wanted from each other, but how much we—or at least I—was willing to do to have it.

"As I say, I have a lot of work to do myself and . . ."

"I'll be here for another hour or so," said Julie in a quiet, even voice. "If you change your mind."

There was still time to catch a plane to San Francisco. I looked at the overnight bag on the floor next to me, but suddenly the idea of going anywhere seemed to require more energy than I had left. I slid my shoulder under the strap and lifted the bag. Back in my room, I sat on the edge of the bed and stared glumly through the gauze-covered windows at the lights outside. With a deep breath that was nearly a sigh, I bent down and untied my shoes. Falling back on the bed, I closed my eyes, vaguely content that I was alone and had nothing I had to do. I let everything run out of my mind until the only thing I felt was a kind of warm, motionless ease as the tension, built up all day, slowly drained away.

The room was dark when I opened my eyes, the only light that which was flickering in from the street outside. I did not know how long I had been asleep, whether it had been a few minutes, or more than an hour. Switching on the lamp, I saw that I still had time. I searched in my pocket for the crumpled piece of paper on which the number had been written.

There was no answer. Julie was gone, and probably gone forever. She might wait for Stanley Roth, but she was not going to wait for me. There was nothing I could do about it now, and it was just as well. Though it was scarcely through any fault of my own, I had told Marissa the truth: I was staying in Los Angeles and I was going to spend all my time doing what I was supposed to do. While other people were out having a good time, I was going to be working on the defense of Stanley Roth, trying to find something that would help me save his life. Nothing is quite so comforting as the promise of your own virtue after you have just missed your last chance for vice.

Alone and silent, stooped over the table, watching my hand slip across the page, filling up one line after another, I worked for several hours straight, and though I was no closer than I was before to solving the mystery of who killed Mary Margaret Flanders, felt better for having done it. It was late when I finished, but I wanted to talk to Marissa, to tell her goodnight, to tell her how hard I had been struggling with what was fast becoming the most difficult case I had ever had. I wanted to hear her voice, the way it came, clear and bright, the tender, sweet music of her soul. Marissa did not answer and I wondered where she had gone.

I tried to go back to work, but I had gone through it so many times, thought about it so often, that I was in danger of making myself crazy with the sheer repetition of all the same facts and all the same questions.

It was after midnight and I was tired, but I knew I could not sleep. I stared at the telephone. Why wasn't Marissa home? If she had just gone out to dinner with a friend, why was she out so late? I picked up the receiver and called Stanley Roth. He invited me over.

"It's a little late," I replied, laughing softly to myself.

"Late for what? You called me."

"There were just a few things I wanted to ask."

"I've got a few things I want to ask you. Come on over."

Suddenly, I remembered what he had done.

"You're still there," I said stupidly. "At Blue Zephyr. How long do you have before you have to leave?"

"I told you before: no one was supposed to know until after the trial. But it doesn't matter. I don't have to leave. I keep the bungalow. It was part of the deal. I keep something else as well," added Roth with a note of satisfaction.

Whatever it was he had done, whatever price he had extracted for his resignation, he was not going to tell me about it on the telephone.

"I'm dead tired. I have to go to bed. But we need to get together."

I paused, trying to think how to put what I wanted to ask.

"I want to spend some more time at the house–your house–The Palms. And I want you there with me."

Roth had only one concern. The Palms had become a place where the curious still gathered to gawk at where Mary Margaret Flanders had been murdered, and if they no longer came in the same numbers they had in the immediate aftermath of her death, there were still enough of them that if Stanley Roth suddenly appeared, reporters and camera crews would not be far behind.

"Let's go early in the morning," insisted Roth. "There won't be so many people."

WHEN HE CAME for me the next morning the sun had barely climbed to the crest of the desolate desert mountain range that ran like a spur just a few miles to the east. Slanting sideways to the sea, the light turned the still air a pale yellow-gold.

Instead of the black limousine in which we had been chauffeured together back and forth to court, or one of the late model Mercedeses or Bentleys that dotted the studio's executive parking lot, a dilapidated, faded blue four-door Pontiac pulled up in front of the Chateau Marmont a few minutes before seven.

Roth looked as down and out as the car. He was wearing a faded green polo shirt as wrinkled as if he had slept in it, and the same nondescript tan windbreaker he had thrown on the night he had taken me from the bungalow at Blue Zephyr out to the beachfront park in Santa Monica. His pants ended high above his ankles, bare except for the straps of a pair of leather sandals. He had not shaved and he had not bothered to run a comb through the tangled mess of gray hair that flowed out from under a blue baseball cap. Small gold-rimmed black glasses fit snug against his eyes. He looked like an aging beachcomber, a hippie, a middle-aged man who still sees the world the same way he had when he was twenty-five. I would not have recognized him if I had passed him on the street, and anyone looking for a celebrity would not have looked at him at all.

Stanley Roth did not want to be recognized, not anymore. He had become, for a all intents and purposes, a prisoner, unable to go anywhere except his bungalow where he was safe behind the gates of the studio, and to the courthouse where every day he ran a gauntlet of obstreperous reporters and crude, catcalling spectators who, behind the police lines set up in front, taunted him with their insults and accusations. This early morning journey to the house he had purchased as a wedding present for his new wife, the house so famous it had a name of its own, the house that from now on would be known less for the movie star who had lived there than the one who had died there, was the closest thing to a holiday Stanley Roth had had in months. Who could blame him if he wanted to go his way undistracted by the cruel and thoughtless demands of strangers?

There was no one in front of the gates that guarded the entrance to The Palms. Roth swiped a magnetized plastic card through the narrow slot on the black metal box. It also housed the intercom by which visitors had to identify themselves before someone inside would activate the mechanism that opened the gate.

"You don't use the combination?" I asked, gesturing toward the key-pad located on the same metal box.

"This is faster," explained Roth with a shrug. He put the card back inside his wallet. "I don't even remember the combination."

"Who uses it, then? Who would you give it to?"

"A few people–not too many. Mainly people who worked here: the gardener, the pool man, the security people . . . a few friends. Louis, of course."

"Did Wirthlin have it?" I inquired as Roth drove toward the enormous brick-and-mortar mansion at the top of a long, twisting drive lined on both sides with thick Spanish date palms.

"Wirthlin was never a friend." Roth paused, a deeply cynical look on his face. "Not a friend of mine, anyway. But, no; I don't think she would have given him the combination."

He glanced across at me, the cynicism less severe, but for all that, leaving the impression of something that was a more permanent part of what he had now become.

"But you never know, do you?"

"You didn't . . . ?"

"Know about Wirthlin and Mary Margaret? Not until you dragged it out of him. Well, it had crossed my mind . . . when I wrote *Blue Zephyr*. I thought about what could happen between people like that: an actress who didn't want to think she owed her career to anyone, and someone rich and ambitious who would do anything to have her."

We pulled up to the front of the house and Roth turned off the engine. He lay back against the seat, with his eyes shut, rubbing the bridge of his nose. When he opened his eyes, he stared into the middle distance.

"Maybe I did know. Maybe that's how the idea–the thought of it–came to me." Roth turned to me, certain I would know what he meant. "The way you know something has changed without quite knowing what it is: a look, a glance, a kind of distance, a slight hesitation, a caution in the way someone talks–suddenly more careful." He paused, smiled, and then added, "Or far less careful, as if they wanted you to think they had no reason to conceal anything. I knew, I just didn't know that I knew–if that makes any sense–until you forced him to admit it."

Inside the house, Roth stood in the middle of the living room, pointing at the thick overhead beams.

"They came from an old castle, somewhere in Yorkshire, hand-hewn from English oak," said Roth, turning the corners of his irregularly shaped mouth into an appraising look. "Then, four hundred years later, a drunken actor who got famous and rich making movies no one remembered ten minutes after they saw them thinks he has to have a home that will be something to remember him by."

I left Roth in the living room and went outside and stood by the pool, gazing at the spot where Mary Margaret Flanders had been murdered. The pool had been drained to get rid of the blood. A little rain and the runoff from the sprinklers on the lawn had left a foot or two of water at the deep end. Dead leaves and debris, some of it scraps of yellow plastic tape that had been used to seal off the crime scene, had choked the drain. After a few minutes I went upstairs to her bedroom–their bedroom when Stanley Roth did not have to get up before dawn to get to the set. The clothes she had worn to the party had been accounted for: the dress was hanging in her closet; the shoes were on the rack where she kept them; the jewelry was back in the black velvet case inside the dresser drawer. There was not a rip, not a tear, nothing to suggest that someone had attacked her, torn off her clothes, and then, for some reason, neatly returned them to where she always kept them. She had taken off her clothes and was found naked in the pool. But if she had gone there to take a late night swim why had she not at least taken a towel? None had been found anywhere near the pool. She must have been meeting someone–or was already with someone. She did not go out to the pool to go swimming: she went out to the pool because it was far away from the upstairs bedrooms in which her husband was already asleep, and was the safest place on a warm California evening to make love–right there, on a chaise lounge, listening to the soft muffled sound of the water lapping gently against the edge of the pool.

But what about the stocking, the stocking found wrapped around her neck, the stocking used to hold her fast from behind while the blade of the knife flashed through her throat? Had she undressed in front of him–the man she was going to sleep with, the man who killed her–teased him with it, made him grab at it, and then, when he caught it in his hand, led him silently out of the bedroom, careful not to awaken her husband a few rooms away; led him down the hall, down the stairs, outside to the pool? Or had she undressed alone and taken it with her when she went outside, taken it because that was the sort of thing they did together, the way she taunted him, excited him?

I left the bedroom, following the path she must have taken, seeing it both ways in my mind: Mary Margaret Flanders, the only article of clothing the single stocking she held in her hand, a wisp of silk floating in the air as she descended the stairs–or pulled taut as someone clutched the other end tight in his hand. Alone, together, they both ended up here, at the side of the pool. They never got to the chaise lounge; they never fell into each other's arms. The police had been over everything, had searched everywhere for evidence of sex. It was the great unspoken mystery of her murder: Why didn't the killer have sex with her first? She was young, she was gorgeous, her picture had been on every magazine cover in America as the most desirable woman in the world, and the man who murdered her didn't touch her.

The police and the prosecution of course did not think it was a mystery at all: Stanley Roth killed her and that explained everything. It explained why she was naked, and it explained the stocking: she was getting undressed; they were having an argument; he grabbed her by the wrist and pulled her behind him down the stairs and outside. He took her stocking because he already knew what he was going to do to her. Or he tied the stocking around her throat and pulled her along that way. The stocking made the case for premeditation: It proved he did not kill her in a blind rage without any thought that he was going to do it. The stocking, and of course, the knife. He had not struck her with his fist, or picked up something and hit her with that. He had not in a moment of anger seized a gun that was lying within reach and shot her dead. No, Stanley Roth, according to the police and the prosecution, had tied that stocking around her neck and then with a knife he must have brought with him, cut her throat.

But if it was not Stanley Roth, if someone else had killed Mary Margaret Flanders, then the question was still there, waiting to be answered:

Why had she not been touched? Had she said something, out here, at the side of the pool, something that drove him–whoever he was–to a lethal act of violence? And if that was it, how had he happened to have a knife? That was the one fact that could not be gotten around: She was killed here, outside, next to the pool, with a knife. Whoever killed her had come here, to this place, with a weapon he meant to use; or brought it with him because he thought he might use it, but had not yet made up his mind. Could it have been an act of jealousy, an act of revenge? Had she decided to stop seeing someone, but then agreed to see him one last time–sleep with him one last time–and then, when he could not talk her out of breaking it off, he killed her because he could not stand the thought of her being with someone else, could not stand the thought that instead of leaving her husband, she was going to stay married to Stanley Roth? Perhaps he had already told his own wife he was going to leave her. Perhaps . . .

"Haven't you figured it out yet?"

Startled, I looked up. Stanley Roth was standing on the other side of the pool, leaning against the doorway, his arms folded loosely over his chest, one foot crossed over the other. A casual, almost indolent smile flickered across his mouth.

"You were concentrating so hard I thought you might forget where you were, take a step and fall in."

My eyes followed his to the edge of the pool, half a step from where I stood.

"You really haven't figured it out yet?" asked Roth, squinting against the sunlight that poured down from the blank white sky.

I moved back from the edge.

"No, I haven't figured it out," I admitted. "Why? Have you?"

"Yes," he replied, "I have."

With the baseball cap clutched in his hands, Stanley Roth took one last look around. He bent his graying head first to one side, then the other; surveying the scene the way I imagined he must have learned to measure a camera shot, studying the angle that would give it the meaning he wanted. His eye ran the same circuit three times at least: the doorway to the house; the sand-colored cement deck where his wife had been murdered; the pool, now empty, into which her body had fallen, or perhaps been thrown; and then, each time, darting back to the doorway to the house.

"Do you think it was Michael Wirthlin?" I asked across the empty weed-cluttered pool.

Roth was gazing intently at the doorway to the house. He did not hear me.

"You think Wirthlin killed her because she wouldn't leave you? You think he killed her and then decided to protect himself by framing you for the murder?"

If he heard me, he paid no attention. He looked across his shoulder, beyond the swimming pool to the close cut grass sloping toward the heavy, impenetrable shrubbery that covered from view the black spike fence on the perimeter of the property. I was not sure whether he was measuring the distance or imagining something that had taken place on the lawn itself. Retracing the path, his eyes came back to the pool. I started to ask again if he suspected Michael Wirthlin. He held up his hand to stop me before I could interrupt his thought.

When he finally looked at me, and he saw how irritated I had become, he put the cap back on his head and with a helpless shrug threw both hands in the air.

"Sorry.

"Have you seen everything you need to see?" he asked, suddenly anxious to leave. He looked down at the pool and shuddered. "I don't like coming back here." His gaze stayed fixed on the spot where, when it was full of water, his wife's body had been found. He put his hands in his pockets and slowly raised his eyes.

"I'm never coming back here again," solemnly insisted Roth. "When the trial is over, I'm going to sell it."

I was still waiting to hear whether it was Michael Wirthlin or someone else Stanley Roth was so certain had murdered his wife, but it was clear that he was not going to talk about it until we had left. When we got to the car, he handed me the keys and asked if I would drive. Though there had not been anyone at the gate when we arrived, he was certain there would be now.

He was right. Tourists and troublemakers, people who had come to stare and shrewd-eyed peddlers hawking T-shirts and buttons with short-worded slogans that ran from the mildly amusing to the utterly obscene, had gathered in front. By the time I was far enough down the driveway to see them, it was too late. The gate was opening and there was nothing I could do. Roth had climbed into the back and lay down on the floor, hiding beneath an old brown blanket he had brought along for that very purpose. I wished I had taken his advice and put on that awful-looking mustache and beard.

The crowd moved back as the gate opened, and then slowly parted as I eased the car into the street.

"It's the lawyer!" a voice cried out.

"Antonelli!" someone shouted.

The crowd began to surge forward, surrounding the car, those in front pushed by those behind. They were fighting with each other, grabbing the shoulders of the ones in front of them, trying to pull them away so they could get closer. One moment a woman in her fifties was right next to my window; the next moment she disappeared, and another face, a man in his forties, was pressed up against the door, laughing that he had won, that he was as close as a single pane of glass. They were all around me, clawing at each other, shouting, swearing, screaming, without any idea why they were doing it except that everyone else was doing the very same thing.

If I stopped, I might never be able to move; if I didn't stop, somebody was going to get hurt, thrown down in front of the car and perhaps even killed. I slammed on the brakes and leaned on the horn. The sudden stop, the sudden noise, stunned them. I rolled down the window and with all the calm I could summon smiled and said that if they did not want to be arrested and taken to jail they had better let me pass.

"How did you do that?" asked Roth, peeking out from beneath the blanket as we moved safely down the street. Making sure we were out of the sight of the crowd, he crawled into the front seat.

"I didn't think we were going to get out of there–not after they started shaking the car. How did you do that?" he asked again, straightening his jacket which had gotten all twisted up.

"They didn't know what they were doing," I explained as if it had been something I had thought about in advance. “So when I told them what to do, they didn’t have any reason not to.”

“Well,” he shrugged, “it worked.”

“You were a lot of help,” I remarked dryly.

Roth looked out the window. “You should have worn a disguise. You’ve become damn near as famous as I am.”

20

I STARTED TO DRIVE back to the Chateau Marmont, going the same way we had come. Roth continued to stare out the window, sunk into thoughts of his own. Suddenly, he sat up and in an unexpectedly cheerful voice suggested we go out to the beach.

"No, really," he insisted with a kind of boyish enthusiasm when I tried to beg off. "After what I did to you this week, least I can do is buy you lunch."

The beach Stanley Roth had in mind was not a place we were likely to encounter anyone he knew; or, for that matter, anyone who, if they had recognized him, would care that he was there. On Venice Beach, everyone was too preoccupied with their own absence of inhibition to notice much of anything about anyone else. Shining in the clear, sun-speckled air, girls with blue vacant-eyed stares and painted permanent smiles glided by on skates. The sight of those gorgeous barely dressed young women made me start to envy those bent-shouldered men with weathered faces who looked as if they never left the beach and, without all the troubles of normal, civilized life, had lost all sense of time.

We walked along, Stanley Roth and I, unrecognized, a part of the crowd, on the wide cement promenade separating the beach from the storefronts painted with reckless intensity every wild, lurid color in a box of crayons. On an asphalt court in the middle of the sand, shirtless tight-muscled young men whooped out loud as they floated in the air, flicking with their outstretched fingers a basketball high above the rim. A little farther on, broad-shouldered men with tiny waists and bulging bow-shaped legs grunted encouragement as they took turns raising iron bars that drooped at each end with circular weights. Out toward the edge of the sand, where the waves came in with barely a ripple, small children romped in the white, swirling ankle-high surf. Weight lifters, bodybuilders, jumpers, runners; young men, old men, middle-aged men with hair bleached blond by a shadowless sun; women and children; all of them in constant, smooth flowing motion; and everywhere that look, that blank-eyed smiling look of a single-season year in which there are no yesterdays and no tomorrows, only the limitless day stretching out forever, a permanent present, where the only things that matter are how you look and how you feel. Stanley Roth seemed right at home.

Roth jerked his head to the side and cut across the promenade. He stopped abruptly and with his hand held me back. Crouched low over her skates, a teenage girl, oblivious of everything except the music beating into her brain from the headset she wore, sailed past us like a missile launched from somewhere offshore. Roth dropped his hand, and with a few more steps we were in front of a dark green stucco building. A pink flamingo and a pale green palm tree flashed with neon brilliance in a small square window to the left side of the door.

Roth entered with the self-assurance of someone who had been here before. It took a moment for my eyes to adjust to the darkness. We were in a small bar and café. Four tables were jammed together along the wall directly opposite the bar, two more around the corner from it. The bartender, with wiry, unkempt gray-streaked hair, and tired, rheumy blue eyes, could have been as old as sixty or as young as forty. Wearing a blue and maroon Hawaiian shirt, he stood listlessly behind the bar, his hands in his pockets, like someone standing on a corner on a Saturday night waiting for something to happen. He seemed not to notice us at all until we sat down and put our elbows on the bar; then he greeted Stanley Roth the way you would a familiar stranger, someone you had seen often enough to know you had seen him before. That was all he knew. From the expression in his dull eyes, I doubted it would have meant anything to him if Stanley Roth had told him his name.

We each ordered a beer and he brought us two bottles. Mainly, I think, to see what he would do, I asked for a glass. He nodded, turned around, took a glass down from a shelf and set it down on the bar in front of my bottle. He did not ask Roth if he wanted one.

Smiling to himself, Roth raised the bottle to his mouth, took a swig, and then wiped his wet lips with the back of his wrist.

"Could we get a couple of burgers?" asked Roth, more at ease in this dark hole in the wall than I think I had ever seen him.

The thin arms of the bartender flapped inside the square sleeves of the Hawaiian shirt as he slowly shuffled along the raised latticelike wooden flooring to a greasy black grill.

"You won't get a hamburger like this in Beverly Hills," Roth assured me.

"I'll bet," I replied with a dry laugh.

Two girls, barely twenty years old, if that, had been watching from a table at the far end of the short bar, whispering to each other, laughing in a way that suggested one of them was eager to do something the other was not. They sensed I noticed. They stopped talking and their eyes drifted toward us and then stayed on us, waiting for a sign that we were interested. Biting my lip to stop the smile that was beginning to spread across my mouth, I poured what was left of the bottle of beer into my glass.

"Want to buy us a drink?"

I looked up. One of the girls was standing just behind me. I started to shake my head.

"Sure, why not?" said Roth. "What would you and your friend like?"

Roth gave the bartender the order, and we moved to their table. He introduced himself as Joe and I went along with it when he introduced me as Stan. In a maze of slow motion, the bartender placed two hamburgers on the bar and then, as if he had taken them ready made out of a refrigerator, the drinks Roth had ordered for the girls: iced glasses full of froth, dripping with the sweet scent of tropical fruit.

"Where you from?" asked Roth as he munched on his hamburger like a teenager out on a date.

The answers were vague and ambiguous, given with a kind of reluctance, as if where they came from, what they had done in the past, had no bearing on what they were now or what they wanted to become.

"The Midwest," said one.

"Back east," said the other.

Roth paused between bites. "What do you do?" he asked, searching the eyes of first one, then the other. I was surprised at how interested he sounded.

"We're actresses," said the one who called herself Shelley. She was blonde, good-looking, with cynical eyes. She had sharper features than her friend and was more assertive. She answered every question first.

"Not yet," quickly corrected the other one–Wilma, a quiet girl, with short brown hair and dark, rather mysterious eyes. A shy smile seemed to apologize for the embellishments of the other girl.

Roth put down the hamburger and leaned forward. "Maybe one of you will be the next Mary Margaret Flanders."

He said it calmly, without emotion, like an older, experienced man offering harmless encouragement to someone just starting out. In a way that I cannot quite describe, it was almost shocking, the utterly detached way he used his dead wife's name. He could have said Greta Garbo or Elizabeth Taylor or any of a dozen other famous movie stars and it would not have had anything like the same effect on me. But then, as I immediately realized, no other name would have had the same effect on these two young women. All pretenses at sophistication fell away; they were suddenly two starstruck girls.

"She was so beautiful!" uttered Wilma in a kind of ecstasy.

The other girl gave her a patronizing glance, and then, proud and defiant, turned to Roth. "Maybe I could."

I wondered if Roth was thinking about the way he had made Marian Walsh into a star, and if he thought he could do it again with a girl like this. How much different was she really from what Mary Margaret Flanders had been when he first found her? A little less educated, a little less polished? What did that really matter when other, far more fashionable people would decide what she would wear, and when every word that came out of her mouth would be written by someone else? The only question was how she looked–not sitting across a table in a dark, deserted bar–but through the lens of a camera.

"Maybe you could," said Roth, seeming to agree with her own view of what she might eventually do. "Did you see her last movie? I missed it. Was it any good?"

"It was wonderful!" said the other girl.

Her dark eyes shimmered with a kind of possessive pride, as if she had taken over and made a part of herself what she had seen. It was, I realized, the same look I had witnessed on those rare occasions when I had taken my eyes off the screen and glanced at the faces around me, so completely caught up in what they were watching they had forgotten that none of it was real.

The blonde girl, Shelley, was sipping on her drink through a straw, her gaze fixed on Stanley Roth. With a dry, rasping gurgle, she finished it. Teasing the end of the straw with her tongue, she waited for him to ask if she would like another.

"She was wonderful," continued Wilma with a furtive, sad-eyed smile. "I don't understand why her husband would have killed her, someone that beautiful, that nice."

"Because the guy's a jerk," exclaimed Shelley with a harsh, brittle laugh. "Because he wanted her money. Because she was sleeping around." She turned her head and confronted Wilma directly. "If you were her–you were that famous–wouldn't you?"

The question, which would have offended most of the women I had known–women, it was true, of a different generation–did not appear to offend this dark-eyed girl who had quite clearly idolized Mary Margaret Flanders.

"No," she replied very seriously. "I wouldn't throw it all away like that. Why would she? If she didn't love him, she wouldn't have married him."

Shelley's mouth, which could one moment break into a dazzling smile of artificial sincerity, tightened into a coarse, caustic grin. She gave her friend a pitying glance.

"She married him because he's Stanley Roth."

"I don't believe that," said Wilma, shaking her head with utter conviction. "And I don't believe he really killed her, either," she continued after a short pause. "He couldn't have done that–not to her. He loved her–he must have."

She lowered her gaze, a little embarrassed by how vehement she had become. "Don't you think he did–loved her, I mean?" she asked, raising her eyes.

She was looking at me, but I was not the one who gave her the answer she seemed almost desperate to have.

"I'm sure of it," said Stanley Roth with an air of quiet confidence. "And I don't think he killed her, either."

Shelley was not that interested in continuing a conversation that had nothing directly to do with her.

"What do you do, Joe?" she asked Roth. "Do you live here–in L.A.?"

Roth asked Wilma if she wanted another drink. She had barely touched the one she had. She thanked him and said no. Roth went to the bar and waited while the bartender produced from out of nowhere another Polynesian concoction and then brought it back to the table. With the straw in her mouth, Shelley smiled and with her blue eyes tried another flirtation.

"What do you do?" she repeated, squeezing the tip of the straw between two fingers. Her nails were painted pink.

Roth lifted the beer bottle and took a short drink. "I'm a movie producer," he said in an even voice, gazing back at her.

She laughed. "No, really," she insisted. "What do you do?"

He shrugged his shoulders. "I just told you: I'm a producer."

It threw her off. A shadow of a doubt crossed her eyes, but only for a moment. She was certain he was lying. What would a producer–or anyone famous–be doing in a place like this? Famous people–movie people–went to expensive private places in Beverly Hills. If she had seen him in a place like that, even with the dark glasses and the baseball cap pulled low over his eyes, and the rough gray stubble on his unshaven face, she would have known he was what he said he was, and known she had seen him somewhere before, and then, if she had not yet realized it for herself, recognized him at once when someone told her who he was, that he was the great Stanley Roth. But not here, not in a place where everyone made up stories about who they were and where they came from and what they were going to be.

"Come on," said Roth to me as he got up from the table. "We have to get going."

Shelley looked up from her drink, her lower lip pressed against the tip of the straw. "You want to go somewhere with us?" she suggested.

"We have to go," said Roth, turning toward the other girl. "I enjoyed talking to you. I'm sure you're right about Stanley Roth. I know you're right about Mary Margaret Flanders."

"Have to get back to the studio, huh?" said Shelley, concealing the disappointment of a failed seduction behind a taunting, knowing laugh.

Outside the bar, as we blinked into the blinding light, Roth remarked:

"She could be the next Mary Margaret Flanders." He sensed my doubt. "Not the blonde, the other one: the quiet one with the dark eyes. You notice that dreamy look, that way she has of drawing you toward her, of making you feel something about her, of wanting things to end up all right for her? You sympathized with her, didn't you? The other one–you almost want her to fall on her face. That's the difference. That's all it is–but you can't teach it, you can't produce it. You have it, or you don't. Mary Margaret had it–maybe more than anyone I ever knew."

I followed Roth as he walked onto the beach, my shoes sinking into the soft sand with each step I took. On a wooden bench next to a small playground where a couple of young boys were trying to see which could go higher on the swing set, Roth stretched out his legs and gazed idly toward the water's edge. The sun, barely started on its afternoon descent, seemed to burn a hole through the sky. Roth fell into a long, brooding silence. A beach ball bounced in front of us. A boy of five or six hurtled by in stumbling pursuit. Roth did not seem to notice. He kept staring with narrowed eyes at some point in the distance, working his jaw slowly back and forth.

"You asked me–back at the house–if I knew who killed Mary Margaret," said Roth finally and quite unexpectedly. "You really haven't figured it out yet?"

"Who do you think did it?" I insisted. "Wirthlin?"

There was nothing in his expression, nothing in the way he looked at me, that gave me so much as a hint as to what he thought. And from the next thing he said, I wondered if he had even heard the question, or whether, like an actor who knows only his own lines, he had been concentrating solely on what, as soon as I had finished speaking, he was going to say.

"You read *Blue Zephyr*. I told you I wanted to do something as good as *Citizen Kane*. I'll tell you a secret. Whenever I write a screenplay, I always start with the ending. I know what's going to happen–how it is going to end–before I start the beginning. I didn't do that with *Blue Zephyr*. I couldn't. I couldn't let the story take care of itself, because I started with the character, the main character. And because I wanted him to be like Kane–a modern day version of Kane–I had to let it, the character, develop by itself, so to speak. But then I couldn't decide how it should end–not exactly. You read it. There are two endings. They aren't that far apart: in both of them Welles dies, but in one he's murdered, and in the other he has a heart attack.

"I decided to go back to the beginning, work my way all the way through it–treat it like it was nothing but a rough first draft, instead of something finished except for that one little detail about which ending to use. That's when I realized that there was something missing: the action. Don't you see? The action. Welles can't just die. He has to be put into an impossible situation. He can't just have things happen to him–his movie-star wife leaving him to run off with his partner and start another studio–he has to have done something himself. He has to be accused of something. Welles doesn't die: his wife does."

I saw where he was going and I wondered why I had not thought of it before. Everything for Stanley Roth–even Stanley Roth–had meaning only when it could be told as a story, a story that could then be made into a movie.

"And Welles is accused of her murder," I said, finishing the thought. "And then Welles goes to trial. Is that the action you're talking about?"

Roth was eager to tell me more. I stopped him with a different question.

"Welles didn't do it. Who did?"

A cryptic smile flickered on his lips, like a secret that will tell you only that it exists. "Do you remember that other Orson Welles picture?"

I thought he meant the other one we had once talked about, *Compulsion*, but that was not it at all.

"*The Third Man*. It was made in Britain. They say it's the best British movie ever made." Roth shook his head in a kind of despair. "Welles was twenty-six–twenty-six, for God's sake!–when he made *Citizen Kane.* Then, seven or eight years later, he stars in *The Third Man.* I'm twice as old as he was when he made Kane and . . ."

He shook his head again, accompanied this time by a short, self-deprecating laugh.

"The camera angles were always at an angle. That sounds odd, but I mean it. Two people are having a conversation. The camera is on one of them–only one of them–and the camera is looking at that person, not straight in front the way you normally look at someone who is talking, but from an angle below, looking up; then, from above, looking down; and then tilted at a forty-five-degree angle. The effect is to isolate whomever the camera is on, show them in their individual characters; but also, to show things so nothing is ever seen the same way. And that of course is related directly to the action of the movie, to the mystery of the third man. You remember who the third man is? Three men carry away the dead body of Harry Lime after he is hit by a car. Two of them are identified. A witness sees the third man. Who is the third man? It is always there, right in front of your eyes–the third man. Remember?" asked Roth, a strange, almost mocking look in his eyes.

I wanted him to go on, but he said nothing more and so I asked what I had asked before: "Who is it? Who is the 'third man'? Who murders Welles's wife in the new version, Stanley? Who is 'right in front of your eyes'? Who murdered Mary Margaret?"

I think he had been getting ready for this moment, rehearsing it in his mind, since the first time I asked him, when we were still standing next to the empty pool where the dead body of his wife had been found.

"If I told you," he said as he rose from the bench, "it would ruin the movie."

21

THERE WAS TOO MUCH at stake for Stanley Roth to keep secret what might help to save his life, but every time I asked him who he thought murdered his wife, he started talking about the motion picture he was now more than ever determined to make. He would not tell me because he did not know, and all the rest of it, the look suggesting he knew things at which I could only guess, the reminder that he always knew the ending before he started the beginning, was just false bravado, an attempt to convince himself that he was still in charge, that he could still create a world of his own in which everything made perfect sense. The odd part was that I believed him, not that he knew who had done it, but that someone had. I wanted to think it was instinct, something infallible on which I could always rely, something acquired after years of testing the reaction, the response, of people accused of things they swore they did not do; but perhaps it was only a refusal to look facts in the face. Whatever the reason, I could not let go of the belief that Stanley Roth was innocent and that someone else had murdered Mary Margaret Flanders. No one else believed it, especially after the way things had been going at trial.

The second-guessing had begun the day I attempted to impeach the credibility of Jack Walsh by insisting that, contrary to his testimony, his daughter had reported her husband's assault to the police. No one could quite remember a case in which the defense attorney, instead of the prosecution, had insisted on portraying the defendant as someone fully capable of an act of violence. The criticism had been severe; but it was nothing compared to what all those attorneys turned television experts had to say after I helped the prosecution establish a motive of jealousy and rage by forcing Michael Wirthlin to admit that he had been sleeping with Stanley Roth's wife. I could almost feel them watching me, pencils in hand, all those lawyers who knew they should have had this case, waiting eagerly for their chance to show how much more they knew about how to conduct a defense.

The jurors tried to appear indifferent, but not all of them could entirely conceal their intense curiosity at the appearance of Walker Bradley. They might have heard of Michael Wirthlin–some of them might even have seen his picture in the society section of the local papers or inside the pages of a movie magazine–but all of them had watched Walker Bradley in the movies. Some of them must have felt about him the same way I had felt about Mary Margaret Flanders: a stranger more familiar to them than most of the people they knew. A young woman in the first row of the jury box, the one who had once darted a quick smile at Stanley Roth, leaned forward as Bradley took the oath. She could barely wait to see what he was going to do next.

The prosecution had called Bradley to testify about things that had happened during the filming of Mary Margaret Flanders's last motion picture, the one that had not yet been finished at the time she was murdered. Dressed as if she were meeting someone important for lunch, Annabelle Van Roten wasted little time getting to the point.

"This was not the first time you had worked with her on a motion picture, was it?"

Walker Bradley moved his head a little to the side. His mouth partly open, ready to reply, he waited until she had finished the question. Lacing together the fingers of his two hands, he tapped his thumbs against each other.

"No," replied Bradley in that whispered, hesitant voice that had made him famous. "We had been in five or six films before that."

Van Roten stood at the side of the counsel table, one high-heeled shoe pushed slightly in front of the other. She smiled demurely.

"Was there anything about the way she behaved–anything she might have said–that made you think she might be worried about something?"

With the same breathless look, Bradley waited until the last echo had faded away and he could step into the silence, knowing that every eye had now turned to him.

"Mary Margaret was always the complete professional," he explained, moving his head to face the jury. "She never let anything get in the way of her work. But this time, something was wrong. She had a hard time concentrating; she'd forget her lines; right in the middle of a scene, she'd burst into tears."

While he spoke, Van Roten stood off to the side, the sympathetic observer, waiting with the next question.

"And did you finally do something to find out why she was behaving in this manner? Did you try to find out what was wrong?"

Bradley had a gift for the anguished expression, the look of regret for failing to understand what no one could have known. It was a way of feeling bad for something completely out of your control, a way of showing compassion for other people's misfortunes. If you knew nothing else about Walker Bradley, you could be certain that, given the chance, he was sure to feel sorry for you. No one could have felt more sorry about what had happened to Mary Margaret Flanders, that gifted actress and irreplaceable friend.

"Yeah," said Bradley with reluctance, "I finally asked her."

Her hands folded in front of her, Van Roten was gazing down at the floor. "And?" she asked, lifting her eyes.

Bradley shifted position. Looking across at Van Roten he dropped his head to the side and turned up his hands.

"She did not want to say, not at first; but I kept after her until she told me. She said she was going to leave him–leave Stanley–that she couldn't take it anymore, that she had to get out."

With a penetrating stare, Van Roten insisted he be sure. "She said she 'couldn't take it anymore'?"

"Yes."

"And she said–definitely said–she was leaving him, her husband, Stanley Roth?"

"Yes, she was very upset about it."

"That must have come as a great shock to you, didn't it?" I asked as I got to my feet to begin my cross-examination.

Bradley mumbled an answer. I did not understand what he said, but I did not care enough to ask that he repeat it.

"A great shock, because in addition to your friendship with her, you had for a long time been a very close friend of Stanley Roth, hadn't you?"

My right hand grazed the top of my empty chair. I moved a step to the left and took a position directly behind the defendant. When Bradley looked at me, Stanley Roth was directly in front of him.

"I'd known Stanley . . ."

"We're in a court of law, Mr. Bradley," I interrupted with irritation. "This isn't some dinner-table conversation. You'll please refer to the defendant as Mr. Roth."

Startled, Bradley drew back. His mouth twitched nervously.

"I'd known Mr. Roth for quite a long time. That's true," he said, quickly regaining his composure.

Placing my left hand on Stanley Roth's shoulder, I started to smile. "'Known him for quite a long time'? You weren't close friends?"

Bradley tried to dismiss it as a matter of minor importance. "I'm not saying we weren't friends."

"Close friends," I persisted, smiling at his attempt to distance himself in public the way he had in front of Michael Wirthlin and the others last week at the home of Louis Griffin. "That's what you used to tell everyone, isn't it, Mr. Bradley? That you and Stanley Roth were close friends?"

I stepped back to my chair and picked a glossy magazine out of a folder.

"That's what it says here," I said innocently as I opened it to a marked page and held it up for him to see. "Right below the picture of the two of you. You have your arm around him here, don't you, Mr. Bradley? Shall I read what it says–about how proud you are to have Stanley Roth as one of your–yes, it says it right here–one of your 'closest friends.'"

I tossed the magazine onto the table. "But of course that was before your 'close friend' was put on trial for murder, wasn't it? It was when Stanley Roth could still do something for your career instead of embarrassing you with all your other 'close friends.'"

In a single, fluid motion, Annabelle Van Roten rose majestically from her chair. Standing tall in her black-strapped high-heeled shoes, she lifted her finely framed eyebrows into an attitude of overburdened patience.

"While Mr. Antonelli's disquisition on the degrees of friendship might be a fascinating subject for a graduate seminar in psychology, this is, after all, a court of law; and this is–or at least I thought it was supposed to be–a cross-examination of a witness. The last time I looked, cross-examination takes the form of question and answer: not endless speeches to the jury."

Van Roten waited for the judge to tell me to move on, but Honigman did not say a word. The grating smile that had floated so easily onto her mouth became awkward and self-conscious, and then faded away. Her long black lashes blinked with nervous uncertainty; her lips twisted into a tense, cramped expression.

"And the last time I looked," said Honigman after this lengthy, dramatic pause, "an objection needs to be stated as such."

Her mouth split back into a rigid, condescending smile; her eyes flared open. She almost spat out the words:

"I object, Your Honor!"

Slowly, with that false, benevolent smile still on his broad mouth, Rudolph Honigman turned his head until his eyes met mine.

"You are supposed to be asking questions," he reminded me gently; more mindful, I thought, of what those watching would think of the way he had delivered this admonition than of any effect it was likely to have on me.

His gaze stayed on me a moment longer, not because he wanted to see my reaction or hear my reply, but because it was expected that he would wait to make sure I understood what I had now been directed to do. I made no response; not so much as a brief, indiscernible nod of my head; nothing to suggest that I had paid the slightest attention to what he had said. He seemed not to notice. He placed his hand on the side of his face and lowered his eyes to the notepad on which he occasionally jotted down something he wanted to remember. I turned back to the witness.

"You used to describe yourself as a close friend of Stanley Roth. Now you seem to suggest that you were never really that close. Which is it, Mr. Bradley?" I asked, picking up where I had left off. Out of the corner of my eye I caught a glimpse of Van Roten sitting at the table, her face locked in a smirking stare.

Bradley retreated, but only a little. He acknowledged that Stanley Roth and he had known each other a long time and that they had been friends.

"Good friends," I insisted one last time and let Bradley's determined silence speak for itself.

"We were talking, Mr. Bradley, of how shocked you must have been when your friend, Mary Margaret Flanders, told you she was going to leave her husband. But as you seem rather insistent that you and the defendant were not such good friends after all, perhaps I was wrong. Were you shocked, Mr. Bradley, when you learned from Mary Margaret Flanders that she intended to leave Stanley Roth?"

"I'm not sure 'shocked' is the word I would use," replied Bradley with a baffled expression. "A little surprised, I guess."

"You testified that she gave as her reason that she–I believe the phrase was: 'couldn't take it anymore.' What did you assume she meant by that? Couldn't take what?"

Bradley's head hung down at an angle on the left. With the back of his fingers he stroked the side of his throat as he thought about the question.

"Well, you know–Stanley. She meant she just couldn't take Stanley anymore."

"No, Mr. Bradley, I'm afraid I don't know; and I'm sure the jury doesn't know. What do you mean, she 'just couldn't take Stanley anymore'?"

"Stanley isn't always the easiest person to be around," said Bradley, lifting his head as he changed positions. He started to cross his legs, then placed both feet firmly on the floor. With his weight on his arms, he bent forward. He began to fidget with his fingers, tapping them against each other, then sliding them back and forth. He could not seem to sit still for more than a few moments at a time.

"He can be quite demanding at times," added Bradley. There was a look of discouragement on his face, as if to underscore his disappointment at having to say something so critical about someone he knew. "Stanley is a brilliant man, and maybe that's why he expects so much out of other people. I don't know."

I let go of Stanley Roth's shoulder and moved around to the end of the counsel table. I was close enough to touch the first row juror farthest from the witness stand.

"Then when she told you she couldn't take it anymore, she didn't mean she was in fear of her own safety, did she?"

"No, she never said anything like that."

"Did you ever see Stanley Roth strike her?"

"No, of course not."

"Did you ever see Stanley Roth threaten to strike her?"

"No."

"Have you ever seen Stanley Roth act in a violent fashion toward anyone?" I asked with a civil smile, as if the question answered itself.

He looked at me, searching my eyes, wondering how I wanted him to take the question. He crossed one leg over the other, dropped his head down and pretended to study his hands.

"Let me ask the question this way, Mr. Bradley. Are you aware that Michael Wirthlin recently testified that he had never seen Stanley Roth commit an act of violence?"

Bradley raised his eyes and nodded. "I read the papers."

I kept smiling, allowing Bradley time to wonder where I was going with this, how close to the edge of the truth I was willing to go. I went back to the empty chair at the counsel table. My hands plunged into my pockets, I glanced down at Roth, then across to where Annabelle Van Roten was sitting.

"And we both know–don't we, Mr. Bradley?–that Michael Wirthlin was lying."

My eyes stayed on Van Roten, watching as she tried hard not to react.

"I'm not sure I know what you mean."

"You don't know what I mean?" I asked, wheeling toward him. "You were there, Mr. Bradley. We were both there that night last week at the home of Louis Griffin when Stanley Roth assaulted–or tried to assault–Michael Wirthlin. You did see that, didn't you?"

Bradley seemed mystified, not about where he had been and what he had seen, but by what I was doing, asking something so clearly detrimental to Stanley Roth. He did not doubt, however, that he better not agree that Michael Wirthlin was dishonest. The same impulse that had driven him to distance himself from Stanley Roth drove him closer to the new controlling authority at the studio.

"But he–I mean Stanley–didn't actually hit him, did he? Michael was probably just trying to protect Stanley. Stanley had too much to drink.

Michael knew he didn't mean it. He knew what everyone would think. He knew they'd say it proved Stanley had a violent temper."

"Yes, yes," I agreed, "they would–and perhaps they will; but, as I reminded you once before, Mr. Bradley, this is a court of law. We're not here to put the best face on things; we're not here to cover up our mistakes; we're here, Mr. Bradley, to tell the truth, and the truth is that when Michael Wirthlin told the jury that he had not only never seen Stanley Roth strike anyone, but he had never seen him attempt to do so, he was lying, wasn't he?"

Bradley had been sitting on his left hip; he changed positions and sat on his right.

"I don't think it's my place to comment on what someone else said," he replied with a helpless shrug.

"You saw Stanley Roth attempt to strike Michael Wirthlin. Is that, or is that not, correct?"

"Yeah, I saw him," Bradley grudgingly admitted.

"You've known Stanley Roth a long time?"

"Yes, a long time."

"Had you ever seen him attempt to hit anyone before that night, last week, when he tried to hit Michael Wirthlin?"

"No, never."

"And you've already testified that if he had ever engaged in violence, or threatened violence, against his wife, she never said anything about it to you. Correct?"

"Yeah."

"Did you ever observe anything–anything at all–that made you think Stanley Roth had ever physically abused Mary Margaret Flanders?"

"No, I didn't," said Bradley, squinting his eyes in a way that wrinkled his nose. He scratched the side of his head and then looked down at his shoes.

"You were very close to Mary Margaret Flanders, weren't you?" I asked in a sympathetic tone.

Bradley looked up. "We were good friends. I thought the world of her. She was the best."

"She would have told you, then, if Stanley Roth had threatened her, wouldn't she?"

"I don't know. I think so," said Bradley, scratching his head again.

"Did you know she had been having an affair with Michael Wirthlin?"

"That's not the kind of thing she would have talked about, even with me."

"Whether or not she talked about it," I persisted, "did you know?"

Bradley shook his head and said he had not known anything about it until it had come out in court. I listened attentively to his answer and moved a step closer to the witness stand.

"If you didn't know she was having an affair with Michael Wirthlin, does that mean he didn't know that you had been having an affair with her as well?"

It was like an abrupt change in the weather, a storm that gathers so quickly there is barely time to run for cover. The silence in the courtroom was suddenly weighted with tension. Every eye was on Walker Bradley as everyone concentrated on the answer he was about to give. Everyone, that is, except Stanley Roth: He was staring up at me, a troubled, questioning look on his face. I kept watching Walker Bradley, boring in on him, attempting by sheer force of will to make him speak. His mouth, parted the way it always was when he was listening, had fallen farther open still. He blinked once, and then he blinked again.

"You were sleeping with Mary Margaret Flanders, weren't you? As a matter of fact, you had been sleeping with her on and off for years. Isn't that true, Mr. Bradley?"

He stretched out one hand, his fingers spread far apart, the beginning of a gesture meant perhaps to convey the essential frailty of the human condition and the need not to judge too harshly those who might have strayed from the rigid requirements of a strict morality. It only got as far as that. Before he could say anything, Annabelle Van Roten stopped him with an objection.

"The victim isn't on trial here, Your Honor. Unless Mr. Antonelli can show some connection between this alleged relationship between Mary Margaret Flanders and Mr. Bradley, this line of questioning is not only irrelevant but improper, an attempt to defame the deceased in the hope, I suppose, of suggesting . . . What, Mr. Antonelli?" She pivoted on her heel until we were face-to-face. "That she deserved to die?"

"No, not that she deserved to die," I countered, returning her condescending smile with one of my own; "but that while she was married she had relationships with other men–that is men, plural–and not one man. Which is to say, Your Honor," I went on, turning toward the bench, "that the fact of multiple affairs, if you will, argues against infidelity as a motive for murder–at least a motive that can be ascribed to her husband, the defendant in this case."

Van Roten could not contain herself. She wheeled around, staring at me in disbelief, before she turned back to Judge Honigman.

"This is the strangest case I've ever seen, Your Honor. The defense insists the defendant is violent, and now wants to show that the affair the victim had with one man could not have been the motive because she had an affair with another. About the only thing Mr. Antonelli hasn't done yet is insist that his client can't have killed the victim on the day in question because he murdered her the day before!"

Mocking her with an exaggerated look of admiration, I bent toward her and in a stage whisper said: "That was really quite good. Are you sure you don't want to have dinner?"

"Your Honor!" she protested, howling her indignation.

"Sorry, Your Honor," I said quickly, flashing a bright, repentant smile. Before Honigman could say anything, I turned serious.

"This is a murder case, Your Honor. The defense is entitled to explore questions about the conduct and the character of the victim; questions which no matter how unorthodox or even unsavory they may seem are necessary to rebut the contention, implicit in the testimony elicited by the prosecution, that the defendant had a motive to murder his wife. And as far as I'm aware," I added, darting a defiant glance at Annabelle Van Roten, "there is nothing that requires I do this in a manner first approved by counsel for the other side."

Stung by this reproach, Van Roten retorted: "It has to be done in a manner permitted by the rules of evidence!"

Raising his hand, Honigman brought discussion to a close. "The objection is overruled," he announced after a solemn pause. "But please keep to the point, Mr. Antonelli. I'm going to allow you some latitude, at least until I see where this is going–but only some latitude. I won't permit any line of questioning offered solely for the sake of sensationalism. Are we understood?"

"Perfectly, Your Honor."

I rested my hand on the railing of the jury box and stared down at the floor, creating some space between the colloquy that had engaged the attention of the jury and the testimony to which we were about to return.

"I don't mean to embarrass you, Mr. Bradley," I said, slowly raising my eyes. "But there is more at stake here than whatever discomfort this may cause you. Now, again–is it not true you at least on occasion slept with Mary Margaret Flanders?"

Casting a questioning glance at Van Roten in the hope that there was still something she could do, Bradley hesitated. But Van Roten pretended to be busy, making a note to herself. Bradley scratched his head, shrugged, and with a bashful, self-deprecating laugh, made a halfhearted reply.

"Yeah, well, there were a few nights . . . when we were on location . . . It wasn't anything serious. We weren't having an affair, or anything like that."

Bradley lowered his eyes and stretched out his legs, slouching like a sullen adolescent intent on ignoring every attempt to inquire further into something he had done.

"You were sleeping with her, but you weren't having an affair with her. Would you then perhaps describe the relationship you had with Mary Margaret Flanders as one of 'casual intimacy'?"

I had moved back to the table and placed my left hand on the right shoulder of Stanley Roth, as if to comfort the injured husband of an unfaithful wife.

Frowning, Bradley lifted his head. "Yeah," he said, biting the inside of his cheek. "I guess you could put it like that."

"And was Mary Margaret Flanders the only woman with whom you had this kind of relationship? 'Casual intimacy,' we agreed to call it."

He gave an angry start. The furrows in his forehead deepened. Exasperated, he turned his face upward, seeking some form of protection from the court.

"Do I have to . . . ?"

"Again, Your Honor," I insisted with the air of someone forced to a thankless task, "this goes to the same issue of the conduct and character of the victim, which in turn goes to the question of motive."

Van Roten had gotten to her feet, signaling her readiness to renew her objection.

Honigman seemed less than persuaded by what I had said, but after narrowing his eyes in a silent admonishment, he let me go on.

"Do you want me to repeat the question, Mr. Bradley?"

He turned to me with a look of growing irritation. "No." But that was all he said.

"Then answer it."

"Yes."

"There were other women with whom you had this same kind of 'casual intimacy'?"

"Yes," he mumbled.

"Louder."

"Yes," he almost shouted, shoving himself up in the chair.

"How many?"

His head jerked back and looked at me with contempt, as if only someone completely naïve–or a complete hypocrite–could think to ask such a question of him.

"I don't know."

"Dozens? Hundreds? Thousands?"

"I don't know," he repeated in a surly voice.

"In other words: a lot. Did Mary Margaret Flanders know this? Did she know that you were often involved–in terms of 'casual intimacy'–with lots of different women?"

Van Roten again objected, but Honigman, bending forward, his eyes fastened on the witness, extended his arm and with an impatient motion of his hand overruled her.

"Yeah, I suppose she knew."

"So she wasn't sleeping with you because she thought there was something more involved than the 'casual intimacy' which, as you've testified, was all it was to you? In other words, Mr. Bradley, she wasn't seduced into sex by the promise or the expectation of love?"

Bradley tried to put the best face on things he could. "We were good friends. We worked a lot together. There were times when we were a little more than friends."

"I take it that is a yes. She was perfectly willing to sleep with you just because she wanted to?"

It struck at his vanity. Without thinking, he replied indignantly: "I certainly didn't force her."

"She was a woman, then, who did what she wanted?"

"Yeah, she did what she wanted."

"She wanted to sleep with you, so she slept with you."

"Yeah," he answered, wondering why I would even bother to ask.

"And if she wanted to sleep with Michael Wirthlin, she slept with him?"

"Yeah, I guess."

"And if she wanted to sleep with anyone else, she did? How many other men did she sleep with, Mr. Bradley? As many men as you have slept with women?"

"Your Honor!" cried Van Roten, but Honigman ignored her.

"I don't know what she did," said Bradley.

"But you knew that you and Michael Wirthlin weren't the only men with whom she had slept during her marriage to Stanley Roth, didn't you?"

Bradley took a deep breath and let it out as a long sigh. "Well, you know . . . you hear things."

"And you heard things about Mary Margaret Flanders?"

"Yeah."

"You heard, didn't you, Mr. Bradley, that she slept with almost everyone? Isn't that the truth of it?"

Walker Bradley turned up his palms and shrugged. "You hear a lot of things in this town. It doesn't mean they're true."

"But we do know one thing that is true, don't we, Mr. Bradley? The real Mary Margaret Flanders, the woman you knew, wasn't anything like the woman the rest of us thought we knew, the woman we all saw so often on the screen, was she?"

22

STANLEY ROTH WANTED ME to see for myself. He would not say what it was or why I had to see it with my own eyes, only that when I saw it, I would not believe it. The driver turned into the street that led to the entrance to Blue Zephyr. Roth tapped the fingers of his right hand nervously on the leather seat. He glanced across at me, raised his eyebrows and nodded rapidly as if he were afraid I might miss what I was supposed to see. When he saw that nothing had yet registered, he lost patience.

"There," he said, nodding faster as he shifted his eyes toward the front of the car, just beyond the chauffeur's shoulder. "See it now?"

We were less than a block away. There was a car ahead of us at the gate. The guard was saying something to the driver, probably giving him directions after he had first checked to make sure it was someone authorized to pass inside. I felt stupid because nothing seemed any different from the way the front entrance of the studio had looked before. Roth was incredulous.

"You don't see it? It's right in front of your eyes. Look again."

It had been a long, difficult day in court: I was not in the mood to be treated like some witless child. I whipped my head around, ready to let him know what I thought of this little game of his when I realized what I had just seen. I turned back to be sure.

Immensely pleased that he had been right, that I would react the way he had thought I would, Roth leaned against the corner of the spacious back seat and rested his hands in his lap.

"When?" I asked, looking at him over my shoulder.

"This weekend."

With a solitary wave of his hand, the guard let us through. The gate shut behind us, the gate that no longer led to Blue Zephyr Studio. The wrought-iron sign under which everyone entered now read WIRTHLIN PRODUCTIONS.

"Remember when I told you that I kept the bungalow and that I kept something else besides? The name. I kept the name. Blue Zephyr. It belongs to me. I told you–remember?–the first day you came here, that I could teach you more in a couple of weeks about running a studio than that idiot could learn in a lifetime."

The driver dropped us at the bungalow. Roth instructed him to return in an hour to take me to the hotel. We went inside and I fell into a chair in front of Roth's desk while he made us both a drink. The murmured sounds of quiet conversations drifted through the open French doors as the working day at the studio Stanley Roth had built almost single-handedly came to a close.

"Wirthlin Productions," grunted Roth as he sank into the chair behind his desk.

He seemed completely without bitterness over what I would have thought must have been an emotionally wrenching turn of affairs. His apparent indifference seemed strange in light of the fact that, as it turned out, his resignation had not been necessary at all. He had allowed Michael Wirthlin to have his studio to prevent him from telling the jury that Stanley Roth had only the other night tried to kill him. And then, after Wirthlin had given him not only his silence but lied under oath about having ever seen him attempt to assault anyone, his own lawyer had proven out of the mouth of another witness the very fact he had paid such a high price to conceal. Yet all Roth seemed to care about was that he had managed to keep the name, Blue Zephyr, for himself. He could not stop talking about it.

"The name was everything, but Michael has too big an ego to see it. 'Wirthlin Productions'!"

Roth put his feet up on the corner of the desk and held the drink with both hands in his lap. The late afternoon light softened the lines that cut deep across his forehead, lending a kind of thoughtful melancholy to his expression. He rolled his head to the side and for a moment looked at me as if he was deciding whether to let me in on a secret that was too good not to share.

"Have you ever done something, or tried to do something, and it worked exactly the way you wanted, but then something happened, something you did not anticipate–something you could not have anticipated–and it ends up working out even better than you hoped? That's what happened here."

"That you were able to keep the name–Blue Zephyr?" I asked as I sipped on the scotch and soda he had given me.

Roth stared pensively out the French doors. After a while he lifted the glass to his mouth. He held it there, after he had taken a drink from it, pressed against his lower lip. A smile, sad, certain, and a little cruel, stole across the rough contours of his mouth.

"Louis made me see it," Roth began, slowly shaking his head, chagrined that he had not been able to see it for himself. "That night–after you stopped me from beating Wirthlin's brains out. I was furious, beside myself. We bring him into Blue Zephyr and he's telling me I have to resign? Then Louis showed me how to use it–how to use Wirthlin's ego against him."

Roth paused, reflecting on what he had just said.

"Do you have a friend?" he asked quite seriously. "Someone you can count on, no matter what–someone you know will always do anything they can for you, not because of something you can do for them, but because . . . well, because that's just who they are?"

The only person I could think of was Marissa, but it seemed somehow improper, as if I were betraying her again, to assume that kind of unselfish devotion. I remembered other people I had known, other people who had trusted me as well, but they were gone now, dead, or far away, living a life of which I was no longer a part.

"No one like Louis Griffin," was my reluctant reply.

"It was finished with Wirthlin," continued Roth. "That was not as clear to me as it was to Louis. Maybe it was because of Mary Margaret. I don't know. But Wirthlin was determined to break me if he could. The choice was either let him walk away, and try to hang onto the studio without his money and the money he can raise–or let him have the studio for himself. With me it was personal; with Louis it was business. I wanted to kill Wirthlin for even thinking he could have what I built;

Louis wanted him to have a business that even with Mary Margaret's last picture was so far in debt we might never dig our way out of it. Louis put it all together. He knew exactly the way Wirthlin would react. He went to him the next morning, as if he was there to apologize for what I had done. It wasn't the first time Louis had done that. He told Wirthlin that he knew how he felt, how angry he must be, but that there was too much at stake–that I was on trial for murder–and that he couldn't let anyone know what had happened. It would make people think I might be guilty after all."

Roth hesitated, as if there was something he was not quite sure he should tell me. He shook his head and laughed quietly.

"You know what the son-of-a-bitch said? 'Everyone already thinks he's guilty.'"

With a weary, troubled sigh, Roth lowered his eyes to the glass, searching for more clarity there than he had found in the things that had happened.

"Anyway, you see what Louis did. He made Michael believe that he had the upper hand. Just to be sure, Louis told him he knew things could not go on the way they had and that I understood that, too. He told him that while I didn't want to, I realized now that there was really no other way; that, given what had happened–that's what he said: 'given what had happened'–I was willing to resign."

Roth looked up, a smile, shrewd, calculating, full of admiration, on his mouth. "Louis wasn't done. He knew there was something more Wirthlin would want. 'I know you'll want to make a fresh start here,' he told him. 'I'll of course resign as well.'"

Roth pulled his feet off the corner of the desk and sat up. Placing one elbow on top of the desk, he rubbed the knuckle of his forefinger back and forth across the hollow between his chin and lower lip.

"Do you have any idea how good it makes someone like Michael Wirthlin feel when they think they can force someone out? They think they're indestructible. They think they can do anything. They think the first thought–any thought at all–that comes into their head is the pinnacle, the very summation, of human wisdom. They think they can give lessons to Machiavelli. 'You want to keep the name Blue Zephyr? Why not?

Why would I, the great Michael Wirthlin, want a name someone else thought of? Why would I want any name, except my own?'"

His eyes wide with wonder, Stanley Roth threw out his hands and sank back into the chair.

"Everything went perfectly. It couldn't have gone better. At least I didn't think it could until you decided–though I have to admit I'm still a little unclear why you decided–to prove to everyone that poor Michael is a liar." A grim, satisfied expression entered his eyes. "One of the few times in his life he actually tried to keep a promise and all he gets for it is to have everyone think he perjured himself. Well, that won't bother him much," said Roth reflectively. "Not with 'Wirthlin Productions' to run."

Roth reached for the half-empty glass sitting on the edge of the desk. He brought it to his lips, but then, changing his mind, brought it down to his lap and wrapped both hands around it. He sat there, with lowered eyes, gnawing gently on his upper lip as he meditated on something that appeared to trouble him more deeply than anything connected with Michael Wirthlin. The longer he stared at the glass, the more disturbed and withdrawn he seemed to become. His eyebrows drew closer together. Two parallel lines deepened into perpendicular grooves down his forehead to the bridge of his nose. He clenched his jaw, relaxed it, and clenched it again, faster and faster. Then it stopped entirely. He opened his mouth, just enough to take in a single short gasp of breath.

"You made her sound like a whore," said Roth with a puzzled, plaintive glance. "Did you really have to do that? Make everyone think of her that way?"

I put down my glass and turned in my chair, facing him directly.

"You told me that you assumed that she had had affairs with other men. You were quite explicit about it: whenever she was on location. That's what you said. Don't you remember?"

"I know what I said," replied Roth, gazing again down at his glass, a subdued expression on his face.

His tone was one of regret, whether at the thought of what his wife had done, or because in a moment of candor he had told me about it, I did not know. He raised his eyes.

"But I don't know why you had to use it."

I stared at him, at first in disbelief, and then, without quite knowing why, started to laugh. "Because I felt like it," I said in a whispered shout. "Because I thought it would be fun." I bent sideways until my elbow reached the desk. "Because I thought the trial was getting dull and I thought we should liven things up with a little sex. Why did I do it? What do you care why I did it?" I asked, starting to become angry. "We're in a murder trial, your murder trial–a trial, I might remind you, in which all the evidence points to you–and you seem mainly interested in telling me how you and your good friend Louis outwitted Michael Wirthlin; how you managed to saddle him with all the debts and all the obligations while you get to keep the name–Blue Zephyr–and of course this wonderful place you like to call home," I said with a gesture meant to take in the limited interior of the white stucco bungalow where Stanley Roth lived and worked. "We're in a murder trial and there is a very good chance you're going to be found guilty, and you're upset that people might not think quite as highly of Mary Margaret Flanders as they did when all they knew about her was what you showed them on the screen and what they read in movie magazines?"

I moved forward to the edge of the chair and spread open my hands, trying to get him to see that nothing less than his life depended on what was taking place in that small cramped courtroom downtown.

"I'm sorry, Stanley, but the best thing that can happen right now is for that jury to believe that she was sleeping around and that you had known about it for a long time. Because if you hadn't known about it, if you had only just found out about it–found out she was sleeping with Wirthlin, or with Bradley: it doesn't matter who–then you have a motive, you have a reason, one of the oldest reasons there is, to murder your wife. But if she had been sleeping with other men–the kind of 'casual intimacy' Bradley was forced to admit to–and you had known about it–or hadn't known about it, but had always assumed it was something she did–then why would you suddenly decide to kill her for something that you had always known?"

Roth lifted his eyebrows, pursed his lips. He nodded gravely, as if he had understood and agreed with everything I had said.

"Unless," he said, as he turned to me and drew himself up, "I finally just got tired of it, got tired of all the lying, all the cheap betrayals."

He said it with a kind of cold rationality, the way someone without a conscience might explain the intricate mechanism with which he had set off a bomb in a crowded public place.

"I wouldn't be the first man to kill his wife out of embarrassment and humiliation, would I? If you were the prosecutor, wouldn't you argue that there is a limit to how many times a husband can forgive an unfaithful wife?"

He was watching me, scratching his chin with the back of two fingers, curious to see what I would say. I began to suspect that he was not talking about himself at all; that he was trying out different possibilities, testing my reaction.

"For the sake of argument," he added when I did not immediately respond. "You told me that was what you liked about being a lawyer. Remember? The argument."

I was no longer angry, but I was still annoyed. "I told you why I did what I did today, why I made Walker Bradley say what he did about your wife. I didn't know Bradley had slept with her. All I knew is what you had told me, and so I took a chance and asked him. I had to ask him. There wasn't any choice, and not just because of what I said earlier. We don't have a case, Stanley; nothing we can offer that shows, that proves, it wasn't her blood on your clothes or that you were somewhere else when the murder took place. That means we're left with their case, the prosecution's case. We have to give the jury every reason we can to make them think that case isn't that good; make them believe that someone is lying and that it isn't you. Bradley lied about what you did, or tried to do, to Michael Wirthlin; and he tried to lie about what he had been doing with your wife. Wirthlin lied; and the cop, Crenshaw, lied."

Roth held up his hand to stop me. "And most of the lies they told–Wirthlin lying about what happened that night–were lies that helped."

"But the point is they lied. I'm going to put you on the stand and you're going to tell the truth."

"And does the truth always win?"

"Almost never," I replied, suppressing a grin; "but it's a lot easier to remember."

Roth thought for a moment. "Sometimes when they tell you that a picture you think is going to be great is really awful–they're right."

The telephone rang. Roth picked it up before it rang twice. He held it to his ear and without saying hello, listened.

I knew who it was. No one else used that line. Whatever was being said, Stanley Roth seemed to expect it, and more than that, feel some obligation to make it go as easily as possible. His eyes softened and a gentle half-smile of something like regret formed on his mouth.

"It's a mistake," he said finally. "I understand you think you have to do it . . . but it's a mistake." He listened a while longer and then interrupted. "This isn't a good time. We'll talk about it later. When? I don't know when. After the trial, I guess."

He raised his arm, ready to pull the telephone away from his ear. "Really, I understand. No, not tonight. I have to finish this thing I'm working on. After the trial. Good night," he said curtly as he hung up.

For a moment, Roth stared straight ahead, tapping his fingers together under his chin. Then his eyes came back into focus and he explained that Julie Evans had just informed him that she was going to stay on with "Wirthlin Productions."

"She'll come back," he said, trying, as I thought, to put the best face on things he could. "After the trial."

After the trial. That was the one constant, the one thing that never changed: this absolute certainty that he could not possibly lose. It was not that he thought people were never convicted of things they did not do. No, it was something more than a blind belief that things always turned out right in the end: it was the belief that things would always turn out right for him. His wife had been killed; he had lost the studio, Blue Zephyr, the studio he had spent so many years waiting to have; now he was on trial for murder; and yet he acted as if his life was no different than one of the screenplays he had written, one in which, as he had once tried to explain to me, he already knew the ending, and the ending was just the way he wanted it to be.

Perhaps that was the reason Julie Evans was in love with him, this sense that while most other people live their lives dealing with their own fears and insecurities, Stanley Roth always seemed to know in advance what was going to happen. Wirthlin had offered her more than she was ever likely to get from Stanley Roth, even if he was eventually acquitted and could start up some new enterprise of his own. She had to take what Wirthlin was willing to give. She would have been a fool to bet everything on Stanley Roth when the odds were so much against him and he had done so little to make her think he was going to change the way he felt about her. But that had not made it any easier to tell Stanley Roth she was abandoning him for a position with the new Wirthlin Productions.

If I had had time to think it through clearly, to consider all the difficult, conflicting emotions with which Julie Evans must have had to deal, I would not have been quite so surprised to find her waiting for me in the lobby of the Chateau Marmont. Who else did she have with whom she could talk about what she had done? Not Stanley Roth, and certainly not Michael Wirthlin.

Blonde and sleek, with that half-smile that made you think she was already secretly laughing at you, Julie looked like she did not have a care in the world. She rose from the dark green chair in which she had been waiting and walked straight toward me, one foot in front of the other, a teasing sparkle in her clear blue eyes. That I had not gone with her to Santa Barbara seemed more than ever a triumph of self-deception and I wondered how I could have been so stupid.

She rose up on her toes and with one hand laid gently on my shoulder, brushed her lip against my cheek. "Take me to dinner," she whispered in a way that made it sound like a dare. "I've lots to tell you."

We went to the restaurant Julie had taken me to lunch the first day we met, the day the police arrested Stanley Roth, and were given the same table, the one she apparently had every time she came. On the drive over she had avoided any discussion of the way in which our weekend plans had come apart. Nor had she said anything about her decision to take Michael Wirthlin's offer. Now, after we ordered, she began to talk about Santa Barbara, but without any regret that she had gone alone. To the contrary, it had been just as well that I had not come. She said this as if it were an objective fact, about which she had no personal feelings one way or the other. It had given her time to think, she explained with a bright smile to indicate that she knew I understood.

"And you decided to take Wirthlin's offer, to head up the new studio–or the old one with the new name: 'Wirthlin Productions.'"

The half-smile on her mouth was replaced with a look less certain of itself. She was not sure whether I had simply assumed it, or whether I actually knew.

"You were there–at the bungalow–when I talked to Stanley?"

When I nodded that I had, Julie looked at me for a moment, hesitant, hoping that of my own volition I would tell her what Stanley Roth had said. The waiter brought the salads and, lowering my eyes, I began to poke around in it with a fork. I could feel her watching, waiting for me to say something.

"What did he say?" she asked finally, as if she were only following where the conversation had led us.

If she could pretend indifference toward Stanley Roth, I could do the same thing with her. Everything about her–the way she looked, the way she held herself when she walked, the coy self-confidence that kept everyone at the distance she wanted, the astonishing heat she generated in bed–made you want to do everything you could to make her think she had not been able to get to you after all, that you could have her one night and not think about her until the next time you happened to run into her when, if you were in the mood, you might spend the night, or part of it, with her again. It was the cruelty of self-defense, the knowledge that if you were not careful you would not be able to think about anything else, the aching, longing certainty that if you let that happen she would break your heart and not give it a second thought. She was in love with Stanley Roth, and so long as she was, she would treat other men the way he treated her.

I put down the fork and looked up. "You want to know what Stanley Roth said about your decision to go with Michael Wirthlin, instead of staying with him? What makes you think he said anything?"

I stretched my left arm over the back corner of the chair. With a cool, appraising glance, I asked her a question that I thought would put everything in perspective.

"You've been with him for years. Have you ever known him to think about anyone but himself?"

The long lashes that stood in such defiant posture seemed to weaken and then collapse, falling halfway down her eyes.

"He said something, didn't he?" she asked in a choking voice.

I should have seized on some convenient lie, something that would make her feel better about having done what she had. If she had been anyone else; if she had been someone with whom I had not become intimately involved; someone I did not despise myself for wanting as much as I did; I would have told her what I knew she was desperate to hear—that Stanley Roth understood that she had to make the choice she had and that he only wanted what was best for her. Instead, I told her the truth, because, to my discredit, I knew it would hurt. I looked her straight in the eye.

"All he said was that you'd come back after the trial."

She twisted her head to the side, searching my eyes until she was sure of it. She began to laugh, a low, furious laugh.

"That I'll come back after the trial!" she exclaimed, her eyes flashing with anger. "That is so much in character for him. He thinks I'll do anything. Tell him I won't. Tell him I'm not coming back—after the trial or ever!"

She clutched her napkin in her hand, struggling with herself. "Do you know what he told me, right after Mary Margaret was murdered? Do you know what he said?"

"What did he tell you?" I asked, grasping her wrist to get her attention as her eyes darted past me.

She was still looking over my shoulder, but her eyes kept climbing higher. There was a strange, puzzled expression on her face. Someone was standing right next to our table. Amazed at the intrusion, I looked at him sharply, expecting him to go away. Then I realized who it was. Jack Walsh was standing above me, looking all around the restaurant, making sure everyone had stopped what they were doing to watch.

"How can you do this?" he demanded, shaking his fist at me. "Defend someone you know is guilty? Question the police, when you know they did everything right? Question the integrity of people who were just doing their jobs? Did you ever see my daughter?" he snarled. "See how beautiful she was? You go into court, dressed in your expensive suits and your expensive shoes, and you don't care who you hurt, do you? Just so long as you convince some jury to acquit someone everyone knows is guilty. And you don't care how you do it, either–do you? You don't care if you have to drag my daughter in the dirt; you don't care what you do to her reputation. You don't care about anything, do you? You don't care that Stanley Roth murdered Mary Margaret Flanders!" he exclaimed, his eyes burning with rage. "All you care about is winning. You're the only person in the country who wants to celebrate letting a killer go free," shouted Jack Walsh as he picked up the glass from the table in front of me and threw the water in my face.

I bolted to my feet, using the napkin to wipe the water out of my eyes. Walsh had already turned and begun to walk away. There was a stunned silence in the restaurant, and then, as I stood there gaping, some people began to clap, applauding Jack Walsh for what he had done.

23

AFTER WEEKS OF TESTIMONY, weeks of listening to among other things the smug self-certainty of experts in the various so-called sciences of forensic evidence proving what no one had ever really denied, that the blood found at the scene of the crime and on the clothing of the defendant belonged to the victim, the prosecution ended its case with a series of witnesses who together described Mary Margaret Flanders's last day alive. The maid, the same one who the next morning would find her floating facedown in the pool, woke her at 8:00 A.M. After breakfast, Mary Margaret drove into Beverly Hills for an appointment at a hair salon. The stylist, sworn in under the name John Baker, but known to his wealthy and exclusive clientele as simply "Eduardo," said she arrived at 10:15 and left an hour and a half later at 11:45. Gesturing with both hands, he said he thought she had looked "simply fabulous," and then added with a sigh, "She always did."

According to her publicist, an energetic woman in her early forties who kept blinking her eyes and fidgeting with her fingers, she and the star were joined for lunch at The Bistro by two women, one a writer, the other an independent producer. They wanted to talk to her about a project they thought would allow her to show a side of her talent she had not been able to show before. Mary Margaret was interested and agreed to look at the screenplay, but that was all.

"Was that the first time she had met with anyone from outside Blue Zephyr?" asked Annabelle Van Roten.

It was not. In recent months, the witness explained, the actress had appeared restive, eager to try something else, something new. She was bored with the kind of thing everyone now expected her to do, the same formula, over and over again, because everyone thought she was good at it and because no one wanted to risk losing the audience she had.

Though the publicist could not be precise, she thought it must have been close to two-thirty when they finally left the restaurant. Mary Margaret drove home and, an hour later, the publicist followed. From four to six in the afternoon, Mary Margaret Flanders hosted a reception on the grounds of The Palms to raise money for the children's wing of a local hospital.

Dimming the courtroom lights, Annabelle Van Roten instructed a technician to show the videotape that had been taken. There were hundreds of people, women in large floppy hats, men in blue blazers with open-collar shirts, standing around the pool and out on the lawn, chattering among themselves. There were several famous faces, and more than a few that you thought you knew but could not quite place. There was one face, however, that made you forget about everyone else. Her first husband, Paul Erlich, had perhaps noticed it first, the night he had gone with her to the party at the home of some now forgotten producer: the way that when she entered a room everything around her seemed to stop, and not only stop but fade into the background or, rather, become the background. Watching that tape, taken from one of the surveillance cameras that were always in use when there was a gathering on the grounds–taken, in other words, without any thought to the artistic values of a motion picture–was like staring at a still photograph in which everything except the principal subject is blurred, slightly out of focus. She had that gift, given to the beautiful and not always to them, of making you feel more alive just by the sight of her. When the lights came back on in the courtroom, the muffled sounds of private mourning were all around me.

The last guest had left sometime after six-thirty. At seven-thirty, in a different dress, Mary Margaret Flanders arrived at the home of one of the last of the Hollywood moguls, the men who had brought together the different strands of entertainment and by their control, first over the performers and then over the media in which they performed, turned it into an industry. She was one of the several dozen invited guests on the occasion of the old man's eighty-seventh birthday. In testimony that lasted only a few minutes, Louis Griffin, the last witness called by the prosecution, told the jury that he had seen Mary Margaret Flanders leave around eleven. He was certain she had left alone.

When the courtroom doors shut behind Louis Griffin, Annabelle Van Roten rose from her chair. With an air of grim satisfaction, and in a solemn voice, she announced that "The People rest, Your Honor."

She stood with her head held high, savoring the moment, extracting from that formal statement of completion all the advantage she could. If she had any doubt about how well she had done, how airtight the case she had built, she concealed it better than any criminal ever hid his crime. With the intense sincerity of a woman insistent on righting a wrong, she kept her eyes focused on the judge. She was steady, certain, absolutely confident that no matter what the defense might now try to say, she had made the case, proven beyond any question that Stanley Roth was guilty of murder.

Judge Honigman asked if the defense would be ready to begin the next morning. The moment gone, Annabelle Van Roten sank into her chair and began absently to pull together the notebooks and papers scattered over the table in front of her. A cruel smile of self-confidence hovered over the edges of her mouth. She knew she was going to win. She was thinking ahead to the way her own life might change after victory in a case of this magnitude and notoriety.

That night, alone at the hotel, trying to work my way through what I was going to do the next day when I called the first witness for the defense, I remembered what I had seen on the face of Annabelle Van Roten. It was the look of someone of modest means, quick to despise the thoughtless and undisciplined habits of the rich, who suddenly and unexpectedly finds herself wealthy. It is a little unsettling to realize how much of what we think and feel depends on the conditions in which we live, and how easily we abandon at the first opportunity everything we thought we believed. It was apparently what had happened to the witness I was going to call. Richard Crenshaw did not become a police officer because he thought it would give him a chance to become a screenwriter; but as soon as it did, he forgot all about what he was supposed to do as an officer of the law.

Crenshaw was to be the first witness for the defense and Stanley Roth was to be the last. That was all I had, two witnesses, and both of them put on for the purpose of showing that Mary Margaret Flanders had once called the police to protect herself against her husband and that Stanley Roth had on more than one occasion attempted to hurt someone. It was one of the few cases I could remember where the only thing left to the defense was to insist that everyone tell the truth. It seemed a strange and perhaps ironic twist of fate that I was going to do it in the only place in America where make-believe, a game for children, was the serious business of adults.

THE NEXT MORNING, instead of taking her accustomed place at the small desk below the bench, the clerk whispered a few words to Annabelle Van Roten. Then she walked the few steps to where I was sitting next to Stanley Roth.

"Judge wants to see counsel in chambers," she said curtly.

"What is it about?" I asked.

"How should I know?" she replied as she turned on her heel and trudged back to the doorway at the side through which she had entered.

Rudolph Honigman was waiting behind his large plain wooden desk. A dozen or so black-and-white photographs of the judge standing next to various figures, posing with the stiff formality of local civic leaders, hung on the wall behind him, forcing themselves on the eyes of anyone who occupied, as Van Roten and I were now doing, the two blue-cushioned wooden chairs in front. On the wall behind us, metal bookshelves were filled with the sequentially organized reports of the state appellate opinions.

"We have a bit of a problem," he began, choosing his words carefully. "The bailiff reported that one of the jurors has complained that another juror has been making statements about the case."

"What kind of statements?" asked Van Roten, immediately suspicious.

Honigman drew his lips together in a way that lengthened the line of his jaw. With his thumb and all four fingers he stroked his chin.

"The first juror–the one who brought it to the bailiff's attention–said the other juror had said she didn't think Stanley Roth could have done it, or words to that effect."

"Then she has to go; she has to be replaced," insisted Van Roten, making an emphatic gesture with her head.

Honigman smiled benignly, less for Van Roten's benefit than as a sign, made mainly for his own pleasure, that he had anticipated–word for word, if the look of satisfaction in his eyes was to be believed–her reaction and had already done something to forestall it.

"I've talked to her–the juror complained of. The bailiff reported this to me last evening. I had her in here first thing this morning. She claims all she said was that she still had some doubts and that she wasn't going to make up her mind until the defense had had a chance to put on its case."

That was not good enough for Annabelle Van Roten. She fairly bristled as she reminded Honigman that the juror had no business saying anything about the case at all.

"She was told–you told her, you told them all–not to discuss the case even among themselves, not until they had heard all the evidence and the case had been sent to them for deliberation. I think she should be replaced. We have two alternates," she added to show how simple it would be.

I was not eager to lose a juror who, so far as I knew, might be the only one who had not already decided Stanley Roth was guilty. As I had been reminded so forcefully in that restaurant when Jack Walsh accosted me, almost everyone thought Stanley Roth was guilty.

"Did she say why she said it?" I asked, hoping to somehow encourage Honigman to do what I thought he wanted to do all along.

"She said some of the other jurors had been making remarks to the effect that with the evidence the prosecution presented there did not seem to be much doubt about what had happened."

So much for the presumption of innocence; so much for the promises I had extracted from each of them not to make up their minds until they had not only heard all the evidence but had carefully deliberated with all the other jurors. They felt so comfortable with their conclusions that they were sharing them with each other, making it that much more difficult for any one of them later to change his mind. I was in trouble, and I knew it.

"I don't think it means anything, just some casual remarks," said

Honigman with the bland expression of someone who prefers not to look too closely at things for fear it might involve too much additional work.

However large the number of those who had at least provisionally decided Stanley Roth was guilty, the prosecution needed all twelve of them to convict. Van Roten renewed her demand that the talkative juror be removed.

"For all we know, she's only saying that about the others because she thinks it's the best way to defend herself against what she said."

I made a suggestion I knew she could not possibly accept.

"To be fair, let's bring them all in, one by one, and ask them each whether they have expressed any opinion, made any kind of statement, and then throw off any one who has. That way," I added with a sidelong glimpse at Van Roten, "we won't just be getting rid of jurors who haven't yet made up their minds."

"That's ludicrous, and you know it," she said, staring daggers at me. "There is one complaint–only one complaint–about the misconduct of a juror. That's the only thing we're here to discuss."

Honigman stopped me before I could reply. "I've talked to her," he said with an air of finality. "I'm convinced it wasn't anything serious, and I don't see any reason to dismiss her. I called you both in to let you know what happened and the way in which I dealt with it. That's all."

"Which juror is it?" asked Van Roten rather too insistently, as if the district attorney's office might want to investigate further.

"I do everything I can to protect the anonymity of jurors. I know you would never reveal her name," said Honigman, with what I thought was a slight trace of irony; "but someone in your office might. Besides," he added as he got to his feet, "I've already decided she did nothing wrong."

Honigman had left us both with something to worry about, but while Annabelle Van Roten might have to fret about a single skeptical juror, I had to convince what might already be a majority that they were wrong to think Stanley Roth guilty beyond a reasonable doubt of the murder of his wife. Nor was it just the simple disparity of numbers that was to Van Roten's advantage. Majorities have a way of imposing their will on a minority. It is difficult enough to speak your mind in the presence of people you barely know, to hazard the chance of finding yourself isolated and alone if no one else agrees; but to insist upon your own opinion, to refuse to follow the judgment of others when everyone is against you, requires a strength of conviction, a moral certainty not found nearly as often as we might like to think.

Back in court, I waited while Detective Crenshaw was put under oath for the second time, wondering if I could lead him into the kind of damaging admission that would make the jury begin to move in the direction of the defense instead of the prosecution.

"When you were here before, Detective Crenshaw, as a witness for the prosecution, I asked you several questions about the extent of your acquaintance with both the defendant, Stanley Roth, and his wife, the victim in this case, Mary Margaret Flanders."

From the table below me I picked up the typed pages of the trial transcript I had asked the court reporter to prepare.

"So there is no question about what you said, let me read it back to you."

Whether or not it was because of the comment I had made about his expensive-looking suit, this morning he was dressed again in a sports jacket and slacks. He seemed relaxed and not the least concerned that he might have said something he would have any reason to regret.

"Question: 'What was she like?'

"Answer: 'What was who like?'

"Question: 'Mary Margaret Flanders. You worked with her. You told Ms. Van Roten that you knew her. What was she like?'

"Answer: 'She seemed like a very nice person. She was certainly very nice to me.'

"Question: 'Did you talk to her very often?'

"Answer: 'No, not very often. A couple of times, perhaps–not more than that.'

"Question: 'On the set?'

"Answer: 'Yes.' "

I looked up and searched his eyes. I skipped forward a few pages and read again:

"Question: 'Who hired you to be a consultant on that picture?'

"Answer: 'Someone from the studio. I don't remember the name.'

"Question: 'I see. Then it wasn't Stanley Roth, because I assume you'd remember his name, wouldn't you?'"

I stopped reading.

"You didn't bother to answer that question, Detective Crenshaw. I have just a little more to read."

I thumbed through several pages to the one I wanted.

"Question: 'When you served as a consultant on that one movie, the one during which you first met Mary Margaret Flanders, did you review a script–to make sure what it said about police procedure was accurate, or at least not too far removed from the way things are actually done by police detectives?'

"Answer: 'Yes.'

"Question: 'You have some familiarity, then, with the mode, the style, or perhaps I should say, the way in which a script is organized, the way each scene is described and the dialogue written within it. Is that correct?'

"Answer: 'Yes, I have some familiarity with that.'

"Question: 'Did you ever think that perhaps you could write one of your own, one that was at least as good as the ones you had seen?'

"Answer: 'I wouldn't mind trying that someday. I think it might be interesting.'"

Placing the typewritten pages on the table, I gazed thoughtfully at them for a moment before I looked again at the witness. He had had plenty of time–weeks, in fact–to consider what he had said. He had to have known from the way I first asked those questions that Stanley Roth had told me all about the circumstances in which they had first met and what had happened as a result. He certainly must have heard about what I had almost shouted in the face of Jack Walsh. Everyone in Los Angeles had heard about the way I had practically convicted my own client by insisting that not only had he once hit Jack Walsh's daughter, but that she had called the police to report it. Crenshaw had lied under oath, not once, but repeatedly; and yet, as I looked at him, trying to guess what might be going on in his mind, I could not detect the slightest trace of concern. He was as cool, as utterly unflappable, as the day he walked into court, the key witness for the prosecution.

"When you said you had only talked to Mary Margaret Flanders 'a couple of times,' and always on the set, that was not true, was it, Detective Crenshaw?"

He did not blink his eyes; he did not fidget with his hands or move around in the witness chair; he did not change expression at all. His voice was calm, steady, that same well-modulated voice that after a while made you want to scream with impatience because it seemed so impervious to any real feeling or emotion.

"I did speak to her several times on the set, just as I said."

"But you had spoken to her before, hadn't you?"

Again there was no change in his demeanor, nothing to suggest anything except that he was completely in charge, if not of the proceedings, then at least of himself.

"Yes, I had."

Out of the corner of my eye, I caught a glimpse of Annabelle Van Roten. Her head was bent over a note she was making. The pen in her hand had come to a stop.

I had called Crenshaw back to the stand as a witness for the defense, but everyone knew he was a witness for the prosecution. I did not so much as bother to ask the court for permission to treat him as hostile before I began to subject him to the kind of leading questions reserved for cross-examining a witness for the other side.

"The first time you talked to her was at her home, wasn't it?" I demanded as I stepped round the end of the counsel table.

"Yes."

He said it with such indifference, such inexplicable unconcern, that for a brief, passing moment, I wondered if I had gotten so lost in the question I wanted to ask that I had asked him something else, some routine, preliminary question that he could of course answer without embarrassment.

"At her home, The Palms?" I asked, to be sure.

"Yes."

I stopped, gave him a quick, searching look and then took a step toward him.

"You were there because Mary Margaret Flanders had called the police and said her husband, Stanley Roth, had assaulted her, weren't you?"

"Someone had called 911. She gave the address, then apparently hung up. She didn't give her name. A patrolman was sent to the address to inquire."

"Yes, yes; and when the patrolman arrived and could not get through the gate, you arrived–isn't that correct?" I asked irritably.

"Yes. I convinced Mr. Roth to open the gate, and I went up to the house."

"And that is when you first met them, Mary Margaret Flanders and Stanley Roth, not at the studio, not on the set of a movie on which you were working as a consultant?"

"Yes."

"In fact, that was the only time you ever talked to Mary Margaret Flanders. You never talked to her on the set of a movie, because you were never really hired as a consultant, were you, Detective Crenshaw?"

"No, that's not correct. I was hired as a consultant. You can check the records at Blue Zephyr. And I did speak several times to Ms. Flanders on the set. You can check with her assistant."

"I'm aware of the way the payment made to you was carried on the books at the studio, Detective Crenshaw. We'll come back to that. Right now, however, I want to ask you about the night you came to her home. You came in your capacity as a police officer. You weren't invited there, you weren't a guest of theirs, were you?"

"No."

"You came there because there was a report of domestic violence and because the patrolman had not been able to gain access to the house?"

"Yes."

"And when you got to the house, you told the patrolman he could go–that you would handle things on your own, correct?"

"It wasn't a situation that required more than a single officer."

"But instead of letting the patrolman handle it, you stayed yourself, didn't you?"

"Yes. In some situations it's easier for a plainclothes officer. I knew who Mr. Roth was, and I knew who his wife was. I could tell it wasn't anything all that serious, and I didn't see any reason why they should have to be embarrassed by what had happened."

I started to ask the next question, but Crenshaw wanted to explain something.

"That was the reason there was never any formal report. I talked to Ms. Flanders, alone, and she told me she was all right; that it was as much her fault as anyone's. She asked me not to do anything. She begged me not to do anything. She said that if some reporter found out, the tabloids would get hold of it and blow everything out of proportion. At the time," he added, a look of regret in his eye, "it didn't seem too much to ask."

It was at this precise moment that I realized how seriously I had underestimated Richard Crenshaw. He was subtle, shrewd, completely aware of what he was doing and, more importantly, of what I was trying to do. He had thought it all through, considered each point in his prior testimony where he had either not told the truth or not told all of it. He was not going to deny anything. I knew that now. Had he decided to lie about it, he would have lied about going to the house, about meeting Mary Margaret Flanders the night her husband hit her, about his failure to file a report about what had happened. No, he was not going to lie; he was going to do something more dishonest still: He was going to take each fact I threw at him and give it a different meaning, put each thing he had done in a new light, one entirely to his own advantage.

I went back to my question, repeated it, insisted he repeat the answer, this time without the elaboration.

"Instead of letting the patrolman handle it, you told him to leave–isn't that correct?"

"Yes."

"You knew this was the home where Stanley Roth and Mary Margaret Flanders lived, didn't you?"

"Yes."

"And that was the reason you decided to handle this matter yourself–because of who they were: Stanley Roth the producer, the director, the head of Blue Zephyr; Mary Margaret Flanders, the actress. Wasn't it?"

"It's what I said before. I could tell it wasn't a dangerous situation. No one was running around, waving a gun. I didn't need any assistance."

"And you thought it would be perhaps your only opportunity to meet Stanley Roth, didn't you?"

Crenshaw permitted himself a tolerant smile. "I was there because there was a call to 911, and because the officer first on the scene had not been able to gain entrance to the house."

"You told Stanley Roth that you had written a screenplay and that you had not been able to find anyone who was interested in it?" I returned to the counsel table and retrieved a thin manuscript of not much more than a hundred pages from my briefcase. "This screenplay," I said, holding the bound copy shoulder high. "The screenplay that you testified under oath you had never written. You remember that, don't you, Detective Crenshaw? You remember–I just read it back to you and I can do it again if you like–you said, when I asked if you had ever thought about writing a screenplay of your own, that you 'wouldn't mind doing that someday'? But here it is, already done; the screenplay you wanted Stanley Roth to read; more than read, to use, to make into a movie, a major motion picture, Detective Crenshaw; a motion picture that would make you famous, that would make you rich, that would make you into the kind of celebrity for whom cops want to do favors, instead of staying one of the cops who want to do them. That is what was going on that night, wasn't it? You were there to convince Stanley Roth that the only chance he had to keep what happened between he and his wife out of the papers was to buy your screenplay, and that was the only reason you were there, wasn't it?"

Crenshaw shook his head emphatically. "No, that's not true," he said without rancor. "That is not true at all. That isn't . . ."

"It isn't? It isn't true that Stanley Roth agreed that night to read your screenplay? It isn't true that the very next day you were sent a check . . . This check," I said, pulling from out of the briefcase the cancelled check Blue Zephyr Studio had issued to Richard Crenshaw. "A check in the amount of $250,000. Have you forgotten, Detective Crenshaw? Do you get a great many checks for that amount?"

"No, that's the only check like that I've ever received. I haven't forgotten."

"That was the payment for your silence, wasn't it, Detective Crenshaw? That was the price you got for your agreement to make sure that no one–not even your own police department–ever found out that Stanley Roth had in a moment of anger struck his wife, wasn't it, Detective Crenshaw?"

Clasping his hands together, his eyes widened into a blank stare. It struck me as odd, the way he looked, like someone sitting on a train, watching out the window, lost in thoughts of his own, as the scenery rushes past. I was almost shouting, but I was not sure he had heard a word of it.

"Did you ever talk to her?" he said.

"What?" I asked, startled. At first I did not understand what he was asking.

"Did you ever meet her–Mary Margaret Flanders? Did you ever talk to her, hear that voice of hers when she was looking right at you, asking if you would do something for her?"

"I'm sorry, Detective Crenshaw, you're here to answer my questions, not the other way around. Now, answer the question I asked. The payment of $250,000 was payment for your silence, wasn't it?"

"No," he replied, shaking his head again in that same slow way. "I was there, at their house, talking to her, trying to make sure things were going to be all right. I wanted them to relax. Mr. Roth was very agitated. I wanted to make some connection with him, put things on a different footing, make him feel that he wasn't being questioned by a cop. I had been working on a screenplay–that's true. I got the idea when, as I told you, I was approached about that police show, when they sent me to that acting class. It wasn't finished; it was only a draft. I had not sent it to anyone; I hadn't even thought of sending it to anyone. I brought it up only because it was something we had in common. No, not in common, something in which the authority was all on his side. You see, I was a police detective talking to someone involved in a potential domestic abuse situation. That put me in charge, but it also put him in a position where he wasn't going to feel comfortable talking about anything. I wanted him to feel at ease, able to talk. That's why I brought it up. And it worked. He started telling me how difficult it was when you were just starting out, how difficult it had been for him when he first came to Hollywood. He told me that almost everyone who had become a success in the business could point back to something that happened–someone who had seen them work somewhere, seen something they had done. Then he told me he'd like to see what I'd done, read what I'd written. He said he couldn't promise me anything, only that he'd give it a fair reading. That's what happened. That's all that happened. There was no deal, no arrangement. I never said anything to him about what I was going to do about what had happened between he and his wife. That was between she and I."

While Crenshaw spoke, Stanley Roth shoved his chair a foot back from the counsel table, crossed one leg over the other. Intensely interested, he studied Crenshaw with a close scrutiny, as if he were watching an actor in a scene he wanted to get exactly right. His eyes were all over him, examining each movement, each gesture, ready, as it were, to insist on whatever small correction he thought necessary. I was much more interested in what Crenshaw was saying.

"And he read it, and the very next day sent you a check for $250,000?" I asked, doing nothing to conceal my incredulity. "For your screenplay–your unfinished screenplay–your first draft of a screenplay?"

"No."

"No?"

"No, not for the screenplay; not alone, anyway. It was for the rights to the screenplay and to serve as a consultant."

"Stanley Roth asked you to work–hired you to work–as a consultant at Blue Zephyr?"

"No. She did."

"Mary Margaret Flanders?"

"Yes."

"When?" I inquired, trying to hide my surprise.

"She called me the next day. She told me her husband–Mr. Roth–had received the screenplay, that he liked it, that it had promise, that with some work it might become a successful picture. She said they were working on a picture that was just about ready for production. It was a mystery. She played the part of a woman trying to find out who was really responsible for a murder for which her husband had been convicted. She asked if I'd like to work as a consultant on it."

Crenshaw turned toward the jury. "The check was for both–the option on the screenplay and the fee to work as a consultant. I had already told them both that I did not see any reason to file a formal report."

"So your testimony now is that you were hired as a consultant–as you originally testified–and paid for this screenplay," I said, picking up the script from the table, "which you did not mention in your original testimony?"

"Yes, that's correct."

"And that this all came about because you happened to arrive at the Roth residence to assist with a routine domestic disturbance, and that the way it was handled–the decision not to make it part of the public record–was taken independently of the offer to take an option on your screenplay and hire you as a consultant. Is that correct?" I asked with icy skepticism. "Is that now your testimony, Detective Crenshaw?"

"Yes."

"The screenplay–the one Stanley Roth was supposedly so eager to have–it's never been made into a movie, has it?"

"No, not yet."

I threw up my hands, despairing of my inability to understand. "It was all so innocent, all so straightforward, and yet you came in here, a police officer, sworn to uphold the law, sworn again as a witness to tell the truth, and you tell the assistant district attorney, and you tell the jury, that you were acquainted with Mary Margaret Flanders and with Stanley Roth because you had met them during your work as a consultant on a movie. Will you at least admit, Detective Crenshaw, that your testimony was misleading?"

He did not even argue the point. "Yes, I agree; it was, in that respect, misleading."

The script was still in my hand. I dropped it onto the table and put one hand on each side of where it fell. Leaning as far forward as I could, I fixed him with a piercing stare.

"And the reason you did that, Detective Crenshaw, the reason you misled the jury, was because you didn't want anyone to know that you might have a motive to want Stanley Roth accused of the murder of his wife. It wasn't just a draft, a not-yet-finished screenplay, you gave to Stanley Roth, was it, Detective Crenshaw? You had poured your heart and soul into it, you had worked on it, done everything you could with it. It was going to make your name, it was going to make you famous. Stanley Roth gave you the money, but he didn't give you what you really wanted, did he? He didn't give you the movie. It was worse than that, wasn't it? When you tried to find out how things stood, when something might happen, when you could start to work on the movie itself, he wouldn't even return your phone calls, would he? That's why you hurried out there, the first detective on the scene: to get even for what he had done to you, for the way he had treated you. After what you had done for him–saved him from the public humiliation of being labeled a wife-beater and worse in every supermarket tabloid! You get there, the first detective on the scene, and all you can think is that Stanley Roth must have done it. He was the only one there and he had assaulted her once before. Stanley Roth is guilty! You're sure of it, so you grab a shirt from his closet, wipe it in the blood–the blood that was all over the place next to the pool–and you put it in the laundry hamper, because, after all, Stanley Roth is guilty, and why not make certain you can prove it?"

Breathing hard, my face burning, I pushed myself up from the table and glared hard at him. "It's true, isn't it? That's what happened. That's the reason you lied about when you first met Mary Margaret Flanders!"

Crenshaw looked down at his hands, still clasped together. "You never met her," he said in a distant voice, slowly raising his eyes. "I think if she had asked me that night to file a report that said she had assaulted her husband, I would have done it. I don't know if it was because she was Mary Margaret Flanders the movie star, or if it was just something about her, something about the way she looked at me: as if she had always known me and known she could trust me. I don't know. But I did what she asked me to do. I didn't think it was asking too much. I believed her, I believed what she told me about what had happened. I did."

Crenshaw straightened up. An apologetic smile crossed his mouth. "You want to know why I didn't tell you, didn't tell the jury about when I first met them? Cowardice, pure and simple. I didn't want to have to admit that I'm the one responsible for her death. I could have prevented it. If I hadn't done what she asked, if I had gone ahead and filed a report, charges might have been brought, something might have been done–and maybe none of this would have happened. I was the first detective on the scene. You're right, I went there the moment I heard about it, but it wasn't because I wanted to do something to make sure Stanley Roth was convicted of murder–I kept praying that it wasn't Stanley Roth. Don't you see?" he cried plaintively. "If it had been someone else–anyone else–it wouldn't have been my fault! Having Stanley Roth guilty of the murder of Mary Margaret Flanders is the worst thing that has ever happened to me!"

24

ROTH SAID HE WOULD never go there again, but he had no choice. While the police held back the pressing crowd of busy narrow-eyed reporters trying to find something to write and gawking wide-eyed tourists eager to see whatever they could, the overworked engine of the ancient public facility bus hissed and groaned as it rumbled through the just-opened gate of The Palms. We were a strange looking bunch, the judge and the jury, the clerk and the court reporter, the bailiff, the prosecutor, the lawyer for the defense, and, sitting all alone behind the driver, Stanley Roth. Everyone had a full seat to themselves and under instructions not to discuss the case no one had said a word during the forty-five minutes since we first boarded the bus outside the courthouse downtown. Someone passing by us might have thought we were on our way to an obligatory company picnic in which all the employees had worn casual clothing while their employers, who took themselves much more seriously, wore the same coats and ties they wore every day to the office. I grew up watching movies in which juries were always made up of well-dressed men; I could count on the fingers of a single hand the times anyone had worn a suit and tie in any trial of my own.

These average men and women, brought from the obscurity of their everyday, anonymous lives to sit in judgment on Stanley Roth, had never seen anything quite like the private splendor of the gated estate that only film stars and their wealthy and powerful friends had been allowed to step inside. The Hearst Castle had become a public park, a place where uniformed tour guides gave the impression it had been vacant for years by remarking that Marion Davies, the mistress of William Randolph

Hearst, had been a film star in the "early days of Hollywood." Though just as old, The Palms was a place where people, famous people, actually lived, and if not with the same massive opulence, with something that was still far beyond the scale of the normal aspirations of the great American middle class. From the rapt expressions on their faces, this is what the jurors had imagined; almost, I think, what they had hoped for.

The one person who seemed to have no interest at all in a closer look at the scene of Mary Margaret Flanders's murder was Annabelle Van Roten. She had opposed the request that the jury view the place where the murder occurred with a combination of moral outrage and caustic charm.

"What's next?" she asked, throwing up her hand. "Do you want to exhume the body so they can view the corpse?"

We were in chambers, a word, with its suggestion of dark, quiet places filled with leather-bound volumes and leather-backed chairs, that scarcely conveys the ugly simplicity of Rudolph Honigman's tin-box office. With his ordinary expression of benevolent boredom, the judge raised a single eyebrow and looked at me.

"That's been done already," I said. "Surely you remember all those photographs you insisted on introducing at the beginning of the trial. If you thought it necessary that the jury see what she looked like when she died, it is a little difficult to understand why you don't want them to see where it happened."

Van Roten's head snapped up. Her coal-dark eyes flared.

"Those photographs showed the manner of her death. What you're proposing is nothing more than a sideshow, a diversion." She turned to Honigman. "It doesn't have any evidentiary value whatsoever."

"A little outing might improve your mood," I could not resist suggesting. "A little fresh air would do you good."

She flashed a taunting smile. "After the trial we can go to the beach. You know how much I love listening to your voice.

"It's a waste of time, Your Honor," she said, turning immediately back to Honigman.

"It's anything but a waste of time," I insisted. "We've had testimony about where the victim was found and how she was killed. We've had testimony about where the blood-soaked clothing of the defendant was found. We've had testimony about the location of the bedrooms. The jury needs to have a clear understanding about distance and direction, how far it is from one place to the other in that house and the route you have to travel to get there. A diagram on a blackboard, or even a scale model of the layout of the house, won't provide anything close to what the reality of it is. It's a murder case, Your Honor," I pled. "This won't take more than half a day."

Annabelle Van Roten sat on the bus, gazing through her dark glasses out the window with the petulant look of a reluctant tourist, a woman accompanying her husband only from the fear that in her absence some greater mischief might occur. This was not the first time I had noticed that look. It was always there, just below the surface, a kind of habitual discontent; a sense of dissatisfaction, I thought, with the way things were–not with the trial, but with herself: the fact that she wasn't doing something else, that she wasn't someone else. When we climbed off the bus and assembled in front of the house to listen to Honigman instruct the jurors about where they were going to be taken and what they were going to be shown, I looked over my shoulder and saw her standing a few steps off, facing the other way, taking in the view of everything that had once belonged to Mary Margaret Flanders. While Honigman droned on, I moved next to her.

"Did you ever dream about being a movie star when you were a kid?"

She turned, looked past me to make sure no one was watching, and then, for just a moment, put her hand on my arm. "Every time I went to the movies," she said quietly, passing in front of me as she rejoined the group that was just about to enter the house.

With Judge Honigman in the lead, our small party made its way along the prearranged route upstairs to the second floor hallway and the bedroom that Stanley Roth had sometimes shared with his wife. The bailiff opened the door to the bathroom and waited while, one by one, the jurors were shown the location of the laundry hamper where, according to Detective Crenshaw's testimony, Stanley Roth's clothing, stained with the blood of Mary Margaret Flanders, had been found. While they waited for the others to take their turn, several of the women on the jury wandered around the bedroom, glancing at the photographs of Stanley Roth and his wife, taken in various famous places, sometimes the two of them alone, sometimes with a few of their well-known friends. Certain no one was looking, the juror who had done a bit of acting and had once smiled at Stanley Roth craned her neck to glimpse through a door left partially open a large walk-in closet filled with dresses. Our eyes met and she knew I had seen what she had done. She began to gaze all around the room, as if the look inside the closet had no more meaning than anything else.

At the other end of the hall, facing the front of the house, the jury was taken into the bedroom where Stanley Roth claimed he had spent the night. One of the men on the jury, impressed with the solid thickness of the door, gripped it between his thumb and forefinger. He had done the same thing with the master bedroom door. Someone could have been crying for help inside one of those rooms and, if the door had been shut, no one would have heard a sound.

"Be careful," cautioned Judge Honigman as he grasped the handrail and began to descend the gray stone staircase, each step sloping toward the middle after what was now close to a century of use.

Outside, the bailiff, thoroughly schooled by Honigman, stood next to the swimming pool and with an economy of words described where, the witnesses had all agreed, the body of Mary Margaret Flanders had first been discovered. Consulting a diagram held in his hand, he pointed to the spot on the poolside deck where blood had been found. The upstairs curiosity; the chance to look behind the scenes at how people like Stanley Roth and his movie-star wife had lived; the close attention to the manner in which the physical characteristics of the house might in some measure affect the meaning of the evidence offered at trial; all of it faded from the jury's eyes at the first mention of death. They huddled together in respectful silence while the bailiff, moving slowly the few feet from one place to the next, continued his spare recitation of the geography of a murder.

When the bailiff bent down to point out the location of the blood spatters on the cement deck, Stanley Roth, who had been standing right beside me, turned away. I found him a few minutes later, leaning against an oak tree next to a goldfish pond at the side of the house. He was looking out across the lawn that swept in a gentle arc down to the barely visible iron fence below, an empty expanse that had once been crowded with guests. Instinctively, my eye moved to the spot, just a few yards away from the pool, where the surveillance camera had caught Mary Margaret Flanders, surrounded by what seemed utterly anonymous faces, in the middle of that late afternoon event, only hours before she died.

A cynical smile played on Roth's mouth, as if he had just become certain of an unpleasant fact. When he heard me coming, he looked over his shoulder and shook his head.

"She was screwing him," said Roth, as we began to walk toward the front of the house where the bus was waiting to take us back to the courthouse. "That explains it," he added cryptically.

"Who are you talking about? What does it explain?"

He looked at me, not with anger or disappointment or any other emotion you might expect on the face of an injured husband, but with an odd sense of triumph.

"It doesn't matter," said Roth, lowering his eyes as we approached the jurors lined up at the bus.

He was doing this more and more now: saying things as if they explained something important, and then, a moment later, acting as if they did not explain anything at all. It was all part of what was happening to him: the months spent protesting his innocence while he waited for the trial to begin; the dawning realization that people he thought he knew and could trust suspected he might not be telling the truth; the unflattering photographs on the covers of magazines with made-up stories about some secret life that supplied the motive for his murdering his wife; the jeering courthouse crowds that chanted his guilt. No one could go through that and not be affected.

Stanley Roth looked older, a lot older, than when I first met him. The lines in his forehead were deeper and more pronounced. His hands, which had started to tremble some months before, did so more often now. But what had happened to him physically was not the biggest change. He was now the most famous name in America, but except for the conversations he had with me, and those he sometimes still had with Louis Griffin, he did not talk to anyone. Isolated and alone, working long hours into the night, Roth lived more and more in a world of his own invention in which, like every work of fiction, everything connected neatly and inevitably with everything else. In putting him on the stand to testify in his own behalf, my biggest fear was not that he might become angry or confused under what I knew would be a withering cross-examination–I had prepared him for that–but that in a moment of what he thought inspiration he would suddenly go off on some strange, wandering monologue of his own, describing with that look of shrewd certainty how Mary Margaret Flanders had been murdered and why. It only shows how little I still understood Stanley Roth.

"WOULD YOU PLEASE STATE your name and spell your last for the record," I said as soon as Roth had finished taking the oath and settled into the witness chair.

The courtroom was packed. Reporters, part of the pool allowed in each day, sat forward on the edge of the benches, notebooks braced against their knees. Jack Walsh, having given his testimony, was back in court under his asserted right as the victim's father. Louis Griffin, solid and reliable, the only friend Stanley Roth had left, was in what for all practical purposes had become his reserved seat in the first row, directly behind the counsel table where I stood next to the defendant's now empty chair. A few feet away, at the other counsel table, Annabelle Van Roten leaned forward on her elbows. Her hands held together under her chin, she joined both index fingers in the shape of a steeple, the apex pushing against her brooding lower lip. The clerk, with half-shut eyes, glanced at her watch.

"Mr. Roth, did you murder your wife?"

"No," replied Roth firmly. He was all business and, for one of the first times since the trial started, fully engaged.

"Mr. Roth, did you ever at any time strike or otherwise assault your wife?"

"Yes, I did."

Moving behind the counsel table the few steps to the end of the jury box farthest from the witness stand, I asked him to describe what he had done and the circumstances in which it had happened.

"That was the first time you knew your wife was pregnant–the day you found out she had had an abortion?" I asked when he finished, doing what I could to underscore the extraordinary nature of the event that had precipitated this single act of violence.

"Yes," he said, with a trace of both sadness and regret in his voice. "She hadn't said anything to me, not a word."

"She knew you wanted a child?"

"It was the reason–the main reason, anyway–we got married. Yes, she knew I wanted a child. She knew I wanted that more than anything."

"If she had told you that she wanted an abortion, that whether because of her career or some other reason she wasn't ready to have a child, would you have gone along with that?"

Roth did not answer right away. "I don't know," he admitted finally. "If she had said she wanted to wait–for a year, for some specific, definite period of time–if she had talked to me about it, about when she wanted to have a child, then . . . maybe. But if she had just left it vague, like it was something she wasn't really serious about, then I'm not sure. I don't think the marriage would have survived it."

"But she didn't talk to you about an abortion: she just did it. And when you found out about it, confronted her with it, you got so angry you hit her. And at that moment, the moment you hit her, you wanted to hurt her, didn't you?"

"Yes, I did. I admit that. I was in a rage. If I had been younger, stronger, quicker, I might have hurt her . . . more than I did. What she had done had hurt me, more than anything anyone had ever done to me before," said Roth with a bitter look in his eye. "I didn't do the right thing, but at that moment I didn't care about that. I wanted to hurt her back."

"And then, after you hit her, she called the police?"

"Yes. I told her to." He paused. "That isn't quite right: I dared her to do it. We were screaming at each other. Isn't that awful?" he added, casting an embarrassed glance toward the jury. He lifted his eyebrows, an expression of disgust on his face. "Two grown adults, with everything anyone could ever want to have, screaming at each other like a couple of spoiled children who can't have their way. It was sinful the way we behaved."

Roth looked down at his hands for a moment. A slight shudder ran through him as he thought about what he had done.

"She was screaming," he went on, still staring at his hands, "telling me how she was going to call the police. 'See what the world thinks of the great Stanley Roth then,' she said, taunting me with it. 'Arrested for beating his wife!' "

Roth lifted his head and in a disparaging gesture waved his hand back and forth in front of him. "I told her to go ahead, call the police. I'd be glad to go to trial and get convicted just for the chance to tell all her adoring fans how she was too damn worried about the way she looked on screen to have a child of her own."

With both hands on the arms of the chair, Roth opened his eyes wide. A pensive expression formed on his mouth.

"I don't think she would have done it, if I hadn't said that, dared her that way. That was one thing you could never do with Mary Margaret: threaten her with any kind of consequence if she did something you didn't want her to do. She was, I think, the most willful woman I ever knew. It's what made her so good on the screen: the way she imposed her personality on everything around her, made you think she was the only one there, at least the only one worth paying attention to."

I was afraid he was about to go off on a tangent, something that made sense in his own peculiar scheme of things but had no obvious connection to the issue at hand, but he did not say another word about it. He looked at me and waited for the next question.

"Describe to the jury, if you would, what happened when Detective Crenshaw arrived."

Set off by the dark blue fabric of his suit, Roth's gray hair had a kind of silver sheen which, along with the deep-set eyes and craggy forehead, added to a general sense of authority, of someone used to making decisions. Or perhaps it was the other way round, and what we knew about him, what we knew about the famous Stanley Roth, gave the meaning to the way he looked.

Roth cleared his throat. “Mary Margaret regretted what she had done,” he said in a full, rich voice. “We both regretted what had happened,” he added, nodding thoughtfully. “When the police officer first called from the gate, I tried to explain that there had been a misunderstanding, that everything was all right. He insisted he had to come up to the house. I’m afraid I wasn’t very polite. A few minutes later, Detective Crenshaw called from the gate.”

With what I suppose must have been a director’s eye for detail and a screenwriter’s ear for dialogue, Stanley Roth described the way in which Richard Crenshaw had, without ever saying it, made clear what he wanted.

“Let me be certain I understand this,” I said when he was through. “He brought up this business about his screenplay before he said anything about the way he was going to handle the incident he was supposedly there to investigate?”

“Yes. As I said, he didn’t seem all that interested in what had happened. He didn’t want to talk to Mary Margaret alone to make sure that I wasn’t trying to intimidate her; he didn’t ask how it happened, or even if I had hit her. Nothing. He wanted to talk about his screenplay. I didn’t have any choice but to tell him I’d take a look at it.”

“And once you told him that–told him you would be interested in seeing his screenplay–that was it? He didn’t take a statement from your wife? He didn’t take a statement from you?”

“He didn’t do anything. He told Mary Margaret she should have her eye looked at. Then he left. Mary Margaret walked him out to his car. He sent the screenplay to the studio the next day.”

I turned and faced the jury. “Did you read it?”

“No.”

“But you bought it, didn’t you? Bought it for the studio?”

“Yes.”

“How much did you pay for it?”

“We talked on the telephone. I asked him what he wanted for it. I paid him what he asked.”

“And how much was that?”

“Two hundred fifty thousand.”

"How was this expenditure listed on the books of the studio? As a payment for an option on a screenplay?"

"No. A decision has to be made whether to renew an option. I didn't want anyone at the studio to know about this. It was put in the books as a consulting fee."

"Did Detective Crenshaw work as a consultant on any movie produced by Blue Zephyr?"

"No."

"So, in other words, you paid Detective Crenshaw a quarter million dollars not to report what had happened that night, not to report that on that one occasion you struck your wife?"

"Yes."

"In other words," I asked, turning my head until my eyes met his, "Detective Crenshaw blackmailed you?"

Roth thought for a moment. "No, at least not in the normal sense of the word. You see, I'm convinced he thought his screenplay was worth every penny I agreed to pay for it. I don't think he thought there was anything wrong with taking advantage of the fact that he found himself with the chance to talk to me about the screenplay that he hadn't been able to sell. When he testified here the other day that in his own mind the two things–the failure to file a report and the decision about his screenplay–were completely separate and apart, I think he was telling the truth. I think from the moment he realized Mary Margaret didn't have anything more than a bruised eye he knew he wasn't going to file a report. He wanted to do us a favor. Maybe he hoped I would do him one in return. I didn't think this at first. I thought he just wanted the money. But later," he went on, nodding in a way that signaled a conversation we had once had about it, "I began to realize that it was more than that. He wanted it made into a movie. He called me, repeatedly, left messages, asking when a decision was going to be made, when someone would tell him if any more work needed to be done on it."

"You never replied to those calls, did you?"

"No. I hadn't even read it. I paid him the money because that was the price–what I thought was the price–to keep what had happened out of the papers."

"You never read it? No one ever read it?"

"Last week. I got it out of the files, just to see what it was like."

"And?"

Roth slowly raised his eyebrows, as a rueful expression settled on his mouth. "It wasn't bad."

I began to pace back and forth, a few steps each way, in front of the jury box.

"So, he comes to your house, the night you struck your wife; he decides to do both of you a favor–keep it out of the papers by not making a formal report–and you tell him you'd love to see the screenplay he's written."

I stopped still and gave him a searching look. "He sends it to you. You call him, tell him the studio–Blue Zephyr–the most prestigious studio in Hollywood, wants to take an option on his script."

I paused and the look on my face turned to one of utter incredulity. "Not only that, not only does Blue Zephyr want it, you want it so badly you'll pay whatever he wants for it. You've dealt with writers, with actors, producers, directors–people trying to get their first big break–he must have been ecstatic, on top of the world. Stanley Roth loved his screenplay! Blue Zephyr is going to make it into a movie! Richard Crenshaw–Detective Crenshaw–working homicide division on a civil servant's salary is going to be famous, he's going to be rich, he's going to have a whole new career. And then you wouldn't return his phone calls. How long do you think it was before it finally dawned on him what had happened: that you probably never bothered to read it, that you probably tossed it in the trash, that you were only interested in keeping him quiet? How long before he realized that he had tried to do you a favor and you in turn were treating him like a crook?"

Roth let the question answer itself.

"He must have hated you for that; hated you enough to make sure he was the first detective on the scene when he heard of your wife's murder; hated you enough to make sure there was enough evidence to convict you by making certain some of your wife's blood would be found on your clothes!"

"Objection!" cried Annabelle Van Roten as she shot out of her chair.

Before Honigman could sustain it, I kept the substance by surrendering the form. "Withdraw the question," I announced with a smug smile of satisfied indifference.

I walked to the counsel table, opened a thick black loose-leaf notebook in which were organized all the materials I needed for trial and, once I had found the one I wanted, made a show of carefully studying the page. It was a way of buying time, a way of making sure nothing else was allowed to intrude upon the jury's silent reflection on the accusation of misconduct I had just thrown at the main witness for the prosecution. I could feel Van Roten's eyes boring into me across the short distance that separated us. She was seething, angry at what I had done and angrier still that there was not yet anything she could do about it.

"Now, Mr. Roth," I said with renewed intensity as I looked up, my finger still pressed against the page, "you've been working for some time on a screenplay of your own, haven't you? A story about the way Hollywood really works. You call it *Blue Zephyr*, the same name as the studio, don't you?"

"Yes," replied Roth. "It was the name of the studio."

"It's the story of someone rather like yourself, isn't it? Someone who started out with nothing, did what he had to do to survive while he learned everything he could until he got his chance. He becomes successful, creates his own studio, takes an unknown actress, makes her into a star and marries her. Isn't that what happened to you? You made Marian Walsh into Mary Margaret Flanders, didn't you?"

Stanley Roth placed his left elbow on the arm of the witness chair. He spread his thumb and forefinger around the contour of his chin. With an abstracted gaze, he thought for a moment.

"She wasn't particularly well trained, and she hadn't had any real experience. She had something you can't teach, and no amount of experience can ever give: she drew you toward her. You couldn't help yourself. When she walked into a room everything stopped. The effect on the screen . . . well, you've all seen her," said Roth, addressing himself directly to the jury. "There weren't many actresses who wanted to be in a scene with her–not many major actresses, I mean. It didn't matter that it was their scene, that they were the ones speaking the lines. If Mary Margaret was anywhere in the shot–standing off in the distance somewhere–

they knew that everyone in the theater would be looking at her, waiting to see what she was going to do next." Roth shrugged his shoulders. "There's no good way of explaining why it happened. It wasn't because she was the best-looking woman anyone had ever seen. Who knows why we feel drawn to one person and not another, why every once in a while there is someone like her, someone who seems to draw everyone's eye. All I know is that more than anyone I had ever seen on camera, Mary Margaret had that ability, that gift."

"But you were the first one to see that, weren't you?"

"I knew she could be a star."

"In the screenplay, the one you've written, the movie-star wife runs off with her husband's partner, and together they start a studio of their own–correct?" I asked, with my head down, moving toward the jury box.

"Yes."

"He loses not only his wife, but his studio as well–or rather is about to lose it–right? And he decides to risk everything on one last picture, one that is going to expose the whole thing–what they did to him–his partner and his wife–and expose a lot of other things as well. He makes the movie, but the movie never gets shown. Why is that? What happens in the end?"

Stanley Roth smiled. "He dies."

"Someone kills him?"

"In one version."

"To stop anyone from ever seeing the movie?" I persisted.

"Yes."

"Your wife was sleeping with your partner, wasn't she?"

Roth looked at me and did not answer.

"You were here, in court, when your partner, Michael Wirthlin, admitted it, weren't you?"

"Yes."

"You didn't know about it at the time?"

"No."

"But you knew–or you suspected–that she had affairs with other men, didn't you?"

Roth nodded grimly and then, abruptly, shook his head. "Mary Margaret needed attention, constant attention. She needed to be told how much everyone loved her; she needed to feel that. You may think that strange," he said to the jury, "that a woman like that, a woman as well-known and admired as she was, would need that. She was incredibly insecure. If you get just below the surface, they all are–all those famous faces you see in the movies. Millions of people go to see them, but they don't have an audience when they work. No one applauds; they don't get standing ovations when they do something particularly well. They do the same thing, shoot the same scene, speak the same few words, dozens, sometimes hundreds of times, before the director decides it's the way he wants it to be. Mary Margaret needed to know she was wanted. Did I know she was having an affair with Michael Wirthlin, or with Walker Bradley, or with anyone else? No. Did I think that she had never slept with anyone else while we were married? I never asked, and I tried not to think about it."

I put it to him directly. "Did you have Michael Wirthlin and your wife in mind when you wrote *Blue Zephyr*?"

"Yes, but not because I knew there was something going on between them, or even suspected it. It was because I knew Michael was completely ruthless when it came to getting what he wanted. It was also because, like a lot of men in this business who only think in terms of money–especially the ones who got into the business only because of the money they already had–he found the idea of sleeping with a famous movie star irresistible."

Folding his arms, Roth crossed one leg over the other. He noticed a piece of lint on his pant leg and flicked it off with the back of his finger.

"And because," he continued, "Mary Margaret had the kind of driving ambition that I wanted to capture in the character I was creating: a woman who can't stand the thought that she can't decide everything for herself."

"If *Blue Zephyr* were made into a movie, would Michael Wirthlin recognize himself as the partner?"

The expression on Roth's face changed immediately. His eyes sparkled and a mischievous grin shot across his mouth. He bounced up in the chair.

"Michael Wirthlin wouldn't recognize himself in the mirror. He thinks he's a creative genius; he isn't even a very good bookkeeper."

"Would other people who saw it think it was Michael Wirthlin?"

"I don't know, they might."

"Wirthlin knew about the screenplay, didn't he?"

"Yes."

"Michael Wirthlin had an affair with your wife?"

"Yes."

"Blue Zephyr–the studio–the studio you built–no longer exists, does it?"

"No."

"Michael Wirthlin used the fact that you were on trial for murder to take the studio away from you, didn't he? He threatened to pull his own money and make sure you couldn't raise it anywhere else, didn't he?"

"Yes."

"That was the reason that at the home of your other partner, Louis Griffin, you got into a fight with Michael Wirthlin, isn't it?"

"Yes."

"So, because you're on trial for the murder of your wife, your partner, the one who had been having an affair with your wife, takes away your studio and, if you're convicted of that murder, won't have to worry about anyone seeing a movie exposing him for what he is. Does that about sum up the situation in which you find yourself? It's almost as good as the ending you wrote, isn't it? Except of course that your partner didn't have to kill anyone. Or did he?

"No further questions," I said before Annabelle Van Roten could finish objecting to what I had just done.

25

IF I HAD EVER thought that this was going to be like any other murder trial, that, despite the almost morbid fascination with which millions of people followed each day's developments, there would be no substantial departure in the way the case itself was conducted, Annabelle Van Roten now showed me just how wrong I was. Another defendant, someone no one had ever heard of, one of that vast, largely anonymous, horde of violent predators charged with taking a life, might have been treated with the same withering contempt which she now lavished on Stanley Roth, but it would have been over in no time at all and it would have concentrated on the weakest points in the defendant's own account.

Few lawyers, and scarcely any prosecuting attorneys, take seriously the first rule of cross-examination, which is not to do it unless there is not any choice. It has become, for many of them, the way to prove their own importance, this itching eagerness to tell a witness to his face that he is lying, or through the skepticism in their voice or the look of incredulity in their eyes show the jury that they know the witness is not telling the truth. But if there are not many lawyers left who understand the advantages of limiting the number and the nature of the questions they ask, most still recognize that there is some point at which things have to come to an end and some need to organize their inquiry around the issues crucial to the case. Annabelle Van Roten seemed to want to know everything there was to know about Stanley Roth whether it had anything to do with the murder of Mary Margaret Flanders or not. She began to ask questions before I had quite settled in my chair, and she continued to ask them with scarcely any pause between all the rest of that day and through most of the next, probing first one aspect of Stanley Roth's life, then another, circling around the witness stand, her dark eyes flashing, gesturing with her long-fingered hands like some rapacious shiny-feathered bird of prey.

How much time must she have spent thinking about this moment, lying awake late into the night, watching the way it was going to be, the moment she matched wits, not with some inarticulate criminal, but with the great Stanley Roth, who had taught an entire generation, if not precisely what to think, then certainly what to feel. It was the chance of a lifetime, the chance to become nearly as famous, nearly as much a celebrity as Stanley Roth himself. Famous people had been killed so that the sick souls who killed them could share in their fame by becoming permanently associated with their deaths. Annabelle Van Roten could accomplish the same thing not only without infamy but with honor by connecting her name with the death, the execution of Stanley Roth, not a man she had murdered, but a man who had murdered his wife.

It did not much matter whether she tricked Stanley Roth into a damaging admission or caught him in a deadly half-truth. It was not even necessary that he make one of those small mistakes, something so subtle no one at first notices: the single, seemingly minor inconsistency that shows that everything was a lie. The lengthy and grueling cross-examination of Stanley Roth was not done because there was either a need or an expectation that he was going to make a mistake. It was done so that when he was convicted, everyone would remember how for the better part of two days Annabelle Van Roten had subjected him to this remorseless, withering attack, hammering him hour after hour with accusations of his guilt. Even among those who had been there every day and had heard every word of testimony and seen every witness testify, few would remember much about what had happened in the middle of the trial, but all of them would remember what had happened at the end when that woman, that deputy district attorney with the blazing black eyes went after Stanley Roth in a way they had seldom seen anyone go after a witness before. They would remember–everyone would remember–that Stanley Roth had been convicted of murder and that Annabelle Van Roten had been the one who did it.

"I'm a little confused," said Van Roten, practically laughing in his face. "You knew, but you didn't know, your wife was having an affair?"

"No, I said I didn't know that she had affairs, but that I think I always assumed that she had."

"You assumed she was having affairs? You assumed–just assumed–your wife was sleeping with other men; and yet, despite this assumption, you never confronted her, never asked if it was true?"

"No, I never asked."

Roth never took his eyes off her. They followed her when she wheeled around to face the jury or when she stalked away, waving her arms in a gesture of disbelief. He looked right back at her and, though I was probably reading into it something that was not there, seemed almost amused when she tried to stare him down. There were moments when I thought he had forgotten he was in court, a witness at his own trial, and imagined himself studying through a lens a scene he was attempting to film. Once or twice I thought he gave an answer for no other reason than to see the effect it would have on her.

"You never asked?" repeated Van Roten in a vengeful tone.

Roth waited with an indulgent smile while what had by now become her patented look of incredulity began to freeze into an awkward, twitching, self-conscious stare.

"As I explained before," finally replied Roth in a calm, patient voice, "there are some things you're better off not knowing."

"You knew she was going to divorce you, though, didn't you?" asked Van Roten, anxious to distract attention from what had been a momentary embarrassment.

"If Mary Margaret was going to divorce me, I would have known about it. I didn't know about it."

Van Roten had just turned toward the jury. With her chin held high, she whirled back around.

"She told her father, though, didn't she?"

Stanley Roth laughed. "Jack Walsh? He wouldn't know the truth if it hit him in the head." Roth bent forward, his eyes narrowed. "If Mary Margaret had ever thought about getting a divorce, the last person in the world she would have told was . . . I was about to say her father, but she never thought of him as that. Jack Walsh abandoned her as a child and then, years later, when she's famous and he thinks she can do something for him, he shows up and asks for money."

Van Roten turned toward the bench. "Your Honor, would you please instruct the witness that . . ."

"And she gave it to him," continued Roth, talking over her objection. "But he kept asking for more, and finally she refused to see him. I told him that, told him not to come around anymore."

"Your Honor . . . !"

"Maybe he's the one who killed her. Did you ever think of that? He thought she owed him. You imagine that?–After what he did to her. You think he was content just to walk away, be cut off from all that money his daughter had?"

"Your Honor!" insisted Van Roten.

Honigman had done nothing to stop Roth from saying what he wanted. When he was finally finished, the judge leaned toward him and issued a mild reproof:

"The witness is admonished that he is to restrict himself to answering the questions put to him. He is not to make statements on his own."

Roth nodded like someone seconding something that had been his own idea. Van Roten flashed an irritated smile at the judge and then glared at the witness.

"Do you have any proof that Jack Walsh murdered his own daughter?"

"Do you have any proof that I did?" Roth shot back as if they were sparring over a matter that had no serious consequences for himself.

She had him now. "Yes, more than I need."

"From the mouth of the admitted liar, Richard Crenshaw?" he retorted with a confident grin. It drove her a little crazy.

"From the mouth of a distinguished and decorated police officer who once made the mistake of trying to do you a favor. And," she added, arching her neck in a way that made her eyes look positively lethal, "from the expert testimony that the blood found on the clothing you tried to hide in a laundry hamper was blood that streamed from the slaughtered body of the woman you killed!"

"Objection!" I cried, rising quickly from my chair. "Who is making speeches now?"

She gave me a sharp look, as if to tell me that I had no business telling her what to do. She turned immediately back to the witness, ready with the next question. The judge stopped her.

"Counsel will please refrain from arguing with the witness." Honigman moved his mouth from side to side, not quite satisfied with what he had done. "This is cross-examination," he said presently, "not closing argument. Ask questions. And if you don't have any more you want to ask, then sit down. Do I make myself clear?"

Van Roten replied with a quick, cursory nod, a gesture that bragged indifference. She moved a step closer to the witness stand.

"Do I make myself clear?" asked Honigman, furious at what he took to be a deliberate act of disrespect.

"Yes, Your Honor," at once replied Van Roten. "I'm sorry," she added with an innocent, apologetic smile. "Didn't I say that?"

His mouth pinched tight, Honigman slowly lifted his eyebrows, subjecting her to the kind of close unfavorable scrutiny judges often employ before imposing a prison sentence of the utmost severity.

"No, you did not," he replied.

With that same implacable smile, Van Roten waited until she was sure she would not interrupt him. "May I resume my questioning of the witness, Your Honor?"

"Yes. Questioning," said Honigman, repeating the word as a warning.

Van Roten stepped back to the counsel table. She briefly consulted the notes she had made on the lined page of a light gray legal pad.

"Mr. Roth," she said, lifting her eyes, "is it your testimony that you didn't know your wife was having an affair with your partner, Michael Wirthlin?"

Roth looked straight at her. "Yes."

Van Roten stood up. "And it is also your testimony that you were not surprised when you found out that she had?"

"Yes."

Van Roten walked behind me and took a position at the end of the jury box.

"You wrote a screenplay about a man whose partner had an affair with his wife, a man who loses his studio when his wife–his movie-star wife–leaves him for his partner and they start a studio of their own. Is that correct?" she asked with a pleasant smile, as if she was talking Hollywood gossip with an old friend.

"It's something I've been working on for a long time."

"I take it that's a yes?"

"There's more to it than what you've described, but . . ."

"It's what you testified when your attorney asked, isn't it?" she insisted more irritably than she meant to.

Roth had better instincts–his work had given him better training–than most witnesses, certainly better than most defendants. He knew she had not wanted to let down the mask and he was not about to help her put it back on. He did not answer. He just looked at her, as if he half expected her to apologize for the interruption.

"It's what you testified, isn't it?' she repeated more calmly.

"Yes." He paused, then added, "But there's more to it than what Mr. Antonelli described. The wife of the main character–his name is Welles, by the way–has an affair with his partner. That's true, but that's only part of the story, and the story–I should tell you this right away–isn't the same story I started out with. In the new version, his wife doesn't leave him. She's murdered and he's framed for it. Instead of *Blue Zephyr*, perhaps I'll call it *Falsely Accused.* Pretty good title, don't you think?"

Everyone had been sitting in the courtroom silence, listening intently to each exchange, measuring the meaning of every shift of tone, every nuanced glance, whether from the witness, the prosecutor, or the judge. Now, suddenly, Stanley Roth had, if only for the moment, taken their minds off the grim realities of a murder trial and made them think of things in the more comfortable guise of pure fiction. A quick breath taken in as a head lifted up; a short burst of air blown out the nostrils as a shoulder rolled forward; everywhere the audible sounds signaling a kind of approbation for the manner in which Stanley Roth had woven together what had happened to his life and what his life had been all about. Then it was as quiet as it had been before, everyone again listening intently, for fear they might otherwise miss the next thing said.

"You didn't know about your wife's affair with Walker Bradley?"

"No."

"But you weren't surprised?"

"No."

"You never asked her if she was having an affair with Walker Bradley?"

"No."

"You never asked her if she was having an affair with Michael Wirthlin?"

"No."

"But you're not surprised?"

"No."

"You never asked her if she was having an affair with anyone?"

"No."

"But you're not surprised?"

"No."

"You wrote about someone like yourself in this screenplay of yours–whatever title you want to give it–whose wife has an affair?"

"Yes."

Van Roten pulled her mouth back at a crooked angle, giving herself the look of someone confirming a suspicion.

"And I suppose he didn't know about it, but when he found out–he wasn't surprised?"

Before Roth could answer, she held up her hand and shook her head. "No, it doesn't matter. We're not here to talk about your movie; we're here to talk about the murder of your wife."

Van Roten had begun to pace nervously. She stopped and fixed him with a puzzled stare.

"If you weren't surprised to find out that your wife had been having affairs with other men, why were you so surprised when you found out she had had an abortion?"

For the first time, Roth seemed to have been caught unawares. He gave her a blank look, as if he had not understood the question.

"What I mean, Mr. Roth," explained Van Roten, moving a step nearer, "is this: If you had always assumed that she had been having–what was it called earlier?–relations of 'casual intimacy'–why would you not have assumed, or at least wondered, whether instead of having an abortion because she didn't want to have your child, she had an abortion because she didn't want to have some other man's child?"

Stanley Roth drew himself up to his full height. Twisting back his head he gave Van Roten an icy stare.

"It was my child," he insisted in a stern voice.

With one hand on her hip, Annabelle Van Roten arched her black pencilled eyebrows. "Really?"

"Mary Margaret was too smart not to take precautions, precautions she did not take with me."

"So far as you know."

Roth started to say something, but then changed his mind. His gaze, which had been sharp and clear during the long hours of cross-examination, seemed to soften and lose at least something of the confidence it had until now projected. His shoulder sagged forward, and his head dropped onto his chest, forfeiting for the moment the sense of strength produced by his erect and at times rigid bearing on the stand. A look of anguish swept across his eyes.

"Why do you keep trying to make her sound like a whore?" he asked. "She wasn't. She had her faults; she had her failings. She wasn't this perfect creature you saw on the screen. She was just like you and me, someone who made mistakes. No, she wasn't perfect, but she was a lot better than the people who took advantage or tried to take advantage of her; she was better than that miserable father of hers who only wanted her money; she was better than that power-crazy former partner of mine who only wanted her because she was famous and because sleeping with someone's wife is the only way he can ever think of himself in the same league with her husband. There are men like that, you know; men who sleep with the wives of famous men because they think it gives them something in common. You don't believe me?" asked Roth, becoming enraged and distraught. He clutched the arms of the witness chair. "You want to taunt me with my murdered wife's infidelities? You want to give me a condescending look when I tell you I knew it was my child? You want to suggest that Mary Margaret was going to leave me–or that I would have or should have left her–because of that phrase you picked up: her 'casual intimacies'? What about Walker Bradley? Where was all your self-righteous indignation when you had him on the stand? Good God, he slept with every woman in Hollywood–but that doesn't matter, does it? He's Walker Bradley. He has that boyish charm–even now, at his age–and it doesn't matter what he does, how many lives he ruins, because there is something about him you like. He sleeps with my wife, takes advantage of her need to be wanted, and you stand there and talk about her as if she were some cheap streetwalker!" Roth shouted. Fighting back the tears, he buried his face in his hands.

Stunned by his outburst and, like the rest of us, mesmerized by the speed and force with which he had spoken, Van Roten had stared in open-eyed amazement. She realized the moment he finished she was in danger of losing control. The sound of Roth's voice was still echoing in the courtroom when she moved to reestablish her authority. He was bent over, his shoulders heaving, sobbing silently into his hands. She could not pretend not to notice; but she could pretend that it did not matter, that it was nothing more than another lamentable instance of a guilty man trying to act as if he had a conscience.

"You testified that you went to bed early that night because you had to be up early to be on the set of a motion picture you were making?" she asked in a harsh, unforgiving voice.

Roth drew his hands a little away from his face. With his thumbs set against his cheekbones, he pushed the heavy, deeply lined skin back and forth on his forehead. He dropped his right hand, then his left, and with an effort raised his head. He looked around, a weary search that ended when his eyes came to rest on Annabelle Van Roten. With the back of his hand, he wiped away a tear.

"You went to bed early that night?" she reminded him.

"Yes," he said in a husky, barely audible voice.

"You'll have to speak louder," snapped Van Roten.

Roth straightened up, blinking his eyes as he struggled to regain his composure. "Yes."

"Because you had to be on the set early the next morning?"

"Yes."

"You didn't sleep in the same room with your wife–you slept in a different room that night?"

"Yes, that's right."

"When you got up–early the next morning–you showered, dressed, and went straight to the studio?"

"Yes."

"You didn't have breakfast?"

"No."

"You didn't have even a cup of coffee?"

"No, I didn't have anything. I went straight to the studio. I had something there."

"I see. So you didn't go into the kitchen at all?"

"No."

Van Roten was looking down at her shoes. She moved one foot slowly in front of the other; then, just as slowly, brought it back.

"How long had it been since you had last seen your wife?" she asked, pushing the other foot forward. When he did not answer, she looked up.

"You had been working on this movie for some time, hadn't you? You were leaving early every morning–and from what you tell us it was your habit to occupy that other bedroom during these periods when you had to be up that early–so how long had it been since you had last seen your wife? A day–two days–a week–a month? How long, Mr. Roth?"

"A couple of days," replied Roth.

"A couple of days!" exclaimed Van Roten with enthusiasm. "Not: 'We had dinner the night before,' 'We had lunch the day before.'" Van Roten's head snapped up, a dark, malicious sparkle in her eyes. "Not: 'We made love the night before'? You hadn't seen your wife in a 'couple of days,' and you didn't bother to so much as stick your head inside her door to see if she was all right before you left that morning–is that your testimony, Mr. Roth?"

"I didn't kill her," said Roth, a faraway look in his eyes.

"I'll repeat the question, Mr. Roth. You didn't look in on your wife before you left?"

Roth blinked, and then looked at Van Roten as if he had just realized she was there. "No," he said, "I didn't want to disturb her."

"Isn't it rather because there wasn't any point to it? Isn't it rather that you knew she wasn't there? Isn't it rather that you knew she was outside, facedown in the pool, where you had left her after you killed her?"

Roth shook his head and did not say a word.

"You went to bed early and you got up early. Did you wake up during the night?"

"No."

"Nothing woke you up?"

"No."

"You didn't hear an alarm go off? You didn't hear the noise of an intruder?"

"No."

Van Roten peered at him with suspicious eyes for what seemed a long time and then turned her gaze on the jury, nodding at them, as if she wanted them to pay particular attention to what she was about to ask the witness.

"You're a violent man, aren't you, Mr. Roth?"

Roth shook his head. "No, I wouldn't say that."

An eyebrow shot up, but Van Roten's eyes stayed fixed on the jury. "You wouldn't say that. You yourself testified that you struck your wife, didn't you?"

"Yes," replied Roth, a little reluctantly.

Van Roten emitted a cruel laugh. "And you're the one who insisted on bringing to our attention that it was sufficiently serious that your wife called the police–dialed 911–for help. Isn't that what you testified?"

There was no response.

"You have to answer out loud, Mr. Roth. This isn't some movie where some silent gesture is all that's needed."

Stanley Roth had begun to recover from his earlier distress. His eyes were clear and his manner had some of the same self-assurance as before.

"Yes," he said, "I insisted on telling the truth."

It made her angry. She turned on him with a vengeance.

"You beat your wife, and then, while you're on trial for murder, you tried to kill your partner, Michael Wirthlin, didn't you?"

"No, I didn't try to kill him. I got into a fight with him. That's true, but I . . ."

"You didn't want to kill him for trying to take away your studio? You wanted to kill your wife for taking away your child!"

"No, that's not true. I didn't . . ."

"No more questions, Your Honor!" she shouted over Stanley Roth's attempt to make himself heard.

On redirect I gave Roth the chance to say what he had wanted and then asked him a few more questions in an attempt to explain away some of the damage the prosecution had done. I asked him one last time the question only the jury could now decide.

"Mr. Roth, did you murder your wife, Mary Margaret Flanders?"

He looked right at the jurors, taking his time, making eye contact with every one of them. "No, I did not."

I thanked him and turned to the bench. "Your Honor," I said in a solemn voice, "the defense rests."

I thought it was over, that all we had left were closing arguments and then the long wait while the jury, in their own mysterious way, decided the verdict. I had started gathering up the things I had to put back in my briefcase when I heard Van Roten's voice.

"Your Honor, the People wish to offer a witness on rebuttal. The People call Julie Evans."

26

I HAD NOT SEEN Julie Evans since the night we had dinner, the night Jack Walsh threw a drink in my face. If she had known she was going to be a witness for the prosecution, she had not said anything to me. Whenever Julie first knew, whenever she was first served with a subpoena compelling her attendance at trial, she had not bothered to give Stanley Roth or me a warning. Perhaps, after everything that had happened, she had decided that both of us deserved a little surprise.

The questions, at least at the beginning, were all about Detective Crenshaw and the formal agreement into which he had entered with the studio.

"This was a contract under which Detective Crenshaw was to serve as a consultant on a single motion picture, is that correct?" inquired Van Roten with an air of casual indifference, as if the question, and not just that question, answered itself.

Julie sat easily on the witness stand, one long leg crossed over the other. She was dressed in a tan silk skirt and jacket. Her blonde hair was pulled back and she wore a pair of large round glasses. Everything about her suggested a conscious effort to look businesslike and efficient. I tried not to think about what she had looked like that night she had taken me back to her place, but even here, in a courtroom filled with daylight, I could not entirely put out of my mind what we had done. With the strange premonition of a chance not taken, with the bittersweet certainty that something worth having had been lost, I listened half conscious to her soft, thrilling voice as she gave answers to questions, wishing I had gone off with her to Santa Barbara and not worried about whom it might hurt.

"Yes," said Julie; "it was a consulting contract. Mr. Crenshaw–Detective Crenshaw–was paid $250,000 for his work."

Annabelle Van Roten nodded her approval, and then asked: "Were there any other agreements between the studio and Detective Crenshaw? Let me be specific: Was there a contract for an option on a screenplay written by Detective Crenshaw?"

Making all the noise I could, I pushed back my chair and got to my feet. "Your Honor, the defendant testified that instead of an option on the Crenshaw screenplay, there was a consulting contract. And he also explained why he did it that way. There is no rebuttal in anything this witness has said."

Van Roten lifted her proud chin and with a brief smile announcing imminent vindication, informed the court that the very next question would challenge the veracity of a key statement made by the defendant. Honigman waved his hand impatiently and urged her to move things along as quickly as she could.

"You can answer the question," Van Roten advised the witness. "Was there an option on a screenplay?"

"No, there's no record of one."

"Now, Ms. Evans, to your knowledge, did Detective Crenshaw serve as a consultant on a motion picture in which Mary Margaret Flanders was the star?"

Julie drew her eyebrows together and bent her head to the side.

"Let me rephrase the question," said Van Roten in the face of Julie's puzzled silence. "During the filming of that motion picture, how many times–according to the records kept at the main gate of the studio–did Detective Crenshaw enter the studio?"

"Fourteen."

"He was there fourteen times while that movie was in production?"

"Yes."

"And on each of the fourteen occasions Detective Crenshaw entered the studio, was Mary Margaret Flanders on the set?"

"Yes."

"So, in other words, he was there when work was going on, work on the movie for which he had this consulting contract, correct?"

Julie was careful. "On the days he was there, Mary Margaret was there, yes."

Van Roten glanced at the jury to make sure they understood the full implications of what had just been said. Then, briefly, she looked at Stanley Roth.

"And tell us this, Ms. Evans: Did you ever yourself see Detective Crenshaw on the set with Mary Margaret Flanders?"

"Yes, I did."

"Once, or more than once?"

"More than once, but just how often, I can't be sure."

"Did you ever see Detective Crenshaw talking to Mary Margaret Flanders?"

"Yes, at least once that I remember."

"What were they talking about, do you know?"

Julie shook her head. "No, I wasn't close enough to hear anything."

With an encouraging smile, Van Roten asked: "Could you tell what kind of conversation it was? I mean, were they having an argument, exchanging words, anything of that sort?"

"No, nothing like that at all. They seemed quite friendly."

"The kind of conversation someone hired to give advice might have with one of the actors or actresses in a movie?"

"I suppose," replied Julie with a shrug.

Van Roten turned away and walked the few steps to her place at the counsel table. I thought she was about to announce that she had no more questions. I was trying to decide what I should ask on cross, or whether I should ask anything at all. It was odd that Crenshaw had been there, on the set, and that Stanley Roth had not known anything about it. Or was it? Stanley Roth would not return his phone calls, but that did not mean that Mary Margaret Flanders had not. Perhaps Crenshaw had called her; perhaps he had told her that he had been hired as a consultant, that he really thought he would enjoy it. What was it Stanley Roth had said? People would do almost anything to get into the business. He had said something else as well: Crenshaw had practically stood at attention that night at The Palms when Mary Margaret Flanders, holding an ice bag to her eye, walked into the room. He had done her a favor by keeping the press from finding out what had happened, saved her from the consequences of her own impetuous act. If he wanted to play at being a consultant–and he was certainly getting enough money for it–what did it matter to her if she was surrounded by one more adoring fan?

I was halfway out of my chair, ready with the question I had decided to ask, when Annabelle Van Roten looked up from the table toward which she had bent her head and asked:

"Did Stanley Roth ever tell you that he wished he had killed his wife?"

With a worried look, Julie quickly shook her head. "Yes, but he didn't mean it. He was angry, hurt–he . . ."

Van Roten cut her off. "He told you that he had hit her, hit his wife, Mary Margaret Flanders–isn't that true?"

Julie Evans was used to having people go out of their way to make her feel comfortable. More than that, she was used to being in charge. Stanley Roth might interrupt her before she had finished what she had to say, but that was different. Stanley Roth was . . . well, Stanley Roth, not some poison-tongued lawyer who drove a used car and bought her clothes off the rack. She gave Annabelle Van Roten a cold-eyed stare.

"Stanley was very upset about what had happened," replied Julie. She spoke much more slowly than before, as if she had decided that Van Roten lacked the intelligence to understand something said more quickly.

It seemed almost to amuse Van Roten, this attempt by some expensively dressed woman to assume an attitude of superiority while being questioned in a murder trial.

"And after he told you he hit her, he told you he wished he had killed her?" asked Van Roten, measuring out the words exactly the way Julie had done.

If Julie disliked interruption, she hated mockery. Her blue eyes smoldered with resentment.

"Ms. Evans," said Van Roten impatiently; "you're here under subpoena. It simply doesn't matter that you don't want to be here or that you don't want to answer the few questions I have to ask. There's no choice–not if you want to stay out of jail for contempt. Now, did Stanley Roth make the statement that he wished he had killed his wife–yes or no?"

"Yes," replied Julie reluctantly. "He did, but . . ."

"No, Ms. Evans, not 'but.' He made that statement. He said he wished he had killed his wife."

Smiling to herself, Van Roten took a step in the direction of the jury box. "Finally," she sighed under her breath, "an answer." Pivoting on her next step, she turned to the witness. "You worked for Stanley Roth a long time, didn't you?"

"Yes."

"Worked closely with him?"

"Yes."

"He confided in you?"

"Well, I . . ."

"No, Ms. Evans. You just testified that he told you he hit his wife. You just testified that he told you he wished he had killed her." She paused long enough to hold out her hands and turn up her palms, a gesture meant to suggest that the answer was plain on the face of it. "He confided in you."

"There were things he told me, and there were things he did not."

Van Roten shrugged. Folding her arms, she studied the tip of her toe as she pushed one foot slightly ahead of the other.

"Among the other things he told you, did he tell you that he quarreled frequently with his wife about–other men?"

"How do you mean?"

Van Roten brought her head up quickly, a frown on her face. "Did they, or did they not, quarrel about her involvement with other men? Yes or no, Ms. Evans!"

"Yes, they sometimes quarreled about that."

"So it would not be true to say that Mr. Roth didn't concern himself with the possibility that his wife might have had affairs with other men, would it?"

"I wouldn't know how to answer that," coolly replied Julie.

"You wouldn't know how to answer that," Van Roten muttered to herself as she shook her head in derision. "They quarreled about it, though, didn't they?" she fairly shouted. "Isn't that what you just testified?"

"I testified that they sometimes quarreled about her involvement with other men," Julie shot back. "You'd have to ask him how concerned he was about it!"

Van Roten threw up her hands and stared incredulously. "And those quarrels," she said presently, "did they ever become violent?"

I almost could not watch, it was so insidious, the way Annabelle Van Roten took advantage of the one weakness Julie Evans had. She was still in love with Stanley Roth–I suppose she would always be in love with Stanley Roth–and she was, despite herself, so eager to help him, or at least not to hurt him; and then, on top of that, she had such contempt for the woman posturing here in front of her, the woman who was trying to send Stanley Roth to his death. She could not stop the look of triumph that raced through her eyes as she realized what she had been given the chance to say.

"Yes, they became violent. Mary Margaret once threw an ashtray at him and hit him on the side of his head. It could have killed him. It would have, too, if it had hit him just a little lower, on the temple. It took a dozen stitches to close the wound. He didn't call the police. Maybe he should have."

She was almost breathless at the end. Her blue eyes darted toward Stanley Roth, hoping for some sign of approval, some sign that she had done the right thing. Roth never saw it. He was peering down at his hands. Julie's gaze became stoic as she looked back at her interrogator who was waiting silently, her hand resting on the cheap wooden railing of the jury box.

"So Stanley Roth hit her," said Van Roten, nodding wisely, "and wished he had killed her, and she became so angry at him she threw something at him that, as you put it, came within an inch or two of killing him. Tell us this, Ms. Evans: Given this history of violence, when you first heard that Mary Margaret Flanders had been murdered, wasn't your first thought that she must have been killed by her husband, the defendant, Stanley Roth?" she asked, shouting the end of her question over my vigorous objection.

"What the witness did or did not think is irrelevant to any issue in this case, Your Honor, and Ms. Van Roten knows it every bit as much as I do."

"Sustained!" thundered Honigman, both to make himself heard and to quiet the boisterous crowd.

"In addition to what you've been told about the defendant's violence, you've witnessed it yourself, haven't you, Ms. Evans?"

Julie gave her a blank stare.

"You were a guest in the home of Louis Griffin the night the defendant assaulted his other partner, Michael Wirthlin, weren't you?"

"Your Honor," I said, springing back to my feet, "the defendant has testified to the fight he had with Mr. Wirthlin. This is supposed to be rebuttal testimony."

"Ms. Van Roten?" Honigman inquired.

"The testimony is offered to rebut the defendant's characterization of his encounter with Mr. Wirthlin, Your Honor."

Honigman stroked his chin, then stroked it again. "Very well," he announced. "For that limited purpose, I'll allow it."

Van Roten looked at Julie Evans.

"Yes, I was there."

"Mr. Roth was drunk, wasn't he?"

"He had been drinking, yes."

"He threw a chair at Mr. Wirthlin, didn't he?"

"He didn't hit him with it."

"Mr. Wirthlin managed to duck and the chair flew into the glass door behind him, shattering the glass–is that correct?"

"The chair hit the glass, yes."

"Then Mr. Roth grabbed a wine bottle and raised it, ready to strike Mr. Wirthlin with it–isn't that correct?"

"I didn't see that," insisted Julie.

"You had dropped to the floor?"

"I'm not sure. I just remember pulling my arms in front of my face, closing my eyes when the glass broke."

"But you saw what happened next, didn't you?"

"What do you mean?"

"You saw what happened: you saw who stopped Mr. Roth from hitting Mr. Wirthlin with that bottle, didn't you?"

"Stanley wouldn't really have hit him," Julie tried to insist. "He never would have . . ."

"You saw what happened," insisted Van Roten with a grim stare. "You saw Mr. Roth's attorney, Mr. Antonelli; you saw him, sitting on the other side of the table; you saw him dive over the table and wrestle Mr. Roth to the floor, didn't you? Mr. Antonelli saved Mr. Wirthlin's life, didn't he?"

"Stanley wouldn't have hit him," protested Julie, her eyes open wide.

"Mr. Antonelli jumped over the table, didn't he?" demanded Van Roten.

"Yes."

"And he wrestled Mr. Roth to the floor, didn't he?"

"It was more like they both ended up on the floor because of the collision."

"A collision that knocked Mr. Antonelli unconscious, a collision that resulted in a cut over his eye, didn't it?"

"Yes."

"Thank you, Ms. Evans," said Van Roten, spinning on her heel. She looked up at the bench. "I have no further questions, Your Honor."

She took a step toward the counsel table and then, as if she had just remembered something, stopped and turned her head to the side. With a haughty, teasing sparkle in her coal dark eyes she looked at me and said loud enough for the jury to hear:

"And to think you said you slipped and fell because you were thinking of me!"

In the space of less than an hour, Annabelle Van Roten had destroyed what little defense we had. She had taken my ill-advised promise to tell the truth, no matter who it hurt and no matter how ugly it might be, and made it seem the criminal confession of someone who, versed in the arts of concealment, admits a lesser evil to disguise the commission of a greater one. With all the evidence against him, the only chance we had was to somehow persuade the jury that, despite all appearances, Stanley Roth really had nothing to hide. Now, because of what Van Roten had been able to get Julie Evans to say, the members of that jury must have wondered if Stanley Roth had told the truth, or at least the whole truth, about anything. When I rose to face Julie Evans several of the jurors shifted uneasily in their tightly cramped chairs, several others coughed uncomfortably. For one of the few times during the trial, the court clerk lifted her tiny eyes to watch.

"You and I have been acquainted for some time now, haven't we?" I asked, smiling gently as I stood in front of the counsel table.

Julie looked at me like someone grateful to find a friend in a room full of strangers. She seized my eyes with her own and did not let go.

"Yes," she replied, smiling back.

"Acquainted from the very beginning of the case, starting the first day I met the defendant, Stanley Roth, correct?"

"Yes."

"You were Mr. Roth's executive assistant, and in that capacity you helped me become better acquainted with his various business dealings as well as other matters that had some relevance to his defense, didn't you?"

"I tried to be helpful, yes."

"We have spent a lot of time together, haven't we?"

Julie tilted her head back to the side, the way she often did just before she opened her mouth to speak. Something–a glimmer of light, a slight change of color, a warmth that wasn't there a moment before–appeared in her eyes.

"I wouldn't say a lot," she said in a soft, soothing voice that suggested she had not gotten tired of it.

I felt my face redden, and for a moment felt compelled to look away. Suddenly, on an impulse, but an impulse guided and given shape by the situation in which the three of us–Stanley Roth and Julie Evans and I–now found ourselves, I told the one truth no one would think to question:

"You knew–didn't you?" I asked, gazing at her again. "I started falling in love with you that first day I saw you–and you knew it, didn't you?"

In open-mouthed astonishment, the jurors temporarily forgot all about Stanley Roth and the murder of his wife. While everyone looked at her, Julie looked at me, a subtle smile on her mouth, the cryptic confession of all the things she knew and would never say aloud. Annabelle Van Roten broke the silence.

"Your Honor," she said in a droll, languid voice, "while you can imagine how utterly heartbreaking this revelation is to me personally, I must at the same time question what conceivable relevance Mr. Antonelli's infatuations have to the issue before us."

With an upraised eyebrow, Honigman waited for my response.

"I'm getting there, Your Honor," I said with an irritated glance at Van Roten.

Honigman shrugged and rolled his eyes. "Please hurry."

"I'm not trying to embarrass you," I said to Julie. "But there's a reason

I have to ask you this. I was falling in love with you, but you were already in love with Stanley Roth–isn't that true?"

"Your Honor . . . Really!" exclaimed Van Roten from the counsel table behind me.

His eyes riveted on Julie Evans, Honigman swatted away Van Roten's objection with his hand.

"Yes, that's true. I was in love with him for a long time."

I wondered if she had meant it, that use of the past tense as if it was something she had finally gotten over, or whether she used it because she was still trying to convince herself.

"He knew you were in love with him, didn't he?" I asked with all the seriousness I could command.

"I'm sure he must have."

"And because of that–because he knew you felt that way–he confided in you, told you things about himself that he would not have told anyone else. Isn't that true?"

"You mean things about his life at home? Things about his marriage? Yes, I'm sure he never told anyone else."

"All the questions you were asked by the prosecution–you answered all of them truthfully?"

"Yes."

"So you told the truth about Stanley Roth?"

"Yes."

"But not the whole truth?"

Though Julie thought she knew what I meant, she waited until I explained.

"Because the questions you were asked didn't allow you to tell the whole truth, did they? For example, while it is the truth that Stanley Roth made that remark Ms. Van Roten finds so infamous–that he wished he had killed her–he said it to you in private as an expression of how frustrated he was with everything that had happened. He didn't say it the way someone would who was actually contemplating taking someone's life, did he?"

"No, that's true. He didn't say it anything like that. I knew he didn't mean it."

"Because if he had wanted to kill her, he could have done it easily enough that night, couldn't he? But instead, after he struck her that one time in anger, he was mortified, angry with himself–isn't that correct? Isn't that what he told you–if not in those exact words, in words to the same effect?"

"Yes. That was how he described the way he felt about what he had done. He was disgusted with himself."

"And about that business with Detective Crenshaw–you are aware, are you not, that he did in fact send a screenplay to Stanley Roth?"

"Yes, I am."

"Was anything ever done about it? To your knowledge, did anyone–Stanley Roth or anyone else at Blue Zephyr–even read it?"

"Not to my knowledge."

"You testified that there was a consulting contract between the studio and Detective Crenshaw. Was the amount he was paid under that contract at the high or the low end of those kind of agreements?"

"The high end."

"Had you ever seen one that high before?"

"No."

"Have you ever seen one that high at any time since?"

"No."

"You testified that according to the studio records, Detective Crenshaw was at the studio a dozen or more times; you also testified that you had on one occasion seen him on the set talking with Mary Margaret Flanders. And though you didn't hear what was being said, it was your observation that this was a friendly conversation as opposed to an angry confrontation, is that correct?"

"It wasn't a confrontation."

The next question came of its own accord; the first I consciously thought of it was when I heard myself asking it.

"Did you ever see them together, having a friendly conversation, somewhere other than the set?"

She said she had not and I moved on, wondering to myself what it was I was missing, what without knowing it I must have seen, that made me ask that question.

"Did you check the records concerning Detective Crenshaw's visits to the studio because Ms. Van Roten asked you to do so?"

"Yes."

I played a hunch. "And did Ms. Van Roten also ask you to check the studio records for any information you could find that would support Detective Crenshaw's claim that he actually worked as a consultant on a movie in which Mary Margaret Flanders was the star? I mean apart from the number of times he visited the studio."

"Yes, she did."

I turned to the jury, a skeptical expression on my face. "And did you find anything–notes, letters, written critiques of the script–anything at all?"

"No, I did not."

"Finally, then, about that night Stanley Roth came to the home of Louis Griffin and got into an altercation with Michael Wirthlin. You were there with me, weren't you? You picked me up at the hotel and we drove there in your car, didn't we?"

"Yes, we did."

"And during dinner–before Stanley Roth showed up–Michael Wirthlin made very clear his belief that Stanley Roth had to go if Blue Zephyr was going to survive, didn't he?"

"Yes, he did."

"He went further than that, though, didn't he? He insisted that Stanley Roth was finished and so was Louis Griffin. And it was just then–wasn't it?–that Stanley Roth showed up, just as Louis Griffin was getting ready to throw Michael Wirthlin out of the house. Isn't that what happened?"

She agreed, but it was now Wirthlin Productions, and she had to be careful. "Yes, but a lot of things were said no one meant."

"Stanley Roth was angry because Wirthlin had left him a letter of resignation to sign?"

"Yes."

"You testified that Stanley Roth had been drinking?"

"Yes."

"Did he have a gun?"

"No," she replied, surprised anyone would ask.

"A knife?"

"No."

"Did he have any kind of weapon, any kind at all?"

"No."

"So he came to the house without a weapon and traded insults with Michael Wirthlin. Is that what happened?"

"Basically, yes, that's what happened."

"And in a fit of anger, Stanley Roth threw a chair through a glass door?"

"Yes."

A rueful smile crossed my mouth. "When I tried to break up the fight, I was knocked out. Was Stanley Roth knocked out?"

"No, he wasn't. He lay there for a moment and then got up. Then, I remember, he knelt down next to you to see how you were."

"So if he had wanted to hit Michael Wirthlin, he could have done so, but he didn't, did he?"

"No, he didn't."

I pressed my fingertips together and for a moment thought about the way I wanted to phrase the next question.

"Michael Wirthlin wanted Blue Zephyr for himself–he wanted a studio of his own–isn't that in effect what he said that night at Louis Griffin's home?"

"Yes, I think everyone there would have to agree that is what he said."

"A few days after this happened–after Stanley Roth had this altercation with Louis Griffin–Mr. Roth resigned, didn't he?"

"Yes."

"And Mr. Griffin has left as well?"

"Yes, he has."

"What is Blue Zephyr now called, now that Mr. Roth and Mr. Griffin are gone?"

"Wirthlin Productions."

"You've been in this business a long time, Ms. Evans. You were in effect second in command at Blue Zephyr, and now you're in charge of day-to-day operations at Wirthlin Productions. Tell us this, if you would. Based on your knowledge of the motion picture industry and your knowledge of the strengths and weaknesses of the three men in question, could this have happened, could Michael Wirthlin have forced out Louis Griffin and Stanley Roth from the studio they started, if Stanley Roth had not been accused and put on trial for the murder of his wife?"

She did not have to answer. It was written in her eyes.

27

"I DIDN'T KNOW she was in love with me," protested Stanley Roth.

"Would it have made any difference if you had?"

I was not really interested in whether it would or not. I was too concerned with the damage Annabelle Van Roten had done and how little the answers I had been able to coax out of Julie Evans had done to repair it. Stanley Roth would never have deliberately injured Michael Wirthlin–isn't that what Julie had said?–but his lawyer, the one who was arguing that he could not possibly have murdered his wife, had thought the only way to stop him from killing his partner was to dive across a table and take a few stitches in the head for the trouble. Everything that had seemed to make so much sense, everything that had seemed so clear, so logical, while under the intoxicating influence of my own courtroom performance tasted like ashes now that the audience was gone and, like a drunk who wakes up sober, I remembered what I had done.

The more I thought about it, the worse it seemed. Stanley Roth had felt so bad about hitting his wife that he told Julie Evans he wished he had killed her! Of course he had not really meant it: he said it only out of frustration. Besides, it was not as if this sort of thing had not happened before. They argued all the time, and about nothing more often than whether she was involved with other men, the very thing Roth had told the jury he had not wanted to know anything about. That did not matter, though, did it? Not when you realized that Mary Margaret Flanders had been at least as willing to use violence as her husband. After all, she was the one who had narrowly missed killing him when she hurled that heavy cut-glass ashtray across the room at his head. What did Roth tell the jury? That if his wife had been thinking about getting a divorce, he would have known it? The only thing right I had done all day was something I did not do: I did not ask Julie Evans whether she thought Stanley Roth could have killed his wife. Just in time, I remembered that I had asked her that question once before and I remembered what she had said.

Roth was still thinking about what I had asked. "I might not have told her some of the things I did," he said finally. "I wouldn't have told her about a couple of the arguments I had with Mary Margaret. She made them sound more important than they were."

Roth looked out his window as the limousine moved at a slow, steady pace along the freeway, the sunlight on the side of his face softening the lines etched deep across his brow.

"You work with someone every day. Once in a while they notice you're not in quite the same mood, that you're a little preoccupied or a little depressed. They ask if anything is wrong. You mention you had an argument with your wife. That night you take your wife out to dinner. You don't remember why you had the argument in the first place, and you can't imagine that you'll ever have another one. But you do of course–weeks later, months later–and you mention it again."

Roth turned and looked straight at me. "You don't mention all the good times in between, all the normal things you've done. All that other person knows are the arguments you've had. You see what I'm getting at? Julie didn't know what my marriage was like. She knew there were arguments–I told her that–and if she thought she was in love with me, then the idea that the marriage was not very good, was even in serious trouble, becomes almost irresistible, doesn't it? Yes, I said 'thought' she was in love with me. She wasn't. She was in love with Stanley Roth–you know, the Stanley Roth who used to run the movie business. She wasn't in love with me. Remember what I told you about growing up in the valley? Julie Evans was the good-looking girl who went out with guys that came from wealthy families and drove new cars. She wouldn't have looked at me . . ." He laughed. "I was going to say 'twice,' but forget that–she wouldn't have looked at me once. She was in love with me? What did she do when Blue Zephyr became Wirthlin Productions?"

Roth laughed again, a defiant laugh that seemed false and hollow, as if he were trying to conceal a deep sense of hurt that despite his failure to give her any reason to stay, or even to ask, she had decided to leave. For some reason I could not have explained and did not really understand, I felt compelled to defend her against any suggestion of disloyalty.

"She didn't want to testify."

"Yeah, well, no one wants to do anything," observed Roth with a trace of self-pity. Aware of it, and perhaps aware as well of how easily that emotion can threaten the ability to function, he abruptly changed the subject and, with it, his mood.

"Look at it this way," said Roth as if he had suddenly put everything into perspective. "You get to win this thing with your closing argument. It's perfect. Everyone thinks the defendant did it; all the evidence says he did it; and then the defense attorney, in the greatest summation of his life, convinces the jury that they can't possibly convict an innocent man. Too bad it's a trial," he added as he looked out the window. "It's a great movie."

His voice was strong and full of confidence, as if he really were talking about a movie he had seen or a screenplay he had read, instead of a trial that had every chance of sending him to prison for the rest of his life if it did not send him to his own execution instead. Then I noticed his hands lying in his lap, trembling so slightly he was not even aware of it.

When I got back to the hotel I went right to work, or rather I tried to work. I sat at the table where I had spent hours every night preparing for the next day at trial and sought to find some new angle, some new approach that would, as Stanley Roth had put it, convince the jury that they could not possibly convict an innocent man. I paced the floor, still wondering if he was innocent, and, if he was, what I had missed. I lay down on the bed and searched the ceiling for an answer, someplace where I could start. There was nothing, nothing at all; my mind was a blank page on which would suddenly appear a few ill-chosen and irrelevant words, the random, fragmentary thoughts of my own disordered imagination.

Julie Evans was not really in love with Stanley Roth; she only thought so because he was Stanley Roth. What then had he thought about his wife? Did he think she would have looked at him–even once–when he was an awkward, plain-looking kid growing up in the valley? What had he been thinking that day at The Palms when he seemed to take a strange, almost perverse pleasure in my failure–a failure that was likely to cost him his freedom and maybe his life–to figure out what had happened the night Mary Margaret Flanders was murdered? If he had known anything, he would have told me; but he didn't tell me, so he could not have known something that would help. But then that look he had on his face, as if he could, but for some reason would not . . . It was too late now. Stanley Roth was right: the only chance left to win was to give the greatest closing of my life. I did not have even the faintest idea where to start.

I picked up the telephone to call home, to talk to Marissa, but I could not think of what I wanted to say. I wondered if she had heard anything, if there had been anything on the news, about what I had said in court, and how I was going to explain it away, or if I even wanted to try. I put down the receiver and made up my mind I had to write some kind of outline of what I was going to say on closing. I went into the other room and sat at the table and struggled again to find an argument that might convince the jury that the case against Stanley Roth had not been proved after all.

The next morning, when I woke up and started getting dressed, I took my time, concentrating on each thing I did, trying to keep my mind from wandering back to all the questions I had not been able to answer and all the riddles I had not been able to solve about the murder, about the trial, about my own dubious existence. On the way to the courthouse, Roth and I barely exchanged a word. He thought I was thinking about what I was going to say; I thought he was thinking about what would happen if we lost. Shoulder to shoulder, our heads bent low, we pushed our way through the raucous, enveloping horde of waiting reporters and, for what would be the last time until the jury came back with its final verdict, took our places in that impoverished courtroom so different from the opulent private places in which Stanley Roth and Louis Griffin and Michael Wirthlin and all the other titans of that strange, mythic world so many people were so desperate to be a part of, lived their lives.

"Did you write it out last night?" asked Roth, as much to make conversation as anything else.

"The closing argument? No."

Roth's eyes widened with admiration for what he then assumed I must have done. "You memorized the whole thing, without writing it out first?"

He had not always been particularly curious about what was going on in court, but he was always interested, and at times, I thought, even a little obsessed, with technique.

"No, I didn't memorize it."

He stared at me, half smiling to himself, perhaps out of sympathy for the difficulty, which I was sure he had experienced himself, of finding the right words, or even figuring out what it is you want to say. It was unfair to leave him without at least some assurance.

"I thought about it."

"Sometimes it's better," said Roth, nodding thoughtfully. "Better not to write everything down, not to try to memorize every word; better just to let it work itself out in your mind–let it simmer for a while. Then, when it's time to do it, it comes out better than you could have written it."

It was too late to reply. The clerk, scowling defiance, stalked into the courtroom, perched on the front edge of her chair, ready to rise again the moment the bailiff, who had come in right behind her, announced the arrival of the Honorable Rudolph Honigman.

"Keep your hands in your pockets or under the table," I told Stanley Roth as we both stood up. "I don't want the jury to see them trembling."

"My hands don't tremble," he protested as Honigman took his place on the bench and instructed the clerk to summon the jury.

Annabelle Van Roten could scarcely wait to get started. She sat at an angle, one arm resting on the table in front of her, the other thrown back over the chair. Her head was held high, her mouth drawn tight across her teeth. There was a kind of eager malice in her shiny black eyes, the ravenous look of a predator closing in for the kill. I turned toward her and smiled, hoping to catch her off guard and perhaps cause her to lose just a little of her concentration. I was not more than three feet away; it might as well have been three hundred. I could have shouted at her and she would not have heard. When the judge told her she could begin, she sprang from the chair and bolted right past me.

She was casebook perfect. She reviewed and summarized the testimony of the witnesses, reminding the jury by an allusion to something they had worn or some eccentricity they had displayed about witnesses the jurors could after all the long weeks of trial have easily forgotten. Beginning with the maid's discovery of the naked body of Mary Margaret Flanders floating face down in the pool, her head covered in a cloud of blood, Annabelle Van Roten described in simple, straightforward language each piece of evidence that had been produced by the prosecution and explained why, taken together, they left no room for doubt that Stanley Roth and no one else had murdered his wife. When she began to talk about the clothing found in the laundry hamper, she stepped back from the jury box and pointed, not at the defendant, but at me.

"Mr. Antonelli has tried to turn your attention away from the fact that the clothing belonged to the defendant and that the blood on them belonged to the victim. Who can blame him? He can't deny the facts: Those were Mr. Roth's clothes and that was Mary Margaret Flanders's blood."

She tucked in her chin and stared at me with a kind of mock sympathy, letting the jury know that I had tried to get away with something, but that I had failed. "Stanley Roth did not kill his wife: Detective Crenshaw just wants us to think so." With a taunting, scornful laugh, she turned back to the jury. "And just why is it that Detective Crenshaw went to all this trouble: ran upstairs–you've been to the house; you've seen how far it is to go–rummaged through the closets until he found something that Mr. Roth might have worn, ran back downstairs, went outside, dragged the clothing through the blood, and then ran back down the hall, through the master bedroom into the bathroom–by the way, without knowing where the laundry hamper was, or even if there was one–where he put those clothes so he can turn right around again and claim to find them there!"

Van Roten sighed, and then rubbed the back of her neck, a puzzled expression on her face. "That's a lot of trouble to go to, isn't it? And for what? Because after being paid a quarter of a million dollars, Mr. Roth had not yet made his screenplay into a movie! That, after all, is the reason–the only reason–the defense managed to come up with. And what evidence have we been given for this? Why, Mr. Roth, of course! He told us–do you remember?–that while he didn't really think so at the time, he now realizes–he now realizes!–that Detective Crenshaw might have become a little unhappy that Mr. Roth had not done anything with his screenplay. This of course is the same Mr. Roth who insisted–do you remember?–that despite the fact that the contract Detective Crenshaw had with the studio was to serve as a consultant, Detective Crenshaw never did any consulting. Yes, well, the studio's own records prove something rather different, don't they? And so does the testimony of Mr. Roth's own executive assistant, doesn't it?"

Dropping her head, she moved one foot in front of the other, intent on what she wanted to say next. "What Detective Crenshaw did was wrong," she said with a solemn expression, looking each juror in the eye. "He should have reported that act of domestic violence. It wasn't his place–he didn't have the right–not to report it, no matter how decent his motivation may have been; and he should have told us about it right away, instead of waiting until he was confronted with it during the trial; but none of that changes the facts of the case. Detective Crenshaw found clothing belonging to the defendant and that clothing was covered with the victim's blood and there is not a shred of evidence that he did not, nothing except the irresponsible allegations of the defense, desperate to find some way around the evidence that proves beyond any doubt, reasonable or otherwise, that Stanley Roth murdered his wife.

"Why did he do it? After everything we've heard, the real question may be: Why had it not happened earlier? Stanley Roth is a violent man, married to a woman too indignant–too strong-willed, if you prefer–to become an object of his abuse. They argued all the time. No, they fought all the time. The defendant told you under oath that he didn't know about any other men, though," she added with a caustic sneer, "he admitted he was not entirely surprised when he heard of her involvement with both his partner, Michael Wirthlin, and his wife's frequent co-star, Walker Bradley. He didn't want to know–that's what he told us. He told Julie Evans, whom he trusted implicitly, something completely different, though, didn't he? He told her–and she told us–that they fought all the time about other men.

"Why did he kill her? Jealousy. Jealousy, and greed as well. Her father, who had no reason to lie, told us that Mary Margaret Flanders was going to divorce Stanley Roth. Walker Bradley told us that she was going to leave him. By his own admission, Stanley Roth hit her and wished later that he had killed her, when she decided–what she had every legal right to decide–to abort a pregnancy she did not want. What do you think his reaction must have been when he discovered that she did not want anything more to do with him? And even if he did not know she was going to get a divorce, we know for an absolute certainty that Mary Margaret Flanders had affairs with other men and that she and Stanley Roth had arguments, some of them violent, because of it. We know, in other words, that Stanley Roth was jealous; we know that he was violent; we know that financially he had a great deal to gain and nothing at all to lose by his wife's death. And we know something else as well, don't we?"

Annabelle Van Roten paused and with a look of intense confidence stared at the jury. "We know that he killed her. We may never know what finally drove him to it, what words may have passed between them that fatal night, but we do know that Stanley Roth and no one else murdered Mary Margaret Flanders. Even without the blood of the victim on his clothing, clothing he tried to hide, Stanley Roth was the only one who could have killed her, because Stanley Roth was the only one who was there."

When it was finally my turn I had for the first time in my career the sense that it was already too late, that I had missed whatever chance I might ever have had to save Stanley Roth. That is what I had been thinking about when I should have been trying to get something down on paper to use at closing: what I had missed, that single piece of evidence that might have led me to the real killer. Annabelle Van Roten was right: all the evidence was against Stanley Roth. And yet, despite the fact that I knew he had not always told me the truth or the whole truth; even despite the fact that I had been a witness, and in a way, a victim, of his temper, I found myself at the end almost certain that he had not done it. It was nothing more than a feeling, an instinct, a hunch; nothing I could put into words, at least in a way that was likely to persuade anyone, especially a jury that had listened attentively to months of testimony making the case against him, that someone else had murdered Mary Margaret Flanders. But I tried.

I stood looking around the courtroom, filled with spectators packed so close together they had as little room to move as the jurors crammed into that pathetically undersized jury box. Some of their faces had become familiar, regular visitors to the daily proceedings, more conversant with the details of the case than either the dull-eyed bailiff or the sullen-eyed clerk. Jack Walsh was sitting in the back row, craning his neck, perhaps to get a better view or, more likely, doing everything he could to be seen. He saw me look at him. The dull expression on his face changed immediately to one of open hostility. In the front row, sitting in the same place he had occupied for at least part of nearly every day of the trial, Louis Griffin, dressed as usual in a dark business suit, returned my glance with an encouraging smile. I turned back to the jury and for a moment looked each of them in the eye, or tried to. A number of them would not look back. It was not a good beginning.

There was nothing to be gained by denying the obvious. I summarized the prosecution's summary of the evidence and suggested by the way I did it that it was something of a mystery to me why Annabelle Van Roten had spent so much time on what no one doubted was true. Was it, I asked at the end of my brief recitation, because she did not want us to think too much about the questions she did not want us to ask because they were questions she could not answer?

"Stanley Roth hit his wife. The defense, not the prosecution, told you that. He hit her in a rage when he found out that she had without his knowledge aborted the child she had not told him he had. Under that rather considerable provocation he did what he should not have done. He lost his temper: he didn't think about it; he certainly didn't get a knife; he didn't drag her down the stairs outside to the pool; he didn't wrap a stocking around her neck and with his knee on her spine pull her head back and slash her throat.

"The prosecution told you that he was angry, beside himself, because–well, why exactly? Because she had been having an affair with another man? Because she had an affair with Michael Wirthlin? Because she had been sleeping with Walker Bradley? Or was it because of all the other men with whom she had apparently engaged in acts of 'casual intimacy'? But how," I asked, scratching the back of my head, "can you murder someone out of rage over something the prosecution insists Stanley Roth had known about for years?"

Standing at the end of the jury box closest to the empty witness stand, I cast a sly glance toward Annabelle Van Roten. Impassive and utterly unimpressed, she stared back.

"Was it because, as Stanley Roth himself had written in that screenplay—that screenplay on which he has been working for years, the one he calls *Blue Zephyr*—the movie-star wife was going to leave him for his partner who was then going to start a studio of his own?"

Still gazing at Van Roten, I smiled to myself. "Murder her after she had already broken it off with Michael Wirthlin? No," I said, turning away as Van Roten began to glare at me; "if anyone had a reason to murder her for what had happened then, it was Michael Wirthlin, not Stanley Roth; Michael Wirthlin, rejected and made a fool of by a woman he loved, married to a man he hated.

"The question of motive is not the only one the prosecution would prefer you not explore. There is also a question, a very serious question, about the evidence itself. Some of you may have noticed—and all of you need to consider when you begin your deliberations—that for all the talk about all the evidence the prosecution was able to assemble, Ms. Van Roten has been strangely silent about what after all is the most crucial piece of evidence in this case: the murder weapon, the knife used to slash the throat of Mary Margaret Flanders. Where is it? Why has it never been found? Because Stanley Roth hid it somewhere? The same Stanley Roth who had so little fear of discovery that he nonchalantly tossed his bloodstained clothing in the laundry hamper and went off to work?"

I stepped away from the jury box so they would have a clear view of the counsel table where Roth sat with his hands folded in his lap, following with an earnest look everything that was going on.

"You watched Stanley Roth answer every question the prosecution could think to ask him. You've seen him sitting here every day, listening to what other witnesses had to say, not all of it things he would have wanted to hear. Whatever else you may think about him, I think it fair to say that Stanley Roth is not a stupid man. He surely isn't stupid enough to hide a weapon and not bother to get rid of his own bloodstained clothing."

Some of the jurors who had not been willing to look me in the eye when I started, were now gazing right at me, waiting to hear what I was going to say next.

"The prosecution tells you that Stanley Roth must have killed his wife because they had sometimes argued about whether she was doing things she should not have been doing with other men. Then the prosecution tells you that Stanley Roth must have killed his wife because he was the only one there that night. But if Mary Margaret Flanders was involved with other men–and whether or not her husband knew about it at the time, there is no question but that she was: with Walker Bradley, with Michael Wirthlin, with God knows who else–then all the more reason to believe that she brought someone home with her that night, and took him upstairs to her bedroom. You've been to that house–you've been to The Palms–you've seen how large it is, how far it is from the master bedroom to the bedroom in which Stanley Roth was asleep; you've seen how thick those solid oak doors are. What happened after she took him upstairs, after she got undressed, we may never know; whether this man she had with her started strangling her there in the bedroom, then dragged her down the stairs and outside to the pool; or whether she came down with him, or whether he was already outside, waiting for her. What we do know is that all the evidence produced by the prosecution to prove the guilt of Stanley Roth could as easily be used to prove the guilt of anyone else who had a motive of–what did Ms. Van Roten say?–jealousy or greed or both? All this so-called irrefutable evidence would prove the guilt of Stanley Roth's partner, Michael Wirthlin, for example, if he were the one brought there that night by the woman with whom by his own admission he had been having an affair, the woman–the very famous woman–who apparently did not want that affair to continue.

"Stanley Roth killed her out of jealousy–or Michael Wirthlin killed her out of jealousy. Stanley Roth had something to gain financially from her death. The studio had a policy on her and the studio collects. The studio released her last picture and the studio made money on it. Stanley Roth started that studio, but Stanley Roth was accused of murder and forced to stand trial and Michael Wirthlin has taken control of the studio and driven Stanley Roth out."

I looked across my shoulder at Annabelle Van Roten. "Someone put blood on Stanley Roth's clothing. Maybe it was not Detective Crenshaw after all. Maybe, despite all his tortured testimony, some of which clearly bordered on perjury, he really did find the clothing where he said he found it. Maybe Michael Wirthlin put it there. He would have had every reason to do so, if he was the one who murdered Mary Margaret Flanders. The point is: if you grant the possibility that someone else killed Mary Margaret Flanders, then all these things the prosecution wants you to believe prove the guilt of Stanley Roth, don't prove that at all, do they? It is only if you begin by assuming, not his innocence as the law says you must, but his guilt, that they do."

I kept going back over it, the way the evidence could prove either the guilt or the innocence of Stanley Roth, depending on what you wanted to believe; reminding them, over and over again, that when the evidence could do that, all that had really been proven was that there was a reasonable doubt and a reasonable doubt meant they had no choice but to acquit the defendant.

"We have heard a great deal about the reasons why Stanley Roth might have wanted to murder his wife. Let me tell you the reason why he would not. We know what we make, and we love what we know, and Stanley Roth made Mary Margaret Flanders. He took someone no one had heard of, a young woman of unproven talent with the unlikely name of Marian Walsh and made her into Mary Margaret Flanders, the most famous movie star in the world. He no more wanted to destroy this woman he had made than a parent wants to destroy his or her own child. He made her almost the same way a parent makes a child, and in the same way the parent loves what she makes–this creature that she knows so well because she is part of everything she is herself–Stanley Roth loved Mary Margaret Flanders. It was more than the way a husband loves a wife. He loved her as a woman, but he also loved her as part of himself. To kill her would have been in that sense to kill himself: It would have been less a murder than a suicide."

Stanley Roth had been right after all: I had not thought of it–at least had not heard myself think about it–until I said it.

With the prosecution's privilege of rebutting the defense's only closing with a second closing of its own, Annabelle Van Roten moved immediately to dismiss what I had done.

"He almost makes you want to believe him, doesn't he? He makes you for a moment forget all the things you know, all the things you learned, all the evidence that, contrary to what Mr. Antonelli would like you to believe, points unequivocally to the guilt, not of Michael Wirthlin or some unknown secret lover Mary Margaret Flanders brought home, but of the defendant, Stanley Roth."

28

WHEN I WAS JUST starting out, fired with all the enthusiasm of youth, I tried a case in which the prosecutor was so arrogant and overbearing, and the defendant, who should not have been charged in the first place, so humble and inoffensive, that the jury never left the jury box. At the close of the judge's instructions, they stood up, ready to move to the jury room, but then, as if each of them had been thinking the same thing, they looked at each other and sat down again. The judge stared at them with a puzzled expression. A juror in the first row explained that they had a verdict and that they had a question. The verdict, he went on, was not guilty. The question was whether the district attorney's office didn't have something better to do than go around prosecuting people who clearly weren't guilty of anything.

I had other juries that were out for only twenty or thirty minutes, just long enough to elect a foreman and have a quick cup of coffee, but that was the only jury I ever had that returned a verdict that was not only unanimous, but instantaneous. I did not expect that or anything close to it from the jury that was to decide the fate of Stanley Roth, but neither did I expect them to be out as long as they were.

Rudolph Honigman had given the jury their instructions Wednesday afternoon, immediately after Annabelle Van Roten's second closing argument. For the next two days there was not a word, nothing to indicate what they were doing or how long they were going to do it. Late Friday, in the cryptic language of the courts, we were told that the jury had decided to work through the weekend. All we could do was wait.

Stanley Roth stayed at the bungalow behind the gates of the studio that no longer belonged to him. I stayed at the Chateau Marmont waiting for the telephone to ring. I tried to watch television to keep my mind off things, but all I seemed to find were the self-assured absurdities that passed for expert commentary on the all but completed trial of Stanley Roth. Everyone claimed to know what the jury was going to decide. The ubiquitous Jack Walsh not only insisted that his daughter's murderer was sure to be convicted but, through tape delay, could be seen doing it on several different channels at once.

I began to wonder what would happen to him when it was finally over and the world moved on to the next scandal that would dominate the headlines and become the principal subject of discussion until it, too, faded into the oblivion of yesterday's news. What happened to people like Jack Walsh, someone suddenly famous, someone to whom everyone else pays attention, and then, just as suddenly, no one knows their name? What must it feel like to call the people who had been calling you every day for weeks and never hear back from any of them? I did not mind, in fact I took some pleasure in the thought that this was almost certainly going to happen to him. Jack Walsh had done a little too well by the death of his daughter. He had abandoned her when she needed him the most; it served him right if he was now abandoned in turn.

Saturday came and went and Sunday, too. On Monday, after lunch alone in the hotel, I called the court just in case they had tried to reach me while I was downstairs.

"You'll be notified," the clerk snapped as if I should have known she had more important things to do.

On Tuesday morning, the court called. The jury wanted to review part of the testimony of two witnesses, Detective Crenshaw and Julie Evans. At one-thirty, we were in court again, listening as the court reporter read back Crenshaw's account of his financial relationship with the studio and Julie's report that the studio's own records proved that he had been there and her statement that she had seen him on the set talking with Mary Margaret Flanders. There could be only one reason they wanted that read back to them: They wanted to be sure Stanley Roth had lied about it. I went back to the hotel and, more worried than ever, waited again for the telephone to ring.

At eleven o'clock the next morning, a week after the case had gone to the jury, the call I had been dreading finally came. I picked up the receiver and heard a single, hurried, unfriendly word: "Verdict."

I took my time. I called Stanley Roth and told him I would meet him at the courthouse in an hour. He suggested we go together, but I convinced him it would be easier to slip in through the back entrance and avoid reporters if he drove there by himself. I said I would take a cab. The truth was I did not want to see him; did not want to have to offer an encouragement I did not feel. There was an old belief that the longer a jury was out, the better it was for the defense. If the evidence was that great, if the prosecution's case was that strong, so the reasoning ran, the jury would not have to take long to decide. I had tried too many cases and watched too many juries to believe you could read anything into how long they spent locked in the jury room.

From the backseat of the cab I looked out at the skyline of Los Angeles, shimmering silver and gold in the dry, dusty midday sun. On a corner, waiting for the light to change, a slim-waisted woman in a black, tight-fitting dress, wearing dark glasses and a broad-brimmed white hat, held a leisurely grip on the leash of a black-faced, cream-colored Afghan hound. Standing a few feet away, a young Hispanic in running shoes and jeans balanced a tall stack of pizza boxes in his right hand, ready to race across the intersection. It was nice to know there were a few people left in L.A. who apparently did not care what was about to happen in a small courtroom just a few blocks away.

When I arrived, Stanley Roth was waiting for me. He stood up, put his left hand on my shoulder and, looking me straight in the eye, shook my hand.

"Whatever happens here today, thanks," he said in a clear, firm voice in which I could not detect the slightest uncertainty or fear.

Annabelle Van Roten came in just behind me. She put her briefcase on the floor next to her chair and with a look of cool confidence stared straight ahead. A moment later, the clerk entered, followed immediately by the bailiff. At the sound of his voice, we were all on our feet, waiting as the door at the side opened and Rudolph Honigman walked briskly to the bench.

Even here, in this squalid, barely functional room, this wretched tribute to public indifference, there was a sense of solemnity that I have never felt anywhere except in a courtroom or a church, the two places where most of the serious ceremonies of existence are held, one for good, the other for evil. There was something cathartic about standing here, part of the ordered formality by which, year after year, down through the generations, a dozen average strangers decide calmly and without emotion whether someone is guilty and whether someone has to die. And then, having done their duty, they go back to their own interrupted lives and never see each other again, and perhaps only later wonder if they got it right.

We sat down and waited for the jury. If I did not know what to read into how long they had been out, neither did I know what to make of the way they came in. I once had a juror so eager to let the defendant know that his ordeal was over, as soon as she took her place in the jury box she looked at me and smiled. Things like that almost never happened. Juries knew that in every trial someone won and someone lost; they knew whatever they decided, someone was going to be disappointed. They never laughed and they seldom smiled; they always looked serious. It was what made you believe in them; it was what made you think that with all the deficiencies, all the shortcomings, all the blatant stupidities of judges and courts and lawyers and, yes, all the awful inadequacies of the law itself, there was, at the end, something to hold onto, something that allowed you the hope that justice would be done; this look they always had on their faces, this fixed and forward stare that said they had done all they could, all anyone could, to make it come out the way it should.

This jury looked more serious than most. Not a single juror looked at Stanley Roth or at me; none of them looked at Annabelle Van Roten. They did not look anywhere except down at the floor as they filed slowly into the jury box, like mourners making their way into a pew.

Honigman took a deep breath as he pulled himself to his full height. "Has the jury reached a verdict?"

Holding the verdict form in his hand, the heavyset juror in the back row, the one who had spent the entire trial with his knees wedged against the seat in front of him, rose awkwardly from his chair. He was on his feet, but he had not yet raised his eyes. He stood there, nodding thoughtfully, staring at a point on that dull scuffed linoleum floor between the jury box and the bench. Finally, he looked up. Gazing steadily at the judge, he shook his head.

"No, Your Honor," he announced, "we haven't reached a verdict."

"You haven't reached a verdict?" inquired Honigman, surprised. He tried to hide his disappointment. He cleared his throat and asked: "Is there any chance that you might be able to reach a verdict with further deliberations?"

"No, Your Honor; no chance at all. We're completely deadlocked," said the jury foreman grimly.

The courtroom began to buzz. Honigman stopped it with a sharp look. He thought for a moment and then, with a civil smile, turned to the foreman.

"If this jury doesn't reach a verdict, then the case will have to be tried again with a new jury, one there is no reason to think will be better equipped than the twelve of you to decide the issue before us."

If Honigman thought this observation, sound so far as it went, would make any difference, he was wrong. The foreman's large mouth clamped down tight, his gaze narrowed into the look of a shrewd-eyed appraisal.

"Your Honor, we could meet till kingdom come and never reach a verdict."

Honigman raised his eyebrows. "I see. Very well. Then there is nothing we can do." Seizing the gavel, he looked around the courtroom filled with faces, tense and expectant, staring back at him, waiting to see what he would do next. "In the matter of the People v. Stanley Roth," he said, speaking in a formal voice, "I hereby declare a mistrial."

The gavel came down. I watched it fall and I saw it strike the hard wooden surface of the bench, but it did not make a sound. I had the strange, uncanny sensation of observing a singular, inexplicable breach of one of nature's laws. Then I realized, instead of silence there had been a sudden explosion of deafening noise coming from everywhere at once. Everyone was shouting at everyone else, trying to make sense out of what had just happened; looking at each other with startled expressions that betrayed their surprise and in some cases their anger and even outrage.

Cursing under their breath, reporters tripped over each other, struggling to get outside to be the first to report what in a matter of minutes everyone who had on a radio or a television would know. I caught a glimpse of Jack Walsh, standing at the back of the courtroom, shaking his fist while he shouted some impotent obscenity no one could hear. Annabelle Van Roten had sprung from her chair. Bent forward, her hands on the table, bracing herself as if she was about to spring forward again, she stared in speechless astonishment. Heads down, as if they expected at any moment to be assaulted by a rock-throwing mob, the jury retreated to the jury room. Judge Honigman had already vanished behind the door to his chambers. The clerk, moving at her accustomed pace, knitted her brow in disgust at all the commotion, as she made sure her chair was in the proper position behind her small desk before she waddled slowly out of the courtroom.

Amidst what was pure bedlam, Stanley Roth remained completely calm. There was no visible sign of any feeling of relief; indeed, nothing to suggest he felt anything at all. He found Louis Griffin, waiting on the other side of the low railing behind the counsel table. They shook hands and whispered a few words that, though I was only a few feet away, I could not hear above all the courtroom noise.

With Roth right behind me, we fought our way through the courtroom until we got to the doorway where Jack Walsh tried to stop us.

"Get out of my way," I shouted as I shoved him aside.

"You murdered Mary Margaret," he yelled as we stumbled through the doorway. "You're not going to get away with it, Roth!"

Roth loosened his grip on my arm and started to turn around. I grabbed him and pulled him with me into the hallway.

"Don't say anything when we get outside," I instructed as we walked at a rapid pace, people all around us, all of them trying to get a closer look.

"There won't be another trial," said Roth without expression.

"Of course there will," I replied, looking straight ahead.

The door that led outside was just a few steps ahead of us. Through the glass I could see a vast spreading circle of microphones and television cameras surrounding the willowy silhouette of Annabelle Van Roten. I could not see her face or hear her voice, but there was not any doubt in my mind what she was saying or how angry and defiant she looked while she was saying it.

"You don't really think she's going to walk away from this because one jury couldn't agree, do you? It was a mistrial, not an acquittal. What do you think she's telling them right now? She's making a promise that they're going to try you again and she's promising them that this time they'll get a conviction," I said as I pushed open the door.

As soon as they saw us, they came after us, running away from the prosecutor to encircle the defendant, like an army lifting a siege on one place to impose it on another.

"What do you think it means that the jury couldn't reach a verdict?" one reporter shouted above the rest.

With my hand on his sleeve, I held Roth to my side and slightly behind me, while I took a half step forward.

"Obviously it means that the prosecution wasn't able to make its case beyond a reasonable doubt. Remember," I went on, raising my voice to forestall the next question, "the defense doesn't have to prove anything; the prosecution has that burden and they couldn't meet it."

"At least some of the jurors must have thought so!" came the shouted retort. "Otherwise they would have brought in a verdict of not guilty!"

"We don't know how many jurors felt that way, and we may never know. All we know is that inside that jury room there was a reasonable doubt and that because of that reasonable doubt the prosecution didn't get the conviction they kept promising everyone they were going to get."

"How do you feel, Mr. Roth?" asked a female reporter as I finished.

I tightened my grip on Roth's sleeve, ready to pull him away if he started to say something he should not. I need not have worried: His reply was perfect.

"More determined than ever to prove my innocence."

"You still insist you're innocent?" yelled someone from the back of the crowd. "Everyone else thinks you're guilty."

Pulling Roth with me, I started moving down the steps. "The jury didn't think so," I shouted back as I elbowed my way through.

I could not see who it was, but it was the same voice as before, a voice filled with cynicism and contempt.

"Want to bet that most of them did?"

It had been a guess, a stab in the dark, intended perhaps as nothing more than a reporter's provocation, an attempt to get a reaction, an angry response that could be put in quotes and, taken out of context, made to seem controversial. That reporter had no more knowledge than the rest of us about what had gone on behind the closed doors of the jury room. Within hours of being dismissed, however, a few of the jurors had begun to talk, and they all told the same story.

From the first ballot taken, immediately after the selection of a foreman, a ballot taken for no other reason than to see how matters stood before they began to discuss the case, to the ballot taken just before they decided that the vote was never going to change, eleven jurors had consistently agreed on a verdict. There was one holdout, the same one each time. The eleven members of the majority had tried every argument, but nothing worked. They thought the testimony read back to them would at least cause this lone dissenter to acknowledge the possibility they might be right, but it had no effect. Eleven members of that jury were convinced beyond a reasonable doubt that Stanley Roth was guilty, but they could not convince the twelfth. It was a mark of their own essential decency that not one of those who had been so certain they were right would divulge the identity of the juror they were convinced had been so wrong.

It did not seem to bother Stanley Roth that he had been saved from the executioner by the slimmest of possible margins or that it might be only a temporary reprieve. When I suggested we start planning for the next trial, he replied with a touch of irritation that there was not much point to it until we knew for certain there was going to be one. The way he said it, not just with impatience, but with that same strange insistence with which he had said to me in the courtroom right after the jury had been dismissed that there would not be another trial, seemed almost ludicrous in light of what we now knew about how near he had come to conviction.

I decided it must be the strain. Accused of murdering his wife; subject to the constant and unrelenting scrutiny of a media that, perhaps because it had once nearly worshipped him, had turned on him with a vengeance; compelled day after day to sit in silence while a parade of witnesses questioned his honesty and made a mockery of his marriage–

who could blame him if he had started to imagine that with a mistrial, whatever its cause, his troubles might finally be over? I decided to let him lose himself in his work for a while. It would do him good not to think about what he was going to have to go through all over again: It had been hard enough the first time. I told him I would be back in touch when I knew something more definite. Then I made plans to leave Los Angeles and go home. Before I left, however, there was someone I had promised myself to see.

I did not know how much of what Mary Margaret Flanders had said to Louis Griffin was true, and how much the result of nostalgia, the thought of things as they might have been, instead of the way they really were. Was her first husband really the only man with whom she had ever been in love? He was the only one with whom she had been willing to have a child. But that was long before she was famous, long before she had to think about what it might do to her career. Perhaps she had said it because with Louis Griffin, who had lost a daughter, she could make the kind of confessions she imagined someone like Marian Walsh might have made to the kind of father she wished she had had. It was too late to know, but it was not too late to tell Paul Erlich what she had said. I suppose I thought it might give him some solace, not so much for himself, but for the child he had in her mother's absence raised alone. Had I had a child, I would have liked to know that the child's mother loved me more than she ever loved anyone else again. Or so at least I told myself as I walked under the blossoming trees on my way across campus to Erlich's tiny, anonymous office.

The door was open. Erlich was talking to a student, an earnest-looking young man sitting in the rigid posture he thought the mark of formality he was supposed to convey. Smiling to myself, I leaned against the cinder block wall next to the door and listened with growing admiration as Paul Erlich, schooled in the ways of stammering adolescents filled with infinite promise, put him at his ease.

"Don't worry if you find this material difficult," he said in a quiet, comforting voice. "Only worry if you're not."

I wished I could have seen the young man's face. With a kind of instinctive sympathy, I recalled my own look of grateful astonishment the first time I had been given a similar assurance that with time everything would become clear.

"Mr. Antonelli," exclaimed Paul Erlich with only mild surprise when I stepped into the doorway after the young man, his face flushed with barely suppressed excitement, had gone. "I heard about the verdict–or should I say lack of one? What's going to happen now?" he asked, motioning for me to take the empty chair at the side of his desk. "Another trial?"

"I'm afraid so," I replied with a rather dispirited shrug. I scarcely knew him; we had talked just once before; but I found myself at ease in his presence, without the need to mask my feelings or measure my words. "The only real question is how long it is going to be before we start all over again. I'm not looking forward to it."

Sitting forward, the fingers of his hands intertwined, he seemed to study me for a moment, a faint, rather shy smile on his finely sculpted mouth.

"But you must have learned something from the trial, something that will help you in the second one."

"I think I know less about the case now than I did at the beginning," I confessed, glad for the chance finally to tell someone the truth of it. "There is one thing, though, that I learned; which is the reason I'm here."

I told him what Louis Griffin had told me and explained the circumstances in which Mary Margaret Flanders had come to confide so much about herself. He listened, staring into the middle distance, an earnest, wistful look in his eyes.

"We were young," he said, his gaze coming back to me. "We didn't see what was going to happen when other things started to seem as important as what we felt about each other, when being in love stopped being the only thing that mattered.

"I had never known anyone like her. I haven't met anyone like her since." He paused before he added: "She wasn't what you saw on the screen. Or maybe she was."

He thought about this last remark, wondering, it seemed, whether it was true. Then he let it go, another question that could never be answered.

"You came all the way out here to tell me that? What an extraordinarily kind thing to do. I'm sorry, I wish there was something I could do to help."

I examined him closely, trying to discover if he meant what I thought he did.

"You don't think Stanley Roth killed her, do you?"

"No," he replied calmly and without hesitation.

"Everyone else seems to think so. Why don't you?"

"Because I stood across from him at her grave and I looked into his eyes and the grief I saw there was real. I think he still loved her, the way I had still loved her, even though I knew the marriage was over."

I did not understand what he meant. What did the fact that Paul Erlich had still loved her after he knew they were going to divorce have to do with the way Stanley Roth had felt?

"They had already agreed to separate," explained Erlich when he saw the look of confusion on my face.

"How would you know a thing like that?" I asked, stunned at the utter self-assurance with which he had said it.

"She told me," he replied, for some reason surprised at my reaction. "You didn't know they were separating?"

Alert and suddenly intense, I bent toward him, searching his eyes. "When did she tell you this?"

"That morning."

"Which morning?"

"The morning before she was killed. She called me. She had never done that before. She said she wanted to see me. She said she and Stanley were splitting up. They hadn't actually decided on a divorce, only a separation, but she made it clear the marriage was over."

"And she wanted to see you?"

"Yes, that afternoon."

"Did she say why?"

"She said she was worried about something. She said something had gotten out of control and she wasn't quite sure what to do about it."

"But you don't think it was about Roth?"

"No, I think it was something else. It wasn't a very long conversation. She asked me if I could come by. She said there was a charity event of some kind at the house late that afternoon and there would be a lot of people but that it would be easy for her to step away inside and we could talk then."

"But you didn't go?"

"No."

"Why?"

His gaze went to the only photograph he kept in his office. "Because she never once asked about Chloe, and because the whole time she was talking to me I kept seeing in my mind what she had done that day I brought our daughter–her daughter–to see her at the studio."

I knew what he was thinking and I tried to get him to stop. "It wouldn't have made any difference had you gone to see her."

"Are you sure? If I had gone there that afternoon, the way she asked–talked to her, listened to her–how do you know what would have happened? Maybe she would have done something else that night . . . gone somewhere else . . . stayed somewhere else. It was the only time in all the years after our divorce that she had ever asked me for anything, and all I could think about was getting even. It isn't much to be proud of, is it?"

29

A WEEK AFTER standing on the courthouse steps, shaking with anger as she swore to try the case again, Annabelle Van Roten, true to her word, filed on behalf of the prosecution the formal request for a retrial in the matter of the People v. Stanley Roth. An intelligent and resourceful lawyer who in all the endless distractions of the first trial had never lost sight of the principal issue at hand, she was so convinced of Roth's guilt, so certain she had proven it, so determined to prove it again, that I think she was genuinely puzzled that the court did not share her sense of urgency about when the second trial should begin. It was not, as she seemed to think it was, simply a matter of impaneling another jury. There was a tremendous backlog of cases, civil cases in which the parties had been waiting for years for the chance to have a trial on the merits, criminal cases in which imprisoned defendants, after all, were entitled to a speedy trial. The second trial of Stanley Roth would have to wait its turn, and the earliest opening was almost eight months away, just around the corner in terms of the way the judiciary looked at such things; a lifetime, if the ashen expression on Annabelle Van Roten's disappointed face was any indication; and a date without any meaning at all from the shrug of indifference with which Stanley Roth greeted the news.

I had given up trying to interpret the sometimes enigmatic reactions of Stanley Roth, or perhaps I had just grown tired of his shifting moods, the sudden enthusiasms, the rapid descents into a kind of restless discontent. Whenever I asked him a question now, the answer tended to be vague, ambiguous, as if his mind were somewhere else and he could not be bothered with what I wanted to know. I asked about–rather I confronted him with–what his wife, Mary Margaret Flanders, had told Paul

Erlich the day before she died. He dismissed it with a show of impatience, suggesting that anyone who knew her knew that what she said one day was not anything like what she would say the next day or the day after that. I thought it was probably more true about him.

The plain fact was that we were both tired, and tired of each other. I was only now beginning to realize just how exhausted I was. I had been running on adrenaline since the trial stopped. All I wanted to do now was go home and sit out on the back deck with the breeze off the bay in my face and not think about Hollywood or Stanley Roth or anyone else involved in this case; just sit there and clear my mind of all of it until it was time to get ready again and I could start to see things in a new and different light.

It does not seem like much, sitting alone at home, with just Marissa to keep me company, thinking about something other than Hollywood and Stanley Roth, but it was not nearly so easy as I had imagined or as I had hoped. Annabelle Van Roten had not wanted to wait to try Stanley Roth again; neither, it seemed, did anyone else. Writers who wanted to be famous; famous people who wanted to be writers; anyone who had ever known and loved Mary Margaret Flanders–and of course anyone who had known her now claimed to have loved her–anyone who had known and if not always hated, at least distrusted, Stanley Roth, was writing a book, or gave an interview, or lent their name to someone who did. Several of the police who investigated the crime, several of the witnesses who testified at the trial, as well as at least two members of the jury, hired agents and tried to sell their stories. Unable to find a publisher willing to come up with the kind of money he thought he deserved, Jack Walsh gave an exclusive interview to a national newsmagazine, released the same day as a twenty-minute segment taped for television, in which he blamed the jury's failure to convict on the shameful incompetence of the prosecution. Detective Richard Crenshaw made no public comments of any kind. He was rumored to be somewhere in Arizona, working on a screenplay about the case.

It was a form of genius, really; an instinct for the main chance, a perfect grasp of the way things had come to work in America. What was the point of becoming a name everyone knew–or a name that could be connected with a name everyone knew–if you did not take advantage of it while you still could, before you and what you knew, or claimed to know, became yesterday's news and no one could quite remember why you had once been someone they thought they could never forget? What was the point of waiting eight months if you were someone who had already given up nearly a year of your life following the case against Stanley Roth because you knew you could write a bestseller if you were the first, or one of the first, to write the story of the murder of Mary Margaret Flanders? In a second trial, coming that long after the first, what would be left of the tension, the heightened sense of awareness, all the things that had riveted the attention of that vast celebrity-intoxicated public that had as its only fear the fear of not knowing what everyone else was interested in knowing right now, today, not yesterday or the day before that? No, if you were going to write a book it had to be the kind publishers had to have because it was the only thing the public at that moment wanted to read. Two months after the first trial of Stanley Roth ended in a mistrial, the number one bestseller in the country was something called *A Death in Beverly Hills: How Stanley Roth Murdered Mary Margaret Flanders.* The book jacket promised "shocking and previously unreported details of the crime." Everyone talked about the author's three-million-dollar advance; no one talked about what it all might do to Stanley Roth's chance for a fair trial.

"Come watch this," said Marissa the evening I started it. "There's something you should see," she added with a teasing sparkle in her eyes.

I was lying on the bed, my head propped up on two pillows. Taking the hand she offered, I followed her into the den where the television set was on and sat next to her on the sofa. An aging actress who years earlier had married a famous and aging leading man, an actress who had not made a movie in years, was insisting to a somewhat startled talk-show host that she had quite unexpectedly become the chosen instrument of God, capable not only of curing the sick, but of bringing love to the world. She said all this with something like the exuberant enthusiasm of a quiz show winner, someone who had just won the biggest prize of all.

Clapping her hands in glee, Marissa seemed to smile several different ways at once. "Isn't that wonderful! You knew sooner or later it had to happen. All these formerly famous people on all these hour-long things that play in the middle of the night, and now, finally, the first infomercial for God!"

She stopped long enough to ask: "What was it Stanley Roth told you about that business–that people would do anything to get into it?"

Marissa turned off the television. There was a slight trace of melancholy in her eyes. "They won't just do anything to get into it; they'll do anything to stay in it, won't they? Once they've known what it's like to be on camera and imagine themselves the center of attention for millions of people who want to be just like them, or like what they imagine them to be."

I thought about that when I went back to *A Death in Beverly Hills*: the way in which it seemed not to matter what you did so long as it kept you at the center of public attention. Movie stars no one wanted to pay money to see any more could find something on television, featured parts if they were lucky, commercials for products sold to an older audience, if they were not. Those who had been really famous could put their names on ghostwritten books that told how Hollywood used to be for those who suffered nostalgia for what they thought they still remembered. Others, like that aging actress, could claim some spectral power to heal the living or make contact with the dead, turning what had once been sold only at carnivals into what in the age of television was applauded as the honest expression of a genuine spirituality. It was pathetic what once-famous people would do to remind people that they were still around and still worth watching. There was more self-respect in quitting things altogether, the way the owner of that English Tudor mansion where Louis Griffin later built his own home of stucco and glass had done. Watching on old reels of film someone he would never be again, he drank himself into oblivion and burned the house down all around him and died in the fire, but he had at least the decency to do it alone.

It was too bad that he had not written something about his life and the changes he had seen when movies began to talk and people began to fly and everyone started to think they had to hurry not to fall behind. It would have been a more interesting book to read than the one the one I was reading and all the others that were being rushed into print. It reminded me of the long-forgotten and perhaps mistaken observation by

Schopenhauer that with the advent of newspapers and journalists anyone could write for publication, and everyone else could read themselves stupid.

Marissa came into the room and I closed the book and put it down. She sat on the bed next to me and picked it up. Opening it to a random page, she began to thumb through it. Something caught her eye. She held the book open on her knee and with an eager, gleeful look began to read.

"It's about you," she said, glancing at me as she closed it. "I'm going to read it. Everyone is reading it."

I smiled, and then I laughed. "I told you it wasn't any good."

Marissa raised her chin and tucked the book under her arm. "I want to see what else he writes about you."

Marissa knew about what I had said in open court to Julie Evans, and I think she knew much more than that, but she never asked what had happened and I was certain she never would. She did make one remark, however, one that I found both touching and a little sad. She said that one of the things she liked most about me was how willing I was to fall in love with beautiful women about whom I knew nothing. Marissa knew so much more about me than I did myself. She was right. When I was with her, I did not think about anyone else; but when I was away somewhere, when I was in Los Angeles, for example, I was always doing that, falling in love with beautiful women I did not know and never would; the same way, I suppose, I had once fallen in love with Mary Margaret Flanders.

She was almost to the doorway before she remembered.

"Did you see the package that came for you? I left it on the table in the hall."

I started to get up, but she said she would bring it to me. It was a fairly thin package, mailed overnight from an address somewhere in Los Angeles. There was no name, nothing to indicate who had sent it, but when I opened it I knew at once who it was. There was a brief cover note asking me to call. For a long time I stared at the title on the cover of the screenplay. It was called *Blue Zephyr*, but as I realized before I had finished the first page, it was not the same *Blue Zephyr* Stanley Roth had given me before.

Everyone was writing a book that told everyone what they already believed; Stanley Roth was intent on making a motion picture that would force people to see–literally to see–that what everyone believed was wrong, and not just wrong about what they thought, but guilty themselves for having been so quick, so eager, to condemn him for something he did not do. Orson Welles had used the radio to convince those who listened to the broadcast that Martians had landed in New Jersey; Stanley Roth was going to use the motion picture screen to convince those who watched that instead of a man who murdered his wife, he was as much a victim as the woman who had been killed. I did everything I could to talk him out of it.

I FOUND STANLEY ROTH living in Culver City, in a rented two-story condominium, a place without a view on a flat, wide four-lane street that whichever way you looked looked the same, a street that seemed to go on forever and yet never go anywhere at all. I parked the rental car next to the curb in front of a treeless brown-spotted lawn and walked up a crumbling sidewalk to the front door. The door was open a crack. Instead of knocking, I called his name. There was no response. I opened the screen door and stepped inside.

The hardwood floors were stained and dirty and the blinds that were drawn on the windows to keep out the stark daytime heat were covered with a heavy layer of dust. The air was stale, stagnant with the dull, depressing scent of open half-empty liquor bottles and cheap smudged glasses filled with the warm water remains of melted ice.

I looked around at the rickety furniture and the grim, barren walls, the walk-in kitchen and the narrow threadbare staircase just to the right of the front door. I started to feel what it must be like not only to fail, but to know that it was all over, that you had run out of chances, that all you had left were the bitter memories of what you might have been. It was the kind of place someone who had once been famous and had not saved a cent might be found living, surrounded by the indifference of strangers, none of whom remembered his name. It was all too close to what I sometimes thought might happen to me; too close to what had happened to more than one person about whom I had cared: abandoned and alone, forgotten by everyone who had once clamored to be their friend, driven each day a little more crazy by the certainty that nothing, absolutely nothing, was now ever going to change.

I heard a noise upstairs, the sound of a door being shut. I thought it must be Stanley Roth, but then, when someone started down the stairs, I knew from the echo of the footsteps that it could not be him. Even when she was at the bottom of the staircase, her hand draped on the railing and her head tilted back, that familiar smile on her mouth; even when I knew that it had to be her, that it could not be anyone else, I hesitated, held back by a kind of last-minute doubt. The sparkle, the clear-eyed radiance, the high-spirited mischievous self-assurance, all of it had gone. Julie Evans looked like a woman on the edge of exhaustion. She greeted me with a kiss.

"It's good to see you," she said quietly. "Really good," she added, squeezing my hand.

Perhaps she read in my eyes the reaction to the way she looked, or perhaps she would have done it anyway. With an apologetic and half-embarrassed smile, she moved slowly from one window to the next, first raising the blinds and then opening them to let in the air. Plunging her fingers inside them, she gathered up the glasses and carried them to the sink. It was almost eleven in the morning and she looked as if she had just woken up.

It was none of my business, but I could not help asking: "You're living here, too?"

She tilted her head to the side and frowned as if not quite certain what to say.

"Not really," she said finally in a tentative voice. "Stanley needed a place where he could work in private, somewhere no one could find him. He sleeps here, too–when he sleeps."

I did not understand. He had the bungalow at the studio; he had The Palms. What was he doing here–what were they doing here–in this awful end-of-the-line place?

"It isn't that bad," Julie assured me.

She was becoming more alert, her movements less lethargic. Something of the cheerful quickness I remembered came back into her eyes.

She poured us both a cup of coffee and we sat down at a small circular table shoved up against the kitchen wall.

"The bungalow was better, of course. It had the kind of privacy he needed. But after what happened at the trial . . ."

A kind of wistful half-smile floated over her mouth as she remembered what happened.

"Let's just say that Michael wasn't happy when a certain defense lawyer tried to make him out to be the killer. He gave orders that no one was to let Stanley through the gate."

"It was part of the contract, part of the deal," I objected.

"Yes, it was," mused Julie, looking at me over the cup she held with both hands in front of her mouth. "And Michael said he could sue him about it if he wanted, but until he did there was no way Stanley Roth was going to set foot on the property of Wirthlin Productions again. I had to go over and get all of Stanley's things out of there. I think Michael would have had all of it thrown away."

"But what about The Palms?" As soon as I asked I remembered the last time I had been there, the day the jurors had been taken to see for themselves where Mary Margaret Flanders had lived her supposedly fairytale life and died her awful, gruesome death. I could see him standing there, gazing out across the lawn, anxious to leave.

"It's been sold," said Julie, breathing slowly. "Louis made all the arrangements. No one knows about it yet. Stanley insisted on that. He still has one more scene to shoot there."

That explained where some of the money was coming from. Louis Griffin had meant what he said that night to Michael Wirthlin: He and his old friend could always find the money to do one more picture. I glanced at the dull, dingy walls and found myself feeling if not exactly admiration then a kind of renewed respect for Stanley Roth. There were not many people left willing to trade in all the luxury of their comfortable affluent existence for nothing more than the chance to keep on with their work. Roth had been for a while one of the wealthiest men in America. Who would have believed that the money had never really meant a thing? Stanley Roth was a throwback, or perhaps a figment of his own inspired imagination, a character of the kind he used to see in movies when he was a kid growing up: a man who never did anything for money, a man who would tell anyone with money to go to hell if they tried to tell him what to do.

"That's where he is now–at The Palms–shooting the last scene." She saw the confusion in my eyes. "It is the last scene that has to be shot; it isn't the last scene of the picture. Stanley left it to the end because he didn't want anyone to put the whole story together until he's ready to show it."

"Stanley isn't here?" I asked, annoyed but not entirely surprised. "I told him I was coming; I told him I had to see him–and he's at The Palms shooting a scene?"

Something in her eyes told me I was wasting my time and that the only question was why I did not know it.

"That's the reason you're here, isn't it?–to tell me that Stanley is off shooting somewhere and that he isn't going to be able to see me."

She shook her head, not in disagreement with what I had said but over what it meant.

"He didn't know until late last night–or I suppose I should say early this morning. God, I don't know anymore if it's day or night," she sighed with a weary, self-effacing smile. "You know what he was like during the trial–working every night until three or four in the morning and then all day and half the night on the weekend. It's worse now. I don't think he sleeps more than two or three hours at a time and there are days when he doesn't do even that. He's obsessed with this thing, and the strange part is he seems to thrive on it, this single-minded determination to do it, make the movie, do this one picture the way he's always wanted to–the way he always thought he could."

She kept drinking coffee and the more she drank the better she seemed able to concentrate on what she was saying.

"We don't really live here; we work here. There are two bedrooms upstairs. Stanley watches film in one and then in the other, on a desk next to the bed, he makes the changes he thinks he needs in the script. I got to bed this morning a little after seven, just after Stanley let the crew know he wanted to shoot the same scene they did yesterday. He didn't like one of the camera angles. The shading wasn't quite what he wanted," she explained with puzzled amusement, as if she could not quite understand how after all it had taken out of her she could still find so fascinating his compulsive attention to detail.

Reaching across, I took her wrist in my hand and held it firmly on the table.

"He can't do this. He can't make this movie. If he does–if he goes ahead with it–I can't save him. I read the script, Julie."

Gently, she pulled her wrist out of my hand.

"You didn't read all of it. He didn't send you everything. No one has seen the whole script."

"Have you?"

She finished her coffee and put down the empty cup. She blinked her eyes and then looked around the dismal room as if she was seeing it for the first time. Suddenly, a smile flashed across her mouth.

"Isn't Hollywood glamorous?"

She got up from the table and rinsed out her cup in the grime-covered stainless-steel sink.

"Nothing can stop him from doing this. It's too late for that." She thought about what she had just said. "It's always been too late. I think he decided to do this–make this picture–the moment he first realized they were going to charge him with her murder. I think he decided he was going to do this before he asked you to come down and talk to him about becoming his lawyer. He's put everything he's got into this, and I don't mean just his money. Everything. All his energy, all his emotion–his heart, his soul, his mind–everything. I live here, but only so I can do whatever he needs me to do. It's the same as it was when he had Blue Zephyr, except then I went home at night. Now there isn't any night; there is just the work, the picture that has to get made."

"The trial is only months away," I reminded her.

"That's why he's driving everyone so hard. It's going to be released before the trial starts."

"Which means I'm not going to be able to find a juror who hasn't seen it; which means I'm not going to have anyone on this second jury who won't be sitting there thinking what a liar Stanley Roth is while they're listening to the testimony about what really happened. He's making a movie about his own trial for murder and there isn't a thing in it that's true!"

Leaning against the sink, her slender hands folded in front of her, Julie gave me a strange look. "Stanley thinks it is," she said after a while. Then, before I could reply, she laughed. "The lawyer saves his client. That part is true, isn't it?"

I stared at her, speechless. "True?" I gasped. "We had a hung jury, remember? One juror–only one–didn't think Stanley Roth should be convicted. Saves his client? It's a miracle he isn't already on death row! And now he's making a movie in which the jury brings in a verdict of not guilty and you think it's true?"

It had no effect. She kept looking at me with that smile that insisted she was right and I was wrong and that one day I would know it.

"But Stanley is innocent, so the jury should have returned a verdict of not guilty."

It caught me completely off-guard, though I don't know why it should have. That was, after all, the difference between what they did in the movies and the way things really worked in the world. It was the whole reason people went to the movies: the expectation that there was a logic in the story, a reason that made sense, a reason you could understand and accept, for the way it ended. Stanley Roth was innocent: The jury had to bring back a verdict of not guilty. A hung jury, a mistrial, months later a second trial with an outcome no one could predict: that was not the formula for a box-office success.

"Stanley wanted me to bring you out to The Palms. He thought you might be interested in watching them shoot. He said to tell you that the scene was not in the script you saw."

I had come to try to talk him out of making the movie, not to watch him do it.

"No," I said as I got ready to go.

I wanted to make some cutting remark, something that when she passed it on to him would convey how angry I was at the risk he was taking; but what I could easily at that moment have said to him I could not bring myself to say to her. It was true what I had said to her that day in court: I had started falling in love with her the first day I met her.

"Tell him I didn't have time, that I had to get back."

"You'll come to the premiere, won't you? You have to do that," added Julie when she saw I was about to offer some excuse. "How would it look if you didn't? Besides, I need a date." She looked up at me, a whimsical smile curving along her mouth. "I know I look a mess now, but I clean up pretty well."

"You have a date," I reminded her, and realized at once that it sounded like the jealous complaint of someone who wished it was not true. She realized it, too.

"I'm here because he asked me to, and because I couldn't live with myself if I didn't help him to do this one thing, this thing he's wanted to do all his life and that he thinks he has to do now while he still has the chance. I'm not in love with him anymore. I'm not. I know that now."

She opened the door and we stepped outside into the white glare of the midday sun. Julie put her hand on my arm.

"So come with me to the premiere. You need to be there anyway," she said as her blue eyes began to dance with mischief. "Don't you want to see what Joseph Antonelli looks like played by Walker Bradley?"

Whether Stanley Roth finished the final scene that day or the next or the one after that, he finished it; and eventually the world knew that all the whispered rumors were true: Stanley Roth had been making a new motion picture and, according to a few usually well-informed sources, it was all about the murder of his wife. The story of what Roth had managed to do in almost total secrecy dominated the news. In the Sunday papers, front-page stories written by investigative reporters revealed what they had been able to discover about how without a studio of his own Stanley Roth had somehow produced a motion picture that those who had been involved in it were saying privately might be the best thing he had ever done. The reference to his impending second trial for murder, if there even was one, came only at the end, a kind of obligatory footnote, an empty formality that would barely register on the eye.

From the day word first leaked out that the picture had been made until the day the picture was released, it was impossible to pick up a paper or turn on the television without seeing or hearing something about Stanley Roth and the movie *Blue Zephyr*. The familiar face of Walker

Bradley was everywhere, flashing that famous bashful, hesitant smile; waiting with his mouth partway open until the question had been asked and he could give the same practiced answer he had given a dozen different times that same day.

"What made you decide to take on this role?" he was invariably asked, though never with any suggestion that he had been wrong to do so.

"When Stanley asked me, I couldn't say no," explained Bradley. "Stanley Roth is one of the few geniuses I've ever known, someone I've been fortunate enough to be able to call a friend. I couldn't pass up the chance to work with him again."

Not everyone who interviewed Walker Bradley had forgotten, or failed to research, his testimony as a witness for the prosecution. One or two of them suggested he might want to explain the apparent discrepancy between what he had said then and what he was saying now.

"You seemed a little reluctant to call Mr. Roth your friend when he was on trial for murder."

With an indulgent smile, Bradley assured the questioner he was wrong.

"What I said was that I had never seen Stanley Roth threaten, much less strike, his wife, Mary Margaret Flanders."

It is difficult to attack sincerity, even when it is disingenuous. The questioner moved on.

"What was it like to play the defense lawyer, someone who, if I remember correctly, gave you a pretty rough time on cross-examination?"

Bradley lifted his eyebrows. A reluctant smile stretched slowly across his lips.

"He was just doing his job. I think it was only after I started working on the part that I understood how difficult a job it is–ask a question, take the answer, then without a moment to think, ask the next one, and go on like that, one question after another, sometimes for hours. I have a hard enough time remembering my lines," he added with a modest laugh. "I could never do what he did."

Shall I admit it? Despite myself, I was beginning to like Walker Bradley.

If Bradley seemed for a while to be everywhere at once, he was not the only member of the cast made available to the media. In a limited number of tightly controlled and always teasingly brief interviews, the young woman chosen to play Mary Margaret Flanders was introduced to the public and allowed to say a few carefully scripted words about what it felt like to play someone that famous in the first acting job of her career. Her name, or rather the name she had been given, was Dawn Cohelan, and as soon as I saw her I knew I had seen her somewhere before. At first I did not think it possible, but then I was sure. Perhaps simply to show he could, Stanley Roth had done it again: taken someone no one had ever heard of and turned her into a star.

"I know her," I said to Julie Evans as we drove from the Chateau Marmont to the restaurant where we were going for dinner the night before the premiere.

Tanned and rested, her blonde, blue-eyed face glowing in the burnt orange light of dusk, Julie kept her eyes on the road.

"Who do you know?"

"The new Mary Margaret Flanders."

Julie tossed her head. A half-smile of something like nostalgia settled gently on her mouth.

"She has that same quality–whatever it is. Stanley saw it right away. You watch her on screen and you can't take your eyes off her. It was eerie. She doesn't look like Mary Margaret–not much, anyway–but she has the same effect."

Julie only now remembered what I had said. "You know her?"

"I met her the same time Stanley did. We were at some crummy bar out at Venice Beach. There were two girls there. One of them was good looking and knew it and thought she could become an actress. She was hustling us for drinks. The other girl–I don't know what she was doing there. She was quiet, shy. She seemed embarrassed by her friend. When we left, Stanley said something about how she'd be good on camera. I thought he meant the good-looking one, the one with all the confidence, but he meant the other one, the quiet one. I've forgotten her name, but Stanley must have remembered. Now she's Dawn Cohelan."

I could still see the other girl sitting there, across the table from Stanley Roth, laughing in his face when he told her he was a movie producer.

All she knew were the lies men told her, but then she had probably never given anyone a reason to tell her anything else.

"I wonder what the other girl thinks now," I said aloud as we drove headlong into the night.

Out of the corner of her eye, Julie watched me as she pulled up in front of the restaurant. She handed the keys to the parking attendant and with a playful smile came toward me on the sidewalk.

"I know this is your favorite restaurant," I said as I held open the door, "but I'm not sure it's the place I would have picked."

We were led toward the same table we had been given twice before, the table that was always available for her whenever she wanted it. The restaurant was crowded, but from the moment we entered conversation stopped, and the only sound was the murmured echo of the whispered questions of those few who did not know who we were. Julie held her head high, her face glistening with the reflected light of all those staring, wondering eyes. We sat down and all around the room the talk started up again, louder, more excited, driven by the need, the desire, to say what they were going to repeat again and again before the night was through.

"It's the movie," explained Julie, leaning across the table so no one would hear. "It's what everyone is talking about. I've never seen such a sense of anticipation. You can almost feel it. No one thought Stanley would ever make another movie, and now they can't wait to see what he's done."

The waiter took our order and a few moments later brought a glass of wine for Julie and a scotch and soda for me. I needed a drink. As I raised it to my mouth I remembered what had happened the last time I was sitting in this chair at this table, watching Julie's eyes lift higher and higher until I turned around to see what she was looking at. I started to laugh.

"What do you think all these people would do if our old friend Jack Walsh showed up and threw another drink in my face? Do you think they'd react the way they did last time–applaud?"

She had to think about it, and even then was not sure.

"They wouldn't applaud. That was during the trial. Now? I don't know what they'd do. Look the other way, I suppose. Pretend it was none of their business. They probably wouldn't be angry at him–they still remember that it was his daughter who was killed–but they wouldn't think he was doing the right thing, either."

We had finished dinner and were having coffee when I thought to ask how they had ever persuaded Walker Bradley to take the part. Julie's eyes darted from side to side, glittering with a secret she was eager to share.

"Louis."

I thought that was all she was going to say. "Louis?"

"Yes, Louis. He told Walker that he knew he didn't want to play the part–Walker had said that night at the house that he didn't want to be involved with anything Stanley might do–but that he thought Walker owed it to Stanley, and owed it to him, to tell them who he thought could do it. Louis gave him the script–the court scenes, the other 'Antonelli' scenes. As soon as he read it he knew it was the best role he could ever have. He told Louis he was willing to do it." Julie paused, shaking her head in admiration. "And Louis told him to forget about it, that there wasn't a chance in the world Stanley would let him do it, not after the way he tried to deny on the witness stand that they had ever been friends, not after he admitted he had been sleeping with Mary Margaret."

"Was it true?"

"That Stanley wouldn't let him do it? Of course not. Bradley was the only one Stanley thought could do it." A thoughtful expression came into her clear blue eyes. "Stanley may have cared about Mary Margaret, but he doesn't care about anything now–only the picture."

She finished her coffee and then raised her eyes until they met mine.

"I'm not in love with him. I was once, for a long time, but I'm not anymore. And what about you, Joseph Antonelli? Are you in love with anyone?"

30

THE NEXT EVENING I sat in the same theater in which I had seen the last picture Mary Margaret Flanders ever made, and watched in amazement the way Stanley Roth had changed beyond recognition the reality I had known. As the movie begins the gate in front of The Palms slides open and the headlights of a dark Mercedes sweep along the drive veering toward the house. The car stops in front and the driver gets out and in the quiet stillness of the night silently goes inside. Upstairs, in the bedroom, sitting in front of the mirror, touching with her finger the corner of her mouth, a beautiful young woman wearing a silk slip is suddenly startled. She looks up and begins to smile.

"Sorry I'm late," says her somewhat beleaguered-looking husband as he bends down and kisses the cheek she offers.

Right from the beginning I could see Stanley Roth at work. Every shot, every scene, was done from a different angle, with the effect that after a while you began to assume that in even the most commonplace things there was something hidden, something you were not being shown, something you had to find out for yourself.

The car comes down the drive and stops just inside while the gate opens again. They drive through the cool Los Angeles night. He tells her that the picture on which he's working is taking more time than he thought: He has to be back on the set by 4:30 the next morning. She tells him that it doesn't matter how early he has to go, she wants him to stay with her, not use the other bedroom down the hall. They go to a small private party, two dozen people invited to celebrate the birthday of an old friend of them both, someone long established in the industry. Several of the guests tell her how much they enjoyed the afternoon, when they were among the guests at the charity event she had hosted on the grounds of The Palms.

The car is again at the gate. Then they are on the stairs, then in the bedroom, then she has her arms around his neck. The camera moves back through the bedroom doorway as the two of them tumble into bed together. And then we see him, hidden in the shadows downstairs in the living room, a pair of eyes, cold, deadly, staring into the darkness, waiting. Upstairs, after she is asleep, her husband gives her a gentle kiss and, careful not to wake her, shuts the bedroom door behind him and goes down the hallway to the room where he will spend what is left of the night. At the sound of the second door shutting, the eyes of the intruder tighten, become more determined, more demonic. The camera moves in a slow half circle, turning the simple act of climbing the stairs into a dizzying, endless spiral.

That was all you saw, the slow circling motion of a figure, dark and foreboding, an apparition of death, until it reaches the top of the stairs and then turns the corner and disappears down the hallway. The camera stays there, trained on that now empty space on the landing, leaving to the imagination of the audience all the grim graphic details of what was about to happen next. It was an imitation of the way movies used to be made, an imitation of something so old it seemed after all this time new and original: a murder is committed and the act of violence is never shown.

An alarm clock rings. Stanley Roth–the actor playing Stanley Roth–turns it off and quickly gets dressed. He walks down the hallway, stops at the closed door to the bedroom where he had made love with his wife, starts to open it, and then, smiling to himself, decides not to bother her this early in the morning and walks away. The headlights of his car cut through the murky gray light of dawn. The gate opens and he drives out. Behind him, behind the gate, behind the house, the body of Mary Margaret Flanders is floating facedown in the swimming pool.

Summoned by the maid, who was reduced to hysteria by what she has found, the police arrive. A few minutes later, while the uniformed officers prowl through the house looking for evidence, a plainclothes detective is peering down at the body, now placed on the deck next to the pool, slowly shaking his head. The look on his face seems to suggest more than the usual professional regret at another senseless killing. Perhaps, like everyone else, he had seen her so often in movies he thinks of her not as a stranger but as someone he knew. Whatever that look means, it is certain that this is not going to be just another homicide case.

At the funeral a young girl tosses a single flower on the casket as it is being lowered into the ground and then, crying quietly, turns away and with the other mourners leaves Stanley Roth alone to say his last goodbye. The camera pulls back and keeps pulling back, and then, as I had seen it all happen once before on television, the image of Stanley Roth grieving for his murdered wife fades away into the golden sunlit afternoon. All around me in the darkened theater I could hear the muffled sounds of short dry coughing and stifled sobs. Julie, sitting next to me on my left, wiped her eye; Stanley Roth, sitting next to her, had a look of satisfaction. It seemed strange and out of place; then I realized that he was not reacting to what he saw but to the effect he had been able to produce. He caught me staring and nodded toward the screen, and with a fugitive smile let me know he was going to be particularly interested in what I thought about what we were going to see next. I felt Julie's hand take my wrist and squeeze it, and I knew she was waiting for the same thing.

Stanley Roth was sitting at his desk in the bungalow. He was watching Joseph Antonelli–Antonelli! How easy it is to surrender your own identity to someone, someone famous pretending to be you! He was watching Walker Bradley as he read the inscription on the Oscar that stood on a bookshelf on the other side of the room.

I shot a glance at Stanley Roth. A knowing smile, one that was not without a certain sympathy, settled over his mouth. His eyes went back to the screen.

I had been in that bungalow, talking with Stanley Roth for the first time in person, more than an hour before the telephone rang and he was told the police had come to arrest him. The scene that I was watching could not have lasted more than three minutes, yet the dozen or so lines of dialogue seemed so far as I could remember an accurate summary of what had actually been said: Roth tells Antonelli that he once hit his wife and he tells him why, but he insists he did not kill her. He explains why he was sleeping in another room, but he can't explain how someone could have gotten into the house without being detected. All the time Roth is talking, Antonelli is moving around the room. Each time he pauses in front of a photograph, the camera, and the audience, see it too, a brief, compressed look at the private life of someone famous everyone already thinks they know.

"She slept with other men," said Roth on screen. "I loved her anyway."

And with that, Stanley Roth turns his dead wife's infidelity into a kind of bittersweet regret, a measure, not just of how much he loved her, but of the remarkable loyalty that could forgive and in a way forget the very betrayal that made it possible. It made Stanley Roth someone to feel sorry for.

It was an odd sensation, watching how the words I remembered speaking seemed now to have a different meaning, and change not just what I had meant, but who I was–or who I thought I was. I sat there, in that dark, crowded theater, watching myself become the figment of another man's imagination, knowing that this was how those who saw the movie would always think of me: ruthless and without conscience, indifferent to the guilt or innocence of his client, willing–no, eager–to take a case because of its notoriety; the lawyer who only gradually and, as it were, reluctantly, becomes convinced that Stanley Roth is one of the few men he has ever defended who is not guilty of the murder for which he has been accused.

Roth did not forget a thing. Outside the bungalow, as they walk toward the front gate of the studio where the police are waiting to take Stanley Roth away, he turns to the man who has just agreed to become his attorney and asks without reproach:

"You don't believe me, do you?" And then adds: "I don't blame you. There is no reason you should. But it's the truth: I didn't do it, I didn't kill Mary Margaret, I didn't murder my wife."

Antonelli watches the police load his new client into the police car and drive off. You can tell from the expression on Walker Bradley's face that he is wondering if Stanley Roth might just be innocent after all.

He keeps his doubts to himself and insists from the beginning that the police have arrested the wrong man. He stands there–I stood there!–outside the gate to Blue Zephyr, and in front of a movie audience that knew I was lying told a crowd of actors playing reporters that before the trial was over they will know who the real killer is. In this respect at least, Stanley Roth had been brutally honest. All through the trial he shows me telling reporters, telling the jury, telling anyone who will listen that someone else did it, and then in those scenes in which the two of us are alone, he shows me challenging him to tell me the truth, to tell me what happened the night he killed his wife.

There was something almost insidious about the way that despite everything I knew Stanley Roth drew me into this remarkable movie he had made. It was remarkable–whatever else it was, it was that–and nowhere was this more apparent than in the manner in which he had handled the problem of time. At first I did not notice. I was too taken with the way in which he had changed the whole visual structure of the courtroom and what went on inside it. Reduced to its elements, a trial–any trial–is nothing more than lawyers asking questions and witnesses giving answers. A judge speaks; a lawyer makes a statement. There is no action, no movement, no great shiny spectacle that captures the eye and makes your blank mind forget that nothing is being said: Everything is being said and you could listen to it just as well if you were blind. I began to understand why Roth had been so excited that day he told me what Orson Welles had done in *Citizen Kane*, and what had been done in *The Third Man* as well. Under Roth's scrupulous direction, the courtroom was turned into a series of what only seemed like random fragments shot from the shifting angle of a camera that seldom stayed still. While a lawyer asked a question, the camera showed the face of the witness or the line of faces in the jury box; when the witness answered, the camera showed the face of the lawyer, or the defendant, or someone in the audience of spectators who filled the courtroom.

That was how he solved the problem of time: by showing something that was happening in the courtroom while the words of the trial were droning on in the background. When the trial begins and the court clerk, who also combines the function of the court reporter, makes her first appearance, the camera follows her every move. She was nothing like the evil-tempered woman I had watched every day of trial make even the simplest task seem a burden. She was younger, and rather graceful; and if she did not have striking good looks, she had elegant, sculpted hands, as lovely as any I had ever seen. The camera concentrated on them, those two hands, flashing silently over the keys of the stenotype machine, taking down every word spoken, measuring like a metronome the constant irrevocable passage of time. A witness who might have been on the stand for hours or even days was there for a few seconds, and as his voice faded away the hands kept moving and the voice of the next witness began to be heard and the face of a lawyer, a juror, a spectator or the judge was there in front of you, shown from a distance, shown close-up, shown in full or maybe only in part, betraying in some subtle fashion a reaction to what was now being said.

It was not until I had seen those hands for the third or fourth time that I realized I had seen them somewhere before, and it was not until the prosecution was calling the detective to the stand and her face was shown in close-up that I remembered where. I grabbed Julie's arm and whispered angrily:

"Did you know about this?"

Startled by my sudden vehemence, she searched my eyes.

"What?" she asked, clearly puzzled.

I glanced beyond her to Stanley Roth, and then beyond him to Louis Griffin. Which one of them had done it, and how had it been arranged, I wondered as I sat back and turned my eyes again to the flickering images on the screen. I had spent all those months defending Stanley Roth and it had never once occurred to me that he would do something like this and that instead of defending him in a second trial, I might now have to defend myself. I tried to tell myself that perhaps no one else would notice. I had not recognized her at first; I might not have recognized her at all if I had not remembered her hands. There had been no cameras allowed in the courtroom; only Annabelle Van Roten and I had really been close enough to see her. Perhaps Stanley Roth and I were the only two people who would ever know that he had bribed a juror with the promise of a part in a movie he had not yet made.

The detective was on the screen, testifying in a voice that in its velvet smoothness was uncannily close to that of the real Richard Crenshaw. The way he looked, the way he dressed, the careful, always conscious way he held himself–even the fluid movement of his head and shoulders each time he turned to the jury–all of it had been reproduced. His testimony, as I realized after he had answered the first few questions put to him by the actress who played the always impassioned and occasionally cruel Annabelle Van Roten, had been taken word for word from the transcript of the trial; not all of the questions and not all of the answers, but those that counted, those that went right to the heart of things. The detective emphatically denied that he had moved Stanley Roth's bloody clothing to the laundry hamper where he claimed to have found it, he denied everything Walker Bradley with a knowing half-smile threw at him with lightning speed during a rigorous cross-examination made all the more intense not only by the short duration it was allowed to last but by the constant alteration of the faces and expressions shown on the screen.

The detective's testimony–Crenshaw's testimony–sealed Stanley Roth's fate. He was the only one there, the only one who could have murdered Mary Margaret Flanders, and her blood was all over the clothing he had tried to hide. Even his best friends think he is guilty. Some, who are not his best friends, try to take advantage of it. His partner, Michael Wirthlin, tries to force him to resign. For the first time, Roth confides in his lawyer that his wife and Wirthlin had been having an affair and that he thought Wirthlin was trying to get her to leave the studio so the two of them could start one of their own.

How many times, I wondered, had Stanley Roth written and rewritten *Blue Zephyr*? How many times had he tried to work out the connection between the movie-star wife and her husband's partner until it came out the way he wanted–until the partner, Michael Wirthlin, was almost evil incarnate, and the movie star, Mary Margaret Flanders, had at least the excuse of having eventually changed her mind?

"Michael is ruthless, but he wouldn't have killed her because she ended the affair. Michael hates me, but he wouldn't have killed her so I'd be accused of it and he could take over the studio."

There is no secret script called *Blue Zephyr*; there are no discussions in which Roth suggests his wife was murdered because someone wanted to harm him; there is no drunken confrontation in which Stanley Roth tries to knock Michael Wirthlin's brains out with a bottle; nothing but that single implicit, seemingly innocent suggestion that Wirthlin might have had reasons of his own to want her dead. It is of course all that the relentless Joseph Antonelli needs to know. From that point forward, everything he does in court, beginning with the cross-examination of Michael Wirthlin himself, is designed to convince the jury that Stanley Roth's partner is the one who had the most to gain by the victim's death.

"You wanted Stanley Roth's wife, didn't you?"

"No, I . . ."

"You had an affair with her?"

Wirthlin turns to the judge, who orders him to answer the question.

"Yes, but . . ."

"You wanted the studio?"

"No, I . . ."

"She broke off the affair. You couldn't have her anymore. But you still wanted the studio. And now that she's dead, you have that, too, don't you?"

Walker Bradley flashes a triumphant smile, wheels away from the witness, and strides back to the counsel table; but as he sits down next to Stanley Roth you can see in his eyes that he knows it was not enough. As he watches the film playing in the courtroom, the one in which Mary Margaret Flanders is on the lawn outside The Palms in the middle of several hundred affluent guests at that charity event for the children's wing of the hospital, a mood of depression deepens the lines of the face now shadowed in the darkened light of the courtroom.

It was not Mary Margaret Flanders, it was that girl I had completely forgotten moments after we left her in that Venice Beach bar, but my eye was drawn to her the same way it had been when, instead of Walker Bradley, I was the one staring at that portable screen from my place at the counsel table during the trial. Roth had staged it all over again, put hundreds of extras on the lawn that spread out from the patio around the swimming pool, all for the purpose of reminding us again how she dominated every scene she was in and made even well-known faces fade into the common anonymity of a background blur.

When the film stopped running and the light came back on in the courtroom, the look on the face of Joseph Antonelli–the other Joseph Antonelli–had changed. Instead of being depressed, he was intense, agitated, barely able to sit still, and at the same time utterly preoccupied.

Annabelle Van Roten announces that the People have no more witnesses to call. The judge instructs the jury that defense will begin its case tomorrow morning. Stanley Roth tries to say something to his lawyer, but his lawyer is in too much of a hurry to leave. Long into the night, Antonelli sits locked in a small screening room, watching over and over again that same film of Mary Margaret Flanders taken outside The Palms late in the afternoon, just hours before she died. When he has seen it for the last time, he picks up a telephone and calls Stanley Roth:

"I believe you. You didn't do it."

He hangs up the telephone, a grim smile on his mouth as he narrows his eyes, anticipating what he knows is going to happen next.

The first witness called by the defense is the defendant, Stanley Roth. He admits he once hit his wife and that she called the police. He describes what happened when the police arrived and how he agreed to pay a quarter of a million dollars for a screenplay Richard Crenshaw had written. Annabelle Van Roten nervously taps a pencil against the edge of the counsel table, waiting to see whom the defense is going to call next.

"The defense calls Detective Richard Crenshaw."

There is something stern, heartless and even savage in the way Walker Bradley sets out on the destruction of the man who had first been called to the stand as the prosecution's most important witness. I had spent hours with Crenshaw in court; Roth cut to the bare essentials and in less than ten minutes produced an effect I could never have dreamed of duplicating. Each time I–I mean Bradley–asked a question, the camera closed in on the face of Crenshaw; each time Crenshaw answered a question, the camera closed in on Bradley. With each question, Bradley, intense, ruthless, unstoppable, becomes angrier, but also more confident, more openly certain about how it will all end; while with each answer, Crenshaw becomes a little more hesitant, a little less sure of himself.

"You testified that you didn't know either the victim or the defendant, that you didn't have any connection with either one of them, but then you admitted that you worked as a consultant on one of their pictures. Isn't that correct, Detective Crenshaw?"

"Yes, but . . ."

"But that wasn't the truth, either, was it? You were at their home, you agreed not to report the fact that Stanley Roth had hit his wife, and Stanley Roth agreed to pay you a quarter million for your screenplay. This screenplay!" exclaims Walker Bradley, waving the blue-bound script in the air. "The screenplay that was never made into a movie. What did that feel like, Detective Crenshaw–when you finally figured out that Stanley Roth had no intention of making it into a movie, that he probably never bothered to read it? Was that the reason you went back to their house, back to The Palms–to get even? Or was there another reason, a reason that had nothing to do with Stanley Roth?"

After a concentrated close-up on the startled face of Annabelle Van Roten, the camera moves in a slow half circle behind her to show in the same frame the two antagonists, the lawyer and the witness, staring hard at each other.

"The next time I was at that house was when I was called there to investigate her murder!"

I could only envy the look of withering disdain with which this actor who had never read a law book or tried a case met this reply. Bradley stood there, three steps from the witness, his face drawn so tight it was actually quivering. When he opened his mouth to speak, the words came like a carefully measured threat.

"The next time you went there she was dead?"

"Yes," angrily insisted Crenshaw.

With a gesture of Bradley's hand, the lights in the courtroom dimmed. On the portable screen Mary Margaret Flanders was again surrounded by a crowd on the poolside lawn of The Palms the afternoon before her death.

"This was shown in court before," said the voice of Walker Bradley as every eye, in the courtroom, and in the theater, was fastened on the smiling actress who had mastered the graceful movements of the actress Marian Walsh had become. When the film reached the point where the projector had been turned off before, Bradley kept it going. "This is where it ended. This is what I want you to see."

But there was nothing to see. Moving in a slow arc the camera covered the same anonymous crowd we had all seen before. Then, at the very edge of it, near a gathering of gnarled oaks, the camera stopped, the frame froze.

"I've had this part enlarged," explained the other Joseph Antonelli as the center of the picture shown on the screen began to expand, forcing out of view everything and everyone around it. There was no mistake. Lost among those hundreds of invited guests was a face we could all now see twice, once on the screen and once on the stand. Richard Crenshaw had been there, at The Palms, not after she died, but just hours before she was killed. The lights came on in the courtroom.

With his left hand resting on the front corner of the counsel table, Walker Bradley bent forward at the waist, and when he did I felt the muscles in my stomach tighten as if I was now imitating him.

"You were there–and you didn't leave. You stayed there, hiding downstairs in the house, waiting until they came home–Stanley Roth and his wife–and then when you heard him shut the door and go down the hall to the other bedroom you went upstairs and you killed her."

Crenshaw shakes his head and starts to deny it. Antonelli holds up his hand and stops him cold.

"You killed her. You met her that night, when you came to the house. You made that deal for the screenplay. Then you started calling her–didn't you?–telling her you just wanted to make sure she was all right. You started going out to the studio–you were seen talking to her on the set–you started seeing her, privately, perhaps innocently at first; then things became more serious–or you wanted them to become more serious. What happened, Detective Crenshaw? Did she sleep with you once and then wouldn't do it again? Did she sleep with you more than once and then, just when you thought she was in love with you, she broke it off, ended the affair? Is that the reason–that and the fact you wanted to get back at Stanley Roth–is that the reason you killed her?"

Bradley is standing at the end of the jury box, shouting at the witness while Van Roten tries to object.

"You killed her, and you covered Stanley Roth's clothes in blood and then you just waited, hid in the house until Stanley Roth had left, until the body was discovered, until the police came. They were too busy to notice that you had not driven up the driveway in your car, that you just seemed to appear at the side of the pool. It was easy, wasn't it? Everyone searching for the murder weapon and you had it tucked safely inside your jacket pocket. You killed her, Detective Crenshaw, but that wasn't enough, was it?" he shouts over the courtroom noise as the crowd erupts and the judge beats his gavel hard. "You wanted to destroy Stanley Roth, ruin him, take everything away–his fame, his reputation, the woman he loved–turn him into someone no one would want to be seen with–turn him into the murderer you are!"

There is no hung jury, no single juror holding out in obstinate dissent from what all the others wanted to do. The jury is out less than an hour. Stanley Roth is found not guilty of the murder that everyone now knows the police detective, Richard Crenshaw, had committed instead. Joseph Antonelli has saved an innocent man. It was in more than one respect quite the most remarkable film I had ever seen, and, as I knew better than anyone else, it was all a lie.

31

I TRIED TO TELL Julie, but I could not get her to listen.

"That's why he shot the whole scene all over again; that's why he paid hundreds of extras; that's why he didn't use the original–the real–tape of Mary Margaret Flanders outside that afternoon: It was the only way he could make it seem Crenshaw was there! My God, why did he do that–accuse him? Just to give a movie the kind of ending he wanted?"

Julie was looking all around, taking in the crowd swirling outside the theater, all those hundreds of people still caught up in what they had just seen, reluctant to leave, afraid they might miss seeing something, or that someone might miss seeing them.

"It was a great movie," said Julie, her blue eyes shining as she continued to search the crowd. Suddenly her eyes stopped moving. "There he is!" she cried.

We had been separated from Stanley Roth as soon as the house lights came on. Applauding, smiling, surging forward to shake his hand, the audience, or that part of it that could get to him, forced us out of the way. Now they were outside, lining up on the sidewalk to see him, all these people who had been so certain that Stanley Roth had murdered Mary Margaret Flanders, people who had only come tonight because they were curious to see what he had done and because everyone else was going to be there.

Julie began to move toward him. I grabbed her arm and held her back. The noise of the crowd was all around us. I had to shout to make myself heard.

"He fixed the jury," I said, searching her eyes to see if she understood the enormity of what had been done. "He made this movie and makes it seem Crenshaw killed her."

She did not care about any of it. "It's a great movie," she repeated, her eyes feverish with excitement.

Julie pulled her arm away and threaded her way through the crowd, determined to tell Stanley Roth that it had all been worth it: the work, the sleepless nights–that it was the best thing he had ever done. All I could do was watch.

Everyone was trying to shake hands with Stanley Roth, eager to tell him that the movie was going to be a great success and that they had always known he had not done it, that he was innocent, that someone else had killed his wife. A few months earlier they would have crossed the street to avoid having to speak to him and now they were almost fighting with each other to get close enough to say a few words they could only hope he might later remember. It had once again become important to be known as someone who could call Stanley Roth a friend.

Julie had disappeared into the crowd. I could not find her anywhere. Then, suddenly, I saw her, her arms around Stanley Roth's neck, kissing him on the side of his face. He kept her next to him, his left arm around her waist, as he began to shake the next hand waiting. I had never seen her quite so radiant, quite so alive. Resting her right hand on Roth's left shoulder, she brushed a strand of hair back from her forehead with her left. Suddenly, her mouth opened and a strange, puzzled look rushed onto her face. Instinctively, my eyes followed hers. Then I saw him, Jack Walsh, just a few steps away, moving forward, a cold smile on his mouth. He was extending his open right hand, as if, like everyone else, he could not wait to acknowledge in person this, the latest triumph of Stanley Roth.

"Congratulations," he said in a booming voice that seemed to freeze everyone where they stood. Taken by surprise, Roth did not have time to withdraw his hand and once Walsh had hold of it, he did not let go.

"You killed her and you think you can wash it all away with a movie?"

At the sound of the first shot, the crowd that was bunched tight around the two of them became a panic-stricken mob, people screaming, knocking each other down as they tried desperately to get out of harm's way. Except for Julie. The moment she saw the gun Jack Walsh was holding in his left hand, she threw herself in front of him, but nothing could have stopped Jack Walsh. He shoved her aside and, as she fell to the ground, fired three more times. With the gun still in his hand, Walsh turned around and looked right at me; but his eyes kept moving, searching for something. When he found it, he dropped the gun and slowly raised his hands.

"He murdered my daughter; he murdered Mary Margaret Flanders," said Jack Walsh in a calm, measured voice as he started to move toward the camera that had begun by filming Stanley Roth in the moment when he reclaimed his place as the leading moviemaker in Hollywood and had now captured forever the moment of his death.

Whether it was outrage at the prospect of Stanley Roth rehabilitated in the public eye, or because, having acquired through his daughter's death a certain celebrity of his own, he thought the world would consider what he had done a justifiable act, Jack Walsh expressed no remorse for what he had done. He insisted that he had to do it to prevent a murderer from going free. He had to do it, he kept repeating, for his daughter. I think he believed it; I think he had convinced himself that it was true; and if he had known what I did he would have been all the more certain that he was right.

A week after Stanley Roth's death, I stood with a handful of mourners as his body was lowered into a grave next to the one where Marian Walsh was buried beneath a headstone engraved with the name of Mary Margaret Flanders. Julie Evans let a flower fall from her hand onto the lid of the casket. Louis Griffin tossed a handful of earth and with that gesture said his final farewell to the man to whom he had always thought he owed more than his life. When it was over and we walked down the hill, I remembered the day I had seen Stanley Roth standing all alone at the graveside of his wife and how, like today, the air seemed to be filled with a fine golden dust as the Southern California sun settled somewhere far out on the Pacific, and I realized he was still as much a mystery to me, still as unknown and elusive, as he had been then. I was too old and had been to too many funerals to think there was anything particularly strange about it. I did not know Stanley Roth, I did not really know anyone, and no one knew me. I wondered how many of us really know anything, even about ourselves, except what we thought we were supposed to show.

We went to Louis Griffin's home out on Mulholland Drive, the house that had been built where those others, each designed to demonstrate the permanence of what had been done, had been built before, and talked about Stanley Roth and what he had done that would last. After an hour or so, Griffin took me aside.

We went into the dining room. I looked through the glass doors at the two swans gliding silently on the mirrorlike silver surface of the pond, moving together, each the shadow of the other. I smiled to myself, remembering what Griffin had said to Michael Wirthlin that night–the night Stanley Roth threw the chair that shattered the glass all over the floor–about loyalty and friendship and how the money did not matter.

"You bribed that juror on your own, didn't you?" I asked. "You made a deal with her–offered her a part–if she made sure he wasn't convicted."

Louis Griffin put his hand gently on my shoulder. A sad, faraway smile passed over his benevolent mouth.

"I've never spoken to her in my life."

At first I did not understand. "Then, how . . . ?"

"I spoke to her agent, but we never discussed the trial. I told him I wanted her in Stanley Roth's next film–if there was another Stanley Roth film. I don't know what he might have told her."

I brushed aside the polished, civilized cunning by which Louis Griffin had tried to keep a distance between himself and what he wanted someone else to do. "But why? Why did you think you needed to do it?"

Griffin removed his hand from my shoulder and sat down at the table. He stared out the window, watching as I had the two swans moving side by side.

"I told you what Stanley did: how he saved my daughter's life. I think you also know he tried to save her a second time."

He paused and seemed to draw into himself, and as he did I could see the signs of age on his hands and around his eyes. He was worn out, exhausted by the effort to set an example, to keep control of himself.

"I would have done that for him if I had thought he was guilty," he said finally. "But I didn't have to. I knew he was innocent."

"I know you were his friend. But how can you be so sure?"

"Julie knows," said Griffin as he led me out of the dining room to rejoin the others. "She'll take you to the studio. She'll show you there."

"The studio? Then you did it? You got it back from Wirthlin?" I asked.

"Stanley always said that Michael didn't know anything about making movies. It turns out, he didn't know much about business either."

A single sliver of reddish orange streaked the horizon of the dark purple sky when we got there. The painters had left their ladders propped against the stone pillars. Wirthlin Productions no longer existed. The newly painted letters arching over the blue-and-gold iron gate again read BLUE ZEPHYR.

"It was Louis's idea," explained Julie as we drove through the gate. "On the brass plaque on the stone pillars it is going to say, 'Founded by Stanley Roth.' That was my idea," she added with a misty-eyed smile.

"I wasn't in love with him," she said in a quiet voice. High overhead, a breeze rustled through the palm trees, chasing shadows across the narrow asphalt street. "Not really in love with him, but I . . ."

We pulled up in front of the bungalow where Stanley Roth had lived and worked during all the long and difficult months of the trial. Julie switched off the engine and in the fading light turned to me, her eyes filled with tears.

"You don't understand. It's my fault. It wouldn't have happened if I hadn't promised Stanley I wouldn't tell."

I started to ask her what she had promised, why it would have made a difference, but she bolted out of the car and, walking fast, headed for the door to the bungalow. I followed her inside and watched in silence as she wiped away a tear and slid a video cassette into the machine in what had been Stanley Roth's private theater. I fell into a chair just below the projector. It was the same scene I had seen in the movie.

"That's what I kept trying to tell you," I said when the scene came to an end and she turned it off. "It isn't real. It didn't happen. That's the reason he didn't use the original film, the one that was shown in court. It's all a lie."

Julie paid no attention. She removed the cassette and put in another. It was the real video, the one taken at The Palms the day before she was killed, the one Annabelle Van Roten had shown to the jury. I was confused. What was the point of it? I had seen it all before. Julie stopped the film.

"That's what you saw in court, right?"

"Yes, but . . ."

"Watch," she said with a strange intensity in her voice.

It was the same thing I had just been watching: Mary Margaret Flanders, surrounded by her guests, hundreds of them, spilling out over the lawn.

"I still don't see what . . ."

Then I saw it, and my heart stopped. Out near the very edge of the crowd, just where Stanley Roth had put him when he staged it for the movie–the movie he had always wanted to make–where you would not look twice at who it was or wonder why he was there, was Richard Crenshaw. Julie turned on the lights.

"He didn't tell us until after the trial," she explained.

I knew the answer, but I asked the question anyway; I suppose because I kept hoping I was wrong. "But he knew before the trial was over?"

"He had the surveillance tapes. He checked them after they showed part of them in court. He said no one would have noticed Crenshaw unless they were looking for him."

Roth was right about that. I could have looked at that tape a hundred times and never seen him. No one standing that far away from Mary Margaret Flanders was ever noticed.

I tried to give Julie what comfort I could, but it did not help very much. She could have told the police, or told me, and then everyone, perhaps even Jack Walsh, would have known that Stanley Roth had had nothing to do with his wife's death; but then there would have been no movie to make, and Stanley Roth would not have been able to do what he had always wanted to do.

"I'm the one that should feel guilty," I said, "not you. Stanley practically told me he knew what happened. He told me he wouldn't tell me because if he did, it would ruin the movie. It never occurred to me he was serious."

In the same way that the murder of Mary Margaret Flanders had drawn huge crowds to see her last motion picture, the death of Stanley

Roth made *Blue Zephyr* another box-office sensation. Stanley Roth was innocent and Stanley Roth was dead, and because of the movie everyone knew, or thought they knew, everything there was to know about everything that had happened. When Jack Walsh was arraigned in court for murder, hardly anyone noticed; and when he avoided the gas chamber by pleading guilty and was sentenced to life in prison no one much cared.

Never one to forget his friends, or those who had tried to help his friends, Louis Griffin invited me to be his guest at the Academy Awards. *Blue Zephyr* had been nominated for seven Oscars. I decided to stay home and watch on television instead. Perhaps because Hollywood wants nothing so much as to keep people coming back for more, the awards for both best picture and best director went to people with many more movies to make. *Blue Zephyr* did pick up one important Oscar. Walker Bradley won best actor for his portrayal of "the ruthless and charismatic attorney, Joseph Antonelli." Bradley thanked nearly everyone it was possible to thank. He mentioned his wife, he mentioned his friend Louis Griffin, and he mentioned the head of Blue Zephyr Pictures which had produced it, Julie Evans. He did not say a word about Stanley Roth.

After it was all over, after the last award had been given, after all the famous flashing faces had waved and smiled their final good-byes into the hollow lens of every camera they could find, I turned off the television set and wandered into the night. For a long time I stood alone on the back deck, staring out across the mystic black waters of the bay, thinking about all the things that happened from the night Stanley Roth called to ask if I would come to L.A. until the night he captured Hollywood all over again and was shot down dead because of it. I kept thinking about what he had told me–I could hear his voice telling it to me again, as if he were standing right next to me, whispering it eagerly in my ear–that great secret of how he made movies: that he always knew the ending before he started on the beginning. It echoed in my mind, haunting me with the question–that dread, awful question–whether it would have made any difference if I had known at the beginning what I knew now, whether Stanley Roth would still be alive, whether I could have done something to make the ending come out the way it should.

I heard the telephone ring inside and a moment later I heard

Marissa's soft whisper of a voice. Still gazing out at the night, I felt her coming, drawing near, moving that way she did: smooth, graceful, her head held at just the right angle, floating across the room and through the open sliding glass door. I turned around and found myself face-to-face with the laughing mischief in her eyes.

"A friend of yours from L.A.," she said with a tender, teasing smile, covering the telephone with her hand. For a brief moment she paused, letting me imagine whom she meant. "Annabelle Van Roten," she said, certain I had thought it was someone else.

Taking Marissa by the wrist, I let her know with a glance that I wanted her to stay. And then in the cool California night I listened to my one-time adversary, the passionate and intelligent Annabelle Van Roten, the woman who had been so damnably certain that Stanley Roth had murdered his wife, tell me more than she had to about what she thought now. When she was finished, when there was nothing more to say, we said good-bye with the strange, bittersweet nostalgia of two old friends who have only learned the truth when it does not much matter anymore.

On the other side of the round glass-topped table, Marissa sat with her chin resting in her hand, waiting for me to tell her what Annabelle Van Roten had said. She had the slightly amused look of an eager schoolgirl trying hard not to show how impatient she felt.

"She called to tell you she was glad the 'ruthless and charismatic' Joseph Antonelli won the Academy Award, didn't she?" she asked in a lilting, pleasure-filled voice, when she could not wait a moment longer.

"Walker Bradley won the Academy Award."

"Yes, but he won it for being you."

Annabelle Van Roten had said almost the same thing. There were times, she had told me, while she was watching Walker Bradley's performance when she thought he was more like me than I was. How strange and incongruous. Even in the world of intimate strangers with whom we live, we are seen as playing parts that might be performed better by someone else. I started to say something to Marissa, to explain what I felt, but it suddenly seemed a useless vanity, this urge to make myself understood. Shaking my head, I looked again out across the bay, toward the city, shimmering bright and mysterious in the distance under a sky filled with a thousand tiny silver stars. For a fleeting moment I had the feeling that we were all on a stage, under the watchful eyes of an audience we could not see, and I wondered if that was what it was like–being in front of a camera that recorded every little gesture, every spoken word, recording it all on film so you could become the center of attention of a vast, limitless audience that you could never touch and never see, but an audience that was always there, watching you, waiting to see what for their amusement you were going to do next.

I kept staring into the night, trying not so much to make sense of things–I had lived too long to think that there was any chance of that–but just to reconcile myself to the fact–a fact that carried with it a kind of solace of its own–that the most important questions could never be answered, at least by mortals like us.

"What is it?" I heard Marissa ask. Awakened from my reverie, I turned around. "What did she say?–Annabelle Van Roten."

"She told me that the detective–Richard Crenshaw–is about to be indicted for the murder of Mary Margaret Flanders." I paused for a moment before I added, "She told me she was glad she hadn't convicted an innocent man."

Marissa read it immediately in my eyes: the doubt, the hesitation, the dissatisfied sense of having failed to get finally to the heart of things. She studied me closely, her gaze becoming more intense, trying to be sure.

"He was innocent, wasn't he? . . . Stanley Roth."

Everyone thought so: Annabelle Van Roten, Marissa . . . everyone. It was the movie that had done it, the movie that Stanley Roth had always wanted to make. It had changed the way everyone thought about what had happened; it had changed the way everyone thought about him, Stanley Roth, the innocent victim of the public's now quickly forgotten mistrust. I remembered watching it, certain that nothing in it was the truth, that everything in it was a lie. But then I had watched that other film, that film of Mary Margaret Flanders surrounded by hundreds of people you did not notice because you could not take your eyes off her, that film that caught Richard Crenshaw standing at the edge of the crowd on the sun-drenched lawn of her Hollywood home, the one so famous it had a name of its own. And then I believed what everyone who saw Stanley Roth's movie believed: that Stanley Roth had, as he had always insisted, been falsely accused.

"He was innocent, wasn't he? Stanley Roth," repeated Marissa, staring into my eyes.

I looked away. "What do you think it says about us," I asked, laughing quietly into the night, "that what we see in a movie–a work of fiction–becomes for so many of us the only reality we know? Stanley Roth innocent? . . . Perhaps. But Richard Crenshaw guilty? . . . Why? Because he was there–at The Palms–late that afternoon, with all those hundreds of other people? Because he was there–at The Palms–the next morning, after Mary Margaret Flanders's naked dead body was found floating in the pool?" I looked at Marissa. "Those are really the only two provable facts." A cryptic smile slid across my lips. "But of course everyone knows more than that, don't they? Everyone knows Richard Crenshaw murdered Mary Margaret Flanders. He was in the house. They saw him there."

Marissa twisted her head a little to the side. A startled, worried expression danced softly in her eyes.

"Are you saying he didn't do it? Are you saying Stanley Roth did it after all?"

I remembered the way Stanley Roth had looked at me that day at The Palms when I asked him whom he thought had killed Mary Margaret Flanders, that look he had when he said he could not tell me because it would ruin the movie. That same look was on my face now.

"No one who sees Stanley Roth's movie will ever think so."